8/29/22

6/2/10

THE LAST
PALADIN

ALSO BY P. T. DEUTERMANN

THE CAM RICHTER NOVELS

The Cat Dancers
Spider Mountain
The Moonpool
Nightwalkers

THRILLERS

Red Swan
Cold Frame
The Last Man
The Firefly
Darkside
Hunting Season
Train Man
Zero Option
Sweepers
Official Privilege

SEA STORIES

Trial by Fire
The Hooligans
The Nugget
The Iceman
The Commodore
Sentinels of Fire
Ghosts of Bungo Suido
Pacific Glory
The Edge of Honor
Scorpion in the Sea

THE LAST PALADIN

P. T. Deutermann

ST. MARTIN'S PRESS
NEW YORK

First published in the United States by St. Martin's Press, an imprint of St. Martin's Publishing Group

For information, address St. Martin's Publishing Group, 120 Broadway, New York, NY 10271.

www.stmartins.com

Design by Jonathan Bennett

Library of Congress Cataloging-in-Publication Data

Names: Deutermann, P. T. (Peter T.), 1941– author.
Title: The last paladin / P. T. Deutermann.
Description: First edition. | New York : St. Martin's Press, 2022.
Identifiers: LCCN 2022009008 | ISBN 9781250279866 (hardcover) | ISBN 9781250279873 (ebook)
Subjects: LCSH: World War, 1939–1945—Naval operations, American—Fiction. | LCGFT: War fiction. | Historical fiction. | Novels.
Classification: LCC PS3554.E887 L38 2022 | DDC 813/.54—dc23/eng/20220225
LC record available at https://lccn.loc.gov/2022009008

First Edition: 2022

10 9 8 7 6 5 4 3 2 1

This book is dedicated to the thousands of Allied officers and enlisted men who spent months at sea fighting an invisible yet lethal enemy: German and Japanese submarines. From the monthlong and frigid darks of the far northern oceans, to the Mediterranean Sea, to the central and South Atlantic Ocean, and all the way out to the endless tracts of miles-deep water in the Far East, these men waged a war of wits, sound, physical stamina, and the constant terror of never knowing when a one-ton, guided underwater missile might slam into the side of their ship at fifty miles an hour, day or night, and send them and all around them to meet their Maker.

I wish to express my personal thanks to the technical staff and professional researchers of the Naval History and Heritage Command, which is located primarily in the Washington Navy Yard, in Washington, DC. They toil endlessly behind the scenes to gather up and preserve the Navy's memories, both good and bad. They facilitate George Santayana's dictum: "Those who cannot remember the past are condemned to repeat it." That means that what they do and the lessons they provide are an extraordinarily useful service, especially for those of us in or about to take up the profession of arms.

THE LAST PALADIN

1

CO

My name is Mariano deTomasi. I'm a lieutenant commander in the US Navy and commanding officer of the destroyer escort USS *Holland* (DE-202), which is presently moored alongside a destroyer tender in Tulagi Harbor in the Solomon Islands. I'm sitting in a dilapidated wicker rocking chair on the veranda of what had to have been a plantation house a long time ago. A fan with at least one bad bearing is grinding away manfully on the ceiling, trying in vain to stir the steamy tropical air. The view from the veranda is not particularly impressive. There's a clutch of weather-beaten jeeps parked haphazardly around the building, several ratty-looking palm trees, and, in the distance, two badly rust-streaked Navy cargo ships anchored down in the harbor itself. Beyond them is my ship, tied up alongside the destroyer tender USS *Wilson* (AD-14) and looking somewhat insignificant in comparison to the 26,000-ton repair ship. There's a row of Quonset huts fronting the harbor piers, their decaying steel sides shimmering in the heat, but there's a surprising lack of activity along the piers. I can hear the *clickety-clack* of typewriters going hell for leather in the office behind me. The never-ending paperwork, I thought. I'm definitely in the rear with the gear, as the Army guys termed it.

Tulagi seems to be a real backwater these days, a far cry from those perilous times in the fall of 1942 when the First Marines had gone ashore on Guadalcanal, whose brooding green bulk across the strait now gave little evidence of the savage fighting that had taken place on that blood-soaked island. At the time, Tulagi had been the Navy's frontline refuge, a small harbor to which battered American warships could limp back from their latest night engagement with the Imperial Japanese Navy. I'd seen some pictures of heavy cruisers with their bows blown clean off parked along this shore and camouflaged with palm tree fronds, while repair personnel worked around the clock to get them seaworthy enough to make it to Nouméa, and from there, to a stateside shipyard. All those herculean efforts had been undertaken between air raids by Japanese bombers looking to finish the job until they were driven off by Marine fighters from Henderson Field, across the channel. Cactus. That had been the code name for Guadalcanal. The air defenses there were called the Cactus Air Force, made up of a mixed bag of Navy carrier fighters, Marine fighter squadrons, and whatever itinerant aircraft that had been available to join the fight.

It was hard to imagine now, looking at the harbor, that back in '42 twin-engine Japanese bombers nicknamed "Judys" came skimming across these waters to drop their fearsome torpedoes, many of which ended up skating across the harbor and nosing up through coral sands at fifty miles an hour before grinding their propellers off on the rocky shore. The shooting war had long since gone north as the swelling might of Fortress America converged in the central Pacific in this summer of 1944. Rumor had it that the next target for Chester Nimitz's central Pacific push would be the Marianas—the islands of Guam, Tinian, Saipan. MacArthur was reportedly closing in on the Philippines, with an invasion probably planned for the fall, and after that, everyone expected a direct assault on Japan itself.

I glanced at my watch and sighed. I'd been kept waiting for just over a half hour since coming ashore in response to a summons from the commodore. We'd arrived a day ago and tied up alongside the destroyer tender, USS *Wilson* (AD-12). I knew I shouldn't be surprised to be cooling my heels. *Holland* was supposed to have been here a month ago, and the commodore's welcome-to-WestPac message had made it clear that Himself was not pleased with our late arrival. The sympathetic expression on the yeoman's face when I'd first stepped into the office and given my name confirmed I was in for it.

I sighed again as I remembered my ship's first swashbuckling days with the Royal Navy, with whom *Holland* had been serving since being commissioned. Heat had not been the problem on the convoy escort runs to Russia, and, as I sat here sweating, I almost missed the icy domains of the far North Atlantic Ocean, with its seven hours of metallic gray daylight, lurking icebergs, monstrous seas, and, of course, Hitler's malevolent U-boats. Almost.

I think the big difference was that the Brits had been fighting Hitler ever since September 1939, and, with their backs to the wall, admin and stuffy protocol had long since gone by the boards by the time *Holland* reported for convoy duty. We'd arrived at Scapa Flow in March 1943, fresh from builder's trials and shakedown at the New York naval shipyard. *Holland* was a destroyer escort of the *Buckley* class, purpose-built to hunt down and kill submarines. My arrival call on British Commodore Halen had been short and refreshingly sweet. A bulky, red-bearded captain, who resembled portraits of Henry VIII, had met me on his weather-beaten flagship's quarterdeck, taken me to his cabin, offered me a large scotch, and then welcomed me and my ship most sincerely to the Tenth Destroyer Flotilla. He'd then informed me that they were sailing the next day to join up with a convoy to Murmansk, and could we be ready for sea by 0930 tomorrow morning? We're ready now, sir, as soon as we refuel. Marvelous, he'd proclaimed. Any questions, Captain? None, Commodore.

Good man, the commodore said approvingly. Drink up, then. There's lots for you Yanks to learn, isn't there, but there's nothing like a run to Murmansk to get you up to speed, eh, what? That said, we are *very* glad to have you with us. A brand-new ship. God's wounds, Captain, all our kit is bloody well worn out. Our people are exhausted; there's not enough food, and we've come to dread the letters from home. We will lean on you heavily just because you're fresh and so is your equipment.

We'll do our best, Commodore, I'd told him. Could we perhaps have a liaison officer assigned for this first convoy run?

Capital idea, Captain. Save us all a lot of time. Especially when we get out to The Gap—that's the bit of the North Atlantic where we'll have no air cover. The only planes that can reach us out there are the Luftwaffe. I know you're an anti-submarine ship, but refresh your people in anti*aircraft* warfare. The threat has been much reduced, but German bombers are not to be trifled with, especially if you don't have some fighters to send against them.

Got it, Commodore.

Very well, sir. Carry on, then. My signals officer will be aboard shortly to give you all the operations bump. Your liaison officer will come aboard no later than 1800.

And then we'd trotted off to Russia the very next day. Just like that.

I heard the screen door open behind me. A chief yeoman stepped out and informed me that the commodore would see me now. Lucky me, I thought, but tried to keep my expression neutral. I followed the chief through the typing pool and down a long hallway to a set of wooden batwing doors. The chief, whose steely face, slight limp, and bright red facial and neck scars spoke volumes about where he'd been for the past few years, stood aside and gestured for me to go on in. I pushed through the doors and then stopped in shock at the sight of the commodore, who looked like a cadaver who'd been propped up at his wooden desk. His yellowish skin stretched over the bones of his face like old parchment.

His uniform shirt hung like khaki-colored cotton drapes over his emaciated frame.

"What's the matter, Captain?" the commodore snapped. "Never seen malaria before?"

"Sorry, sir," I said, trying not to stare. "No, I haven't seen malaria before."

"There's lots you haven't seen, Captain; this isn't going to be like Atlantic convoy duty out here, especially since you've missed the convoy. Why is *Holland* so damned late?"

"The far North Atlantic is not kind to small ships, sir," I replied, wondering if I was going to be invited to sit down. "We needed voyage repairs, and they also needed time to install a hedgehog launcher, a new radar, three new long-haul radios, and make mods to the sonar."

"And the other five ships? Did they get upgrades, too? Because they all arrived on time, unlike you, sir."

"They came from other yards, Commodore," I said patiently. "So, I don't know if they did or didn't. We were in the Norfolk Navy Yard, and, apparently, cramming all the new stuff just took more time than their planners expected. Once we came out of the Yards, we came straight here to Tulagi, via some pit stops for fuel."

The commodore began to tap a fountain pen on his desk as he gave me a stern look. His eyes were sunken, and he looked to be over fifty years old, even though he was probably forty at best. If the commodore felt like he looked, I could partially understand the unpleasant tenor of what should have been a welcome-aboard call.

"Well, you're in the Pacific Fleet now, Captain," the commodore said at last. "AKA, the First Team. The Big Blue Fleet. The one that's going to take this abomination of a war back to that megalomaniac *emperor* who set it in motion. Destroyers out here don't 'escort'; they fight. They take on heavy cruisers. The battleships don't just sail around pretty seas like the Brits do in the Mediterranean, showing the flag and maintaining 'His Majesty's presence.' Out here they fight Japanese battleships, great big bastards, crowded with twice as many heavy guns as our ships carry. Our combatants don't cruise offshore to enforce a theoretical blockade around a German-occupied continent—our combatants fight fleet actions. Carrier versus carrier at two hundred miles. Cruiser formations duking it out at one thousand yards, at night. *We* don't make leisurely transits from point A to point B, like from Halifax to Murmansk, U-boats be damned, like you've been doing. *We* invade occupied and heavily fortified islands, and we deliver thousands of Marines ashore right into the teeth of fanatic Japanese infantry, who believe dying in battle is a higher calling than even victory, and who fight to the death rather than *ever* surrender.

"You're anchored in Tulagi, which is a peaceful backwater now. A distant logistics base. The big show has gone north, on its way to Tokyo via any number of benighted island atolls, which will require more bloody smashing, all of which means I'm damned if I know what to do with a lone LantFleet DE who's unfamiliar with how we operate, where we operate, how we communicate, and against whom we operate, and *late*."

I took a controlled breath before answering, seeing that the commodore was puffing from delivering his diatribe. "We were told," I said quietly, "that we'd been sent out here to provide escort services to whatever big deal was shaping up next."

I paused, determined to maintain control of my temper, then continued. "I assumed they were talking about protecting invasion forces—transports, landing ships, ammo ships, cargo ships, tankers—and *not* going up against Japanese carriers. *Holland* is a DE, Commodore. Destroyer *escort*. Anti-submarine ship. Three-inch guns, not five-inch. We specialize in hunting down submarines and killing them. I don't think all these PacFleet carriers or battleships *or* even your cruisers can do that. And, while I think that Japanese submarines are nowhere near as good as Hitler's U-boats, I seem to recall that one lone I-boat *sank* a carrier, blew a destroyer in half, and punched a great big, go-back-to-the-States-for-repairs hole in a battleship, and all of that with a single spread of torpedoes."

The commodore glared at me. "You've got a smart mouth on you," he said finally, "for the captain of such a little bitty ship. I can have *you* removed with the stroke of this pen for insubordination."

I decided to go on the attack. "Where's my intel briefing, Commodore?" I demanded. "Updated charts? Communications plans? Standard operating procedures for PacFleet destroyer forces? Supply system requisitioning procedures? Current code books? Am I in the wrong office? Do I need to go to somebody else, Commodore, to get these things?"

"How *dare* you!" the commodore hissed. "You work for me, not the other way around, mister!"

"*Mister?*" I said. "The title is 'captain,' not 'mister.' Sir. You know what? I think maybe I should go back to my ship and try out some of those brand-new, long-haul HF radios. Tell the First Team, as you call them, about my reception here, or lack of one. Tell them that I think perhaps your medical condition has affected your mind. They do know the full extent of your physical condition, right, Commodore? Yes?"

The commodore's jaundiced eyes widened. He looked like he would explode, if he could have managed the energy. When I saw he couldn't, I seized the opening.

"Let's do this, Commodore," I said, still in as calm a voice as I could muster. "You assign *Holland* to a patrol station, some place between the Solomons and wherever the next island invasion is going to take place, with general orders: you know, look for submarines. Or act as a distant picket. Maybe even become a mid-ocean weather reporting station. A lone outpost, way out there to cover the First Team's flanks. Give me fuel and supplies for a sixty-day patrol. We'll get out of your hair and take that time to soak up all those PacFleet procedures, while you, or somebody, figures out how you eventually want to employ us. How's that sound, *sir*?"

The commodore gave me what he must have thought was a withering glare. The effort made his eyes tear up. He was a wreck.

"Go back to your ship, *Captain,*" he growled. "I'll give you sailing orders when I'm damned good and ready to. Nothing too taxing, I promise you; don't want to overstress a LantFleet unit on her first time in the real Navy war. In the meantime, get the hell out of my office."

"Aye, aye, sir," I said. "Pleasure meeting you, I'm sure."

I left the office and retraced my steps down the hallway. The same chief met me halfway and escorted me to the door, his scarred face a study in absolute neutrality. As I stepped through the door, I asked if this was the standard welcome-aboard call for LantFleet ships being transferred to WestPac. The chief stopped in the doorway and studied his shoes for a moment before replying. The clacking typewriters behind him never stopped.

"There's more to it than malaria," he said quietly. "Our squadron doc says Commodore Halen'll be dead in a few weeks. He used to be my favorite boss. It's painful to watch. His replacement is inbound, coming up from Brisbane, I think. Until then, we're all going through the motions, pretending there's nothing wrong. The chief staff officer, Lieutenant Commander Carson, is over on Cactus today. He'll set you up on a mission and with whatever logistics you need as soon as he gets back."

"Okay," I said. "Sorry to hear that. I guess I'm surprised they didn't relieve him right away."

"He asked nicely," the chief said. "To be allowed to keep serving, that is. His wife died of cancer just before Pearl happened. He was here for the initial Guadalcanal invasion, including all the battles that gave that patch of water out there the name Ironbottom Sound. Navy Cross. Purple Heart. Had to swim for his life from *two* broken-backed destroyers during those bad old days, late '42, before any of us truly understood Japanese torpedoes. I, myself, got off the *Atlanta* just before she went down. Today's replacement ships and crews can't imagine the ferocity we encountered when we first went up against the Japanese. Those of us who had to be left behind here at Tulagi are still licking our wounds. The tone of your office call this morning was more about us than you, if that's any comfort, Captain. Every time I look out at Ironbottom Sound I start to weep, so he's not the only broken one here. If that makes any sense, Captain."

"All the sense in the world, Chief," I said, recognizing that I'd just been tactfully admonished. No surprise there—in a way, calibrating senior officers was part of a chief's job. "But for what it's worth, the U-boat war up there in the land of the midnight sun wasn't exactly a cakewalk. I will never get the smell of burning men out of my memory."

"Well, that makes two of us, Captain," the chief said with a sigh. "Pray to God once a day, without fail, that you never encounter a Japanese type 93 torpedo. We'll be in touch, sir, and, again, I apologize on behalf of the entire staff for—that business in his office."

"Apology accepted," I replied. "And thank *you* for filling me in, Chief. We'll be standing by."

As I walked back down to the waterfront, I was seething inside. I was a Sicilian. Well, technically, I was not—I was born in Brooklyn into a family of Sicilian immigrants, so I was an American. My family, the deTomasis, had come from Siracusa, a Sicilian city whose history would fit right in with what had happened here at Guadalcanal. I was raised in a multigenerational household—my grandparents, the original immigrants; my parents; my grandfather's firstborn son and his Italian wife. I had two older sisters. I was the youngest. At home we kept to the old-country traditions. We spoke in the Sicilian language. Back in the 1700s our family had been aristocrats, during the time of the French. There were palazzos around Siracusa, magnificent if crumbling, to prove it. That was a long time ago.

Now Sicily was again wrecked. The Second World War was just another chapter in Sicily's bloody history. This island country had been conquered by the Athenians, the Phoenicians, the Carthaginians, the Greeks, the Romans, the French, the Germans, and finally, almost as an afterthought, the Americans. It was a beautiful island nation, filled with farms, vineyards, beaches. Sicily even had its own volcano, Europe's biggest and most fearsome. Roman temples adorned the southern part. Early Christian catacombs stretched for miles underground close to the city of Palermo. The quarries of Siracusa, where the Sicilians trapped an Athenian fleet and its embarked armies in 413 BC, were still there and were not places for anyone to visit at night. Throughout Sicily, the very stones were said to bleed in remembrance of eons of conquest, occupation, war, and subjugation, with only an occasional victory.

One of the central tenets of Sicilian culture was the concept of respect. Sicilians spoke respectfully to their elders and acknowledged betters. They also spoke respectfully to strangers, mostly as a matter of fundamental politeness. The commodore today had behaved disrespectfully. He had displayed his ignorance and his lack of proper manners. He knew nothing of my ship, the *Holland,* except that she had come west on a journey of almost ten thousand miles to join the effort to crush the Japanese. He knew nothing about our experiences in the Murmansk convoys or the hell of watching oil tankers explode in flames, their crews jumping into the icy seas, themselves aflame, or the sudden appearance of German bombers, flying low and fast over the ice-filled sea to bomb ships that could not defend themselves beyond some futile gunfire. All hail Chester Nimitz, the Big Blue Fleet, and all the admirals and commodores; I was truly angry.

2

XO

My name is Ephraim Edmond Enright, US Naval Reserve, and I'm the executive officer , or second-in-command in USS *Holland*. At the moment I'm trying to get my arms around about a foot and a half stack of official mail, dropped on my desk when no one was looking by the tender's mail clerk. We'd been at sea for some time, making the transit from Pearl Harbor to the Solomon Islands. The bureaucrats had been busy in our absence. The captain was ashore, paying a call on the commodore and presumably getting some idea of where we'd be going next, while I dealt with myriad mini-crises that had been popping up since we arrived yesterday. Nothing truly alarming, just the usual stuff that lined the pier when a ship came in from an extended period at sea. The size of the paperwork stack alone made me think there really wasn't a war on out here. Except right across the straits lay Guadalcanal, a name synonymous with the word "war."

There were two new guys waiting for us in Tulagi. One was a fireman apprentice, the other a sonarman apprentice. They were both fresh out of their respective A-schools and *Holland* was their first ship. They were a long way from home and still a bit wide-eyed about their new surroundings. The officer of the deck had had the quarterdeck messenger bring them to my stateroom to begin in-processing.

"I'm Lieutenant Enright, the executive officer," I said. "Welcome aboard *Holland*. The captain's ashore right now, but he'll welcome you aboard later today. How was the trip?"

"Long," the fireman said. "Sir, is this really Guadalcanal?"

"No," I replied. "That's the big, dark green island across the sound. This is Tulagi Island. It's a forward base. You're in the Solomon Islands now. There are hundreds of islands in this chain. Got your service records?"

They both dug into their seabags and produced the manila folders. I scanned them briefly and then summoned our personnelman, PN2 Gordon. I told him one would be going to AS Division, the other to B Division.

"Petty Officer Gordon here will take you to the ship's office and get you checked in. Then your division chiefs will come and get you. They'll assign you lockers, a rack in your respective berthing compartments, and introduce you to your division mates. Right now we're getting some repair work done from the destroyer tender we're alongside. We'll probably be going back out to sea soon, so get checked in, and then someone will take you for a tour of the ship."

Two quick *yessirs*, and then Gordon took them away. The ship was noisy—we were alongside a destroyer tender, a big floating repair ship. There were welding machines hissing topside, the clanging of metal stock coming aboard, the rattle of chipping hammers, and a lot of noisy conversations out in the passageways as our guys worked with the tender's people to get the work done. We'd been originally scheduled to arrive out here a month ago, but there'd been delays. Previous to our PacFleet assignment, we'd been in the Atlantic and on loan to the Royal Navy to hunt U-boats. We'd gone from pretty much eternal cold to unending, oppressive heat and humidity. That's what a nine-thousand-mile voyage could do for you.

Lieutenant Hal Welles, the operations officer, normally called the "ops boss," knocked on my stateroom doorframe and asked if he could get a minute.

"What'ya got, Ops?" I asked.

"The radar pedestal, up on the mast. It's got a big crack in its base. The tender says they can't fix it, but they can install one that was cannibalized from another ship after battle damage. Is that okay?"

"Whatever it takes, Hal," I replied. "We have to have an operational radar."

"They said it's gonna look funny," he said. "It's bigger than the one we have."

"I say again, whatever it takes. We need to get as much stuff done as quickly as possible while we're still alongside the tender. Otherwise, we'll be SOL—there aren't any naval supply centers way out here in the wild west. And remember, get as many spare parts for everything that you can beg, borrow, or steal—especially those big vacuum tubes for the sonar and radar."

"Yes, sir, got it."

We were alongside for what were called "voyage repairs"—nothing spectacular, just the usual mechanical failures of overworked machinery: pumps needing new impeller rings, electronic gear needing new tubes, guns needing their hydraulic motors overhauled, electrical motors needing rewinding. Our time in the Norfolk navy yard had been all about getting new gear on board, but this was about routine maintenance caused by weeks at sea—England to Norfolk, Norfolk to Pearl, Pearl to the Solomons—that required skills and materials just beyond our own capability.

The captain had been gone longer than I'd anticipated. I wondered if the commodore really was mad at us for being late. There was nothing we could have done about that—the delays had all been caused by problems installing a new radar, new radios, and doing electronic upgrades to our sonar system. If the commodore was mad about our being "late," the captain was equally frustrated. Our captain's formal, full name was Mariano Medina Santangelo deTomasi. That mouthful had been a little too much for his academy classmates, so he'd shortened it up to Mike deTomasi. He came from a Sicilian immigrant family in Brooklyn, and he looked the part: intense, almost black eyes, high forehead, jet-black hair, a thin Roman nose, and disproportionately wide shoulders for a man who was five foot eight on a tall day, tops. He was second-generation American who'd been brought up in a traditional Sicilian family of shopkeepers in Brooklyn. At home they spoke the language of Siracusa, the city from which his grandfather had emigrated way back when. In school, and later, at the Naval Academy, his Brooklyn, New York, accent had been sufficiently prominent to conceal a lot of his Sicilian upbringing.

According to him, he'd been a bit of a street fighter in his home neighborhood, and he continued that pastime at the academy in the intercollegiate boxing program, earning his academy nickname of "Sweetie." Other boxers just didn't see him coming, he'd told me. "I was short, had a strange, foreign last name, and I didn't talk much. But when they came across the ring at me, I'd let them get close, and then I'd beat the hell out of them, to the point where the boxing coach often had to intervene." After one particularly violent bout with a senior who was a much larger opponent, the coach had apparently had to drag him back to his corner, where he then turned around, looked at the glowering deTomasi, then only a midshipman third class, and said, "Aren't you just a regular sweetie, Mr. Tomasi."

Apparently, at the Naval Academy, that kind of incident got you your academy nickname. By his senior year, that name was well known in his weight class within the East Coast intercollegiate boxing world. I didn't go to the academy, so all I knew about that was what he'd told me, but there was definitely something about him that made you aware that this was a guy you wouldn't want to trifle with. Not that he came on with some kind of Brooklyn thug manner or tough-guy demeanor; if anything, he was a quiet, reserved man, an officer who cared about his people as long as they did their duty faithfully and to the best of their ability. If you didn't, he could give you an unblinking, narrow-lidded stare that damn well got your attention without him saying a word.

According to scuttlebutt, he was also a man on a mission. He'd been given early command of a minesweeper as a lieutenant. The sweep had been based at Pearl when the Japanese attacked. The ship had been undergoing a routine maintenance availability, similar to what we were doing right now, so she was moored over at the shipyard on one of the smaller piers. As the story went, some Japanese planes came by from the direction of Ford Island, where the world was ending, and one of them dropped a bomb that went off between his ship and the pier. A steel-hulled ship would probably have survived that, but minesweeper hulls are made of wood, so the bomb ripped her open and sank her almost immediately, right alongside the pier. A lot of the duty-section crew had come topside to man machine guns after the big attack started. Unfortunately, it was standard procedure when you went into any Navy shipyard to offload all ammunition except for small arms, so there was no ammo on board.

Everybody topside ended up in the harbor, including deTomasi, which is when two Japanese fighters came by for a strafing run, killing most of the men in the water. He'd ended up trapped under a piece of the sweep's main deck with a broken hand, so he got to watch. He personally had dragged some of his wounded to the pier, only to find that they'd died, literally in his arms. He swore an oath, while still in the water, that he would avenge that barbarity or die trying. Any skipper might have done the same thing, but for someone with a Sicilian heritage, apparently, such an oath is tantamount to a lifetime quest. He was given a medal and command of *Holland* a few months after the attack.

He came aboard while she was still being built and began to assemble his commissioning crew. Once she came out of the Yards and her shakedown, the Navy assigned *Holland* to the Royal Navy for operations on the North Atlantic convoy routes to Murmansk, where Japanese were unfortunately scarce. He'd had to wait until the ship was eventually reassigned to the Pacific Fleet. Now that we were here, some of the chiefs said they could almost see him licking his chops at just the thought of killing Japanese. So far, however, all we'd seen of the Pacific war was the rusting wreckage from the Guadalcanal campaign around Tulagi Harbor. Naturally everyone was anxiously interested in where they were going to send us. Not the least of those, our captain, who by his own account had a blood oath to honor.

3

CO

The *Holland*'s motor whaleboat was waiting for me at the pier. I'd walked down the slight slope to the pier area, still somewhat surprised by how lifeless the harbor operation seemed to be. I'd expected a beehive of activity, even with the main fleet two thousand miles away, but it was as if Tulagi and, indeed, the Solomon Islands themselves, scene of so much vicious combat in the fall of 1942, were now slipping back into their prewar somnolence. Dusty-looking palm trees drooped along the empty crushed-coral roads. Some strange-sounding birdcalls could be heard back in the nearby jungles. Blackened and rusting pieces of beached ships that had been unlucky when the Bettys came. Several ramshackle wooden buildings that looked like they predated the invasion, some with temporary hospital markings, slept in the heat. There was a medium-sized civilian oil tanker anchored in the harbor, not far from the destroyer tender where *Holland* rode quietly alongside. I could hear sounds of industrial activity from across the water, but the big ship's five-inch guns were covered in canvas, a sure sign that the war had most definitely moved on.

"Back to the ship," I said to the coxswain. As if there was anywhere else to go, I thought, as I climbed down into the boat.

The boat ride took five minutes. We pulled up alongside *Holland*'s starboard quarter, where a pipe ladder had been hung. I climbed aboard to the sound of two bells coming over the 1MC topside speakers, along with the familiar announcement: *Holland,* returning. Above us the looming steel sides of the tender seemed unimpressed with the fact that *Holland*'s commanding officer had returned to his ship. My executive officer was waiting as I climbed through the break in the lifelines.

"XO," I said.

"Captain," the exec replied. "How'd that go?"

"Just ducky," I said with a pleasant smile, mostly for the benefit of the quarterdeck watch standers. "My cabin, please."

The captain's cabin on *Holland* was located just beneath the pilothouse. It spanned the entire width of the ship's superstructure, with room for a built-in desk, a metal armchair, a small head, and a couch that turned into a foldout bed. There was a single porthole on either side; they were both now locked open because the ship was not air-conditioned. The temperature in the cabin was just over ninety degrees. The exec dropped his lanky frame awkwardly down onto the couch while I sat at my desk. The entire ship was only thirty-seven feet wide, so my cabin was about twenty-six feet across and maybe ten feet wide. A multi-station sound-powered phone console was mounted at one end of the couch, along with a single, black Bakelite handset that connected me directly to the bridge. The cabin was hot, cramped, and with all amenities, such as carpet or wooden furniture, removed because it was wartime. Even so, it was still the largest living accommodation in the ship.

"The commodore was most unpleasant," I began. "Besides that, he's very sick, with advanced malaria. Utterly contemptuous of all things LantFleet. Only the PacFleet could be considered the First Team. Lant-

Fleet ships that are transferred to the Pacific theater are more of a burden than an asset. Lots more like that."

"I guess we could just go back," the XO offered. "The Brits liked us well enough."

I had to grin. My executive officer, Lieutenant Ephraim Edmonds Enright, III, USNR, was always good for an irreverent quip. He was six three, bony, awkward, and skinny, with a shock of unruly red hair, piercing blue eyes, and the biggest brain I'd ever encountered in the Navy. He was literally the smartest individual I'd ever met. He came from a prominent family in Providence, Rhode Island, and had attended Andover prep school, where he had been blessed with the nickname "Eeep" once his classmates discovered his full name. He completed a bachelor's degree in mathematics in three years at Princeton, and then a doctorate in electronic engineering at MIT. Following Pearl Harbor, he'd been shanghaied by the Naval Research Laboratory in early 1942 to work on advanced designs for both radar and sonar at MIT. He'd been given a draft deferment because of his vital scientific work. In November 1942, however, his older brother, Mark, had been lost in a sea battle, right here in the Solomons, and Eeep Enright had gone down to the local Navy recruiting office the next day and signed up. He was duly sent to OCS and graduated as a lieutenant (junior grade) in deference to his age and degrees. Then the Navy sent him right back to the NRL labs in Boston.

Eeep grudgingly went along until his father, almost sixty and still deeply depressed by the loss of his eldest son, got in his cups one night and asked Eeep why the hell he wasn't out there fighting. "Excellent question, Father," Eeep had replied, and the next morning he'd called the assignment office at the Bureau of Navigation, which handled all officer personnel matters, and demanded to go to sea or he'd resign his Navy commission and go enlist in the Army. The bureau frantically called his boss at NRL, who protested mightily, but just then came an urgent requisition for an LTJG for new construction. That took precedence, and three weeks later, he reported to the newly commissioned destroyer escort, USS *Holland* (DE-202), as assistant operations officer.

He'd fleeted up to becoming the operations officer in six months when the ops boss was drafted for the still-expanding new-construction program. When the incumbent executive officer had managed to fall overboard during a gale in the far North Atlantic, never to be found, I'd made Eeep acting XO. The other department heads were senior to him, of course, but none of them had objected: everyone kind of recognized that Eeep Enright was a special case. The Bureau of Navigation had queried me as to whether or not I wanted a truly qualified and senior lieutenant to be sent in as XO. I told them I was very happy with LTJG Enright. Inexperienced as he was at being a naval officer, he was a quick study; besides that, the crew was a bit in awe of him, especially when they found out why he'd signed up. He made full lieutenant three months later.

We had an excellent relationship, driven in part because we weren't that far apart in age. I was regular Navy, of course, Academy class of 1932 and fortunate enough to have been given early command as a lieutenant. I was also a veteran of the Pearl Harbor sneak attack, which apparently bestowed a certain status among the members of the surface line, even though my oceangoing minesweeper (MSO) had been sunk and most of my crew killed by marauding Japanese planes after they'd destroyed battleship row. One of the marauders dropped a bomb that landed between my ship's side and the concrete-faced pier to which we were tied up. The blast broke her in two, and all of us ended up in the harbor, some in battle dress, some still in their skivvies, when two fighters dropped down in line abreast and began strafing us survivors. I'd been on the bridge when the bomb struck, watching my guys desperately unlimbering machine guns, forgetting that we had no ammo on board because we were technically "in the yards." The blast whipped the forward half of the ship to port, sending anyone topside flying into the air and then down into the harbor, including me. When I came up for air, I bumped my head against a piece of our wooden main deck that had been blown out into the harbor. I grabbed it just as the fighters showed up and then ducked behind it, discovering my hand was broken. I actually felt their 20mm rounds whacking into the other side and even felt one graze my right leg underwater. It was over seemingly in seconds, but when I looked around, all I could see were bodies bobbing in the oily water. I tried to get some of them back to the pier, but with only one hand I made a hash of it.

I swore a blood oath then, that I would avenge them and do so with the same savagery.

"So now what, boss?" Eeep asked, prodding gently as I remembered that horrible day.

"We wait for orders and a station assignment," I said. "Apparently, the commodore's chief staff officer is discreetly acting in the commodore's stead. He's going to make something up, seeing as the convoy train we were supposed to be part of is long gone. So, let's make sure we keep topped off with fuel and feedwater and that we have enough stores aboard for a sixty-day patrol."

"Aye, aye, sir," Eeep said. "Actually, we're topped off with provisions, fuel and water, and since we went cold iron when we came alongside, we're not burning any fuel. The tender's working on number one evap, which should be back up tonight. Depth charges are being barged over from the Tulagi magazines tomorrow morning. We have plenty of three-inch and a full load of hedgehogs, which is fortunate because the tender's gunnery people have never even heard of them. Oh, the radar's pedestal is being replaced. The old one was cracked and leaking oil."

"That thing was brand new," I grumped.

"They're making stuff as fast as they can back home, Captain. Like the chiefs tell me, you want it bad, sometimes you get it bad."

"I believe that," I said. "I have to wonder how long they're gonna keep this base open. Talk about being overtaken by events."

"Any skinny on where the next big push is going?"

"That information is available only to members of the First Team," I replied archly. "And they don't even know we exist."

"Gee, it's just like you said, Skipper: everything's just ducky."

I grunted. "Yes and no, XO. You know the old saying—when the elephants dance, us mousies run for cover. Personally, I don't want anything to do with a battleship engagement and especially a carrier strike from the other side, for that matter. Killing submarines is tough enough, but if that defines us as minor league, frankly, that suits me just fine."

There was a knock on the cabin door, and then a signalman stepped in. "Flashing light from the base tower, Cap'n," the man announced. "Chief staff officer will be coming aboard in one hour."

I smiled. "There you go, XO," I said. "Ask and ye shall receive. Alert the wardroom and then stand by to stand by."

The chief staff officer was a full, three-stripe commander, so protocol demanded that I meet him at the top of the pipe ladder even though I was the captain.

"Nate Walker," the CSO said as he stepped aboard. He was a burly man with blond hair, a friendly face, and a strong handshake. He wore a pith helmet instead of a regulation uniform cap. He was visibly perspiring in the tropical heat, and there were large sweat stains under his armpits. "Please, God, tell me you have air-conditioning."

"Um," I replied. "We do, but only in sonar plot and CIC. Otherwise, we're still thawing out from the Murmansk run."

"That's right," he said, nodding. "You guys were with the Brits. This must be one helluva big change."

"We can meet in CIC instead of the wardroom," I said. "Might be a better place to talk ops stuff. Crowded but cooler than this."

"Capital idea, Captain," he said. "Lead on."

I instructed the quarterdeck OOD to call for all officers to assemble in Combat. Then I led the commander forward and up one level. The Combat Information Center, which was the nerve center for all the ship's sensors and weapons systems, was just behind my cabin, one deck below the bridge. It was only marginally larger than my cabin but stuffed with consoles, plotting tables, communications desks, and large, plastic status boards where watch standers plotted the location of surface and air contacts when we were at sea. By US Navy warship standards, *Holland* was a small ship, only 300 feet long, displacing 1,700 tons, and with a complement of fifteen officers and 198 enlisted men. A regular-sized destroyer, for instance had a crew of 350.

The CSO sat down at the main plotting table, while the wardroom officers stuffed themselves into whatever nooks and crannies were available. I introduced him.

"Afternoon, boys and germs," he began. "I'm Commander Nate Walker, CSO of DesRon Forty-Five. I'm here to give you a short in-brief on the Big Picture. You're new to the western Pacific theater, but even so, we're glad to have you join the PacFleet. I'm told you guys are specialists in anti-submarine ops. That's good because we have all sorts of other specialties out here—fleet air defense, mine warfare, amphibious ops, shore bombardment ships, and good old ship-versus-ship battle forces. You've probably heard that the waters just to the west of here are littered with so many sunken warships from both sides—thirty-six in all—that it's called Ironbottom Sound.

"Things have changed a lot since August of 1942. We got our asses kicked when we first went up against Japanese cruisers and destroyers. In the very first engagement, we lost heavy cruisers *Quincy, Vincennes, Astoria,* and HMAS *Canberra* in the space of a few hours. Thousands of Allied sailors died. Those Japanese cruisers walked all over us, and then left without a scratch. That was followed by an eighteen-month slugfest where the Japanese schooled us on how to fight surface actions, principally at night and mostly with torpedoes. It took us a year and a half—1942 to 1943—to absorb the lessons, while the First Marines underwent a similar experience across the straits on Guadalcanal, which we code-named 'Cactus.'

"Eventually we prevailed. Ironically, the Japanese taught us too well. In a huge simplification, the big difference was that we could replace our losses and they couldn't. We could maintain a supply of food, fuel, planes, ships, and ammo; the Japanese barely could and then, couldn't. So now, this is a safe haven, and the Big Show is going north from here. About two *thousand* miles north. The other LantFleet DEs who came through have been swept up in the movement of vast naval forces preparing for the next island campaign. The Japanese know if they can't defeat that operation, the Philippines will be next. And after that, Japan itself.

"Which brings me to the matter of what to do with one DE, who's very new to PacFleet operations. There seems little point in sending you out to the big carrier task forces getting ready for the next invasion campaign. The bald truth is that you wouldn't contribute much. But there is something we think you *can* help us with, and it happens to be right up your alley, LantFleet or PacFleet. We have intel that the Japanese are going to react to the thrust into the Marianas by dispatching several submarines in the form of a one-thousand-mile-long picket line so that when our big dogs head north, they can: one, alert the Japanese fleet, most of which is in Borneo, and two, maybe thin some of our forces out.

"What we don't have is *where* that picket line might be established. You guys have never been involved in an island invasion campaign, but you supposedly know all about hunting down and killing German pigboats. So that's gonna be your mission. We're going to send you out to some very empty ocean areas in hopes that you can find one of the picket subs. If you can find one, maybe you can find the rest of them and then do some real damage to the Japanese. And by sending a lone ranger, we minimize the chances of your being discovered—the Japanese maintain pretty good airborne reconnaissance coverage of the entire Philippine Sea using great big, heavily armed seaplanes, called *Kawanishi*."

He stopped there to let the officers ask questions. That lasted thirty minutes, after which he asked if he and I could have a private word in my cabin.

"Now for the real story," he began, wiping his perspiring forehead with a handkerchief as he sat down. "As you undoubtedly gathered, the commodore is unhappy about *Holland*'s late arrival. *I* understand the reasons for that; in better times, I think he would, too. It's not like you took three weeks off to go get a tan somewhere. His instructions to me were as follows: Send them out to Point Nowhere. We have neither the time nor the resources to retrain a ship and crew who's only mission so far has been convoy duty. Maybe after sixty days or so Fleet Command will think up something for them to do. Here endeth the lesson."

I took a deep breath, trying for a composed reply, and then decided to just speak my mind. "First, thanks for the candor. Second, you're telling me that we came almost ten *thousand* miles, all the way from the North Atlantic to the far western Pacific, halfway around the goddamned planet, just to bore holes in the ocean?"

The CSO frowned. "That's a little strong—" he began, but I cut him off.

"Bullshit, CSO," I said. "You know what? If I get sent out for sixty days just to twiddle my thumbs, I might just head back east. With sixty days, we could make it all the way back to Norfolk, and from what you're telling me, nobody on your precious First Team would even notice."

"Aw, shit, Captain, don't talk like that," he sputtered. "Look, I know the circumstances are a bit strange, but they will be resolved sooner rather than later. Plus, the truth is we're really in the dark about where the fleet is going to strike next, and that's by design. Look at it this way: Consider your assignment as a training and familiarization opportunity. I'll make sure you get all the current PacFleet op-orders, SOPs, comms plans, and logistics procedures. You spend some highly focused time out there absorbing all that without the distraction of bossy commodores, the busywork of fleet operations, and the constant running hither and to at flank speed. Fleet Command is so big now that it's like a dinosaur: whack it on the ass and it takes ten minutes for the beast to say 'Ow' and another ten to really react. That way, when Fleet Command realizes you're here and sends you hurry-up, hurry-up orders to proceed to X to do Y, you'll actually know how."

I realized I'd been neatly trapped. Putting it that way, the CSO had made it almost impossible for me to argue, not to mention that orders were orders and arguing was not usually an option. "I'd like that in writing," I growled. "Message orders, telling us to do just that."

"Well, of course," the CSO said, suddenly beaming. "Send your department heads over to the HQ building. My staff will organize the paperwork, and I'll verify you're properly supplied to go out for a couple months. We'll make sure you get to an oiler at the end of thirty days to top you off, bring spare parts, food, and whatnot. Who knows, by then one of the big units may get torpedoed and they'll be frantically squawking for all dedicated ASW units to call home. You send me a daily sitrep—the usual stuff."

"Define usual stuff."

"See what I mean?" he asked pleasantly.

I groaned mentally. "Basically," he continued, "distantly stationed PacFleet units send a daily sitrep at noon: current position, fuel remaining, feedwater, potable water, food for X more days, urgently needed parts, medical cases, if any."

"I find this all a bit hard to believe," I said. "I feel like we're so insignificant that we really might just as well go home."

He nodded. "Lemme ask you: How big were the convoy escort forces you were part of up there in the North Atlantic?"

I had to think for a moment. "Typical convoy, maybe as many as ten escorts, all in."

"How big were the convoys?"

"Fifty, sometimes as many as seventy-five, a hundred fifty ships."

He nodded again. "The fleet heading north to hit wherever they're gonna hit?" he said. "There are eight *hundred* ships gonna be involved in that, counting frontline combatants and support ships—you know, oilers, hospital ships, cargo ships, refrigerated stores ships, ammo ships, transports, minesweepers, repair ships for ships, other ones for aircraft, and on and on. Don't feel like you're being picked on, Captain. You're just going to have to get used to the scale of what's happening out here in the Pacific."

4

XO

The captain and I stood on the starboard bridgewing at sunrise five days later, each of us with a mug of really good coffee, admiring the view. The captain's Filipino steward, Petty Officer Third Class Paulino Danilo, made his way down to the engine room every morning with a thermos bottle, where he would wait for the engineers to make fresh coffee for the oncoming six to eight watch in the engine room. The snipes had the same coffee grounds the rest of the ship had, but they made it into coffee by passing low-pressure steam from a boiler drain line over the grounds, twice, and always with a pinch of salt. Glorious.

"We never saw anything like that at Scapa Flow, did we," I said, scanning the perfectly flat, glassy sea. There were bands of color here and there as the sun made its first appearance far to the east, creeping up between towering cumulonimbus cloud formations that looked like writhing, white mountains as they sought the icy reaches of the stratosphere, their ice crystals glowing yellow with the morning sun.

The captain shook his head slowly in obvious wonder. "No, we did not," he said. "That is truly beautiful. The North Atlantic was always just gray."

We were steaming in a giant lazy circle, six knots with two degrees of right rudder, just to make sure we did not establish a straight-line target in case we had unknown company. "Steaming" wasn't entirely accurate. *Holland* had two boilers that did indeed make steam, but they fed four turbogenerators, not high-pressure, steam-turbine-driven main engines like a destroyer. She was an electric-drive ship, which, given her small size, required a much less expensive power plant than that of a full-sized destroyer. Her top speed was twenty-three knots, easily ten knots slower than a fleet destroyer or an aircraft carrier. Submarine hunting was a task done usually at slow, and thus acoustically quiet, speeds. We did that in order to keep the ship's propellers from cavitating and thereby creating distracting noises in the water that might mask the wispy, almost ghostly, sounds made by a submerged submarine. There was a method to the madness of constantly turning: If there did happen to be a Japanese sub lurking out here, he'd be having a tough time computing a torpedo fire-control solution on a ship whose heading was constantly changing.

We were eight hundred miles north and slightly east of the Solomon Islands, literally in the middle of nowhere, as promised. We had only one of our two boilers on the line in order to conserve fuel while we awaited developments. The CSO had come through with a full set of operating procedures and operations orders for Task Force 58, AKA the First Team or the Big Blue Fleet, as others liked to call it. Ever since we'd arrived on station, I'd been conducting training sessions in the wardroom for all the officers. The commodore had been right about one thing, I thought: *Every*thing in the Pacific Fleet was done differently, so there was lots to absorb. That was especially true if one compared PacFleet procedures to those of the Brits, with whom we'd been working since commissioning. I had been reading and studying in the mornings, and then chairing a question-and-answer session after lunch to settle the major differences. Our wardroom was young but experienced. We had four department heads—operations, gunnery, engineering, and supply—fleshed out with a collection of ensigns to head up the various divisions into which the nearly two hundred men on board were divided.

"What are the sonar water conditions?" the captain asked.

"The morning BT drop revealed a slight layer," I replied. "Two degrees differential, at eighty feet and another one, thicker, almost eight degrees, at two hundred twenty feet. If a sub's at two hundred thirty feet, we'd probably never see him with that strong a layer."

"If he's down at two hundred thirty feet, he's not much of a threat," the captain pointed out. "We'd hold him down until he runs out of oxygen or battery. Eventually he *has* to surface, and then he's fresh meat."

"*If* we even detect him in the first place," I said.

"Yeah, yeah," the captain said.

For a small ship, *Holland* was armed to the teeth. There were two three-inch guns, one on each end. Most *Buckley*-class DEs had three main guns, but the Navy had literally run out of them right at the time *Holland* was being built. There was also a single, four-barreled 40mm gun mount, eight single-barreled 20mm cannons on pedestal mounts, one triple tube twenty-one-inch diameter torpedo mount, one hedgehog underwater mortar battery that was mounted right behind the forward three-inch gun, eight five-hundred-pound depth-charge side projectors, four on a side, and two rails on the fantail loaded with five-hundred-pound depth charges. If the ship's sonar system could detect and maintain contact on a hidden submarine, the outcome—between the hedgehogs and the depth charges—was pretty much certain. That "detect and maintain contact on" was, of course, a relatively big if.

The ocean, for some as yet not understood reason, often settled its upper depths into layers of water that were at different temperatures. If the temperature difference was big enough, that layer could reflect our outgoing sound beam, much like a fisherman seeing a fish from the stream bank, except that, because of a trick of light called refraction, it wasn't actually right there. We did a bathythermograph drop, called a BT drop, four times a day. The BT was basically an underwater thermometer that was tethered to the ship by a small wire. It reported temperature versus depth until five hundred feet, at which point it broke its wire. Submarines did the same thing with an instrument attached to their outer hulls. If they found what they called a "decent" layer, they'd make sure to lurk underneath it.

The sound-powered phone at the navigator's table squeaked. A moment later, the quartermaster of the watch announced that there was a CO's-eyes-only message down in Radio Central.

"At last," I offered. "Always did want to see Antarctica."

The captain chuckled and went below to the radio room. There he'd meet the ensign who had crypto duty, who'd be holding a two-foot-long strip of yellow paper tape, the width of a typewriter ribbon, which had text printed along its length. He came back to the bridge five minutes later and showed me the message, which was from *Holland*'s newest admirer, the CSO. I scanned the message. It began with a date-time group, and then identified the sender: in this case, ComDesRon 45. The meat of the message was that one of our long-range PBY night patrol planes had spotted a Japanese I-class sub on the surface and gave the time and position. Go get him. Ack. End text.

The captain called for a message blank. He addressed the reply message to the commodore at Tulagi: Ref sighting message. WILCO, which stood for "I will comply." He sent it marked unclassified since it revealed nothing. He instructed the Radio Central supervisor to find the ops boss, Lieutenant Hal Welles, and ask him to come to the Combat Information Center, known throughout the ship as Combat. We had Ops plot the latitude-longitude coordinates of the sighting on the wide-area navigation chart, which ended up being ninety miles northeast of *Holland*'s current position. We could make sixteen knots on one boiler, twenty-three on two. The captain instructed Main Control to warm up the second boiler on the line in case we needed a sudden burst of speed. He then ordered the officer of the deck to proceed at fifteen knots toward the last reported position of the Japanese sub. We'd get there at 1500 if we stayed at fifteen, which was our most economical speed.

"I'll want to arrive at the actual datum well *after* dark," the captain said. "When he'll hopefully be on the surface recharging his batteries. So when we're within ten miles, we'll slow way down and rig for quiet ship."

"Radar approach?" I asked.

"No, I think not," he said. "Intel says they don't have active radar, but that they might have receivers that can detect our radar signal. We'll creep in and then bring the radar up for one sweep—just enough to see if he's on the surface. I'll want the forward three-inch mount manned and ready. If he detects us, he'll crash-dive, but I want him to do so under a hail of three-inch shellfire."

"Not likely to get a whole lot of hits in the dark," I pointed out.

"On the other hand," he replied, "just one would have him crash-diving with a hole flooding his hull. Maybe two. The deeper he goes, the worse that's gonna get. At the very least, it'll make for a major distraction, which is when we'll make our first hedgehog attack."

I liked it. "You, sir, are a mean man," I said.

"I'm Sicilian, XO. This is killing we're talking about. I've got some scores to settle. Surely that isn't news."

I saw the bridge watch standers grin when he said that. He left the bridge, and I went down to Combat to set things up.

5

CO

I came down to Combat an hour later. Eeep had summoned Hal Welles and the chief engineer, Lieutenant Casey Stormes, to Combat for a briefing. I took a chair in a dark corner and listened in. Eeep explained what was going on and what I wanted once we closed in on the last known position of the enemy sub, otherwise known as the "datum."

"I have little faith in a nighttime surface gunnery attack against a crash-diving submarine," he said. "The single radar sweep will mostly confirm we have a real contact. But the sudden gunfire will rattle them and maybe provoke a diving mistake. After that, it'll turn into a classic seek and destroy."

The chief engineer was a lieutenant (junior grade) naval reservist who'd held an engineering ticket in the merchant marine before the war. "So why warm up the second boiler?" he asked. "From what you're saying, we don't need it to get there when we want to. Just as soon not double our fuel consumption."

"I think it's because the skipper wants the ability to scoot if this guy comes up shooting torpedoes."

"Oh," Casey said. "But once we hook one, we don't usually do sonar ops at high speed."

"We've never gone up against a Japanese submarine, Casey," the captain said from his corner. "The Germans would always try to escape, remember? You know, go deep, go quiet, and creep off in the away direction. Japanese? I don't know, and we've had no feedback from previous encounters. We do know all about their torpedoes, though, and they're genu-wine bastards. So, I think it's worth having a third-gear available."

"Gotcha covered, XO," Casey said, all his reservations vanishing at just the mention of Japanese torpedoes.

"We'll go to condition one AS when we get into about ten miles," Eeep continued. "Intel tells us that the Japanese send their subs to a geographical point station and tell them to stay there, unlike our guys, who operate in a specifically designated geographical patrol area and then go where the targets are. The I-boats go to a designated lat-lon and stay within a few miles of that point. That probably makes it easier for their headquarters to reposition them, but it also makes it easier for us to find them."

Ops then had a question. "I'd heard scuttlebutt that we'd been sent out here as some kind of punishment for our late arrival at Tulagi," he said.

Eeep looked at him. "Does this sound like we're being punished, Hal?" he asked. "A transiting PBY saw a Japanese I-boat on the surface. The commodore's exact words to us were: Go get him. That's what we do, right?"

Ops, suitably abashed, nodded. "We'll be ready, XO."

Eeep dismissed them and then came over to were I'd been lurking in the semidarkness.

"Pre-action calibration complete?" I asked him.

"I believe so, sir," he said. "You'd think we've never done this before."

"Well," I said, "it's the chief engineer's job to worry about fuel, and the operations guys are the biggest rumormongers in the fleet. Remember, with the Brits, we always brought a crowd when we got word of a U-boat sighting. This is a bit different. I think they'll do okay."

"They'd better," Eeep said. "Now I need to go down to Sonar Control to check that they understand what we plan to do. Are you available to sit in?"

Was I available? Well, shucks, I guess I was, as if I had anything else to do. "Happy to oblige, XO," I said.

It was always fun to watch Eeep at work. And that's what I meant by a "good relationship" with my second-in-command. In most cases, we thought the same way. And if we didn't, we both quickly sought to find the reason why. By tradition, the XO always deferred to the CO in deciding what the ship was going to do. But there was something about Eeep's sheer intellectual prowess that had always given me pause when we argued. That was especially true when I was tempted to say "I'm the captain, dammit—we'll do it my way." Instead, I would ask him why he thought whatever he thought. Almost inevitably I would end up concluding that he was right and I was, if not wrong, not as right as he was. Eeep for his part always maintained the "your obedient servant, sir" demeanor of Royal Navy tradition. I believe the Chinese might also have said that he was saving my face. It worked, and I was truly grateful he was the XO.

We left Combat and headed down. Sonar Control was a perpetually darkened compartment down on the third deck. It was positioned slightly forward of the bridge, almost directly under the hedgehog mortar mount and vertically above the keel-mounted hydrophone array. The Sonar gang, called AS Division, consisted of a lieutenant (junior grade) division officer, the chief sonarman, four console operators, two electronics technicians, two seaman apprentices, two torpedomen, and two gunner's mates who were responsible for the depth charges and the hedgehog mortars. Sonarmen were called "sonar-girls" by the other white hats because of their posh working station, which was air-conditioned, low in the ship, and thus comfortable in a seaway, and the fact they were the reason the ship existed. It was all in good fun, because the other way you found out there was a sub nearby was when one of its torpedoes blew the ship in half, so nobody truly resented the Sonar gang.

The acronym "RADAR" stood for *ra*dio *d*etection *a*nd *r*anging. "SONAR" stood for *so*und *n*avigation *a*nd *r*anging. Our sonar system used a large hydrophone array mounted outside the hull in a pod bolted on the keel. It worked by blasting an acoustic wave into the depths and then the listening for any returning sounds caused by that wave striking, say, the metal sides of a sub and reflecting back to the sonar's receiver array. The outgoing wave was called a "ping"; anything coming back, however faint, was called an "echo." The operators could also actually hear the echo, which allowed them to evaluate its validity as a sub, a process known as "classification."

The chief of AS Division was Chief Petty Officer Roscoe "Hammer" Santone. Hammer was a pretty accurate nickname. The chief was a burly, red-faced, profane, loud, and easily provoked individual, fiercely protective of his sonar-girls. They were both scared of him and in awe of him, because Roscoe was an absolute wiz at interpreting often those ephemeral echoes coming back to the ship from the depths. "That's biologic," he'd growl. "But *that,* right there? That's meat." He was also a killer, a trait that I admired and shared with him. He was the one who convinced me to layer the depth charges when we got that U-boat. Most ships set them all for one depth; Roscoe suggested picking a median depth and then setting some charges to go off above and below that depth.

"Just one in his face'll do it, Cap'n," he'd said. "I live for that moment."

Me too, I remember thinking. Especially if they're Japanese.

The chief petty officers in a destroyer-sized ship are the flywheel of the entire organization. They are technically enlisted men but wear khaki like the officers. They've risen through the ranks, from apprentices in their specialty rate to petty officer third, second, and first class, and then, finally, chief, over usually ten to twelve years of service. They had their own mess, where the food and certainly the coffee were superior to anything the officers saw in the wardroom mess. That was because the chief commissaryman, who supervised cooking, baking, and food-handling for the entire ship, was a member of the chiefs' mess.

Most importantly, they were of similar age and experience to me, the captain. I could on any given day amble back to the chiefs' mess and ask if they had any decent coffee. Then I could sit at their table, raise a problem, and seek their advice. Typically they already knew about the problem and were ready with a solution. Sometimes they even extended an invitation for me to join them for lunch, which usually meant *they* saw a problem that I had not yet seen for myself: a bad cook. An officer with a dictator complex. A card shark in X Division, preying on the new guys. A perceived unfairness in the watch bill assignments.

Some of it was penny-ante; some of it was not, but I'd always call in the XO and tell him about what they'd told me. In some ships the XO would have been invited for that kind of meeting, but Eeep was so junior, both in rank and naval experience, that they wanted me to hear it, whatever it was. They had to like you and respect you before that channel would ever open, but it was a godsend when it did. Sometimes I was unknowingly the cause of a problem, due to a policy I'd put in place or something I'd said. That's when I would learn about the law of unintended consequences. When that happened, they were careful to make sure the fix, whatever it was, was broadcast among the crew as happening because I had had a word with the XO. Again, being PacFleet sailors, they, too, knew about saving face. The truth was there were strong chiefs, okay chiefs, and weak chiefs. Roscoe was one of the strong ones, which is why the chiefs had elected him president of their mess. I could send word that I wanted to talk to him, and he'd knock on my door, usually after working hours. He could do the same and we'd meet on the boat deck or some other inconspicuous place. It was a great system.

The Sonar gang was obviously excited that we were finally on the way to do a job of work. Eeep gave them the basic scenario and what we had in mind for the approach to datum. He told them that the flying boat had reported an I-class boat, which meant that we should have a substantial target to hunt for in case we didn't catch him on the surface. Roscoe wanted to know what mode they'd be in when we closed in on datum.

"I want to be slow and quiet," I replied. "Sonar in passive mode. Narrow weave. Only intermittent radar sweeps. If we get a radar contact, we'll slow down even more and try to creep up on him. I'm hoping his listening gear will be deafened by his own diesels, since the only reason he's on the surface is to recharge his battery banks. I want to get close enough for the three-inch to reach him, then light him up and start shooting."

"If he's able to crash-dive and get back under?"

"Then I'll tell you guys to go active, and we'll take the covers off the hedgehogs. Even if we don't get a killing hit with the guns, or any hits at all, seeing as it's gonna be dark, we might scare them into making a mistake instead of starting immediate evasion procedures. Even a glancing hit may scare the diving officer into pulling the wrong lever. However, it works out, I want this bastard dead."

Roscoe nodded. "Sounds good to me, Captain," he said. "XO, you think these Japanese know about hedgehog?"

"We'll probably be making first-time introductions," Eeep answered. "He'll be expecting a barrage of depth charges. In fact, he'll be counting on that, because that much underwater noise deafens our sonar, and that's how they usually break contact and get away. Might just spook the bastard when everything goes quiet."

I found it interesting the chief asked Eeep that question and not me, although I knew why. Eeep, with his academic and laboratory experience, was technically miles ahead of the Sonar gang. They were products of the Navy's training system, which took farm boys who'd never heard of a sonar and taught them the basics of how to operate one. Eeep was the product of first-tier universities and months of technological development experience in the Naval Research Labs. He'd already rewired the display consoles to present a brighter picture. When we'd been in the Yards, he'd been the one supervising the sonar upgrades, suggesting better ways to install and test them to the shipyard folks. Even though he was now the XO, he was still the go-to expert when something went wrong with the sonar. Roscoe considered himself the top dog when it came to interpreting those echoes, but if the electronics went haywire, he and the entire Sonar gang would happily defer to the XO.

Eeep wanted to go over some technical matters with the gang, so I stepped out of the space and headed for the ladder. As I was about to start up, I overheard the chief say something interesting: "This captain wants all Japanese dead," he rumbled. "That man's on a mission for blood."

"Remember Pearl Harbor, Chief," Eeep said. "Who doesn't want blood?"

"Yeah, but everybody knows the captain is a Sicilian, XO," Roscoe said. "I grew up in Red Hook—that's in Brooklyn. Lemme tell you something: When one of *those* black-eyed guys decides he wants blood, stand the fuck by. Absolutely anything goes."

"And?" Eeep said.

"That means we gotta be on our goddamned toes. There are standard Navy procedures, and then there's the heat of moment, understand? Be prepared for goddamned anything, girls."

I smiled as I headed up the ladder. Got that right, Sunshine, I thought.

6

XO

At ten after midnight, I went up to the bridge for a final confab with the skipper before I turned in for a few hours. He was sitting in his captain's chair on the bridge, staring out into the almost absolute darkness. There was no moon and an overcast sky obscured the normally brilliant display of stars. The ship was barely moving as we conducted an expanding square search. The expanding square had two advantages: First, it was the most efficient way to cover a large search area. The second was that the ship never stayed on any one course long enough for a submarine to set up a torpedo solution. Go west for one thousand yards, then turn north for fifteen hundred yards, then east for two thousand yards, et cetera. Doing this on electric drive made *Holland* an unusually quiet destroyer.

We both knew the original position report could have been wildly off. The sub's skipper may have been spooked by that PBY and changed his station position by as much as ten or even twenty miles. The PBY could also have been looking at a breaching whale, for that matter. And yet, the report had called the sighting an I-boat, which was the largest class of Japanese submarine and thus the most recognizable. Combat had orders to bring up the radar for two sweeps every twenty minutes once we'd arrived at the edge of the datum area, but there'd been no contacts. Otherwise, our approach had been radar-silent. I looked at my watch. The crew had been sent to general quarters an hour before we arrived at the edge of the search area. We were assuming a submarine, ours or theirs, would remain submerged during daylight to avoid scouting aircraft, and only surface late at night for battery charging and fresh air, so between now and dawn, everybody would just have to wait it out. Come the dawn, we'd go back into our normal patrol routine of what was called "port and starboard watch-standing": six hours on, six off, with half the crew on station and the other half sleeping or working.

"I swear this is the hardest part," I said. "Waiting."

"Yep," he said, shifting uncomfortably in his chair. The captain was the only person allowed to sit down on the bridge; everyone else stood, whether for a four-hour watch or for a seemingly endless GQ. The chair was indeed a privilege, but I'd tried it once, and comfortable it was not. I think everybody up here needed a cigarette and probably a head call, but this was no time for anyone to leave his GQ station or to light up. On a dark night like this, the flare of a Zippo lighter could be seen for miles. The tropical heat had dissipated somewhat, but everyone in the ship except the Sonar gang and Combat was still sweating. There was no night breeze, and the knowledge we might already be engaged with a silent, invisible predator didn't help. As I was turning to go back below, the red light on the 21MC tactical intercom in front of the captain's chair, known as the "bitchbox," came on.

"Bridge, Sonar Control."

He reached for the press-to-talk switch. "Captain."

"Sir, we have a weak *passive* signal bearing zero nine five, range unknown. Sounds like diesels. He may be up and recharging, but further east of us."

"Bridge, aye," the captain answered and then ordered the officer of the deck to bring the ship to 090. He turned to me. "Alert all stations," he ordered. "Keep the radar in standby while we try to refine the acoustics. Doppler, for one. He doesn't have to move to charge his battery banks, but they usually do, just to get fresh air into the boat. Hopefully we'll get some Doppler."

"If you want, we can start a passive angle tracking plot," I offered.

"No, that takes hours," he said. "Let's head straight for him with a narrow weave. I don't want to know where we *think* he caught a sniff and did an emergency dive. I want to run up on him and kill him with guns, if possible. Make sure the first five rounds are point-detonating, then turn 'em loose with armor piercing."

"Aye, aye, sir," I said, and headed down below. I never did get that quick nap.

My battle station at general quarters or condition one AS was in the CIC. The captain usually remained on the bridge, where he could give instant conning orders, communicate with and physically see other escort ships, and recognize that a dangerous situation was shaping up. My job was to be in charge in Combat, where all of the information coming from our sensors, human and otherwise, was consolidated and then displayed, usually on a lighted plotting table called a dead reckoning tracer. There we could lay out where we were in relation to whatever was happening, as well as where our consorts were, if we had any, and where the sonar or the radar or even the lookouts were saying the enemy was.

The captain on the bridge could simply look out the windows and theoretically construct that same picture in his mind. We in Combat could see the entire tactical picture, but only if our eyes—the sonar, the radar, the ship's gyro, the fathometer, the anemometer, the bathythermograph receiver, the engine order telegraph repeater, the radio speakers mounted on the bulkheads—were all working in concert. That's what the word "center" meant in the term CIC: assembling the Big Picture and getting it up to the captain.

Which rather raised the question—why wasn't the captain in Combat and the XO up on the bridge? One of the main reasons was ownership: the captain owned everything and anything that happened on or to his ship. Since anti-submarine warfare was usually conducted by groups of ships, the risk of collision, as both the target and his tormentors twisted and turned, was always there. Most captains insisted on being able to see with their own eyes where the other ships were and thus be able to maneuver instantly to avoid collision without waiting for Combat to develop a radar track and then evaluate it for a few minutes.

It was different in antiair warfare, where engagements took place sometimes miles away from the ship. AAW, as it was known, was a matter of radar-directed fighters being controlled from a CIC, much like the FAA controls civil airliners. The controllers in Combat would vector our fighters, which were sometimes stationed fifty miles away and twenty thousand feet high, to a position from which they could intercept and then shoot down incoming enemy aircraft. ASW, on the other hand, took place right in front of you. Nobody in Combat could see the wake of an approaching torpedo. The sonar could hear it and sound the alarm, but when the captain had to decide *right now* which way to turn to evade it, it was best if he could actually see its wake.

During routine underway steaming, Combat would be manned up by the CIC watch officer, a radar operator, two plotters for the DRT table, and a telephone talker on a sound-powered circuit with the bridge and the lookouts. But if we were headed in to engage a submarine, there were many more people crammed into the space: extra plotters, gunnery coordinators, the ops boss and the CIC officer, the senior radarman, and talkers to man up other sound-powered phone circuits. We used sound-powered phone systems because, if the power went down, they still worked. My biggest job was to ride herd on all the extra hands while still trying to keep that all-important Big Picture in my head. It was never boring.

7

CO

I leaned back in my chair as the ship headed east. The course change had brought a relative wind from ahead that helped to cool off the sweltering bridge team. A little, anyway. The helmsman executed the narrow weave by slowly bringing the rudder to the right ten degrees, holding it for about fifteen seconds, and then reversing it to the left ten degrees. If we thought the sub was really close, we might change to a broad weave, holding the turn for thirty seconds, and thus presenting an ever-changing course and speed aspect to frustrate the sub's fire-control team, who would be trying to set up a torpedo solution on us. The bitchbox lit up.

"Bridge, Combat, Sonar Control: No Doppler, but the signal strength is increasing. Definitely multiple diesels, bearing one zero zero degrees true. Recommend slowing to creep speed. He's either going north or south; the bearing drift will tell us in about five minutes."

"I concur," I replied. "Remain passive for now."

"Sonar Control, aye." Roscoe sounded a bit excited.

I pushed the button for Main Engineering Control. "Main Control, Captain."

"Main, aye," Casey Stormes answered, the sounds of steam-driven machinery clearly audible in the background.

"We're closing in, and we think he's on the surface, so we're gonna start a deep creep," I said. "But, listen: If he detects us, he'll crash-dive, so stand by for an unexpected big bell."

"Main, aye, Captain. We're ready-teddy."

I was awake now, the head call and the ciggy butt forgotten. I reviewed my tactical approach. The key decision was when to radiate the surface-search radar. Wait too long and we might run right up on the surfaced submarine, rendering guns useless. Come on the air too soon and the sub's receivers, if he in fact had any, might detect the radar signal, giving him time to dive and evade. If that happened, *Holland* would still have a chance to get him, but that damned layer was going to present a real underwater acoustics problem for the sonar if he could get down fast enough.

I drummed my fingers on the armrest. There was another possibility I didn't want to think about: the sub, being on the surface and with a gang of lookouts perched on his bridge using those superb Japanese optics, might have already detected our presence and was preparing a salvo of torpedoes. A destroyer escort bow-on was a tough target, but if he fired enough fish, especially those type 95 torpedoes, the first hundred feet of *Holland* would be blown right off.

"Slow to five knots," I ordered. "Helmsman, maintain the weave but use no more than seven degrees of rudder."

The lee helmsman rang up the ordered bell, while the helmsman acknowledged the order about how much rudder angle he could use. If the helmsman used too much rudder, he could create what was called a "knuckle," which was a temporary whirlpool that could persist for several minutes and actually show up on the sonar, looking like a valid contact.

We were creeping forward in the dark now. I was having visions of us running right up onto the sub. My gut instinct told me it was time to take a radar sweep. I called Combat.

Eeep answered. "Sir?"

"What'ya think—we close enough to light him up?"

"Probably, Captain, but let's turn one way or another so both guns can bear. That way if we're in too close, we'll avoid running into him."

Shit! I thought. I should have thought of that. I ordered the helmsman to come left to course 060 with standard rudder, and then told Eeep to train the main battery out to ready-surface starboard. When the gunnery aspect was correct and the gun crews ready, I ordered a single sweep of the radar. Eeep immediately called up a contact and gave the range, 1,800 yards, and the relative bearing at 070, which put the target on our starboard beam.

Combat called that data to all stations, especially gun control one deck above us, where Lieutenant Kerry "Bat" Watkins, the gunnery officer, waited for the order, and then ordered the signalmen to turn on the big searchlight and point down that relative bearing. Ten seconds later, the white-hot beam from our twenty-four-inch searchlight snapped on and, almost simultaneously, the night exploded into gunfire as our two three-inch guns—one on the bow, one on the stern, and both pre-pointed down the last radar bearing—opened fire, followed by the quad-forty. The painfully bright muzzle flashes from the forward gun destroyed everyone's night vision on the bridge, but that white beam had locked squarely onto the target, which was a long, black, and rounded shape, low in the water. We got a momentary glimpse of the distinctive silhouette of a conning tower before it was entirely enveloped in a blizzard of shell splashes, ugly vertical fans of grayish water erupting thirty feet in the air from a hot red center at their base. Within seconds, the black shape went under in a roil of white water and spectacular plumes of air escaping from her ballast tanks, at which point the guns fell silent.

I quickly ordered the helmsman to come right to the approximate bearing of where the sub had disappeared, and then told Combat to take control. Sonar went active and immediately announced contact, with a new bearing and range. We'd been so close when the guns opened up that the attack team in Combat hadn't bothered to begin a plot. A moment later Combat ordered a small course adjustment to the left, and then the hedgehogs began to ripple-fire, casting the twenty-four mortar rounds in a high arc right over the forward gun mount and out into the sea fifty yards ahead of the ship. I would have loved to follow that up with a barrage of depth charges, but then the sonar would have become useless. Plus, with depth charges, you never knew if they'd hit the sub because they exploded at a preset depth, regardless of their proximity to the submarine, while the hedgehogs would *only* go off if one or more of them actually hit the submarine.

The ship began a wide circle to the left as Combat now took over sending orders to the helmsman via a sound-powered phone circuit. The ship's speed came up to fifteen knots because the objective now was to get some distance between *Holland* and its quarry. If any of the hedgehogs exploded, fine, but we always had to assume they'd all missed and then get set up for another, sonar-directed approach. I could hear men frantically reloading the hedgehog mount down below on the main deck. I looked at the clock above the chart table. If the first attack had placed the rounds exactly right, there should have been explosions by now, but there weren't any. No one had to say anything; we simply advanced to the second phase of the attack, where the sonar would maintain contact on the evading submarine while Combat plotted its movements and then maneuvered the ship into position for another run, coming back around to the right so as not to put the target in *Holland*'s baffles, the acoustic dead zone created by the noise of the ship's rudders and propellers. Attacking with hedgehogs wasn't much different from bird hunting: the plotters in Combat had to calculate the course and speed of the submarine based on a series of ranges and bearings from the sonar. They then had to maneuver the ship to a point where the swarm of silent bombs fired ahead would arrive on top of the sub, not where it was at the moment of firing, but where it *would* be by the time they slid down to the sub's estimated depth.

I figured the submarine skipper would be expecting a volley of five-hundred-pound depth charges about now, which would require that the attacking destroyer pass directly overtop and get slightly ahead of the submarine. Depth charges make a distinctive sound when they hit the water and start down, which was the signal for the submarine skipper to make an immediate turn to frustrate the attack. The hedgehogs were much smaller and streamlined so as to enter the water quietly. Instead of being just a big, dumb underwater bomb, their warheads contained shaped charges. That meant that if they actually hit the sub's hull, they would detonate and project a lance of superheated explosive plasma that could penetrate the pressure hull and create a leak. If the sub was sufficiently deep, a four-inch-diameter leak could flood an entire submarine in less than a minute, and, because the hedgehogs were fired in a circular pattern of twenty-four bombs, if one hit, there was a high probability that others would also hit. There was no way that the sub's crew could overcome the results of multiple holes in the hull at depth, if only because the incoming water would compress the air in the boat to lethal temperatures and pressures in a few seconds. I felt the ship steady up after a wide turn to starboard.

"Commencing second approach," Eeep announced over the bitch-box. "Sonar estimates he's down at two-fifty, maybe two seventy-five. Doppler's all over the place, so he's making constant turns."

"How's the contact?" I asked.

"In and out," Eeep replied. "That layer isn't helping, but we get the occasional solid echo, and that's enough to stick with him. Recommend a fake pass."

"Concur," I replied.

If the sub's skipper didn't know about hedgehogs, then it was time to make a fake depth-charge attack—but without the depth charges. A normal depth-charge attack would have the destroyer trying to place a cascade of five-hundred pounders just in front of the sub's estimated position so that the bombs would have time to sink down and end up all around the target before their fuses went off. Sub skippers knew the tactic, of course, so they would wait until the destroyer was just about on top and then turn hard. If the Sonar gang could determine which way the target was turning, the destroyer would try to turn *inside* the slower submarine's track and fire a hedgehog pattern. We all waited for that turn order to come up from Combat.

"Right standard rudder, aye, sir," the helmsman cried and spun the wheel.

Holland heeled to port and then steadied up on a course sixty degrees to the right of the initial fake depth-charge approach course. Moments later, twenty-four hedgehogs ripple-fired from behind the forward gun mount. Invisible in the darkness they arced 150 feet into the air and then splashed down into the sea ahead of *Holland* in a wide, figure-eight pattern. I held my breath. If the sub was at 250 feet, these bombs would be on him in thirty seconds.

Thump.

Thump. Thump. Thump.

I grinned in the darkness. Four hits. That should do it.

Combat maneuvered the ship so as to maintain sonar contact but also open the range to the target. The sonar would be going passive now as the gang listened for sounds of a growing catastrophe inside the submarine. Four holes in the pressure hull. Seawater blasting in at 150 psi, already beginning to compress the air inside the boat. It didn't much matter where the bombs had hit—even with all the interior watertight doors closed, the men scrambling to contain the flooding would already be experiencing breathing problems, especially as the inrushing water began to also heat the atmosphere within the boat.

"Sonar's lost contact," Eeep announced over the bitchbox. "But we're hearing sounds of hull collapse."

"Wait for it," I replied as the ship swung out on a wide turn to keep the sonar pointed at where the contact had been hit. I could almost visualize what was going on in the sub by now as the air temperature passed four hundred degrees Fahrenheit and the pressure in the boat rose to ten times the pressure in a diesel engine compression stroke. The entire crew collapsing onto the deck plates as their eardrums burst and their lungs were seared. And then, finally, there'd usually be a big boom: as the sub's hull, totally out of control and falling vertically into the vast ocean depths, its crew already dead, was crushed into a long chunk of mangled steel. The final crush usually, but not always, ignited the torpedo warheads stored in the forward and after torpedo rooms.

"Bridge, Combat: Hull collapse heard on sonar."

"Explosion?"

"No, sir," Eeep said. "Big steel crunch, though."

Good enough for government work, I thought. I sat back and breathed a sigh of relief. Got the bastards, I thought. I asked the quartermaster what the ocean depth was here. Three *miles* was the response.

Perfect, I thought. Those Japanese were now falling through the water column all the way to the realm of endless darkness and pressures of *tons* per square inch. Remember Pearl Harbor, I thought. "Amen," one of the bridge crew said. I hadn't realized that I'd spoken aloud.

I decided to remain in the area until daylight. I wanted to see diesel oil and buoyant wreckage before I made my report. I leaned forward and pressed the talk switch on the bitchbox. "Combat, Captain—well done to all hands. Remain within two miles of the sinking, but keep courses and speeds random until we see actual wreckage. Secure from general quarters."

8

XO

The following morning presented itself with a calm sea and hazy sunlight. I went up to the bridge and refilled my coffee mug from the dented pilothouse pot. The captain was already in his chair, enjoying a cigarette. He was asking Combat for a range and bearing to the sinking position.

"Two four zero, range three miles," Combat answered. He looked at the officer of the deck who quickly gave the necessary conning orders. Ten minutes later the ship passed over the last known position of the Japanese submarine. The sea around us was glassy calm and devoid of any signs of what had happened the night before. I stepped out onto the bridgewing and joined the rest of the men looking for signs of debris. Nothing.

"Quartermaster," the captain said. "Is there an ocean current here?"

The quartermaster of the watch, who was a navigation specialist petty officer, scanned his chart. He grunted. "Yes, sir—there is. South at two to three knots, depending on which monsoon season we're in. Should be south now. This water wants to go to Australia."

"Doesn't everybody," the captain said, drawing grins from the watch team. "Officer of the Deck, come to one eight zero, speed five," he ordered. "Alert all hands topside to look for anything in the water."

Twenty minutes later, we no longer had to look. A sudden stink of diesel fuel enveloped the ship. A *lot* of diesel oil. Then reports started coming in to the bridge: "Stuff" in the water. Broken wooden crates. Life jackets. Large batts of yellowish cork insulation, all anointed with a thick, multicolored sheen of diesel oil. Sheets of paper. No bodies, but uniform shirts, trousers, caps. Sodden bags of what was probably rice, bulging obscenely now as the water took its course. The fuel stink was eye-watering.

"Okay," the captain said. "This looks good. XO, tell First Division to get the crab nets out and pick some of that stuff up. Ask the ops boss to come see me."

My eyes were stinging from the diesel oil fumes as I made the necessary calls. "Gotta wonder what they're making diesel fuel out of," I commented, squinting in the sudden glare.

"The Brits say they boil down the bodies of dead POWs to recover body fat," the captain said.

I was revolted. "There are no fat POWs," I pointed out. "And if there was one, the rest of the prisoners would know he was a collaborator."

The captain was giving me a long, patient look until I realized he wasn't being serious. It was well known that I was always serious, which invited an annoying number of pranks from the ship's jokesters, including the captain.

"This is what I want to do," he finally announced. "Head south, as if we're completely satisfied that we got this guy. Start out at eighteen knots—make lots of prop noise. Every fifteen minutes we'll slow down by two knots until we get down to six knots. Keep the radar on the air the whole time and concentrate the search in the oil slick area. Weave as necessary to keep the radar beam unobstructed by the mast. Then, we'll turn around, and we'll creep back at six knots. That'll take most of the day."

"Aye, aye, sir," I acknowledged. As I headed back down to Combat to set up the plot, the officer of the deck, an ensign from the gunnery department) named David "Dutch" Wusthoff, had a question.

"Captain, why are we gonna do that—what you just laid out?"

"Because, Dutch," the captain said, "submariners are notoriously tricky bastards. Back in the days of depth charges, before hedgehogs, they'd wait for the depth bombs to deafen the sonars up top, make a big turn away, and then they'd fire all sorts of crap out of an empty torpedo tube and open a fuel tank's overboard discharge valve, create a 'wreckage' field and an oil slick to make the tin cans think they'd won the day."

"But we got four underwater explosions on that last pass," Harry pointed out. "That means four hits. Shouldn't that do it?"

"Yes, it should," I replied. "Especially if he'd gone deep. But all four of those hedgehogs might have hit the same compartment. Flooded that sucker to the mark, but, with good damage control, you shouldn't lose the boat with just one compartment flooded. We're going back to make damn sure he didn't get lucky."

"How will we know?" Dutch asked.

"Well, a radar contact would be a pretty good indicator. But, absent that, bodies. Dead bodies take a little time to come back up to the surface from three miles down. And the sharks won't get 'em because of all that oil."

Dutch took all that aboard and decided he'd learned all he wanted to know. He thanked the captain and went back to the centerline pelorus, looking a little bit nauseated. I chuckled as I headed through the pilothouse door.

"I heard that, XO," the captain said.

That's right, Dutch, I thought, with a mental smile. This is a mortal, bloody game we're playing. The losers end up bobbing in an oil slick, ballooning up into unrecognizable swollen lumps that even sharks wouldn't touch.

We returned to the area of the sinking at just before sundown. There was a light breeze blowing now, which had dissipated much of the diesel oil slick. Most of the flotsam had also been dispersed, but now bodies were definitely out there. I ordered the ship's photographer to get pictures from the bridgewing.

"Jesus H. *Christ*!" I heard the photographer's mate mutter as he focused his bulky Graflex camera down on the nearest body, which had been to the bottom of the sea and back again, and which now resembled a paper cutout of a human form, with most of what had been inside now dangling outside. He took the picture with a flash, and then a second one of the others floating near the ship, and then, gagging, he fled the bridge. I wanted to join him. The bodies were beyond horrible.

The captain ordered Combat to take us back to our original station and to send a radioman to him on the bridge.

"Combat, aye."

The radioman arrived three minutes later, bringing with him a message pad and a pencil. The captain filled out the "From," "To," "Subject," and "Classification" blocks and then paused to consider how to phrase the report. The commodore had sent us to the edge of nowhere, clearly expecting *Holland* would accomplish absolutely nothing. I knew the captain wanted to crow a little, but he decided on a more prudent option: just report the bald facts and leave it at that.

"Proceeded to last known position of PBY sighting. Caught an I-boat on the surface at 0139. Drove it under with gunfire. Made two hedgehog attacks. Second attack produced four explosions. Photographed debris field with bodies next morning. Returning to station."

He handed the pad back to the radioman and told him to send it out op-immediate, which meant that the message would take precedence over most of the radio traffic flowing through the vast Pacific Fleet communication networks. Then he told me what he'd said in the message.

"Perfect," I said. "Dear CSO: You told us to go get him. That's what we did. Ho-hum. Ask the commodore if there's anything else, your Lordship?"

The captain laughed. "I do believe you're getting the hang of this, XO," he said. "How's the crew reacting?"

"The human remains this morning sobered everybody up," I said. "Hell, they sobered me up. It's one thing to make cold, careful tactical calculations and then fire a hedgehog pattern; it's another to see the consequences of those four booms down below."

"It is, indeed," he said. "Do you think maybe it's time for a homily from on high?"

"Yes, sir, I do," I replied after a moment of thought. "Killing a German U-boat was always a group effort. This seemed a little more—up close and personal."

"Very well; I'll talk to them during noon meal. Listen, I know the crew feels that I'm on some kind of mission of Sicilian vengeance against the Japanese. They're not entirely wrong about that, but it's important that we keep the killing as professional as we can."

"Um—" I began.

"I don't want any of them, young as they are, suddenly harboring feelings of guilt about what we did and will hopefully do again. If one of these subs manages to turn the tables and puts a torpedo into *our* guts, the results in the water are going to look very much the same."

"Yes, sir."

He paused, as if choosing his next words carefully. "I also get the sense that this war is entering the final phase."

"How so?"

"Well, for example, seizure of the real estate that makes it clear we're not island-hopping anymore. We're occupying places that will ultimately allow us to invade their home islands. The Japanese have to know this, I think. There's going to be more of this . . . slaughter. Most of our crew is eighteen or nineteen years old—I need to make them understand that everything is going to get a lot worse before it gets better."

I sensed the captain was right, but I didn't know how to respond to that. He gave me a thin smile. "Don't get all wrapped around the axle, XO," he said. "As some of the goombahs used to say in my old neighborhood, this isn't personal. It's just business."

9

CO

The following morning Radio brought me a personal-for message from the commodore in Tulagi. The personal-for tag meant that only the captain was supposed to see it. It was often used by unit commanders to chastise a ship's CO in private without doing so on the Fleet Broadcast, where everyone in the Pacific Fleet could see it. It was also used to send kudos. I sighed and opened the steel message board to see which kind this one was.

"Am eating crow after reading your report. Very well done. I was wrong about *Holland* and glad I was. Keep up the good work. Halen."

I initialed the message and handed it back to the radioman. Then I called the XO. "You're not going to believe this," I said, and then told Eeep what the commodore had said.

"Can I share that with crew?" Eeep asked.

"Hell, yes," I replied. "I think the consensus is that we're out here because the commodore hated us."

"Indeed it is, sir," Eeep said. "I may indulge in a little poetic license, as in the LantFleet showing the PacFleet how it's done."

I laughed. "Just don't put that in writing anywhere. The rule of ten thousand still applies."

"Aye, aye, sir."

The rule went like this: one *aw, shit* negated ten thousand *attaboy*s.

There was a knock on my cabin's door, and this time it was Hal Welles. He was holding a message.

"What'ya got, Ops?" I asked.

"Something really interesting, Captain. It's from FRUPAC, that's PacFleet Intel back in Pearl. They think the I-boat we got was part of that patrol line the Japanese supposedly were gonna set up to intercept Halsey when he comes north for the next big deal."

I read the entire message, whistled softly, and then told Hal to get the XO for a quick meeting in Combat.

Ten minutes later, the three of us stood around the dead reckoning tracer. Hal had invited Roscoe to join us, which was something I'd forgotten to do. I'd told Eeep to fold Chief Santone in anytime something big was cranking up. We had a wide area chart of the Philippine Sea stretched out on the lighted table. The Mariana Islands were at the top right of the chart, the Solomons at the bottom right; New Guinea was toward the lower left. The Philippine Islands, themselves, were on the top left.

"We're here," I said, putting my finger on the chart. "We killed that I-boat—about here."

Eeep was baffled. "What's up, Captain?"

"We got a TS message in from Pearl. It speculates that the Japanese, anticipating Halsey is coming out with Task Force Thirty-Eight, might indeed have establish that submarine picket line between right about where our station is in a great big arc whose other end is about five hundred miles below the Marianas. They're probably still trying to figure out if Halsey's going for the Marianas, and Guam in particular, or the Philippines. They have a big fleet of battlewagons at Brunei, over—here, way to the west of us. If they can figure out where Halsey's going, they might—might—send the remains of the Imperial Japanese Navy's striking force out to do battle with Halsey. So, let's pretend we're the emperor's top admiral: where would you station a picket line of submarines that would cover *all* of Halsey's likely approaches to both Guam and somewhere in the Philippines?"

Hal spoke up. "Since Japanese submarines are stationed at a certain designated point, not in a wide, operating area like our guys, I'm gonna need more than one or two submarines."

He picked up a pair of navigation dividers, stuck the pointy end into the middle of Luzon Island, and then adjusted them to swing an arc that included the Marianas, most of the Philippine Sea, and ended up a couple hundred miles south of Mindanao. "This would do it; the only question then is the spacing of the submarines."

"It would certainly have to be more than two or three," Eeep said. "I'd want them to be able to mutually support each other."

"Only if they have orders to report *and* attack," I said. "If they're just pickets—early warning scouts—whose only duty is to sound a warning, then . . . no, that wouldn't be necessary. If I knew where the Third Fleet has been holed up, I'd draw two lines. One between there and, say, Saipan Island in the Marianas, and from there to one of the southern islands of the Philippines. Then I'd concentrate my assets on the part of the arc that covers both routes."

We all stared at the chart for another minute, as if it might give us the answer.

"Okay," I said. "Let's assume this—they're stationed on this arc. How many? Doesn't matter. If we head along that arc across the Philippine Sea and up toward Saipan, and we get lucky, we'll encounter a sub. Sink that one, then connect his position to the I-boat's sinking position, i.e., refine the arc."

"There weren't any orders for us to do that in that message, Captain," Eeep pointed out.

"Nor were there any orders *not* to," I pointed out. "Otherwise, why would we have been sent that message?"

There were nods around the table, although I knew my argument was a bit specious: Fleet Radio Station at Pearl didn't order anybody around. I was aware that various CIC watch standers were listening hard while pretending not to eavesdrop.

"Besides," I continued. "That's why God created the UNODIR. Someone get me a message blank."

A radioman appeared in Combat and handed me a message draft blank. I filled in the required fields:

> From: USS Holland (DE-202)
> To: ComDesRon 45
> Subject: Japanese picket Line
> Ref A: FRUPAC 061544
> BT. UNODIR intend to take Ref A for action. Will proceed east along best estimate of the picket station arc and attempt to roll them up. Request logistic coordination for fuel, food, and ammo. BT.

I showed the message to Eeep, who read it and then took a moment to think about it. "We need to include the coordinates of the arc," he said. "That way they'll know what to tell a replenishment ship so he can meet us. But I don't know . . . UNODIR?"

UNODIR was navy radio shorthand for "unless otherwise directed, I intend to do such and such." It provided a way for captains to display initiative. The boss could always come back and say no. If the boss said nothing, then whatever the consequences of what the CO had proposed, good or bad, would be on the CO's head. Good? I knew that would work, the boss could say. Bad? I never saw that UNODIR.

"What's the worst he can say?" I asked.

"No?" Eeep offered. I made a rude noise.

"What's he got to lose?" I said. "First he sends us out here to the back of beyond as some kind of punishment for being 'late.' Now he loves us. That wasn't an urgent-warning action message from Pearl—that was probably the Intel weenies covering their asses in case the Japanese actually have set up a picket line. Halsey probably won't even see it. And if he did, Halsey would probably *tell* the Japanese which way he was coming just for an opportunity to fight the entire Japanese fleet."

I looked around at my officers. Eeep was still thinking about it, which is one of the reasons I treasured him. Hal was nodding. On the other hand, Hal rarely disagreed with anything I proposed to do if it sounded like I'd made my mind up.

"But what if it's true?" Roscoe interjected. "Buncha goddamned subs out there looking for the Big Blue Fleet? One little DE creeping up on them in the dark? They'd never see us coming. Hell, we might get them all."

"Be still my heart." I handed the draft to Eeep. "Send it," I said. "What could go wrong?"

Eeep rolled his eyes and went below to deliver the draft to Radio Central.

In the event, we received a reply three hours later, but it wasn't what we were expecting. The chief staff officer informed us that the commodore had died of complications from malaria, and that he, the CSO, was in temporary command pending the arrival of a new commodore. But that was it. Nothing about my proposal.

There were three possibilities. One, that my UNODIR message might not have been received yet. Or, two, it had, but the commodore's death and the resulting command change down on Tulagi would probably overshadow whatever messages came in from their orphan DE. Or, three, the CSO was turning a blind eye to my message, which was tantamount to saying: Do whatever you want to. If it all goes off the tracks, it'll be on your head, Captain. I explained that to Eeep.

"So, we'll leave station and head east, northeast?" he said.

"Yeah, but before we do, get me an up-to-date summary of our logistic status; if they don't notice that we've left station, they'll surely notice when we come in asking for beans, bullets, and black oil."

"Interesting," Eeep said. "If the CSO is turning a blind eye, how do we know he'll take care of the second half of our message: logistics?"

"I'm willing to wait a few days to see if they arrange something.

That's why I need that summary. We can always send a second message saying we need a replenishment request."

Eeep gave me one of his "You're brave, I'll give you that" looks. Not very bright, mind you, but certainly brave . . . "And our destination?"

"Well, let's use that estimated arc of stations. Until we locate a second sub, we won't know the structure of the arc. But if we do find a second sub, we'll assume some Japanese admiral used a pair of dividers and simply swung an arc, just like Hal did. After that, assuming we satisfy ourselves that they're actually out there, the station spacing ought to become obvious."

"One last question," Eeep said. "The best way to actually find one is to come up on his station at night, when he's on the surface, like we did last night, using intermittent radar to spot him. Which means we have to *not* get there during daylight."

"Wherever 'there' is," I pointed out. "We won't know until we try. But I get your point: arrival time of, say, 0300, will drive the track."

Eeep nodded. "I'll get with Hal and the navigator," he said. "We'll lay out a plausible arc with, I don't know, six stations and spacing that looks reasonable for max coverage. We'll operate off that until we get better data."

"Actually, XO," I said. "*I* want to do that. That way I get a chance to scrub the plan."

His eyebrows rose.

I laughed. "You thought I was going to make you lay that out, didn't you?"

Eeep cleared his throat as if to say something, but I waved him off. "Look," I said. "Of course I'll have you check my work. You're the math wizard; but I'm the killer-diller. Between the two of us, we might actually manage to do some really good work for Jesus with this little caper."

10

XO

By 1800 we had a plan. Using the sunken I-boat's position as the southwestern anchor, I had swung an arc that effectively covered the ocean area that the Third Fleet would have to transit to get either to the southern Philippines or the Marianas, assuming Halsey was coming up from the south or southeast. This being the Pacific, the arc was twelve hundred miles long. If six subs were involved, then the station spacing could be about two hundred miles between each sub. Traveling at twelve knots to conserve fuel, *Holland* would need sixteen hours to make a direct two-hundred-mile transit to where we thought the next boat might be. The captain wanted to arrive at the estimated position of the second station at 0300 the day after tomorrow. If we went at twelve knots for ten hours, that would cover a hundred and twenty of the estimated two hundred miles, leaving eighty, at which point we'd slow way down and creep in toward the estimated position to arrive at the ordered time. I gave the order to leave station at 2100.

There'd been a lot of what-if discussion about the whole plan once the captain left. Maybe the Japanese weren't stationed on an arc but on a flat line. Where'd the arc concept come from, anyway? Maybe there were more subs, or fewer. Or none at all. I had let the officers work through it and argue among themselves. By the evening meal skepticism reigned. Then I acknowledged that the whole operation was based on flimsy information and a lot of assumptions.

"But, guys," I pointed out, "it beats boring holes in the ocean out here. You gotta ask: Why was an I-boat lingering out here in the empty quarter of the Philippine Sea, if not waiting for something? If we find nothing, so what? The real higher-ups don't even know we exist. If we do find a second one and kill it, then we'll probably see a task unit come huffing over the horizon to swallow us up and then go find the rest of them. Either way, good deal. Finalize the plan and the track. I turned to the supply officer. "In the meantime, Chop, you and I will work the logistics summary."

Two further problems needed resolution as we started east at sundown: active sonar or passive? A sonar pinging energy into the water could be heard farther than the sonar itself could hear a returning echo, much like radar, whose outgoing signal could be intercepted well beyond the actual effective range of the radar. I ordered the sonar to be kept in the passive mode. That wouldn't help us if the Japanese sub was submerged and running silently on its batteries and electric motors, but, if he was on the surface like the first one, his diesel engine noise could be detected by our sonar in the passive mode without revealing our presence.

Which led to the second problem: The Japanese certainly knew about the long-range PBY patrols, like the one that had reported seeing the first I-boat on the surface. Ever since the Guadalcanal landings, the Black Cats, the popular name for the twin-engine Consolidated Aircraft seaplanes, had been tearing up Japanese shipping with night attacks. The plane had an operational range of 2,500 miles and could carry bombs and strafing cannons. After the Solomons were secured, they'd been reassigned to long-range scouting missions. This meant that any Japanese subs that surfaced during daylight were asking for it, so they'd adopted a submerged in daylight, surfaced at night routine, just like our guys. No submariner wanted to mess with an enemy airplane.

This was what was driving our approach tactics. Since *Holland* needed to arrive in the best estimated position after dark, when the sub, desperate for fresh air and the opportunity to run their main engines to get a battery recharge, would be on the surface. Basically, we had two choices: go very slow in a straight line in order to arrive after dark at where we thought the second station might be, or draw up a track that went almost there at a nominal speed, and then slow way down to creep up on what we hoped was a surfaced submarine.

For planning purposes, I'd chosen the latter. Once we got into the vicinity of where we thought this guy was, we would initiate a zigzag plan, a truly extreme one. Zigzag plans were designed to frustrate a submarine torpedo fire-control computer team's efforts to develop a firing solution on a surface ship. The prospective target's course and speed were the essential elements of that solution, which would be fed into the torpedo's guidance system moments before they shot it. The disadvantage was if you were trying to get from point A to B, the zigzag maneuvers necessarily made the trip a whole lot longer. Unless, of course, that's what you needed to do—delay your arrival at point B until it was three in the morning.

I was not a fan of going slow in enemy submarine waters; the slaughter of the North Atlantic convoys had been due in great part to the fact that many of the ships in the convoy could barely manage twelve knots. There was a side benefit to using a zigzag plan, however: the wide course variations would point the sensitive "ears" of our sonar in a much wider search cone than a straight-line passage, while giving *Holland* some protection against torpedo attack. Just like we did with the first sub, we'd also manipulate the radar transmissions. We'd keep both the sonar and the radar quiet in a further effort to sneak up on our prey, depending on the sonar to hear those telltale diesel engine noises.

I took the logistics summary to the captain after dinner. Destroyer-type ships observed a cardinal rule when it came to fuel: never get below 50 percent. *Holland* was at 63 percent and looking at a two-hundred-mile transit. I wanted to send out a logistics request to Tulagi now, but the moment we revealed our proposed rendezvous position, it would call attention to the fact that we were no longer "on station." The CSO might send back a what-the-hell query, and I knew the captain wanted to have a second sub in the bag if at all possible before anyone started asking annoying questions.

"How long has it been taking to get a priority-precedence message through out here?" he asked me.

"Twenty-four to thirty-six hours," I said.

"That long?"

"There are a whole lot more ships out here than there were in the North Atlantic," I said. "And I think a lot of them are abusing the precedence system, sending everything op-immediate instead of priority or routine."

The captain nodded. The CSO had said there were now almost eight hundred American and Allied warships in the western Pacific and more coming. At some point the creaky, prewar naval communications system would need to be enlarged, I thought. Right now, ships at sea sent messages to the nearest long-haul naval communications station, which would then forward them, sometimes by radio, sometimes by undersea or buried cables, to a central station in Washington, DC. That station would then rebroadcast that message over what was called the Fleet Broadcast, using transmitter farms placed on both coasts. Every seagoing command guarded (listened to, day and night) the Fleet Broadcast, passing it through a teletype, which printed out every message on a yellow roll of paper. Radiomen then had to screen the entire teletype printout to see if there was anything addressed to *their* command.

This meant a message sent to the destroyer squadron headquarters in Tulagi would be just one of *hundreds* of messages on that day's broadcast. If a sleepy radioman missed it, then the message might go unseen for hours—or days. Our submarines had a similar problem. Once every twenty-four hours, our subs would have to come to periscope depth, raise an HF antenna, and then copy their version of the Fleet Broadcast, slimmed down to contain only submarine business. It seemed cumbersome, but it was an effective way to deliver messages to an entire navy. It also meant that one of the things that was always on a logistics request was teletype paper.

I discussed all this with the captain.

"Results, Eeep," he said. "Results trump a whole lot of bureaucratic bullshit."

"You really think the Japanese have deployed a scouting line?" I asked.

"The Germans wouldn't do such a thing," he said. "They're tactically nimble. The Japanese are a little more hidebound. Admiral-sama wants X, which then becomes the staff's holy grail for the day. Exactly X, not Y and not Z. Just X. Now. And, remember: the German navy had World War I to practice unrestrained submarine warfare. They learned some tough lessons, but they also almost starved Britain into submission."

"So, I'll hold the LogReq until we see what happens?" I asked.

"Or until the day of—if there's nothing there or the bastard gets away, we can always slink back to our exile station. Nothing ventured, nothing gained."

"What could possibly go wrong," I muttered.

"Everything, XO," he said, patiently. "But that's exactly the right attitude. It's wartime—it's up to us to make our own luck."

11

CO

We arrived near the coordinates of the postulated station for a second submarine at just after 0200. The seas remained calm. A light overcast diluted the already weak light from a new moon. Our once-every-thirty-minutes radar sweep had produced nothing. The sonar was similarly coming up empty. The day's tropical heat had not yet dissipated, and there was no cooling breeze on offer. I sat in my captain's chair on the bridge, envying Eeep, who was in Combat, where there was air-conditioning. I'd been to the chart table about a dozen times as we crept into the estimated position, wondering each time if that casually swung arc might not have been another ass-biting assumption. I wished I had a radar gun–director like the big destroyers had for their five-inch gun batteries. It had an intense beam that was no bigger than a pencil lead, as opposed to the wide, and thus very detectable, sweep of a surface-search radar. So now what? I thought. Wild-goose chase? All along I'd been expecting a "Where are you?" message from Tulagi, followed by indignant orders to go back to our assigned station with our tail between our legs.

"Bridge, Combat."

"Captain, aye," I replied.

"Recommend an expanding square search," Eeep said. "Two-mile legs, doubling, to start. Speed seven knots—that's below cavitation speed, so we should remain pretty quiet. Radar sweep every thirty minutes. Sonar passive. At the very worst, we'll eventually end up back on station."

"Make it so," I said, realizing this was now our only option. Our search square would expand north, south, east, and west—a two-mile leg, four-mile leg, eight-mile leg, and so on. The square would eventually get really big. I remembered the instructive story about a wily banker selling a piece of land to a man he didn't like for a penny, payable in thirty days. The only catch was that the penny would double every day for thirty days to arrive at the final price.

We'd end up covering a pretty large ocean area, but if we could find this second bastard, then we'd have a much better picture of the picket line arc. If it was an arc. Or a straight line, or whatever the Japanese had laid out. I decided to slip into my sea cabin and get some sleep.

I almost got to sleep all the way through the night when the phone next to my bed chirped.

"Captain."

"Sir, we have a radar contact, bearing zero zero five, range six miles. Small but distinct. We're turning toward it."

"What time is it?"

"Zero four thirty, Captain. Still dark."

"Is the contact similar to what we had last time, as in an I-boat on the surface?"

"No, sir; much smaller, but we have a definite skin paint."

"Okay, I'll be on the bridge. Notify the XO."

"He's here in Combat, sir."

I smiled, got dressed, washed my face, and went out to the bridge.

The air had cooled down but not very much. I climbed up into my chair and gratefully accepted a cup of chart house coffee from the quartermaster of the watch.

"Bridge, Combat." This time it was Eeep.

"Go ahead."

"Request permission to radiate the surface search continuously," Eeep said. "I don't think this is a submarine. Sonar has no diesel sounds. It's definitely something on the surface, but . . ."

"Okay," I said. "Take us straight in then. Tell signal bridge to get ready for searchlight illumination. Have the forward three-inch ready, as well as the quad-forty. Just in case."

"Aye, aye, sir."

At five hundred yards, the searchlight came on, revealing a ragtag wooden fishing vessel, where several startled men were rising up from the deck and trying to figure out what all this blinding white light was about. I told the OOD to bring the ship alongside and then stop. I told Eeep to muster up the boarding party, which was a team of gunner's mates carrying small arms, led by Chief Gunner's Mate Bobby Garrett. It was easy enough in the flat-calm sea to hold the ship alongside the forty-foot-long fishing vessel. A boatswain mate up on the fo'c'sle threw down a line that was caught and then made fast to keep the boat alongside. I looked east. There was a faint line of color in the sky, which meant that dawn was approaching. I ordered the big searchlight turned off. Within a minute, I could see the boat alongside in the rising daylight.

"XO," I said. "Get Petty Officer Danilo up here and see if he can talk to these guys. Ask if they've seen any Japanese subs. See that old guy? That's probably who he should talk to."

The fo'c'sle crew unrolled a chain ladder and asked the old man to come aboard. He seemed hesitant, but then grabbed the ladder and climbed slowly to *Holland*'s fo'c'sle, where he was helped aboard by one of the boarding team. Eeep approached with Danilo, who began talking to him. I watched from my chair on the bridge. I also called Combat and told them to watch the radar picture; with everyone focused on this boat, a Japanese sub could be setting up a torpedo shot on us with his periscope.

Danilo, being Filipino, was able to communicate with the old man, but apparently the old man didn't understand what Danilo wanted to know. Eeep sent for a silhouette recognition book for Japanese warships. Once he showed the old man the pages for the different classes of Japanese subs, the man reacted. He excitedly pointed north and gabbled away in his native language, which I assumed was Tagalog. Danilo reported that they'd seen a sub like that on the surface just after sundown, north, two days' sailing. The fo'c'sle phone talker relayed this information to me on the bridge. I frowned when I heard that "two days" bit. Then I realized the man was describing the distance covered by a sail-powered, wooden fishing vessel. In these calm airs, that could be minimal.

I told the phone talker up on the bow to put the XO on. "Eeep," I said, "give that man a carton of cigarettes and some candy bars. Thank him very much. Be nice. Be deferential."

A half hour later we were headed due north, the radar back on one sweep every thirty minutes. It was full daylight, so we went slow, executing a zigzag plan, the sonar still in listening mode. I met Eeep in CIC. "Where are we in relation to our estimated arc of stations?"

"Well north," Eeep said. "It may not be an arc but a straight line after all. I think we should loiter here, go in circles, and then start back due north after dark. Go in using the passive sonar. If there's a sub out here, we'll hear him. Keep the radar mostly off the air until we think he's close, and then go get the bastard, just like last time."

"My thoughts exactly," I said. "In the meantime, make sure the crew gets chow and a chance to get some rest. After about 2200, it's gonna be a long night. One last thing: If at all possible, I want to creep up on this bastard—from directly astern."

"You want to arrive in his baffles."

"Exactly, XO. Once you get an actual contact, either by passive sonar or the radar, begin a passive angle track. We need to know his course;

speed not important. They come up, open the hatches for fresh air, and light off their mains. Their course is immaterial to them as long as it's a smooth ride. Time on the surface is everything. But if we can compute that course and manage to get behind him, then he'll never hear us approaching."

"Got it, Captain," Eeep said. "I recommend we brief the wardroom right after lunch so the word has time to get around."

"Concur. Anything from Tulagi?"

"No, sir, but when should I send out that logistics request?"

"We have enough fuel to get back to our exile station if we draw a blank here?"

"Yes, sir, but we'll be well below fifty percent."

"Let's see what happens tonight," I replied. "We bag another one, we can tell them where to meet *us*."

Eeep grinned.

12

XO

I was awakened by a call from the JOOD on the bridge. "What time is it?" I asked.

"Zero three fifteen, XO. We have a radar contact. Bearing zero two zero, eighteen thousand yards. I shut the radar down as soon as we saw it. We're headed that way at five knots, weaving."

"Captain been informed?"

"Yes, sir. He said to slow to five knots and to set condition one AS, silent."

"I'll be right up."

I'd been sleeping in my stateroom, dressed except for shoes. My room was on the main deck, just forward of the wardroom mess. I could hear the sound of urgent feet outside my door as I put my shoes on. The crew was hustling to their general quarters stations, but without the usual clangor of the GQ alarm. One AS, silent, meant that, instead of ringing the GQ alarm, individuals already on watch would be sent down to the berthing compartments to wake the crew, who would then proceed quietly to their stations. The current Navy standard for setting general quarters was three minutes from alarm to all hands reporting on station and manned and ready, and with the ship completely buttoned up. The silent alarm took about fifteen minutes, but it was an orderly process, and, most important, a relatively quiet process. I went straight up to Combat and caught up with the captain at Combat's front door. Up the hatch leading to the bridge I could hear the sounds of the GQ team as they relieved the helmsman, lee helmsman, lookouts, and the two officers of the deck. Our version of the first team was getting on station, but quietly.

We both examined the tactical picture displayed on the lighted maneuvering table. We'd come north through the night, based solely on the fishermen's story. I had explained to the officers that we'd go north on the assumption they'd been telling the truth. If they'd seen a submarine, it was probably Japanese. If he was part of the picket line, he'd still be there. I had no idea of when Halsey and company would bring the Big Blue Fleet up from wherever they were, but I reckoned that a Japanese sub, having been assigned a station, would stay there until told otherwise.

"If we're wrong, then we'll keep looking," the captain said. "By all accounts the Japanese have occupied the Philippines in their usual brutal fashion, so those islanders have no reason to lie to us."

We reviewed the approach phase. Sonar had picked up a passive in-and-out contact to the north. Chief Santone had listened to it for half an hour before classifying it as diesel engines. The confirming radar contact had been eighteen thousand yards ahead. Nine miles. At five knots, it would take almost two hours to creep up on them. We had about two and a half hours left before first light, at which time he'd submerge.

"Increase speed to eight knots," the captain ordered. "Take another single radar sweep in twenty minutes, and then head straight for him. I'd love to arrive at a position directly astern of him, but there's no time to calculate his course and speed now, so forget that. Now I want to get within fifteen hundred, two thousand yards of him, turn broadside, then light him up, and shoot him to pieces with every gun we've got. We'll keep the sonar passive until the guns start up. We'll use a DR track to get in on him. Use the passive sonar bearing to determine if there are any changes on the way in. At twenty-five hundred yards on the DR, light off the radar continuously and we'll drive in on him, silence be damned. I'll be on the bridge."

I remained in Combat and made sure everyone understood the plan of action. Then we informed the rest of the crew via the several phone circuits about how we were going to try to get this guy. The GQ team stations acknowledged and then began making their manned and ready reports. Word went out that every gun—the three-inch, the forties, and the twenties—was going to open fire as soon as the big searchlight came on and they saw something to shoot at.

I climbed up onto a stool next to the DRT plotting table and asked for coffee. Combat, with the plot of the tactical situation as we closed in, would drive the engagement, refining an intercept course on the surfaced submarine, slowing as necessary to keep the *Holland*'s propulsion noises to a minimum. The sonar was in the passive mode, and hopefully the roar of the sub's diesels would deafen them and provide a nice steady directional cue.

The sea felt still, flat, calm. The lookouts were reporting almost total darkness. That jibed with the moon's current phase. The air temperature outside Combat was still up in the high eighties, and I knew everyone was sweating in their battle dress: steel helmets, a bulky kapok life jacket, a long-sleeved shirt, and trousers tucked into their socks. Here in Combat it was almost cold. I had seen pictures of sub sailors at work: khaki bathing suits, T-shirts, tennis shoes, ball caps. Submarines in tropical water were hot, steel tubes. Anti–flash burn battle dress was irrelevant—it wouldn't be fire that killed them. I, along with the entire crew, waited. If we can just luck out and get into his baffles, I thought, we'll surely get him.

There was only one wrinkle in our approach: modern submarines had torpedo tubes both forward and aft. American subs had six torpedo tubes forward and four aft. I wasn't sure what this sub had, not having actually seen him. Intel said an I-boat had stern tubes; the smaller Ro class submarine had only bow tubes. Tactically, we had to assume that the sub's skipper, finding himself under sudden gunnery attack from astern, would simply fire every fish he had back aft. This meant that, when the searchlight came on and the shooting started, *Holland,* which would now be broadside to the submarine, had better kick it in the ass and move sideways out of any approaching spread. The entire American Navy had learned, usually to our great cost, about the devastating effect of Japanese torpedoes. We had to balance the risk of facing a sudden torpedo attack against the necessity to bring all guns, fore and aft, to bear in the few seconds he remained on the surface. Obviously, the captain thought it worth the risk, but it was going to be our job here in Combat and down in Sonar Control to give us warning and to order the correct maneuver to avoid torpedoes. I made a mental note to talk to him about where he should be in a situation like this: up in his chair in the dark on the bridge or down here at the head of the table where he could see the tactical picture being plotted out in front of him.

"Bridge, Combat, Sonar confirms diesel engine noise. Relative bearing is zero zero five. Dead ahead of us on our present course. Range unknown."

Then the captain, who'd heard that report, asked for a course that would put the noise source on our starboard beam instead of right on the bow.

"Zero one zero, true," the senior radarman said, and I relayed that to the captain. But then I realized that, if we turned ninety degrees in either direction, the range to the sub would begin to open, which might put all but the three-inch out of the game. Since all the shooting would be in manual control, we needed as many rounds of all types to be headed his way to make up for the lack of accuracy. I called the captain.

"I recommend we hold course and speed for a little longer," I said. "If we turn now, we may put the forties and twenties out of the action—the moment we turn, the guns' range to the target will start to open."

"Just thinking the same thing. Screw it, let's use the radar in five minutes: if we're close enough, we'll turn and start shooting. If we're too far out, we'll take our chances on his detecting the signal and crash-diving."

"And if he does that, we'll conduct an immediate hedgehog attack."

"Exactly."

Then we waited some more while the electronic techs brought the radar up from its nap. It was truly frustrating not knowing how far out in front of us the sub was. I had visions of colliding with the damned thing. I finally hit the talk switch on the bitchbox. Another minute, the ETs were saying. I called the captain.

"Bridge, Combat."

"You ready to blink there, XO?"

The ETs reported the radar was ready to start shining. "Yes, sir," I said. "Let's take that radar sweep."

"What could go wrong?" he chuckled. "If he's there, and close enough, order the turn. I'll handle the light; you handle the maneuvers."

"Aye, aye, sir," I said. I told the radar operator to bring the radar up into full radiate. His face lit up. "Radar contact: Bearing one zero five, range fifteen hundred yards."

I nodded at my Combat-to-bridge talker, and he gave the order to the helmsman on the bridge to turn left to zero one zero. "Speed fifteen," I added.

I overheard the captain tell the gunnery officer on the bitchbox to activate the searchlight on a relative bearing of zero nine zero and to commence firing as soon as he saw a target. I prayed the gunners *would* see a target and we hadn't jumped the gun, so to speak. Radars can sometime lie.

We couldn't see the searchlight come on, of course, but we could definitely hear and feel the shock of every gun barrel that could be brought to bear opening up: three-inch, 40mm, and even the 20mms poured a stream of fire at the hapless submarine. I just *had* to see this.

I sprinted out of Combat and ran up the ladder to the bridge. There was no longer any need for night vision, not with that intense white light from up above. The submarine was already enveloped in a maelstrom of tracers, explosions, and fountains of water rising higher than her periscopes.

Then the bitchbox erupted. "Torpedo noise spokes!" Sonar Control yelled. "Up-Doppler!"

"Bearing drift?" asked the captain.

We waited for an agonizing ten seconds before Sonar came back with the words we wanted to hear: "Torpedoes drawing right."

Just as we expected, I thought. We should be well out of the way unless he fired again. Then came a blast of incoming machine gun fire as some incredibly brave gunner on the submarine began firing back even as everything around him was being torn to pieces. Two bridge windows shattered, flinging shards of glass everywhere in the pilothouse. I ducked, but then got back up and focused my binoculars on the submarine. I saw four three-inch shells in a row connect just below the sub's conning tower, and then a bunch more punching fiery holes into the top of the pressure hull. Something happened inside the sub that resulted in an explosion of red fire erupting straight up out of the conning tower, and then the boat began to sag by the stern.

We could have stopped it then, but our gunners were tearing this bastard to pieces under the white glare of the searchlight, and the captain was obviously loath to stop the carnage. Suddenly the sub's stern settled out of sight, and the bow came up, revealing those murderous torpedo tubes. The boys kept firing as the sub slowly settled backward into the sea, great gouts of air, fuel, and water blowing out of every orifice.

"Kill him, kill him, *kill* him," I heard the captain mutter as the sub's bow finally stood straight up. Every gun on the ship concentrated on the forward half of the sub as it began its plunge, sliding backward into the sea in a roil of white water and smoke.

"Cease firing," the captain said finally.

It took a full minute for all those vengeful guns to stop shooting, followed by sporadic bangs as red-hot, loaded bores cooked off into the night. All except for one twin 20mm mount, which kept a steady stream of white-hot rounds hammering into the water where the sub's forward section had disappeared. That would be Chief Bobby Garrett's mount, I thought. He'd lost two brothers at Pearl on December 7, and his hatred of all things Japanese exceeded the captain's.

I heard the gunnery officer yelling into his sound-powered phones. The offending 20mm finally went silent. Probably out of ammo, I thought with a cold smile. I made a mental note to tell the gunnery officer not to make a big deal out of that. The air was filled with the sulfurous stink of gunpowder and burned grease as all the gun barrels cooled down. The sudden silence made me aware of a commotion on the level right below the bridge, where the forward quad 40mm mount was.

"What's going on down there?" I asked the OOD.

"Mount forty-one reports one dead, two wounded," the OOD replied. "Mount thirty-one reports several hits on the front gun shield, but no casualties."

Well, *damn,* I thought. In a way that was pretty amazing: one gunner on that submarine's conning tower had fired back at that big white searchlight even as hundreds of rounds came his way and probably killed him in the next few seconds. I had to suppress a spike of admiration for courage like that. Have to admit, I thought, these Japanese were fighters.

We felt and, moments later, heard a deep underwater explosion. The searchlight operator, who had been sweeping the scene of the sinking suddenly locked on to a tight maelstrom on the surface, where large amounts of air were erupting, carrying quite a bit of wreckage. I heaved a sigh of relief; my heart was still pounding at the sight of our murderous barrage. The captain got on the bitchbox and called for the XO.

"Right behind you, Captain," I said. "I wanted to see for myself."

We both stared out into the night for a minute as that rumbling fountain of death and destruction began to diminish.

"All right, douse the searchlight," he said. "Got a casualty report?"

I checked with the gunnery officer. "One dead, one about to be dead, one seriously wounded, one cut up but okay. The gunners said it was probably a 20mm."

"We lost some windows up here," the OOD said. "But no casualties on the bridge."

That was because of all those professionally executed deep-knee bends, I thought. Mine included.

"By the way," the captain said. "Regarding Chief Garrett—"

"Understood, Captain," I said. "I'm sure the gun boss is, understandably, mad, but I suspect not very."

"Good," the captain said. "Now, have the sonar go active, and conduct an expanding square search, five hundred yards first leg, for one hour. I want to make sure that sub didn't have a buddy out here. In the meantime, get a sinking report out to Tulagi, give our current position, and ask them to set up a logistics rendezvous. And then I think we need to recompute that picket line geometry."

13

CO

At sunrise, we conducted a burial at sea for the two gunner's mates who'd been killed the night before. We slowed but did not stop, and I kept the ship in a continuous gentle turn while we gathered on the fantail. I read the service, the gunner's mates performed the rifle salute, and then we dispatched them to the deep, each of them cradling two three-inch shells under their flags to ensure they went down. All officers not on watch plus about two dozen crewmen attended, heads bowed, hats off, and standing there as quiet as I'd ever heard on a ship.

After breakfast that morning, I sat down with Eeep and Hal Welles to reexamine our projections on the picket line. I thought that finding two Japanese subs out here in the wastes of the Philippine Sea lent great credence to the existence of a picket line. Submarines didn't sit out in the middle of the ocean like venomous snakes sleeping off a big meal. They lurked around the major sea-lanes and straits, and the naval bases of their enemies. They ranged ahead of fleets on the move or waited around islands that were being struck by carrier aircraft, ready to rescue pilots in the water. One could argue that the I-boat could well have been going from A to B, but the second one? The fishermen had told us they'd seen one north of where we thought he'd be and so he had. The picket line theory was growing legs.

The navigator had managed to get a good star fix at nautical twilight. Sonar had produced no further contacts, so I collapsed the expanding square to return to the position of the second sunken submarine. The water depth there was 18,500 feet. No wreckage or oil slicks remained; the sea had swallowed them whole, as sometimes was its custom.

"If we draw a line from the first sub to where we sank the second one," Hal said, "it points northeast by east—about zero eight zero. If you carry that out to a thousand miles, it seems like it wouldn't give much warning of an American carrier task force headed toward the Marianas."

"That would be a straight-line projection?"

"Yes, sir, Captain," Hal said.

"What would a great circle track look like?"

The CIC plotters consulted some other charts, made their computations, and laid out a curving line that gradually lifted up to end a few hundred miles south of the Marianas Island group.

"Do we know where Halsey is now with Task Force Thirty-Eight?" I asked.

No one did, which wasn't surprising. The location of the American main battle fleet wasn't something that was promulgated. "Okay," I said. "Let's postulate they're somewhere around Nouméa or maybe even Truk, and then, alternatively, let's assume they're at that new base, Ulithi Atoll, in the Carolines. Draw one track from Nouméa and another one from Ulithi."

"Going where?" Eeep said.

"The Marianas," I replied. "Let's see where they intersect, and then draw a line from our present position to that intersection."

The plotters did what I asked. The intersection of the two most likely

Halsey tracks and the line from where the second sub had been sunk was bearing 083 degrees true from where we were.

"Good a plan as any," I said. "How far was the second sub from the first one?"

"One hundred twenty-five miles," Eeep said after taking a measurement with a pair of dividers.

"How many kilometers is that?"

"Just about two hundred," Eeep said, doing the calculation in his head.

"The Japanese use the metric system," I said. "So that's one station every two hundred kilometers. Nice round number, right? I want to arrive at around zero three hundred again; that seems to be our lucky number. And get a message out to Tulagi explaining our analysis of a possible submarine picket line, which hopefully will ground any static about why we left our 'picket station.'"

"I still think it was exile," Eeep grumped. "But I'll get that out right away."

The first congratulatory message came in at 1630, from the administrative commander of all destroyer forces in the Pacific Fleet, a vice admiral whose title was ComDesPac. This was followed by another "attaboy" from the brand-new commodore at Tulagi. I shared these with the exec and the wardroom; I wondered if our standing as a lone and bothersome Atlantic Fleet DE was rising in the eyes of the almighty First Team. A message from Halsey would have really made our day, but I suspected the big boss wasn't saying anything to anybody as he readied for the Marianas invasions, if indeed that's where the next blow would strike. A second message from Tulagi contained instructions for rendezvousing with a fleet tanker and her three escorting destroyers. The designated rendezvous position was, however, two hundred miles due *south* of our current position, which meant that the search for the next picket station would have to be delayed. I informed the XO, who was not happy.

"They should be coming to us," he snorted. "We're obviously onto something that nobody else has figured out."

"The price of success, XO," I said. "And I suspect that there will soon be other destroyer forces who'd like to horn in on a piece of the action, especially after they read our operational analysis. First and foremost, however, we need fuel, food, and more hedgehogs, if they have any. Turn south."

The rendezvous took place the next day. The fleet tanker was USS *Haw River* (AO-11), a requisitioned civilian Esso bulk oil carrier that had been painted gray, given four twin 40mm mounts and a detail of Navy gunners to serve them, and then sent west. She had an escort of three destroyers, who were part of Destroyer Division 212, complete with a commodore. After the underway replenishment was completed, the entire gaggle of ships turned south to return to Tulagi. *Holland* was ordered to accompany them long enough for me to be highlined aboard the flagship for a quick operational meeting with the commodore. As the two ships, the flagship and *Holland,* closed in alongside each other to a distance of seventy-five feet, I wondered what was about to unfold.

A destroyer squadron had a senior four-stripe captain in command. He was called "commodore" because he commanded a group of warships. The squadrons, consisting of twelve ships, were often organized into two divisions, six ships each, and commanded by a division commander, a somewhat less senior four-stripe captain. He also was called commodore. We must have an abundance of captains out here, I thought, as I climbed into the highline chair for my brief but exciting trip across the turbulent water kicking up between the two ships.

An ensign on the destroyer took me up to the commodore's cabin, which in fact had been the ship's original captain's in-port cabin before the commodore and his staff moved aboard. This custom forced the ship's commanding officer to live in his sea cabin for as long as the staff was aboard, which is why everyone just loved having the staff on board. I shucked my life jacket as I went up a ladder to get to the commodore's cabin and asked the ensign to get it back down to the highline station for my return trip.

The commodore turned out to be a young-looking four-striper named William Martinson III. I assumed he'd just been promoted from ship command to his present position as a DesDiv commander. Martinson pointed me to a chair and commended *Holland* for getting a second sub, but his first question confirmed my suspicion there'd be some quibbling about the two kills.

"Were you able to retrieve any physical evidence from either sinking," Martinson asked.

I nodded. "The first one was a hedgehog kill in very deep water. The human remains that came up weren't anything we'd want to bring aboard, but they proved that those people had made a trip to the bottom of the ocean, if you follow me. The second one we watched sink stern first under gunfire, and we have pictures and one grainy film of that. So, yes, sir, these are confirmed kills: one I-boat, one Ro class."

Martinson nodded, seemingly satisfied. "I saw your message about a picket line," he said. "So did my boss, the squadron commodore. For your information, we, too, have been receiving intel about the *possibility* of such a picket line. The problem is, according to PacFleet headquarters in Pearl, it's nowhere near where *you* think it is. Do you claim to know, or are you guessing?"

"Admittedly," I said, "we've been guessing all along, but we were under the impression that FRUPAC was also guessing, given the number of "might bes" and "possibles" in their detailed message. But having found a second one close, okay, roughly close to where we thought he was, with a little help from local fishermen, I think the likelihood is growing. If we find a third one where we think it'll be, I'd conclude that we're right and Pearl's wrong."

Martinson gave me a disapproving look. "You came from the LantFleet, didn't you?"

I nodded.

"Well, out here, lieutenant commanders, even those in command, don't publicly disagree with Chester Nimitz's intel organization. I would advise you not to start a dispute over who's right or wrong."

"Can I assume then we're going to go back to our original picket station when you and I are done here?" I said.

"And do what, Captain?" Martinson replied, his eyes suddenly cold and suspicious.

"Whatever we're ordered to do, Commodore," I said. "We're just one little DE. The only fights I want to have are with Japanese. I wouldn't dream of disagreeing with Admiral Nimitz's estimate of any situation."

"Good to hear that, Captain," Martinson said approvingly. "You might be interested to know that Tulagi has been ordered to form up a task unit to go run Pearl's estimate of where this purported picket line is. I will command that task unit. Would you like to be part of that?"

I dissembled. "We have yet to be integrated into any PacFleet operational unit," I said. "We'd probably just get in the way."

Martinson beamed. "You know, I think you're probably right about that. I'll advise my boss and Tulagi to get you joined up with the next westbound convoy escort unit as soon as possible. Again, congratulations on sinking *two* Japanese submarines. That's terrific. But a word of advice if I may: Make sure your evidence remains intact in case someone in the chain of command wants a look-see, okay?"

"Absolutely, sir," I said, with as much respect in my voice as I could summon. "Thank you."

"Especially any pictures or films," Martinson went on. "They may want those for our own wartime propaganda programs. You know—home front morale and all that."

"I understand," I said. "Commodore."

There came a knock on the cabin door and a lieutenant stepped in. "Time for the briefing, Commodore; we've received the new third fleet comms annex."

I stood up, made my manners, and followed the lieutenant back down to the 01 level for the return highline trip.

14

XO

I met the skipper when he landed amidships and climbed out of the flimsy looking highline chair at just about noon. He did not look happy. The highline team hadn't dunked him, so I assumed the meeting had been—interesting. I went up to the bridge with him, where he climbed up into his captain's chair and growled for a cup of coffee. He lit up a cigarette and blew angry puffs of smoke into the air for a minute while burning holes in the front windows with those black eyes of his. The bridge crew chatter had stopped altogether when they'd seen his face.

"That good, Captain?" I said, innocently as I could.

"I really liked working for our British commodore," he said. "And the boss in Norfolk was nothing but helpful and a prince of a guy besides. Out here, however, there must be something in the water."

I waited for him to expand on that but then realized that the entire bridge watch was listening hard, as usual. Everything he said would be all over the ship within the hour.

"Pearl thinks we're wrong about the projected arc of the picket line," he continued. "This commodore naturally assumes Pearl's right and, being new to the scene *and* an ex-LantFleet amateur, we're wrong."

"Well, our initial posit for the second station *was* wrong," I pointed out. "Thanks to those fishermen, we corrected it. But I'm curious—how did our message get back to Pearl?"

"Somebody at Tulagi making sure he—and us—were not about to step on Chester Nimitz's intel folks. That's what the commodore called them—Chester Nimitz's intel organization—and then explained to me why I should not pick a fight with them over who's right."

"Wow."

"So now they're gonna form up a task unit and go run Pearl's estimate of where the rest of these bastards are lurking. He even invited us to join that effort, in a "you'll get to see how the varsity does it out here" tone of voice. I thanked him but told him no, that we still hadn't operated with any PacFleet units and that we'd probably just get in the way."

"And he jumped on that with both feet," I said.

"Indeed, he did, XO; indeed, he did. Which means we're free to do whatever we want to. Oh, and he asked about 'physical evidence' of our two kills. I told him what we had and that seemed to satisfy him. For the moment. But he made a point of making sure we didn't lose it."

This time I was the one who was pissed off. "Well, maybe next time," I said, "let's pull some bodies aboard, chop off their heads and freeze 'em. Show the goddamned high-and-mighty First Team how we did things in the North Atlantic—you know, Viking style. That'll shut 'em up."

The captain laughed even as the bridge crew's eyes went out on stalks at the mention of severed Japanese heads in the ship's meat freezers. I could just hear the shocked whispers going out over the phone networks: the XO wants to cut off a buncha Japanese heads and put 'em down on the reefer decks. The XO? Yeah, the XO. That shit sounds more like the captain to me, et cetera, et cetera.

"Well, here's what we're actually going to do in order to keep up the good work and improve our standing in the company," the captain announced. "I want to proceed directly to where we think the next Japanese pigboat might be hanging out. Arrival in the dead of night, like the last time. We've got plenty of fuel now, so whatever speed we need to accomplish that is okay. Did the tanker have hedgehogs?"

"Yes, sir," Eeep said. "And we're topped off with fuel at ninety-five percent."

"God is with us, XO," he said. "But this time, I want to prepare the guys for a submarine that detects us first and has time to generate a solution, unlike the last one who fired everything in desperation. They can do that surfaced just as well as submerged."

"Yes, sir, but—"

"Look, XO," he said, "I'm thinking that these last two were almost too easy. If the Japanese high command has lost comms with the two westernmost pickets, they may have alerted the rest of them that something scary this way comes. We can't prevent an alerted sub from launching a four-fish torpedo attack. I want us to be thinking and talking about what measures we can take going in that would best frustrate that attack."

"Aye, aye, sir" was all I could say. Beyond bolting from the scene as fast as we could and trying not to insult my signalmen—or skivvies—at this moment I had no damned idea of what to do.

That afternoon we held our, by now, usual pre-action planning session, in the wardroom this time. I folded in all the department heads, even the supply officer. My theory was that the more the entire gang knew about what we were doing, the quicker they'd react to whatever our target sent our way. Like four type 95 torpedoes.

The first order of business was the time and motion problem. We'd been pulled way south to meet the tanker, so now it looked that we would have to steam all night and most of the next day *and* night if we wanted to arrive at the third picket station while the sub would still be on the surface. Our chief concern, as usual, was fuel—we were full-up now, but there was no telling if a tanker would be dispatched to a lone and distant station while a three-ship task unit was hunting somewhere else. Destroyer-type boilers had never been designed with fuel economy in mind, no matter what the Bureau of Ships claimed.

"The commodore didn't tell me that we *couldn't* keep on doing what we've been doing," the captain said. "And, of course, I didn't ask. I believe that, right now, all the bosses in PacFleet are distracted by whatever big move Halsey's about to make. Besides, we don't actually work for that commodore, which, for him, means we're someone else's problem. In other words, the closer the next island invasion gets, the less anyone out here will be thinking about what to do with *Holland*." He looked around the table. "Comments?"

No one spoke. "XO?" he said.

I hesitated to contradict him, especially in front of the department heads. But he had asked. "Out with it," he said.

"There's a new commodore down in Tulagi," I said. "He won't be involved in the next big push north, other than to supply destroyers to Halsey as they check into the theater from the States. I would expect that, sooner or later, he's going to say 'What's this LantFleet DE doing way out there all by itself? *Holland,* is it?' And the CSO would say, 'Well, Commodore, that's the one that's just sank two Japanese subs.' 'Okay, CSO, but aren't we supposed to integrate *Holland* into a PacFleet destroyer unit? Isn't that what we do here? Why not send her to join up with that task unit hunting this purported picket line of Japanese subs?' Something like that. And the CSO can either say, 'Because I thought if we just left her alone, she might get another Japanese sub.' Or, he'd say, 'Aye, aye, sir. We'll do that.'"

"Okay," the captain said. "What's your point?"

"If we want a chance to get a third sub, I think we should pour on the gas and get up there well before dawn tomorrow—not the next day."

"Navigator, is that feasible?" the captain asked.

Lieutenant (Junior Grade) Russell "Russ" West left the wardroom to go make his calculations up in Combat, where the all-important large area chart was maintained. Everyone else lit up cigarettes and recharged coffee mugs. West was back in five minutes. "It'll require twenty-two knots to get there by zero four hundred from here," he announced. "We'd have to enter the datum at that speed to beat sunrise, too."

"Hmmm," the captain said. "They'd hear us coming two hours out at that speed, even while they were recharging batteries. Plus, we'd burn up time zigzagging our way in for the last ten miles."

"If he's even there," Hal pointed out. "I understand we may get called off, but a high-speed run-in is asking for an ambush. I would recommend we stick to the present plan and use the deep-creep tactics we've been using." Then he looked over at me rather sheepishly, realizing he'd just made an entirely contradictory recommendation. The captain intervened to defuse any embarrassment.

"I agree," he said. "I'd love to try what the XO's suggesting, but time and distance rules in our situation this far south. So, if we get called off, then screw 'em if they can't take a joke. We'll just follow orders. If we don't get called off, then we'll try to sneak up on the bastard. You all do realize that headquarters' intel might actually be right, don't you?"

"That would be a first," Hal said. "Every estimate I've read for the past year has been off, especially when we were up in the North Atlantic."

"Well, there was Midway, wasn't there," I said. "And then their intentions to occupy the Solomon Islands so they could cut our supply lines to Australia, causing us to invade Guadalcanal. Then—intercepting Yamamoto's airplane and killing their top admiral?"

I paused. I suspected that the captain had seen an opportunity to teach us something.

"Do you remember why a subordinate is required to always follow his superior's legal orders?" he asked. "Because there's always the chance that his superior may know something really important the subordinate doesn't. Look—all these what-ifs are very interesting but, ultimately, way above our pay grade. Let's us snuffies go do what we know how to do and leave the chess-playing to all those grand masters back in Pearl. Okay?"

There were nods around the table. We were certainly aware that what we didn't know far exceeded what we did know.

"Now," the captain continued. "I still think we've been exceedingly lucky the last two times. Like I said, I want to start thinking about approaching an alerted submarine for a change, one whose outer doors are open and whose torpedoes are warmed up."

We discussed approach tactics for the next hour, with the captain pointing out that in this situation, a task unit had a much better chance of success than a lone escort. A submarine being surrounded by three or four escorts would be in dire trouble; a submarine being approached by one destroyer required only a single firing solution to make good his getaway. I reminded them that the Brits never sent just one escort against a U-boat. They always sent a crowd, and just as we were headed back to the States, they were adding a light aircraft carrier to that crowd, meaning that the U-boat was now fighting for its life in two dimensions.

"If we detect and successfully engage a third boat out here," he said, "then that task unit we just gave the slip to will be there the next morning, commodore and all. And that's okay by me. The trick is to get one more, but, as I've said to the XO, the first two were almost too easy. This guy, if he's there, might be on the surface and *not* charging diesels. He may be listening hard on *his* sonar and just waiting for something to show up on the scope. Remember, he can hear us long before we can ping on him. We mustn't get complacent. They've lost two boats to unknown forces. The rest of them may have been told to be on their guard. Hell, they may have withdrawn the picket line, although I don't think so, and that's because the bogeyman is coming with eight hundred ships. I can just see the Japanese high command being willing to sacrifice any number of submarines for firsthand intel on where Halsey's going. We'll meet again in the morning to talk actual tactics, especially on how to best use the sonar."

15

CO

After dinner that evening, I called a meeting of the chiefs' mess. It turned out to be a full house since none of them wanted to miss a séance with the captain; any chief on watch would simply turn to the next senior petty officer in the space and say: you got it. I'd picked a good night: it was Chief Boiler Tender Thomas 'Steamboat' McGruder's birthday, which meant cake was available to go with coffee. They claimed it was a morale booster, but I always thought that it was because the chiefs really liked cake. A crewman having a birthday got a mention in the Plan of the Day.

I sat at the head of the table so I could be face-to-face with all of them. There were six chief petty officers assigned to *Holland*. Roscoe "Hammer" Santone, chief sonar technician; Thomas "Steamboat" McGruder, chief boiler tender; Louie "How" Garcia, chief boatswain mate; Robert "Gunner" Garrett, chief gunner's mate; Tommy "Spike" Carroll, chief machinist mate; and Walter "Skinny" Baynes, chief commissaryman.

Most of them resembled their specialties. Garcia, Santone, and Garrett were big boys. Carroll and McGruder were slim and wiry. Skinny Baynes was anything but. The collection was small enough that everyone got along. On a full-sized destroyer, there might be as many as fifteen chiefs, a large enough group for factions to form. My chiefs were through and through professionals, much respected by the crew.

I began by giving them a briefing on what I knew about the Big Picture: what was happening, what was about to happen, maybe, and the intel we had on the so-called picket line of submarines.

"We got the first one because of a PBY sighting. He was out there where we were, and we got lucky—he certainly didn't expect an American destroyer escort to show up out there in the empty quarter of the Philippine Sea. The fact that we were able to sink him must have truly surprised our fans in Tulagi."

That produced some sniggers. The chiefs were fully aware of the reason behind our being out there in the first place.

"The second one was based on what Pearl had been telling us: there's a 'possible' picket line of Japanese subs out there somewhere. We think they're maybe there to alert the Japanese high command if they can catch a glimpse of Halsey and the Third Fleet driving by. We assume they're stationed on a great arc that covers all the possible approaches the Third Fleet could use to go to either the Marianas—that's the islands of Saipan, Guam, and Tinian—or the Philippines, themselves. We think the arc is possibly a thousand miles long. We think it possibly begins about where you guys sank that I-boat. We assume, we think, we postulate all sorts of possible stuff—you get the idea. They got a tickle, and they faithfully passed it on. Happened to be, *Holland* was the only unit that could 'possibly' respond, which is ironic, seeing how it really was we happened to be out here.

"Now we're on our way to see if we can find another picket submarine, assuming that any of this possibly, maybe, might-be dope is right. That task unit we refueled with today is on its way to where they—actually Pearl—think the next station is, based on Pearl's latest reading of whatever entrails they've been studying. I think we're right and they're wrong, but the only way we're gonna prove that is to get a third sub. But here's the rub: I also think we got lucky on subs one and two. I think there's a good chance that Tokyo may have noticed that two of their subs have gone radio silent. I think they may have alerted the other four that the Americans might be hunting the picket line. Which means, in turn, that when we go creeping in on number three this time, we might be creeping up on an alerted submarine, who'll be sitting there, his diesels shut down, listening carefully for an approaching surface ship with all his torpedo tube doors open and his fire-control team awake and ready.

"So, as we head in tomorrow tonight, be thinking about damage control. Brief your people that this time there may be a fight instead of an easy ambush. Make sure they're properly dressed out for GQ and that they know where the life rafts are and how to deploy them. When we button up, no exceptions for ventilation. No smoking topside. You snipes in particular be ready for anything, including an oh-my-God emergency bell to go balls to the wall, boiler safety procedures be damned. Drag 'em down if you have to, but if I call for an emergency flank bell, give it to me, got it?"

Chiefs Carroll and McGruder nodded emphatically. Flank speed was at the top end of *Holland*'s ability. An emergency flank bell meant that the rheostats on the electric motors would be pressed into their stops. That, in turn, would put an instant surge demand for steam on the ship's boilers as the turbogenerators applied the summoned amps. If the sudden steam demand drew so much steam that the boilers couldn't keep up, the generators might trip off the line, leaving *Holland* with no propulsion power whatsoever. I was telling them to take chances, because I knew full well what a Japanese torpedo hit could do to my ship. Which was to break it in half and sink it in under a minute.

There was a moment of alarmed silence in the mess. I let it build, then smiled and asked if there was any more cake.

16

XO

The next morning, I was greeted by a messenger from Radio Central. The captain had received a personal-for-CO message that he was sharing with me. I contained a groan when I saw it was from Tulagi, but it wasn't quite what I thought.

> *Holland* will soon be ordered to join up with amphibious task force 58.7 to become part of the escort ASW screen. ComDesRon 36 (CTU 58.7.3) will be screen commander. Remain in your current patrol area until further notice. When summoned proceed at most economical speed to join the screen at a position to be designated by (CTU 58.7.3). Review antiaircraft operational procedures, as enemy airstrikes are expected as soon as TF 58.7 comes in range.

In range of what? I wondered. All the rumors still pointed to the Marianas—Guam, Tinian, Saipan, but given the sheer amount of rumors flying around, that could all be one big feint. The good news was that *Holland* wasn't being recalled immediately. If we struck out tonight, then whatever the big deal ended up being, it sounded interesting. I called the ops boss to deliver the news. He pointed out that the task organization numbers had changed to Task Force Fifty-Eight. That meant Admiral Spruance had relieved Admiral Halsey. And how about that "remain in your current patrol area" bit? I told him that the term "current patrol area" meant wherever we happened to be at the time. He accused me of spending too much time with the captain.

That afternoon we reviewed Pacific Fleet antiair warfare standard operating procedures, courtesy of the books and operations orders given to us at Tulagi. *Holland* had a minimal antiaircraft capability. She could barely defend herself against a determined Japanese bomber attack, other than by maneuvering wildly and shooting at anything we could see. Destroyers had radar-directed gunfire capability and multiple five-inch guns. Destroyer escorts had two or three three-inch guns and no director or even an air-search radar. If we were ordered to protect amphibious shipping—troop transports, attack cargo ships, ammunition ships, the best we could do would be to lay practically alongside one of them and add to whatever guns the amphibs could muster. When the captain saw the looks on the officers' faces after he explained all this, he reminded them that there would be carrier-based fighters engaging the incoming Japanese long before they got close enough to start dropping bombs on large, slow-moving amphib transports.

"That said," he continued, "the second word in our ship-type designator is 'escort,' so start thinking about a close-in, last-ditch AA barrage situation. Gunner Garrett can fill you in. In the meantime, tonight's an ASW operation, against a possibly alerted opponent."

For thirty minutes we moved on to the approach plan: radar employment, torpedo evasion maneuvers, sonar operation—passive or active—and what the expected water conditions and the need for constant data on where any thermal layers were.

"We surprised the second one," he pointed out. "But I think the first one detected us and was crash-diving by the time we lit him up. This third guy may already be submerged or decks awash—so he can still suck air for his diesels while waiting for us."

Now that's a lovely thought, I told myself.

After dinner I gathered up the attack team in CIC to talk about an idea I'd had regarding the sonar. I wanted to kick it around with the Sonar and Combat gangs before taking it to the captain, but he wandered in just as I was getting started, so I went back to the beginning.

"We were discussing an idea I've had about how to make the passive mode more effective. To review, our sonar has three modes of operation: active mode-wide angle or what's called omnidirectional search; active mode-narrow beam, where all the energy is concentrated in a three-degree beam; and, of course, the passive mode. Omni means the sound wave goes banging out in all directions except dead astern, i.e., the baffles. Narrow beam means we concentrate all the acoustic energy down that three-degree-wide sector; we use that when we have contact and are trying to keep it while the sub wiggles and squirms to get away from it. Passive means we're transmitting no energy; we're just listening.

"We can listen in omni mode, or we can listen in sector mode. The Brits told us that if a U-boat engineer dropped a large spanner—wrench—on the deck plates of the submerged U-boat, a good destroyer sonarman should be able to hear that. In a perfect world, I'd agree with that, and by 'perfect,' I mean perfectly quiet. The problem is that the deep sea is not silent—it's actually quite noisy: schools of fish, whales, undersea volcanic activity sending clouds of hot gases up from the bottom, and a barrage of noises that nobody can recognize. A submerged submarine running on electric motors, driven by batteries and not a steam plant like us, is pretty damned quiet by sonar standards. If there's a layer, i.e., if the first two hundred feet of depth is at eighty-four degrees, but the next two hundred is at seventy degrees, acoustic energy waves tend to bounce off the layer boundary. Submarines will come to periscope depth and then go back down, measuring the water temperature as they descend to see if there is a layer, and if there is, they make sure they stay below that layer, which can frustrate even an active sonar in narrow-beam mode."

"So, you're saying that, in reality, we're pretty limited unless someone in the sub screws up," the captain observed.

"Yes, sir, we are," I said. "Any destroyer would be."

"And your idea?"

I hesitated, not sure it was ready for center stage. "My idea is to rewire the sonar receiver unit. I want to put some capacitors between the raw signal coming back in from the transducer to act as filters and thereby eliminate as much background noise as possible coming from the deep sea."

That produced a moment of silence around the plotting table. I could see that most of them only vaguely remembered the term "capacitor" from academy or A-school days.

"The trick is to make sure the filters—the capacitors—don't filter out legitimate sounds," I continued. "So, I propose to add a parallel circuit coming from the receivers to the displays. One channel will deliver what we always see, complete with oceanic noise. The other channel will be filtered. We'll set up two operators, one on each channel, and each with the ability to switch between channels. One guy gets something, the other guy can switch and evaluate it for himself."

I sat back on my stool and waited for the captain's response. Modifying wartime equipment without BuShips' permission could get a CO in big trouble. On the other hand, I thought he'd recognize that the filtered circuit might mean the difference between finding or missing a lurking submarine, who was just dying for the approaching destroyer to go active and give them a final torpedo firing bearing.

"How long will this take?" he asked.

Oops, I thought. "Um," I said. "Not too long."

"You've already done it?" he asked.

"I might have already made a brass board," I said, squirming a bit. "I was just waiting for permission to wire it in."

I could see he was way ahead of me. "Does it work, XO?" he asked quietly.

I grinned sheepishly. "Yes, sir, it does."

"Make it so, then," he said. "And just so we can say that we did not modify the BuShips' approved design, make sure you use the word 'experimental' a lot."

"Exactly right, Captain," I said with great relief.

He went up to his sea cabin to get some rest. I finished the briefing with my accomplices, and then I went back to my stateroom to get some sleep before the night's festivities. Passive sonar, I thought, and the captain approves. Up in the North Atlantic, every escort had been continuously banging away in all directions, looking for U-boats, rarely detecting anything. The only time you knew a submarine was lurking nearby was when a nearby tanker in the convoy went boom and lit up the entire night in ghastly flames. I wondered if I could actually get a little sleep before we got there. Once I got back to my cabin, however, getting to sleep wasn't a problem, I discovered. We were all pretty tired.

17

CO

The bridge gave me a wake-up call in my sea cabin at 0130. I got up, washed up, got dressed, and went down into Combat. The watch officer gave me an update of where we were and how much farther it was to the estimated datum. I went to the bridge, cadged a mug of stale, midwatch coffee, and told the officer of the deck to set condition one AS, silent. Even this far out, I wanted quiet. Everything we did was based on sound. Noise could kill you.

Eeep reported from Combat that condition one AS had been set throughout the ship and that datum bore 075 degrees true, range nine miles. I looked at my watch: 0210. "Slow to eight knots," I ordered. "Tell Main Control to go to single-screw ops, but to be ready for twin-screw ops and full power at short notice."

"Combat, aye," Eeep said.

"And, XO? Tell the depth-charge gang to be ready—if this guy shoots at us I'm going to let fly, if only to remind him what the end of the world sounds like."

"But, sir—"

"Yeah, I know. But if we get a torpedo noise spoke from, say, one two zero degrees true, and we evade it, I want to drive back down that bearing at full power and get their attention. Then we'll slink away, go really quiet, and wait for him to make his next move. We'll be deaf after a depth-charge barrage, but so will he. I want him to focus on evading the next depth-charge attack, while we set up for a hedgehog attack."

"Aye, aye, sir," Eeep replied. From the tone of his voice, I knew he wasn't convinced.

The next hour was increasingly nerve-racking as *Holland* crept in to the datum area. There was a light chop on the surface and some low-level flying scud overhead through which a little moonlight glinted. There was a thin layer at ninety feet. The ship was fully darkened, and, as yet, there were no acoustic indications of a battery-charging submarine on the surface. I'd kept the radar off the air; I wanted an acoustic cue before using the radar to nail down an actual range and bearing.

He's been alerted and he's gone down, I kept thinking. Now he's listening for us as hard as we're listening for him. Ninety-foot layer—so he's probably down at one fifty or even two hundred feet.

"Helmsman, put your rudder to three degrees right," I ordered.

"Three degrees right rudder, aye, sir. Rudder *is* three degrees to starboard."

"Keep it so, Helmsman."

"Keep it so, aye, sir."

A steady turn in either direction was the standard defense against torpedoes. If the sub was capturing noise from us passively, it would be displayed as a bearing, but not a range. There was a plotting method called "passive-angle tracking," by which a listener could determine approximate distance to a sound source by taking a series of bearings, then change course and do it all again. It took a lot of time, but if you had nothing else, that's what you did. A ship that was circling in a big enough circle would frustrate that computation.

"Lee helm, indicate turns for three knots."

"Three knots, aye, Captain." There was a quiet clangor of bells. "Main Control answers: seventy-eight turns for three knots."

"Very well."

At three knots and three degrees of rudder, *Holland* would execute a wide circle indeed. The only downside was that at some point, we'd be pointing our acoustic dead zone, the dreaded baffles, right at the target submarine.

"Combat, Bridge: Tell Sonar Control to open the second channel, the filtered one."

"Combat, aye."

I summoned my talker, who wore a phone set and who was in contact with every important GQ station in the ship. "Tell all stations—make zero noise; we are in range of the enemy's torpedoes."

The talker relayed the message, and then reported: All stations acknowledge. Zero noise.

I knew, of course, we could be miles away from our intended prey. Everything we'd accomplished so far had been based on estimated positions, estimated station numbers, estimated every damn thing. On the other hand, that Japanese sewer pipe might be five hundred yards from us. So, we turned and waited.

At 0320, the bitchbox lit up. "Bridge, Combat, this is Sonar Control. The filtered line has detected a continuous squeal on bearing two seven five, true. Intermittent but it's definitely there. Somebody has a singing bearing."

I smiled. "Well done, Sonar. I'm going to bring us to two seven five, three knots, and begin a broad weave. Can you guess at the range?"

Eeep intervened from Combat. "No, sir, they can't, but they can measure Doppler, and if the amplitude of that signal begins to increase, we can narrow it down to a cone of courses. But it's just more guesswork."

"All right, XO," I said. "You and Sonar Control monitor what's happening to the filtered signal. When you think it's sufficiently strong, go active on the sonar. Tell me when you do that, because I'm going to make a radical course change to avoid whatever he might have cocked and ready."

"Aye, aye, Captain," Eeep said.

I then instructed Main Control to bring the second electric drive motor back online. Then I got out of my chair and went back to my sea cabin to pump bilges. Returning to the bridge, I refilled my coffee mug, briefly longed for a cigarette and then banished the thought.

More waiting. It wasn't as hot as it had been. The air was oppressive, as if it was being compressed by something big.

"Bridge, Sonar Control: Recommend we go active."

"Very well," I replied. "Talker—all stations: here we go." My talker repeated that to all the stations: the three-inch guns, the 40mm and 20mm guns, the depth-charge teams, the torpedo mount, Damage Control Central, the signal gang, and the searchlight team.

I could almost hear that first *ping* going out. And then: "Sonar contact! Bearing two eight zero, range fifteen hundred yards."

Followed by: "Torpedo noise spoke! Bearing two eight zero; more than one!"

"Right *full* rudder," I yelled. "All ahead flank—*emergency!*"

The lee helmsman grabbed his engine-order telegraph handles, pressed them all the way forward, then all the way back, and then all the way forward again until the pointer landed on *flank*. Main Control's pointers matched it in one second.

"*Up*-Doppler, at least two fish," Sonar Control announced. The voice on the bitchbox was noticeably higher than it had been.

I felt my ship shudder under the sudden application of full power, followed by a noticeable heel to port as the screws pounded the water beneath the stern.

"*Shift* your rudder, steady on two eight zero," I called. I pressed the talk switch on the bitchbox. "Combat, prepare for a depth-charge attack. Full bag when you think we're over top."

"Full bag, Combat, aye."

"Torpedo noise spokes have *left* bearing drift," Sonar announced. The relief in his voice was almost comical. Almost.

"Well, that's good," I said trying to defuse the obvious tension down in Sonar Control. "Range and bearing to target?"

"Range is nine hundred fifty yards, closing fast; contact becoming intermittent—he's probably going deep."

"Combat, Bridge: If we lose contact, drop depth charges on predicted position; set charges half and half: two fifty and three hundred feet."

"Combat, aye, half and half, two fifty and three hundred." The voice from Combat was no longer Eeep, who was probably doing the computations as to when to throw the book at the target.

"Torpedoes passing down the port side," Sonar announced. "Null Doppler. The display shows possible right turn on target."

"Combat, Bridge: Lead him!"

Even as I said it, I felt the ship, which was humming right along now, heel to port—Eeep had already given the order to put *Holland* on a course to drop just ahead of the fleeing submarine. Forty-five seconds later the first depth charges were blasted out of the ship's side projectors, port and starboard.

"Mark center," Sonar called. "Rolling aft, both racks."

"Left standard rudder," I called. "Slow to ten knots. Steady up on zero nine zero."

"Combat concurs," Eeep said. "That'll put the racket in the baffles."

That's the whole idea, XO, I thought. Twenty-four five-hundred-pound depth bombs were going to make one hell of a racket. I didn't really expect to hit the sub, but they'd be profoundly deaf once all that high explosive let go. Then the first group of side-projected depth charges started to go off at two hundred and fifty feet, beginning with heavy thumps that were followed by several eruptions of white water on either side of our wake. Twenty seconds passed before the second tier, now at three hundred feet, followed suit. I could just about visualize the spherical maelstrom of violently blasted water expanding into a hot bubble of explosive gases that would probably grow to four hundred feet in diameter.

"Slow to six knots and begin a narrow weave," I ordered. Then I called Eeep on the bitchbox. "I want to come slowly around to starboard so that we end up pointed at the last predicted position, and then come to all stop."

Five minutes later, *Holland* lay motionless in the dark sea. The sonar was back in passive mode because there was no point in sending acoustic energy into the rapidly expanding bubble, now the size of a small stadium, of disturbed water. I summoned my talker and twisted the mouthpiece on his phone set so that I could talk directly to all stations.

"This is the captain," I said. "We've come to all-stop to let the water settle down after all those depth charges. We're in the listening mode now. If we hit him, we'll hear breakup noises. If we damaged him, he might start blowing ballast to get back up to the surface. If we missed entirely, he's out there trying to localize us for another torpedo attack. This is where we determine if he gets us or we get him. Sound is everything right now, so maintain absolute silence throughout the ship. That is all."

I released the mouthpiece and settled back in my chair. After a minute, my talker told me all stations had acknowledged. "Quarter-gasket of the Watch," I said in as calm a voice as I could muster. "Make some fresh coffee please. This may take a while."

"Quarter-gasket, aye, sir," the navigation petty officer replied promptly and left to restoke the chart house's coffeepot. His proper title was quartermaster of the watch, but by using the crew's nicknames for various ratings in the ship—quartermasters became quarter-gaskets; radiomen became radio-pukes; sonarmen were sonar-girls; all engineers were snipes; signalmen were skivvy-wavers—I hoped to diminish the fearful tension that was gripping the bridge team. Japanese torpedoes passing in the night had that effect. On the sonar's audio speakers, they'd sound like steam locomotives.

I knew I was taking some big chances by coming to a full stop. Yes, it was a dark night, but there was just enough moonlight for a periscope, especially one containing first-grade Japanese optics, to see us. On the other hand, the sub would have to come to periscope depth to take that look. That would require blowing air into ballast tanks to bring her up, and I was counting on Eeep's capacitor-lined circuits to detect that noise. On yet another hand, if the submarine had survived that barrage of depth charges, her skipper might be doing exactly what I was doing: hovering as quietly as he could down at three hundred feet or so and trying to move in the away direction at bare steerageway on *his* specially quieted electric motors.

The quartermaster returned with fresh coffee that I gratefully accepted. I looked at my watch: it would be daylight before long. Eeep appeared at my side, his face looking like a Halloween mask in the red light of the bridge's instruments.

"What do you think, XO?" I asked.

"I think if he was really smart," Eeep said. "He would have maneuvered back into that area of disturbed water and settled down to wait us out."

"I agree—that's what I would do. But he can't stay there forever, especially if he didn't get a battery-charging hour or two on the surface tonight. If nothing else, he'll eventually need breathable air. We need neither. That's a waiting game he can't win."

"Yes, sir, that's all possible. But if he can make even two knots over the next eight hours on what's left of his batteries, he can be sixteen miles away in any of three hundred sixty directions."

I smiled. "This," I said, "is when I wish we had a crowd to work this bastard. What do you recommend?"

We were interrupted. "Bridge, Sonar Control."

"Bridge, aye."

"The filtered circuit has a faint, single-frequency noise spoke at one eight five; low amplitude, but relatively steady; request the XO come down here to listen."

"On the way," I replied, but Eeep had already gone.

I squirmed uncomfortably in my chair. More waiting, I thought, but at least we had a line on something. Let's hear it for capacitors: Eeep's filtered circuit experiment might be about to pay off again. The ship was unusually quiet; only the sound of the vent fans mounted on the ship's single stack, which pulled hot air out of the main engineering spaces, and the forced draft blowers, which fed the boilers, filled the nighttime air. The breeze had completely died out as the sea prepared to greet the sun in a few hours. I would have loved to eavesdrop on the conversation going on down in Sonar Control right now. Eeep with his mad scientist hat on and the sonar-girls pressing earphones into their skulls, trying to interpret that strange noise. I figured we had maybe another ninety minutes before false dawn, at which point we'd have to move. I heard muffled conversations drifting up from the hedgehog mount down below the bride. Hang in there, guys, I thought. We may have some business for you shortly.

Eeep stepped back out onto the bridge and came over to the captain's chair. "I think it's that same mechanical bearing," he announced. "A very faint squeal on something that's not a very big piece of machinery: a vent fan or a cooling pump. But it's not biologics."

"Due south of us?"

"Yes, sir. No idea of how far, of course, and if there's Doppler, none of us could tease it out."

"Does that bearing intercept where we thought he was when we fired depth charges?"

"Slightly west of that, but not by much. I think he turned west and then glided down deeper to a hover under the depth-charge boil. He's probably making some way to stabilize the hover, so I'd guess west at one or two knots. Probably wants to stay close to all that residual noise down there. He knows we can't see into that."

As in, "I told you not to do that," I thought, but mentally shrugged the implied criticism away. I didn't want to admit to him that I'd been itching to make the sea roar again like we used to do up north. Terrorize the bastards if nothing else. "What's the range to that intersection?"

Eeep had to go back down into Combat to review the plot. He came back out and said it was 3,600 yards.

"Okay, let's assume that's where he is and that he's creeping west, depth unknown, so let's postulate two hundred fifty feet. I'm going to come up to ten knots and head to an intercept point of where we think he'll be once we've covered those thirty-six hundred yards. You go compute that course for me. When we're at two thousand yards, I'll come up to fifteen knots, and then I want you to go active on both sonar and radar. This time I want to make a hedgehog attack. Hopefully we'll gain contact, but if not, we'll shoot anyway. Get the word out to all stations."

"Aye, aye, sir," Eeep replied and disappeared again.

I called the chief engineer and explained what the plan was. "I want you to come up to ten knots now as quietly as you can—no sudden thrashing of our screws. Ease up to it."

"Got it, Captain," Casey said.

"Bridge, Combat—recommend one eight five at ten knots."

"Officer of the Deck—make it so," I said.

I felt a gentle push as the engineers brought the electric motors up to the RPM needed for ten knots. A steam turbine–driven ship couldn't do what I'd just ordered. There'd be a sudden rise in the noise produced by the boilers' steam-driven, forced-draft blowers, followed by even more noise as the steam admission valves were opened on the main engines. Holland's boilers ran two big turbo-electric generators, which spun at constant speed. Coming to ten knots simply meant rotating a really big rheostat to apply more current to the ship's electric motors. Within a minute or so, the boilers would need to start producing more steam, but it would be a gradual—and quiet—process.

At two thousand yards—one land mile—Sonar Control went active and immediately announced a sonar contact. Combat gave the conning officer a new course to steer as the ship surged up to fifteen knots. Quiet operations were no longer necessary—the sonar banging away would make it clear to the submarine's captain that the game had resumed, and also that he was in deep shit. I thought about weaving in case our prey fired more torpedoes, but at this stage, there'd be no time for the submarine's attack team to calculate a solution.

"Bridge, Combat, contact is drifting right; he's running for it. Come right to one niner five."

"Bridge, aye, launch when ready."

Another minute and then came the *pop-pop-pop* of twenty-four hedgehogs as they went flying out ahead of the ship, dropping into the water with deceptively innocent small white splashes. Combat recommended a course change to port to bring the contact through the baffles quickly and position the ship for another run.

It wasn't necessary. *Seven* explosions thumped the sea back on our starboard quarter in quick succession, and I yelled my approval. I ordered the ship to slow to five knots and to continue turning around to point back at our target.

"Combat, Bridge, Sonar Control: Propeller noises and heavy ballast blowing, bearing two one zero. We think he's trying to surface."

I alerted Bat Watkins to prepare to engage and to have the searchlight ready. This time I remembered to turn the ship so that every gun could be brought to bear.

"Combat, Bridge, Sonar: Noises on the bearing are much louder—he's definitely coming up. Bearing zero seven zero *relative*."

"Bridge, aye," I replied and alerted the gunnery team to direct the searchlight seventy degrees to starboard, relative to the bow. Santone was playing really heads-up ball, I thought, to give that last bearing in relative degrees: the searchlight operators did not have a gyro repeater up there on their platform on the stack. Then the beam snapped on to reveal an amazing sight.

The submarine's stern emerged from a hundred-yard-wide boil of white water and escaping high pressure air. Both her screws were turning furiously, and great gouts of water mixed with air were pulsing out of her limber holes along the port side. The searchlight moved right slightly to capture the scene; I could hear the photographer begin snapping pictures from out on the bridgewing.

"Bridge, Gun Control: Request permission to open fire."

"Not necessary," Eeep said from behind my chair. I turned around. "What?" I said.

Eeep pointed at the spectacle unfolding in front of us. "He came up stern first," he said. "Which means all those hedgehog hits were forward of his conning tower. As soon as those screws fully clear the water, he'll start sliding back down again. Why waste the ammunition?"

I gave the order to hold fire.

As if listening to Eeep's prediction, the sub's stern rose into an almost vertical attitude when both those screws cleared the water and began whirling at an impossible speed like a runaway engine, flashing bronze highlights in the harsh, white glare of the searchlight. Then she began to slide out of sight, visibly accelerating as the tons of water flooding her forward half took control now that there was no counteracting force from the propellers. In seconds, she was gone on a vertical dive from which no submarine could ever recover. Ninety seconds later came the rumbling thunder of hull collapse, audible to all hands topside, who were standing transfixed by what they'd just seen.

There was a collective sigh of relief on the bridge. I slumped back into my chair and closed my eyes for a moment. More booming reverberations from the great deeps made their way to the surface.

"Secure from general quarters," I ordered, finally. "Nice job, everyone. That's three, by God."

18

XO

Holland lingered in the area until sunrise, and then we began looking for that commodore's precious "evidence." There wasn't any, not even an oil slick. The captain ordered a small scale expanding square search, but by noon, nothing had come up. He wandered over to the chart table and examined the depth markings.

"Depths in fathoms or feet?" he asked.

"Fathoms, sir."

We both looked again at the numbers. Good God: the waters here were twenty-five-thousand-feet deep. That would explain it, I thought. The photographer's mate had shown me some black-and-white proofs of the sub's stern in the searchlight. That'll have to do, I thought. I thought it was pretty convincing.

I drafted a message report of our third kill and then showed it to the captain. I'd kept it short and succinct, as he had done:

> Gained contact on submerged enemy submarine and conducted a depth-charge attack with unknown results. Lost contact. Began search. One hour later, regained contact. Scored seven hits with hedgehog. Sub broached stern first but then went back down in a near vertical attitude. Sonar recorded sounds of hull collapse. UNODIR, heading east.

"Now, that's gonna bring a crowd," I said. "Pretty obvious our picket line is *the* picket line."

"Yeah, probably," the captain replied. "And it'll also bring a commodore who's gonna tell us how to do this stuff. Fun while it lasted. Work up a LogReq, please, and let's start heading east-northeast."

We gathered in Combat in the early afternoon to lay down the next track on our hunt. The weather was beginning to change, with a steady fifteen knot wind and a rising chop in the sea. The next station on our projected picket line arc was estimated to be just over a hundred miles to the northeast, requiring a course of 075. The next question was speed. At ten knots, it would take twenty hours to arrive in the vicinity of where we thought the next station might be.

"That's too early," Hal said.

"Yeah, but if we go ten knots we'll conserve fuel," I said. "Plus, that allows us some latitude in choosing how to make that final creep."

The captain nodded. "Okay, set it up," he said. "We're at sixty-one percent on fuel; so slowly is better than 'fastly.'"

In the event, everything changed when an op-immediate, personal-for-CO message came in from Tulagi later that night. It began with hearty congratulations on sinking yet another Japanese submarine. Then came the news we had been expecting: *Holland* was to rendezvous with a task unit and report to ComDesDiv 212 for duty. There were three destroyers in the task unit; *Holland* would make four. A replenishment with USS *Escambia* (AO-80) would be set up for the next day. After that, the task unit would proceed as directed by ComDesDiv 212. Again, very, very well done. Wooldridge.

The task unit was considerably southeast of where *Holland* was pointed, so I had to get together with the navigator and compute a new course and speed to make the scheduled rendezvous. I met with the captain at 2230 to review the track.

"I've retransmitted our LogReq directly to *Escambia* just to make sure," I told him.

The ship was rolling and pitching a bit on the new course to make the rendezvous. I had to grab my coffee mug to keep it from hitting the deck. "Weather's picking up," he said.

I nodded. "Nothing serious as far as I can tell," I said. "So far. No big, deep ocean swells, so I don't think there's a typhoon out there somewhere. On the other hand, the chiefs who've been out here in the Pacific before are getting worried. Apparently, this *is* typhoon season. The barometer is dropping, but very slowly."

"Wonderful," he grumped. We'd both read about the Pacific's typhoons, whose cousins, the Atlantic hurricanes, we'd already met. The one thing I remembered was that the typhoons tended to be worse than hurricanes because the Pacific was so much bigger, and thus the storm systems had more time to really wind themselves up. If a typhoon was coming, there'd be no anti-submarine operations; we'd be operating in the survival mode. Ironically, any submarine, ours or theirs, could simply go deep and ride it out in relative comfort. Even the possibility that something like that was coming meant that *Holland* must be refueled so as to be fully loaded down when the monstrous seas arrived.

"Tell the department heads to review their heavy-weather bills," he ordered. "I'm hoping we can pull off that replenishment in the next day or so. But if not, and a big storm is brewing, we'll have to ballast to maintain metacentric height."

Something in my expression must have revealed my ignorance about ballasting. The captain explained that when a ship was facing really bad weather with half-empty fuel tanks down below, it was imperative that you restore the designed liquid load to keep her stable. The only way to do that was to admit seawater into the fuel tanks. Theoretically, the oil and the water wouldn't mix, and the oil would "float" on top of the seawater. Theoretically.

"Casey won't even want to hear that word," he continued. "All engineers believe that's a recipe for getting water in the fuel oil, which can, if not detected in time, extinguish boiler fires. Then you go dead in the water—in a typhoon."

"Lovely," I said, hoping my face didn't reveal that I had no idea what a metacentric height was. I was a ninety-day wonder, with only a few years at sea under my belt even though I was now the XO. The captain had once told me that the exec on his first destroyer had been forty years old with eighteen years in the Navy. Back during the big Depression, promotions moved like glaciers. Someone had to die or retire before anyone got promoted. He said no one complained—they were employed and eating regularly.

"We should hear back from CTU 212 pretty soon," the captain said. "Lemme know when and where to expect a rendezvous."

We joined up the next evening, just before sundown. The other ships in the task unit were already alongside and refueling, so *Holland* had to get in line. The sea was still disturbed, and the night air felt like it was waiting for something. Low scud clouds were really flying by this time, flitting like ghosts across a weak moonlit sky, going from north to south. If there was a typhoon out east somewhere, that would fit. We were above the equator—cyclones would rotate counterclockwise. Their leading-edge clouds would look just like this. The barometer, which had slowed its descent during the day, was falling again.

After refueling, the commodore assigned us a station in the formation, and then the task unit turned north. I had the tactical team meet in Combat at 2200.

"We're going too far to the right," the captain said. "Here"—he pointed to an X on the plot—"is where the next one should be if our projection of the whole picket line is correct." He paused as if he'd just had a thought. "Does the commodore know the details of *our* projection?" he asked.

"We assumed they'd figure it out after we got a third enemy sub," I said. "Three sinking positions—draw a line though them and you'll know where to look for the next one."

"Assumed?" he asked innocently.

There was a sudden embarrassed silence around the plotting table. Naval officers were taught never to assume unless ordered to do so. The word itself parsed into the expression that when you assume, you take the chance of making an ass out of you and me.

He sighed. "Look," he said. "They didn't believe our projection in the first place. They accepted Pearl's version. Now we've embarrassed the whole system. Ordinarily, we'd be—*I'd* be—on somebody's silent shit list for that. The only thing preventing that is three Japanese subs have been sunk. Do this: Send the commodore our entire line of projected positions for the picket line. Make sure they include the positions where we sank the three subs. No recommendations. No advice. No crowing. No 'if you'd just listened to us' stuff. Just the facts. In fact, I'll send that as a personal-for message, from me to the commodore. That way he can walk into his CIC and say: 'Hey, everybody, let's do this instead.' Like it was his idea."

At about noon the next day, the commodore ordered a course change as I came up to the bridge. The navigator plotted the new track and brought it to the captain, who smiled. "Well, how 'bout that," he said. "Now, I want to see how he plans to surprise the next picket with a formation of four ships."

Once again, I had to grab for my coffee mug, which I'd placed on the bridge windowsill. "Something is coming," I said.

"How Garcia asked me if we shouldn't be setting the heavy-weather bill," the captain said. "He's an old PacFleet hand. Says he doesn't like the color of the sky *and* that he feels deep swells."

I couldn't detect the presence of a deep ocean swell train. On the other hand, my only experience, such as it was, had been in the far North Atlantic. We'd encountered gales; dense, icy fogs; icebergs; and whiteouts, but not hurricane-sized wind and seas. We were looking at a twenty-four-hour run to the estimated position of the next picket station. A lot could change between now and then.

"I'll get right on it," I said. "Of anybody, Chief Garcia ought to recognize one when he sees it."

"Yes," the captain replied. "It's a whole lot easier to do it when things are relatively calm, isn't it?"

The heavy-weather bill meant that the crew would begin to tie down and stow anything that could be blown or swept away by typhoon winds and seas out on the weather decks. The bosuns would set up the inboard lifelines, which were steel stanchions screwed into the deck inboard of the ship's lifelines and containing a single wire instead of the four strands of bronze wire and netting in the actual lifelines. All the lifeline netting was removed. The ship's boat was double-griped. The depth charges were covered in canvas, and then strapped down. Anything that could be blown off the ship by 140-mile-per-hour winds was taken inside if possible. All the topside gear—gasoline fire pumps, hose reels, mooring line reels, fire hoses, applicators—were stored inside the superstructure. Down in the berthing compartments, all loose gear—chairs, laundry bags, tables—were tied down. Officers secured everything in their tiny staterooms. The big coffeepots on the messdecks were clamped down; cooking utensils, steam kettles, pans, food stores in the galley were tied down. The gun mounts were covered with extra canvas, and the forward three-inch gun was reversed to point at the bridge because the back of the mount was more watertight. The torpedo tubes were locked centerline and covered. Every man was issued a kapok life jacket, which he had to inspect and then keep within arm's reach.

By 1700 *every*body, even me, could feel the arrival of a deep ocean swell. Pacific typhoons, some of them six hundred miles in diameter, would advertise their forward advance by pushing up the entire ocean. Mariners could begin to experience deep, periodic swells when the typhoon was as much as a thousand miles away. The sea always gave its warnings. The captain told me about a sign he'd seen in the chart house on his first destroyer: "The sea lies in wait for the unwary; it *stalks* the heedless."

These swells were not yet visible on the surface but I knew they could become as much as a hundred feet from crest to trough once the cyclone got close enough.

A message belatedly came in at midnight from the task unit commander directing ships to set their heavy-weather bills if they hadn't already done so. Casey, our chief engineer, was relieved because there'd be no need for ballasting since we'd just finished refueling. By dawn there was no longer any doubt of what was bearing down on us. The barometer had dropped into the 980-millibar range, and the surface winds had increased to forty-five knots. All thoughts of going after submarines were forgotten. The ship was pitching and rolling, but not violently. Yet. The commodore slowed the formation down to ten knots, enough to maintain steerageway but not fast enough to challenge the building seas. A half hour later he told his ships to operate independently to minimize weather damage but to remain within radar range if at all possible. This gave every skipper the latitude to adjust his course and speed to best protect his own ship.

The far eastern horizon began to turn a greenish black, masking the rising sun completely. The mast stays were beginning to whistle and moan. Gone was the daily routine of cleaning, repairing, eating, sleeping, and training. A minimal number of watch standers manned their stations for four-hour watches. The topside lookouts were called back inside the ship. The signal gang was secured. The weather-deck hatches were dogged down, and everyone was told to stay inside the house. For the most part the crew hit their racks and strapped in. The cooks had baked extra bread because bologna sandwiches were going to be the only food they'd be offering over the next forty-eight hours, assuming the entire crew wouldn't be too seasick to eat.

I secured my cabin while I checked my own life jacket to make sure the flashlight, police whistle, and straps were all in order. Then I went up to the bridge to strap in and enjoy the show.

19

CO

The typhoon did not disappoint. Within hours, *Holland* was being assaulted by a wave train featuring sixty-foot-high waves and 90 to 110 knot sustained winds, which were so loud that speech had become impossible. The doors to the pilothouse were dogged down, and all the bridge portholes except the one directly in front of my chair had been clamped shut. I had to hang on my seat belt just to stay in the chair. I spent my time watching those seas advancing toward us like emerald mountains and adjusting the ordered engine speed to ensure that *Holland* could climb the next approaching swell and hang at the crest, but not drive down the back slope so hard she kept on going straight down. The entire ship would shudder when the props came out of the water as we went over one and down into the dark valley between them. The troughs were only visible because of the lightning bolts ricocheting off the face of the next monster we were facing. I had to give engine orders by writing on the back of a clear plastic clipboard with a black grease pencil and then showing it to the lee helmsman, who was strapped to the engine order telegraph in order to remain upright. The helmsman had been sent below; the rudders were not effective in these huge seas and had been centerlined. The officers of the deck spent their four-hour watch hanging with both arms from a thick, braided cable that spanned the width of the pilothouse overhead for that exact purpose.

Down below, the engineers were experiencing less movement, being at the bottom of the ship. They concentrated on making sure the constant roller-coaster motions didn't cause the boilers to lose fuel oil or feedwater suction. Sounding and security watch standers crept through the lower decks, looking for leaks or any accumulating water in remote spaces. The ship was pitching hard, forty degrees up as she rode the mountainous swells and then forty degrees down as the bow cleared the water and then fell with a sickening motion as we began the slide down the back side of the swells, where she'd then bury her prow into the next one, hang there for a scary few seconds while the sea swelled up toward the pilothouse, sometimes swallowing the forward gun mount, and then, almost grudgingly, begin to rise for the next ascent.

Even though it was early afternoon, the daylight failed entirely as the center of the storm approached. Crazed lightning bolts knifed through the sky in all directions, their thunder overwhelmed by the steady shriek of the winds. Saint Elmo's fire buzzed along the mast stay wires outside even as dark green waves came aboard from the bow and swept down both weather decks, on the hunt for anything, human or not, that wasn't tied down. The quartermaster of the watch, strapped to the back bulkhead of the pilothouse on a pull-out stool, finally reported that the anemometer was registering zero, meaning it had either been blown off its mount up on the mast or its prop had been stripped off. The last reading had been 120 knots, or almost 140 miles per hour. I wondered if the radar antenna was next; it had been ordered into a fore-and-aft storm-stow position, parallel to the ship's centerline. Then I looked out the porthole to see a true monster rising in front of us, one of those rogue waves, where one swell manages to catch up with another one and create a wall of water over a hundred feet high.

"Hang on," I yelled instinctively, although I didn't think anyone heard me. The ship tried to climb it, but it was simply too big. *Holland* buried her bow halfway up, swerved twenty degrees to starboard, and then experienced a wall of seawater that swept the length of the ship almost at the level of the bridgewings, submerging the torpedo tubes and all the topside guntubs. I felt her stagger and then stop as hundreds of tons of seawater tried to press her down into the sea.

"Starboard engine ahead flank emergency," I yelled loud enough for the lee helmsman to hear me. That swerve to the right, if unchecked, could put us broadside to the wave train, which could then easily roll us completely over. The lee helmsman pushed the starboard engine order handle to flank, then back to full astern, and then back to flank again. Down below, the engineers cranked the big rheostats all the way to max and then called the fireroom to warn them of a sudden steam demand from the turbogenerators as they poured on the amps. I held my breath as I waited for the sudden surge of power from the starboard screw to push her head back directly into the oncoming waves, and then, using my clipboard this time, ordered both screws back down to ten knots and remembered to exhale. I wondered how the larger destroyers were doing. That had been much too close; my bridge crew was white as sheets.

After another hour of this, a sudden blaze of late afternoon sunlight assaulted our eyes as the ship broke through the eyewall of the typhoon and out into the surreal seascape of the eye itself. The monstrous swells disappeared as if a switch had been thrown, replaced now by an angry and badly confused sea. I could see the distant other side of the eyewall looming twenty miles ahead, laced with lightning ripping up the boiling black clouds that towered twenty thousand feet into the air. I got out of my chair and went out to the starboard bridgewing, where I looked astern. The western eyewall loomed behind the ship like some kind of furious incubus, with coils of hot, wet clouds racing counterclockwise behind us as a veinlike web of lightning burned bright hot in continuous flashes. I realized that it was suddenly quiet, which was even scarier, as if the cyclone was saying, "I'm not done with you yet." I went back in and ordered damage-control central to make a tour of the weather decks to see the extent of the damage after that last monster wave. I scanned the black horizon all around the eye formation, looking for other ships. None were visible. The most frightening aspect was I could see the entire eyewall moving ponderously around this twenty-mile-wide patch of exhausted ocean.

"Ask the galley to send up some food and coffee," I ordered. "And by the way, this isn't over."

The bridge crew just stared at me. They weren't seasick—beyond a certain level of pitching and rolling the brain recognizes there is mortal danger, which trumps nausea every time. The bridge messenger called the galley. Five minutes later a mess cook, who looked to be thirteen years old and whose eyes were still wide with fear, presented me with a wardroom thermos of black coffee and a gourmet bologna sandwich, complete with mustard and mayo. I looked around at the bridge crew.

"If you're hungry, now's the time," I said. "We have about an hour before chapter two starts."

The XO had come up to the bridge earlier but then retreated to Combat. He'd been holed up for the duration in the CIC, wedged between the main radarscope and the port bulkhead, where he'd stuffed his life jacket as a pillow and tried to sleep. He approached my chair as if not quite trusting the treacherous deck to remain horizontal.

"Hungry?" I asked.

Eeep shook his head. "We saw green water covering a porthole when that last big wave hit us," he said. "I thought we were done."

"Me, too," I said. "Except this class has a high metacentric height for a tin can; full of fuel, she bobbed right back up."

"I believe," Eeep said. He looked through the single open porthole in front of my chair. "That the back half?" he asked.

"Should be less intense," I said. "The front half adds the storm's winds to its speed of advance. The back half subtracts that. We'll just ride it out, and then go find the task unit. Heard anybody on the radio?"

"Not a word, sir," he said. "Not that we could have heard much with that wind noise."

"Do a quick all-stations query on damage, leaks, injuries," he said. Then I eyed the approaching eyewall. "Then go back and tell everyone to buckle up. You're not seasick; you should get something to eat."

Eeep just looked at me. I laughed out loud, aware that my bridge team were still frightened out of their wits. I was too, just a little, but this was no time to show it. Besides, *Holland* was a Bath Iron Works–built ship. They made tough ships up there in Maine, especially destroyers. *Deo gratias.*

The back half was less intense than the front wall of the cyclone, but that was a distinction without much of a difference. It was sunrise the next day before it seemed to be subsiding. The ocean looked bruised, with wide areas of blue water lathered in patches of gray foam that appeared to be coming up from deep below. Exhausted seabirds rode the crests of the waves, looking like clumps of feathery rags. But now there was a new problem. As the atmospheric conditions once again permitted radio transmissions, the commodore came up on the task unit tactical net and asked for sitreps—damage, injuries, percentage of fuel remaining, and position. One of the three destroyers from Tulagi failed to answer, even after a number of radio checks. Eeep and I were down in Combat by then, listening to the voice reports from the other ships. *Holland* had some minor topside damage, but the heavy-weather bill, executed early, had done its job. One of the destroyers had lost both its stern depth-charge racks; another reported her after torpedo tube mount was over the side. Otherwise, mostly minor stuff—lost fire hoses, lifelines, life rafts, portable fire pumps.

"Who's not answering up?" I asked.

"*Monaghan,*" Eeep said. "She's a *Farragut* class, launched in 1935. Very low freeboard aft of the bridge."

"Could have lost a mast and all her antennas," I said. "Meaning she can't talk. The commodore wants our posit—do we know where we are?"

"In the Pacific, south of the Philippines, north of the Solomons, east of Borneo."

"That's a no, then?"

Eeep shook his head. "We'll get local apparent noon if the sun breaks through, but that's only latitude; if it's any comfort, the current water depth exceeds the fathometer's deepest limit."

Eeep being funny, insinuating I was afraid we might run aground.

"Well, then, XO," I said. "Dead reckon from our last good fix and make something up. We'll get stars this evening, and then we'll know. I suspect we were blown west from that last posit. Is the radar operational?"

"The ETs say they think the radome has water in it, so they'll need to climb the mast to deal with that before lighting it off."

I eyed the approaching escarpments of wind and water. "Do that ASAP," I said. "We may have a search and rescue mission on our hands."

20

XO

Once the electronic technicians had climbed the mast and drained the radome, we made radar contact with one other ship, which was north of us, right at the edge of *Holland*'s radar range. We drove in that direction and met up with the commodore's flagship, the destroyer *Smalley.* The cyclone was gone, but the ride across the remnants of its disturbance turned into a pretty rough ride at twenty knots. *Smalley*'s radar was more powerful than *Holland*'s, and they had radar contact on one of the other destroyers, USS *Putnam,* who'd been ordered to close the flagship. Once we'd reformed into a task unit we began the painful search for the *Monaghan.* The commodore decided to return to the position where we'd rendezvoused with that oiler and begin the search there. He also made a report to PacFleet headquarters and Tulagi that she was missing. Everyone still held out hope that she'd been battered into electronic silence but was still out there.

The commodore then formed a line abreast with his three destroyers, spaced at three-thousand-yard intervals and began the expanding square search. At nightfall the formation slowed to five knots and posted extra lookouts to listen for cries for help in the darkness. It became apparent by noon the next day that *Monaghan* may have been taken by the storm. The three ships had seen nothing—no oil slick, debris pattern, or anything else to indicate that a ship had gone down. The nearest islands were six hundred miles to the southwest. Tulagi sent out a pair of PBY seaplanes, which could cover a much larger area in a much shorter time, but they, too, reported sighting nothing. *Monaghan* had carried a crew of 328 officers, chiefs, and enlisted men. The search was called off at sunset except for the PBY flights.

The next morning, I convened all hands not actually on watch on the fantail for a short memorial service. The captain read a selection from the Book of Wisdom 3:1–9:

> The souls of the just are in the hands of God, and no torment shall touch them. They seemed, in the view of the foolish, to be dead; and their passing away was thought an affliction and their going forth from us, utter destruction. But they are in peace. For if before men, indeed they be punished, yet is their hope full of immortality; Chastised a little, they shall be greatly blessed, because God tried them and found them worthy of Himself. As gold in the furnace, He proved them, and as sacrificial offerings He took them to himself. In the time of their visitation they shall shine, and shall dart about as sparks through stubble; They shall judge nations and rule over peoples, and the Lord shall be their King forever. Those who trust in Him shall understand truth, and the faithful shall abide with Him in love: Because grace and mercy are with his Holy ones, and His care is with His elect.

He then explained the meaning of some of the more archaic language, putting into context the loss of a ship and its entire complement at the hands of a God-sized storm. He then asked them to join him in reciting the Lord's Prayer and singing the first two verses of "Eternal Father, Strong to Save."

I walked forward with him afterward on our way back to the bridge. "I didn't know you were a biblical scholar," I said.

The sailors we passed seemed to be still somewhat stunned by the idea of an entire ship being swallowed up like that. The captain smiled. "I read the Bible for comfort, not for religion," he said. "Some of the language is immeasurably beautiful, and it makes me realize that nothing we face out here is new."

"How is that comforting?" I asked.

"The people who wrote all that did so because they were confident mankind would somehow survive," he replied. "And so we shall, I think, in one form or another."

"Yikes," I said, experiencing a quick chill.

"Amen to that, XO. Now to the matter of Japanese submarines."

The commodore sent a flashing light message for *Holland* to come alongside *Smalley*. Once there, the *Smalley*'s deck crew fired a shot line over *Holland*'s fo'c'sle, followed by a phone line. The captain stood on the port bridgewing and put a handset to his ear. Seventy feet away, the commodore did the same. I listened in on a phone circuit inside the pilothouse, next to the door to where the captain was standing.

"Dutch Schultze here, Captain," the commodore announced. "We haven't met, but your ship has made quite a reputation for herself. Three subs—that's one hell of an accomplishment."

"Thank you very much, sir," the captain said. "I'm very sorry about *Monaghan*."

"Aren't we all," the commodore said. "She didn't get a full load of fuel during the UNREP. Her fuel system transport pump broke down, so she was probably at only fifty-five percent, with no time to fully ballast. Look, I want to thank you for sending me your estimate of where the rest of the picket line is. What would you suggest in the way of approach tactics?"

The captain was visibly taken aback. Even I knew that commodores rarely solicited tactical advice from mere lieutenant commanders.

On the other hand, *Holland* had killed three subs. "Do your ships have hedgehogs?" the captain asked.

"Negative," the commodore said. "But I see that you do."

"Yes, sir, and the advantage that they give us is that a hedgehog attack doesn't ruin the sonar conditions like depth charges do. There's no bang unless one of them actually hits him."

He then explained our tactic of approaching the estimated position of the target in hopes of catching him on the surface at night, running his mains and thus being relatively deaf. He told him about using passive sonar to listen for the racket of the sub's diesels charging the batteries. "Zero three hundred has been a good time to go in on them," he said. "They'll have been on the surface for a while; his people will be at the ebb of their alertness. He's out in the middle of nowhere, so his guard is somewhat down."

"You use your radar?"

"Sparingly," the captain said. "We've been told they don't have radar, but Intel thinks they can detect ours. We think sound is better. My exec is an electronics wiz, and he's made some modifications to our sonar that filters out a lot of ambient oceanic noise."

I had been splitting my concentration between watching over the conning officer as we steamed alongside each other, well within collision range, and listening to the captain answering the commodore's questions. I now noticed there were also officers on the other ship who appeared to be listening in to the conversation.

"What's your previous experience in hunting subs with multiple ships?" the commodore asked. I covered the microphone end of my eavesdropping handset and told the conning officer to come right one degree; it looked to me as if the ships were drifting in on each other. Two destroyers slicing through the water within sixty or seventy feet of each other created a venturi effect. Without careful attention to the distance between them, both ships could be sucked into a side-to-side collision.

"All of it with the Royal Navy in the North Atlantic, sir," the captain replied. "They'd establish a thousand-yard circle around a sonar contact, which they called 'the fence.' One ship at a time would peel off and go in for a depth-charge attack. He'd then get back out onto the fence, but, of course, he would have lost contact due to all the underwater racket. The other ships would cue him back onto where they still held the target. Once he regained contact, the next ship would peel off and have a go. The idea was always to have one or more ships in sonar contact before sending in the next attack."

"Yeah, that's kinda what I had in mind," the commodore said. "If we can catch him on the surface, our five-inchers can hit him at nine miles, and that's under radar control. Drive him under, go in and gain contact, and then set up a fence."

"Yes, sir, that would work. Our guns are fired manually and under visual control. We don't even carry a gun director. My guys are good, but without the searchlight, we don't have a night-firing capability."

"Yes, I understand. Let's see how it turns out; if we have to, we'll hold him down for a while and then pretend to leave. Then you sneak in and do your passive sonar stuff while we hang around in the near distance. I'll set us up for a zero three hundred ETA at datum, and then, hell, we'll wing it."

"Aye, aye, sir," the captain said. I was beginning to really like this commodore. He clearly understood there were so many imponderables—it might have been a three-sub picket line, not six, or the Japanese had been spooked and called the remaining boats back to base, or the estimated position was wrong, and on and on. Time to stop yakking and just get up there and go to work. The commodore waved goodbye and handed his handset to someone. It took another two minutes for *Smalley* to retrieve her light-line phone line, and then *Holland* broke away by simply putting on five degrees of right rudder and accelerating.

The commodore put his three ships in a line abreast at four-thousand-yard intervals this time. The captain then called the tactical team together and outlined the plan, such as it was. I liked the setup—let the two destroyers go in with radar and sonar banging away. *Holland* would hold back, go super quiet, and wait to see the results. With any luck, the destroyers would successfully jump the bastard on the surface and kill him. Or, the depth charges would take care of business. But if not, my guys knew what to do next.

"I take it this commodore isn't the same one we met originally," Hal, the ops boss, said.

"Right," the captain replied. "I think this one's a fighter. And a realist. Any word on *Monaghan*?"

Hal shook his head. "The black cats have been flying continuously during the day, looking for an oil slick, wreckage, anything. But that storm probably atomized any debris. If she did capsize, I can't imagine anyone surviving seas like that for very long."

"Damn," the captain said. "There but for the grace of God . . ."

Everyone took a moment to reflect once again on the sheer danger of even being at sea. The Japanese were one thing, but Mother Nature had a merciless side, especially if you had the temerity to venture forth into the dominions of Neptune. The Navy hymn, "Eternal Father, Strong to Save," expressed it best: "O hear us when we cry to thee, for those in peril on the sea."

I broke the silence. "I've had an idea on how to refine our attack geometry during the last five-hundred yards of an active sonar attack," I announced.

"Do tell," the captain said, obviously relieved to change the subject.

"Everyone knows that the final five hundred yards of an attack are critical—you're trying to place weapons in the water that will be where the sub *will* be, not where he is, once they get down to his depth. But the sonar loses contact at about four, maybe even five hundred yards because the look angle gets much steeper and we can't tilt or direct the beam.

"The fathometer is also an acoustic transducer. Unlike the sonar, which projects a dome-shaped sound wave into the water, the fathometer sends a powerful acoustic beam straight down, no thicker than a pencil, to determine the depth beneath the keel. If the fathometer shows depth suddenly changing from three thousand fathoms to twenty, we'd know that, for that one moment, we're right on top of him, *and* how deep he was.

"The problem is, if he hears us right over top, he knows we're about to drop depth charges, so he's usually gonna turn hard, one way or the other. That would defeat anything we dropped. But that would be a great time to fire a full depth-charge pattern from both sides. If we discover his depth during the run in, using the fathometer, we'd know precisely when to let 'em go so that they got there when he got there, whichever way he turns."

"I like that," the captain said. "If he successfully evades that, we'll just do it again. Is the fathometer transmitting in an audible frequency?"

"Not to us, but I do believe a submerged sonar receiver might be able to hear it. And, we also could throw some shit in the game with the UQC, the underwater telephone."

The captain frowned. The UQC was a notoriously clunky piece of gear that changed human speech into a signal that could be propagated through the water. The system worked well enough, but the quality of the speech received underwater by, say, a submarine, was usually awful. I tried to keep an evil grin off my face.

"I saw this done once back at the Naval Research Labs," I explained. "We were in a mock-up of a destroyer's Sonar Control room. One of the senor scientists wanted to know what an approaching torpedo sounded like on the sonar. My boss, a destroyer captain who despised submariners for some reason, showed us what he'd done to an American sub with whom his ship had been training. He had one guy key the UQC and hold the transmit switch down. Then my boss went across the Sonar Control Room to the far side, picked up an electric drill, turned it on to full power, and slowly walked back across the room toward where the operator was holding the UQC microphone up in the air. Since he was approaching the microphone, the resulting whirring noise had both up-Doppler *and* rising amplitude.

"Apparently the sub's sonar operator down below had jumped out of his chair when he heard it, and the whole boat had gone to GQ. The sub's skipper even filed a formal complaint to ComDesLant afterward."

Roscoe Santone laughed when he heard that story. "Hell," he said. "You really want to play games, do what one of *my* previous skippers did. We'd be doing these tracking exercises with a tame US sub off the coast. It was all canned. He'd go down to two fifty feet, run a straight course at five knots, and announce movie call. Our student operators would practice gaining contact, classifying it, then maintaining contact. Then we'd make a fake depth-charge run controlled by the student plotters up in CIC. We'd have a guy on the fantail throw concussion grenades into the water to simulate dropping depth charges when Combat called 'mark center.' They'd go off at about twenty feet, and then the sub would evaluate our attack."

"And they'd always tell you that your 'attack' was off by x-hundred yards," the captain said.

"Right as rain, Skipper," Roscoe said. "Lying sonsabitches that all sewer-pipe sailors are. So, after three 'misses,' the skipper himself showed up on the fantail for the next run. He'd brought along a roll of toilet paper. He had the gunner's mate wrap the spoons on six concussion grenades several times with TP, pulled the pins, and handed them to the startled gunner's mate. 'Next time the bridge calls "mark center," he said, 'throw these over the side.'

"We made another pass, with good contact and a good solution, and the gunner's mate did what he'd been told to do when Combat called mark center. He pitched 'em over the side, two at a time. Only this time, the spoon didn't release until the water had dissolved all that TP. When it finally did, those grenades were now down at two fifty, three hundred feet, right where those lying bastards were, watching the flick, when they went off right alongside that sub's hull. Water don't compress, so those grenades sounded a lot like real depth charges. Scary shit—for them. But no more lies after that."

The tactical team laughed at this sea story, and suddenly I got a warm feeling about this bunch. We'd killed three Japanese subs. We were getting used to the taste of blood. We were becoming hardened veterans, emotionally annealed by events such as near-miss torpedoes in the night and the unthinkable loss of *Monaghan*. The captain would remind us, as he had me, that in any battle, land, air, or sea, the enemy always gets a vote. But I sensed they were now beginning to take a keen tactical interest in their current mission, and that was gold. They were turning in to hunters and killers even. I glanced at the captain across the table. I could see he'd come to the same conclusion, and when our eyes met, we nodded at each other.

There'd been this chilling mystique that had grown up around our captain ever since we joined the hunt for Nazi subs. Something about him changed when the hunt began. His voice became quieter, his stare became scarier, his eyes brighter, and his entire demeanor became more stonelike. Watching the captain was full time entertainment for any small, tight-knit crew: eavesdropping on the bridge, looking for signs that someone was about to get "across the breakers" with the boss, gauging what made him laugh and when it was a good time to get your head down and become really busy, preferably somewhere else. I'd finally come to understand that commanding officers were fully aware of all this and played to their audience all the time. That had become especially true in *Holland* once he took me into his confidence and began to tell me how we were going to "play" this situation or that.

But when GQ went down and the canvas covers came snaking off all those steel barrels, there was no more playacting from Lieutenant Commander Mariano Medina Santangelo deTomasi, USN. Somebody else emerged, somebody who still vividly remembered the sight of his boys spouting blood out of their mouths in the shattered waters of Pearl Harbor as Japanese pilots indulged in a little "sport."

I think everyone—from the officers to the chiefs and all the way down to the lowliest seaman—who saw his other face knew that whatever was coming next, it would be as serious as a heart attack. I know I did.

21

CO

The formation split up at 0230, *Holland* slowing down and remaining astern, five miles from the estimated datum, while the other two conducted the destroyer version of a deep-creep approach: surface search radars off, sonars in passive mode—for the moment. The two destroyers were now at four thousand yards interval—two miles—so as not to present a concentrated target if the sub happened to be waiting for them. The commodore had transmitted one change in plans—they'd use their gunfire control radars to sweep the area ahead of them. That straw-sized beam might be detectable to the Japanese, but it would appear as an almost instantaneous blip of energy as compared to that relatively big, wide beam of the surface search that came around every fifteen seconds.

I went down to Combat to watch the plot develop. *Holland*'s own radar was silenced, so the plotters were dead reckoning, or DRing in naval parlance, based on the last known position of the two destroyers ahead of us. If you knew their starting position and their course and speed, you could plot their advance, assuming that nothing had changed.

"Our guys hearing anything?" I asked Eeep.

"They can faintly hear *Smalley*'s propellers," Eeep said. "We're guessing they're badly fouled with marine growth."

"And you know this how?"

"I told Roscoe to record our partners' prop sounds while they were close by, since they'd be going ahead of us. That way if we hear a different set of prop sounds . . ."

"Well, now," I said. "That's some heads-up ball."

We waited to see if the pair of destroyers flushed anything up ahead, but the radio remained silent. Slowly but surely, they drew away from *Holland*, at least according to the DR plot.

Then the bitchbox in CIC lit up. "Bridge, Combat, Sonar Control—we're hearing an unidentified noise passing down our starboard bow, range unknown, bearing drawing slowly right. Very faint, but it's definitely there."

I grabbed the phones away from the CIC-to-bridge talker. "This is the captain: right standard rudder. All ahead standard." I turned to Eeep. "Tell sonar to go active and alert the hedgehog crew. Radar on. Depth-charges stations: pull safeties."

I rose to go back up to the bridge but then hesitated. The plotters were laying out bearing lines to the unknown noise slinking down from our starboard bow toward our starboard beam. I felt the ship accelerating and coming right. I suddenly realized that right here, in CIC, I had the tactical picture. On the bridge all I would have would be my chair in the dark.

"Bridge, Combat, Sonar Control: sonar contact, bearing one five zero true, range eighteen hundred yards. Null Doppler."

I looked at Eeep. "Make a hedgehog attack."

Eeep picked up a phone handset. "Combat has control," he said. "Steer one seven zero."

"Watch his bearing drift," I said. "Whichever way he turns, we'll roll depth charges after the hogs go hunting."

"Aye, aye, sir," Eeep responded, his eyes fixed on the plotters' pencil lines as the sonar sent up continuous ranges and bearings to the fleeing contact and the geometry of death spread across the plot.

"Fire hedgehogs," Eeep ordered. The familiar thumping announced the launch of twenty-four hedgehogs.

"Bridge, Combat, Sonar Control: Contact is beginning to drift right."

I took over. "Right ten degrees rudder. All ahead full. Fire depth charges on my command."

Sonar came up with a new bearing, and I made the computations in my head. The sub was evading to the right, which meant that the hedgehogs were probably going to miss. But *Holland* was going faster than the submarine, even if he'd kicked it in the ass when our sonar lit up. Submerged, he could do eight knots, max. I could do twenty.

"Activate the fathometer," I ordered. "Report depths continuously. Notify the commodore we're in contact."

Another talker switched to the navigation circuit, where the quartermaster, back in the chart house now, began calling observed depths beneath the keel. The talker repeated every reading. Three thousand fathoms; three thousand one hundred fathoms. Three thousand two hundred fathoms. *What?* Repeat? *Forty* fathoms?

"Fire depth charges," I ordered. "Full bag, depth setting: two hundred fifty feet."

There were eight K-gun projectors on each side, each holding a single, five-hundred-pound depth bomb. Sixteen depth charges were lofted off each side by the K-guns, while the fantail crew simultaneously pulled the levers to drop five more out of each of the stern racks.

I ordered a wide turn to the right, then steadied up to gain distance from the imminent underwater firestorm. It wasn't long in coming as twenty-six bombs exploded in quick succession. Even from 250 feet, huge plumes of white water erupted in *Holland*'s wake, creating boils fifty feet across. I knew the sonar gang would have put the delicate hydrophone system in the passive mode as soon as depth charges began to roll; the operators would have removed their headphones to avoid the cascade of painful underwater blasts. Now I felt like I should be up on the bridge, except that there were no other ships maneuvering in close quarters nearby for me to worry about. Here in Combat, I could "see"; this was truly a revelation. I stayed put. We waited for the avalanche of underwater explosions to subside.

"Slow to five knots," I ordered. "Alert the gun crews and the searchlight station in case he comes up. Give them relative bearings to where we marked center."

Then we waited some more. Back on our starboard quarter there was a mountainous roil of battered seawater way down deep, grudgingly expanding into a sphere nearly three hundred yards in diameter as it rose to the surface. There was no point in going active—the sonar would have been acoustically overwhelmed after that barrage.

Then came what I had been hoping for: a single, rumbling underwater explosion that shook the ship, even as far out as she was from the drop point. The rumbling sound reverberated underwater for thirty seconds, creating an eerie sound like thunder in a canyon that seemed to resonate in the steel of our hull.

"Sayonara and goddamn your treacherous eyes," I growled. The GQ crew in Combat all pretended not to hear that. I could imagine them thinking: Not personal? Bull*shit.*

"Tell the commodore we propose to loiter in the area until sunrise," I said. "See what comes up. Drive around in a figure eight—five knots, three-thousand-yard axis. Radar up; sonar off. I want us to be constantly changing course in case we missed and he comes up for some revenge."

"Missed?" Eeep said. "I don't think so, Captain."

"Me, neither, XO," I said. "But some bodies would be nice. I'll be in my sea cabin."

"Shall we notify the commodore that we got him?"

"Tell him we think we got him. See if we can get some pictures first. Tell him we made an attack, are no longer in contact, and are waiting for daylight for evidence of success."

By dawn the other two destroyers had shown up, and we all drove back down to the drop point, where we encountered a huge debris field drifting on a battered sea. The winds were calm, and the Pacific gave no evidence of the typhoon we'd so recently endured, but it gave plenty evidence of a demolished submarine: many bodies; diesel oil in great, greasy patches, almost fluorescent in the rising sunlight; broken crates from the sub's storerooms; life jackets; insulation panels. The photographer's mate dutifully record everything as I enjoyed a cup of coffee in my chair on the bridge. The smell of diesel was really strong, which meant there was a lot of it. It was perfume to my vengeful senses.

The commodore came up on the tactical UHF circuit. "Looks to me like you're four for four," he said. "Congratulations. Again."

"Thank you, sir," I replied. "We detected a contact fleeing datum area at high speed. Dropped hedgehogs, but he was going too fast, so we accelerated and then conducted a full-scale depth-charge attack. From the looks of this, he ran right into the pattern."

"I'll say he did," the commodore said. "I'll get a report out. Come alongside in one hour. Let's talk."

By the time we were alongside *Smalley,* the debris field was even bigger. The only unsettling aspect was that sharks were feasting on the human remains bobbing between the oil slicks.

"Ain't no doubt about this mess," the commodore said once we were hooked up. "You well and truly mangled this bastard."

"We were literally just hanging around when Sonar heard something flying by us," I said. "He was probably cavitating. Once we went active, there he was."

"Did he evade?"

"He did, but my exec had a trick up his sleeve. He turned on the fathometer as we chased him. The sonar detected a right turn, so we turned with him, but we were going faster than he was. When the fathometer suddenly registered forty fathoms instead of three thousand, I waited ten seconds and then let go with hedgehogs. But he was still turning hard, so, once again, we chased him, overran him, and let fly with a full,

Fourth of July pattern. I think he broke up at forty fathoms, and all this just spilled out."

"Well, god*damn*, Captain, like I said, that's four for four. We never even got a sniff. You'd think the Japanese might have noticed by now."

"Yes, sir, I would think that as well. The difference here was three ships instead of a Lone Ranger sneaking up on them. You spooked him, he ran, and we heard him running. If he'd gone in another direction, we'd have never seen him. Are there any Intel updates from Pearl?"

I knew that the commodore would be privy to a higher level of intelligence reporting from PacFleet headquarters, which was why I'd asked the question. *Holland* and the task unit had now conclusively confirmed that there was a picket line, and that *Holland*'s estimate of where the picket stations were was correct.

"Yes, there is," the commodore said. "The Big Blue Fleet's on the move. They've finally confirmed it's the Marianas. They'll come up into the Philippine Sea and hit Saipan first. Once they do that, they expect the Japanese will come out in force with everything they've got left—carriers, battleships, the whole shebang. Apparently, Pearl's been following your exploits, too, and Nimitz wants this picket line wrapped up, as in: now would be nice. We have about seventy-two hours before the whole fleet shows up, and he doesn't want the Japanese carriers to get good targeting reports."

"So, we go northeast to our next best estimated position?"

The commodore grinned. "*We*'re being recalled to the carrier task force. You, on the other hand, are directed to finish off the picket line. There's an oiler coming our way in twenty-four hours. After that, you will be detached to do what you do better than anybody out here: kill Japanese subs."

I remembered hoping that, after the first two kills, we'd be left alone to get the rest, but after last night, I realized that bringing a crowd to an ASW fight really was the better way to do it. If those two tin cans hadn't spooked the Japanese sub into bolting like that, *Holland* would never have found it. It was the one big advantage surface ships had over submarines: they could bring friends and conduct a fully cooperative attack, for days if necessary. A submarine could fight for thirty-six hours, max, and then he'd have to come up and face the music.

"We'll give it our best shot, Commodore," I said. "After all, what could go wrong?"

"Hold that thought, Captain," the commodore said with a laugh. There was a brief pause, and then he had a final observation. "If the Japanese finally have realized," he said, "that somebody is rolling up their picket line, they might tell station five and station six to join forces."

I felt a small chill. That would be an entirely different problem. Creeping up on one sub was one thing. Creeping up on one sub while another waited for you to reveal yourself would be a lot more dangerous. So far, we'd been hunting sentinel ships. Dealing with a two-sub wolfpack, as the Germans called it, meant that the next time it might be us floating in oil-soaked waters, waiting for the sharks.

"Yes, sir," I said. "I will definitely keep that in mind."

"There's one more thing, Captain," the commodore said. "And I can only say this because we're on a ship-to ship-telephone out in the middle of nowhere where nobody can hear us. It's the Japanese First Mobile Fleet coming out to contest our invasion of the Marianas. Ozawa himself is bringing twenty-eight destroyers, five battleships, eleven heavy cruisers, two light cruisers, and *nine* carriers—five big decks, four light carriers—with somewhere near six hundred aircraft total. Be aware that any search planes you see in the next two weeks may not be ours."

"Great," I said, before realizing I was being sarcastic to a senior officer.

"Yeah, right," the commodore said. "Good luck and good hunting. You guys are good—*god*damned good. Go get 'em, tiger."

"I have one question, sir," I said before they disconnected the light line. "If Pearl knows about this picket line, why would he pull your task unit out?"

"I'm guessing they want every destroyer they can get their hands on for this one," the commodore said. "Either way, when the fleet commander says, come here, you go there."

22

XO

I stared at the overall plot of the picket line. Our picket line, by God. Stations one, two, and three had been on a relatively straight line. Number four was where the line began to curve up toward the northeastern part of the Philippine Sea.

"We have to assume that the line will continue to curve up toward the Marianas," I said, as we considered the plot. "Remember that the whole idea was for the picket line to warn the Japanese fleet that Halsey was on his way north. And now we know why—the Japanese battle fleet is coming out."

"Excuse me, XO," Hal said. "But it won't be Halsey; it'll be Spruance. The few messages I've been seeing are now referring to the Fifth Fleet, not the Third."

"You're absolutely right, Hal," I said, remembering I'd seen the same thing. At this stage of the war, command of the Big Blue Fleet alternated between admirals William F. Halsey and Raymond A. Spruance.

When Halsey was in command, it was called the Third Fleet; when it was Spruance, it was called the Fifth Fleet. Supposedly, the idea was to make the Japanese believe America actually had *two* enormous fleets out in the Pacific.

"Well, based on what the commodore told me yesterday," the captain said. "I don't think *we* are going to be of much interest to the fleet commanders of either side, although he did say that Nimitz still wants this picket line knocked out. I'm not sure what any of that means."

"Maybe it has to do with where we are on the picket line," Hal said. "We started almost six hundred miles west of here; now we're headed slightly northeast, closer to the Marianas. We're assuming Halsey—I mean Spruance—is south of us, but the Fifth Fleet could be coming from any direction."

"I think the commodore was also telling us to forget about what the elephants were up to and to concentrate on getting another Japanese sub," I said. "We're back on our own, and we do pretty well on our own."

"There you go, guys," the captain said. "The XO is right. Just so you know, however, the other thing the commodore warned me about was that the last two subs on the line may join forces and come hunting us. It's just possible he didn't want to be here for that interesting scenario."

The team stood around, chewing on that happy thought until they saw the captain grinning his version of an evil grin, and then everybody relaxed. We were all pretty tired. We'd met up with the oiler in the middle of the night, meaning no one got any sleep during a two-hour nighttime underway replenishment. The good news was that we were topped off on fuel, hedgehogs, and even some ice cream. The captain brought us back to the problem at hand.

"Look," he said. "I don't think we would've got a shot at that last sub if those other two tin cans hadn't spooked him into bolting. And if it hadn't been for the XO's idea of using the fathometer, we'd have never been able to localize him like that. He got surprised and ran for it. He wasn't lying in wait for us."

"So, what the commodore said about the stations joining forces?" Bat asked. "Not likely?"

"Not likely," he said. "There are huge naval forces in motion. These picket line subs have been given one mission: advance warning of the approach of the American fleet. That's their *only* job, so I don't think they can leave their stations. If they're tethered to their stations, they can't do much one way or the other about the Marianas except that one early warning. I think we've got free rein here."

Everyone took a moment to absorb all that. I studied their faces, looking for signs of disagreement, but there didn't seem to be any. Okay, then, I thought, but the possibility of two Japanese subs getting together and having their own light line, side by side conversation still bothered me. They would know the precise positions of the picket line. If the Americans had been coming *up* the line in search of the stations, then why not us Nipponese go *down* the line and see if we can ambush them? The captain, apparently wasn't too worried about that.

"I want to head northeast and do exactly what we've done so far," he said. "Sneak up in the middle of the night on a submarine charging his batteries, surprise him, and kill him. That's *our* only mission. XO, set up the track. Zero three hundred arrival at datum. And now, everybody, get some sleep. We need to be fresh and ready."

Out of the corner of my eye I saw Bat Watkins mouth the words "fresh and ready" silently, as if the whole idea were preposterous. The captain saw it, too. "You need to be fresh and ready in case I'm wrong and the commodore was right," he said with a smile. "This time we may have a real fight on our hands. Food for thought, boys and girls."

The captain went to his sea cabin. I went up to the bridge and waited for my eyes to adjust to the darkness. The bosun mate of the watch asked if I needed coffee; I declined. The bridge was quiet as the ship headed northeast at fifteen knots. The weather appeared to have relaxed, at least for the moment; the ship was cruising through glass-calm seas, although there was our familiar overcast layer diffusing the moon's light. I stepped out onto the port bridgewing for some fresh air.

I needed sleep as much as anyone did, but I was uneasy about our situation. Entire fleets were in motion in the western Pacific. Soon there would be carrier battles, huge ships on both sides hurling hundreds of bombers and fighters at each other over equally huge distances. Dozens of transports might already be lumbering toward the Marianas from somewhere—Pearl? Australia?—carrying thousands of Marine and Army infantry. Soon the End of the World would descend on three little islands—Saipan, Tinian, Guam—where thousands more would die on both sides. An inexorable American military vise was closing on the remains of the Japanese empire. Now that I thought about it, it seemed to me that the commodore and his two destroyers had made only a halfhearted attempt to blow up station four. They'd been awfully quick to decamp to rejoin the main event. It was only by blind chance *Holland* had caught an acoustic sniff of the fleeing submarine and killed it. And that last comment by the commodore? It almost made me wonder if these PacFleet sailors had decided that the six-boat picket line was at best a sideshow. Leave it to the new guy from LantFleet, who'd already proved the picket line's insignificance by rolling up four of the six boats like it was nothing.

I just couldn't escape the feeling that something wasn't right, and the more I thought about it, the more I wondered if *Holland* wasn't being set up in some fashion. Because we were "late," I thought. I had always expected that one more DE coming out of the Atlantic, where the U-boat war was just about won, would have been folded into the nearest transport convoy, if nothing else but to add mass to the escort effort. Instead, we'd been stationed in the vast, empty waters of the Philippine Sea and told to investigate a mysterious possibility that there *might* be a picket line of Japanese subs, who *might* be waiting for whatever was coming to *maybe* the Marianas. The only wrinkle was that it had turned out to have been true, and now this little orphaned DE had run up an inconvenient record—one lone ship had managed to destroy four Japanese subs and their crews. I sighed. I was tired. Everybody was tired.

I tried to make sense of it. I tried to think of a different tactic, in case there was an ambush waiting us at 0300. I almost fell asleep on my feet. I went back down to my stateroom and crashed.

I awoke a few hours later and for a moment didn't know where I was. The telephone next to my bed was squeaking. I picked up. It was the watch officer in Combat. I asked what time it was.

"It's zero four fifteen, XO. We just took a single sweep on the radar, and we saw a contact, possibly more than one, some twenty miles to the southeast."

"Twenty miles?" I said. "*South*east? We that far off on this one?"

The watch officer was talking to someone else, then he was back. "Sir, Sonar Control has an acoustic bearing in the same direction. They evaluate it as many ships, moving fast."

Oh shit, I thought, rolling out of my cot, wide awake now. The Japanese are here. But by the time I got up to the bridge, the captain was on the bitchbox with the signal gang. "Sigs, Captain: get ready for flashing light challenges. Use red filters but have yellow available. Radio will give you tonight's challenge plus two backups."

"Sigs, aye," a voice answered.

He punched another button on the bitchbox. "Combat, Bridge: See if you can find Task Force Fifty-Eight's comms plan, and if you can, patch their primary tactical circuit to the bridge. I think this may be part of Spruance's force, and I'd love to be able to talk to them, bridge to bridge, preferably before they start shooting."

"Combat, aye. We have Task Force Thirty-Eight's comms plan, but I don't know about Fifty-Eight. Hopefully they use the same one."

He leaned back in his chair and gave me a worried look in the gloom. Hopefully indeed. The same ships constituted each fleet. If this was the American task group headed north looking for trouble, *Holland* was in danger. Some trigger-happy heavy cruiser might decide to deal with this "unknown surface contact" with a peremptory nine-gun eight-inch salvo.

"Captain," I said. "Recommend bringing up the radar into continuous radiate mode. If there are heavies in this formation, they'll have electronic intercept capability and will recognize an American radar."

"You hope, there, XO, but yes, I concur. Also go active on the sonar, just in case there's a goddamn Japanese sub around here somewhere after all. And sound general quarters."

I went down to CIC to look at the radar picture. Our radar was greatly dependent on good atmospheric conditions. A hot, muggy atmosphere, like tonight, did not love *Holland*'s radar. But when the radar picture on the planned position indicator (PPI) scope clarified, it was an impressive sight. A bent-line screen of eight destroyers preceded a column formation of increasingly bigger ships, if the blips on the scope were any indication. They were ten miles out now and definitely making big tracks. The plotters on the DRT table reported a preliminary course and speed estimate of 010, twenty-five knots. Whoever they were, fuel economy was not a concern. Sonar, being active, could no longer give us any useful passive information. I had a bad feeling; I'd read reports of how the Japanese used to come down the Slot, the main channel through the Solomons chain, toward Guadalcanal from Rabaul back in 1942—column formation, twenty-five or even thirty knots.

When the range to the escorting screen got down to eight miles, the signal bridge finally reported a visual challenge and that they were answering with tonight's reply. I heaved a sigh of relief when sigs then told us they were then exchanging call signs; the "challenger" being satisfied that the "challengee" was legit. After exchanging call signs, they said they were receiving a flashing light message from one of the main body ships, possibly a heavy cruiser.

I went back up to the bridge—the formation was going to pass within six thousand yards of *Holland,* which the captain had brought to five knots and a nonthreatening, northerly course. It took less time to adjust my eyes because the moon was suddenly out now, and here they came. Ghostly gray destroyers swept past us on both sides as the screen came up. Then came the main body: one, two, three light cruisers, then the unmistakable shape of a battleship, no, *four* battleships, one big one, an *Iowa* class, and three older ones, which looked like some of the ones they'd raised from the mud at Pearl. Great gray phantoms with towering superstructures, masts and funnels, their fourteen-and sixteen-inch guns laid flat, and each ship with a bone in her teeth as they rumbled north. I got goose bumps just seeing them. I realized we were getting a light from the *Iowa*-class battleship. Compared to the size of the ship, the signal light looked like someone was using a red-lens flashlight to send it instead of a standard, twelve-inch signal-searchlight. Then came ten, count 'em, *ten* heavy cruisers, all totally darkened. The screen astern consisted of five of the *Atlanta*-class light cruisers, now designated as CLAA's in recognition of their primary job—antiaircraft defenses, followed by a dozen or so more destroyers, one of whom had to maneuver to steer clear of us. *Holland* actually began to roll when their wakes finally spread out. Within ten minutes they had faded from view, and in thirty, they began to disappear off the radar.

"Now that's a sight you'll never forget," the captain told the bridge GQ team. One of the signalmen came onto the bridge and handed him a clipboard with the visual message. He smiled when he read it and then read it aloud.

"'Greetings, Holland. Your designator should be DD instead of DE. You are a sub-killing destroyer of the first rank. Pearl says there are two more out here. Find them. Kill them. Very well done. R. Spruance.'"

"How's about them apples?" he said.

"Wow, indeed," I said. "Spruance himself. But now that they've gone, sir, the waters around here have been so churned up sonar can't hear a thing. Do you want to remain at GQ?"

"Yes," he said. "And I want to leave the radar on. Put sonar back in passive mode and get a BT drop so we know if there's a layer. How far are we from the estimated datum?"

"We're within twenty miles or so," I replied. "Recommend we begin an evasive pattern."

"Concur, and here's what I think's gonna happen. If there is a

Japanese sub around, he would have heard that freight train and probably went deep on general principles. Their orders were to sound a warning, not attack, so I expect a radar contact within the hour. If he comes up within gun range, open up on him immediately."

"And if he's detected but out of three-inch range?"

"Then, shit, fire a torpedo at him; don't worry about a firm tracking solution. Set the depth for ten feet, speed high, and turn it loose. He'll hear it and evade, maybe even crash-dive. Either way, no message gets out to Tokyo that Spruance is coming to pay them a visit."

I nodded. Firing a torpedo at a surfaced submarine would most certainly throw some shit into the game. *Holland* had a single, three-tube torpedo mount on the 01 level. A standard destroyer carried two quintuple mounts, but the DEs couldn't stand that much topside weight. Still, the scream of an approaching torpedo's counter-rotating screws would absolutely spook a surfaced submarine, even if the shot was taken on the fly.

I hustled back down to Combat to set everything up.

23

CO

I remained on the bridge after the XO left. We only had a few hours of darkness left, although the picket submarine might risk a daylight surfacing to get that vital warning out on HF radio. Assuming he was somewhere nearby and not fifty miles away. Assuming he'd even heard all those ships. I asked for some coffee while I reviewed my decisions. The ship came right in response to course orders from Combat. Hopefully sonar would recover their passive ears as we moved away from all that badly disturbed water. I summoned the gunnery officer.

"Bat, I want you to brief the torpedo mount crew to be vigilant. If this sub surfaces to get a radio report out, things are gonna move fast. Coordinate with Combat to make sure they give a *relative* range and bearing to the torpedo control station the moment they get one. There won't be time to compute a solution—just set depth for ten feet, point and shoot. Hitting something is a long shot; my objective is to spook him into either diving or maneuvering so I can get us close enough to use the three-inch or our standard bag of underwater weapons. Most of all, we need to drive him down before he can get that warning message off, okay?"

"Got it, Captain," Bat said. "And, for what it's worth, two fish would be better than one. One on the bearing of the radar contact, the second ten degrees ahead of that if we happen to know which way he's moving. That way he has to decide which way to turn—hell, we might even hit him."

"Our surfaced-launched torpedoes are not famous for hitting anything," I reminded him.

"That was the Mark fourteen, sir; these are the Mark fifteens. We tag him with one of these, all his earthly troubles will be over."

"Fire two then," I said. "Keep one in reserve in case we run into a Japanese battleship."

He grinned and left the bridge.

Then came more waiting. The ship was buttoned up, which meant that belowdecks they were sweltering. Hell, above decks we were sweltering. The ship was moving through the water but not fast enough to raise a cooling breeze. Above the bridge, I could hear a periodic metallic squeak as the radar antenna cranked through its search cycle. Gotta get some grease up there, I thought. I was hungry but knew food wouldn't be available until GQ was relaxed. If I was hungry, the crew was probably hungrier, but this was no time to get distracted.

More and more I'd begun to appreciate Eeep's fascination with the passive sonar approach to catching one of these bastards. A destroyer pinging away continuously without knowing if there was even anything out there was mostly creating a beacon for a listening sub who might want to try his luck. The rule of thumb for counter-detection of radar was almost two to one: someone scanning the electronic spectrum could detect a radar transmission farther than the radar could detect the listener. Why? The signal only had to go half as far. Acoustic signals were similar, although they radiated much less predictably due to water conditions. But it stood to reason that a sound wave banging out into the water at amplitude X would be much more detectable than a returning echo, coming back at one-third strength or even one-fourth, while having to fight its way back to the sonar's receiver through noisy marine life, thermal layers, and other disturbances. Eeep's idea of filtering the background noise had been brilliant; the ocean was definitely a noisy place.

But not right now, I thought. I looked at the chart house clock: nautical twilight in forty minutes; sunrise a half hour after that. Was there a submarine nearby? I got on the bitchbox.

"Sonar, Bridge: What's the current layer?"

"Bridge, Sonar: Last BT drop was an hour ago; it showed a ten-degree layer at three hundred fifty feet deep."

That was a pretty thick layer but also pretty deep, I thought. A Japanese sub might be able to get down there and survive the pressure, but almost every engagement in the past two years had taken place between two hundred and three hundred feet. I had an idea.

"Combat, Bridge: Ask the XO to come up here."

Eeep arrived thirty seconds later. "Sir?"

"There's a layer at three hundred fifty feet, a thick one-ten-degree differential. Any acoustic signal generated from *beneath* that layer would reflect off it, right?"

"I would think so, Captain," Eeep said. "I think our own sonar pulse would also reflect off *that* strong a gradient. You think that task force coming by made him go really deep?"

I ducked the question. "Would it be possible," I asked, "that he wouldn't even hear us right now, as long as we stay quiet and go slow enough not to cavitate?"

Eeep thought about that for a moment. "Yes, sir, especially compared to all that screw-beat and sonar noise that the task force generated."

"Okay," I said. "I want to stir something up, if possible. He may not be anywhere near here, especially if the Japanese have tumbled to what's happened to stations one through four. Or he could be right below us, sweating bullets. I want one depth charge dropped, set for four hundred feet. Once that goes boom, I want a second one dropped, set for three hundred feet. After that one goes off, come up to twenty knots and go active. Pick a direction—it doesn't matter. Run at high speed for five minutes, then slow back down, change course ninety degrees, and go quiet."

"Leave the radar on?"

"Affirmative. Their mission—their duty to the almighty emperor—is everything to the Japanese, even if it involves sacrificing their ship and themselves. I'm hoping he hears those depth charges and comes up to get that report out before we get him, regardless of the consequences."

"He might not hear us," Eeep said. "But he'll sure as hell hear those depth charges if he's anywhere near the predicted datum position."

"Yeah," I said. "That's what I'm hoping. Depth charges mean someone is hunting him. Assuming he heard that task force going by and went deep, the clock started ticking as soon as the task force disappeared. He now *has* to surface to get a message out. The question for him is: When? The safe thing for him to do is to stay down there for another few hours to make sure he doesn't surface in the middle of a second task force. Except that would eat up warning time for the Japanese fleet. We start rolling ash cans, I'm hoping he'll decide to come up and transmit before we get him."

"If he does come up, do we still want to shoot torpedoes at him?"

"Hell, yes, XO. And guns, too. If he's close enough, turn everybody with a trigger loose. Our mission is to prevent that HF transmission. If he comes up shooting, I'll handle the maneuvers. Otherwise, Combat's in control."

"Yes, sir, got it."

It took a half hour to get everything set up. I got on the 1MC and told the crew what was going on and why it was important that they crush the sub's efforts to get a radio message out anyway they could. "If you see him come up on the surface and he's in range, let fly. Open season, boys."

The first depth charge went off as ordered, so deep that only a large boil of agitated water would have made it to the surface. The second one was more vocal but still nothing like a barrage going off at two hundred feet. The ship shook as the snipes poured on the amps, and we were soon galloping to the northeast, the sonar banging away and the radar casting its lethal beams everywhere. After five minutes I felt the ship heel as we came left and slowed to five knots. False dawn was barely beginning to tease the eastern horizon. Suddenly the starboard lookout yelled: "*Submarine! Submarine!* Bearing zero eight zero relative!" In the next instant damned near every gun on *Holland* opened up in an ear-shattering roar, even the 20mm, whose rounds were arcing high into the air in an attempt to reach the ugly black shape that was already dissolving into a firestorm of exploding three-inch shells and 40mm tracer streams. The sub was out of range of the twenties, but they continued to tear up the water between *Holland* and its prey just the same. I barely heard the torpedoes launch, but when one of them apparently hit, the submarine was blown into two pieces, both of which quickly assumed near vertical angles and then began to slide back into the merciful deeps of the Philippine Sea. *Holland*'s guns followed the wreck down, blasting red-hot pieces off her bow and stern halves and firing so flat that rounds were ricocheting everywhere. Within ninety seconds *all* the rounds were ricocheting because there was nothing there to hit.

"Cease firing," I said, but apparently no one heard me because the guns kept at it, shredding the massive upwelling of seawater, fuel oil, and compressed air for another twenty seconds. I didn't bother to repeat it—they'd done their job, without the need for further orders or formal permission. Let 'em shoot.

Finally, all the noise stopped as sunrise finally drew a bright yellow line just under a deck of clouds on the eastern horizon. I ordered the ship to secure from general quarters. I was still hungry, and now the cooks could get back into the galley. But first we had some details to attend to. I ordered the officer of the deck to drive through the rapidly expanding area of oily wreckage at five knots and to get pictures. I was interrupted when the red light on the bitchbox lit up.

"Bridge, Combat."

"Bridge, aye," I said.

"Recommend continuous course changes until we know that station six didn't join forces with station five sometime last night."

"Good call, XO," I said. "Make it so. And tell Sonar to stay active. Set a modified watch in Combat and have a hedgehog crew on station to deal with any surprise contacts. Go ahead and get a sinking report out, too."

"Yes, sir, and by the way, a Fleet Broadcast message has come in. The invasion of Saipan has begun. Don't you think that chasing what's left of this picket line is kinda OBE?"

"Hell with that," I said. "If there's another one of these bastards out there, he might not know that the Marianas are being invaded. I suspect the Japanese high command has more pressing issues to deal with right now, like that doom train that went by last night. Besides, Spruance himself told us to get him, so let's go get him. Make a report of this sinking, and find me an oiler if possible."

"Aye, aye, sir," Eeep said. "Steer course zero seven five, speed twelve when you're ready. That'll put us at picket station six at zero two thirty tomorrow."

24

XO

We got a scare as real daybreak broke. I'd gone up to the bridge for my usual sunrise coffee and message board session when one of the lookouts, the after lookout, who stood his watch back on the stern between the depth-charge racks, reported hearing an airplane. There was a light to medium overcast up at about five thousand feet. The seas were relatively calm with only light airs about. The OOD asked the lookout for a bearing, but he couldn't give him one. He'd just heard it, in the distance, somewhere. In and out; multi-engine; goes away and then comes back. Faint.

I remembered a trick the Brits had taught us, based on their experiences in the early days of the Blitz. First, I summoned one of the sonarmen to the bridge. We then gave him what the Brits back in the days of sailing ships called a "speaking trumpet": a three-foot-long plastic cone-shaped loudspeaker, like the ones the cheerleaders used at a football game. We sometimes used it to shout orders to line handlers down on the pier when mooring. I instructed the sonarman to go out onto the port bridgewing, reverse the cone, placing the mouthpiece end next to his ear, and listen for an airplane. Before radar, the Brits had used much bigger versions of this down on the coast to get an earlier warning when German bombers were approaching.

We were already headed northeast at six knots, killing time so we could arrive at our preferred time. We hadn't bothered to survey the last debris field. Our photographer had managed to get two grainy pictures of the sub's bow and stern folding up into a V. The sonarman went out and listened. I'd chosen a sonarman because their entire job was to listen.

The petty officer came back into the pilothouse and shook his head. "Those blowers," he said. "That's all I can hear."

He was talking about the whine of the boilers' forced-draft blowers: steam turbine–driven fans that provided combustion air down in the fireroom. Underway they produced a constant noise, which bridge watch standers soon learned to block out. If they happened to wind down suddenly when we were at sea, we knew we had a boiler problem.

"Go back aft to the after lookout station and try again," I ordered. He dutifully took his cone and left the bridge. I asked Combat to make a radar sweep, which produced nothing. Not surprising, since it was a surface-search radar. Destroyers carried an air-search radar, designed to look up; not DEs.

One of the bridge talkers spoke up. "After lookout says the sonar-girl—um—sonarman—hears something. Bearing two four zero relative. He thinks it's an aircraft and that it's coming our way."

"Sound general quarters," I ordered as I called the captain. "Tell the signal bridge to put the Big Eyes on that bearing and begin a horizon search."

The Big Eyes were binoculars, really big binoculars, 20 x 120, made by the Kollmorgen Optical Company up in Massachusetts, who also made most American submarine periscopes. They were mounted on their own pedestal up on the signal bridge, one set on each side. They were there to make sure the signalmen could read a distant flashing-light message or a signal flag hoist during low visibility conditions. If there was an aircraft out there, our radar wouldn't be able see it unless he was down on the deck, but someone on the Big Eyes might. The captain came out onto the bridge just in time for me to report that the ship was manned and ready for GQ. I told him what we had.

"Brief all stations that this could be an enemy aircraft, a scout, or even a bomber," he told me. "Tell the gun stations to review their antiair procedures, and break out some VT Frag for the three-inch."

The bridge watch standers' eyes got big. Submarines were one thing, but no one wanted to hear anything about bombers.

"We're small and maneuverable," he told me. "Get me a Japanese aircraft recognition sheet."

"I got him!" yelled one of the signalmen on the Big Eyes. "Bearing three zero zero relative; position angle three. High wing; four engines; inbound, I think."

Hal came up from combat with the silhouette recognition sheet for Japanese aircraft. High wing; wing pontoons, four engines. "That's a *Kawanishi* flying boat," he said from over my shoulder. "Code name: Emily."

"Scout or bomber?" I asked.

"Both," Hal said with a strained voice. "Carries 20mm cannons, machine guns, bombs. And torpedoes."

By then both the captain and I were scanning the bearing, but neither of us could find it with our 7 x 50 binoculars. Everyone else on the bridge with binocs was scouring the hazy sky too. Then the bitchbox lit up: "Bridge, Gun Control: I have it. Bearing three zero five relative; he's out of range. Request we start with able-able common, max range, set on time. Maybe scare him off?"

"Permission granted; if he keeps coming, switch to VT Frag as soon as he gets in range. Stand by for maneuvers."

"Control, aye."

The three-inch guns began blasting away at about forty-five degrees elevation. They were using antiaircraft common shells, which had fuses, so they'd fly a certain distance and then explode, putting flak bursts into the air. Any pilot headed toward us would see those and know we weren't friendlies and we weren't asleep. I still couldn't find the target, but the gunnery folks had more powerful binocs than the bridge. Our two three-inch mounts could reach out to six miles, so if he did keep coming, we'd switch to variable time fused, fragmenting rounds. These had a tiny radio transmitter-receiver set in the nose and sent out a continuous stream of pulses once fired. If they got an echo back, they'd go off, sending a swarm of white-hot metal fragments everywhere. They were going at 2,700 feet per second, so an immediate detonation was necessary. Then I finally was able to see the plane.

It was big, with a distinctive seaplane high wing, four engines, and painted almost black. I couldn't understand why I hadn't been able to see it before. I could also see the first AAC rounds going off between us and the Kawanishi. Our rounds were falling short, which meant he was still out beyond our guns' range, but from what I could see he was still inbound. The captain didn't want to maneuver until he knew what was coming—iron bombs, or worse, far worse, torpedoes. This guy's appearance had to be related to what was going on at Saipan, or maybe they were looking for the American DE that had sunk five of their submarines.

The captain called Main Control and told them to stand by for a flank bell. I kept scanning the sky, finding the approaching plane, then losing him again. The flak bursts were more numerous now, so I knew that the Japanese pilot knew he was within VT Frag range. Then I found him again. He was much lower now. Combat reported they had him on radar, range nine thousand yards, bearing 300. They relayed that info to Main Battery Plot so they could refine their gun orders. Then suddenly he turned away, in a big, swooping, climbing turn, pursued by flak bursts. He'd obviously known all along how close he could get to us.

Almost immediately, Sonar Control reported incoming torpedo noise spokes. The captain gave the order for all-ahead flank and for a hard left turn to put us lengthwise to what was coming, if nothing else to reduce the size of the target we presented. We lost visual contact on the Kawanishi, but I knew that didn't mean he'd left for good.

"Bridge, Sonar Control: Torpedoes remain on steady bearing, *very* high Doppler." Shit, I thought, these had to be type 93s—one-thousand-pound warheads howling through the water at almost sixty miles per hour.

I realized then we'd made a mistake—the captain should have kicked her in the ass and then stayed on that course to give us maximum lateral separation from the incoming torpedoes. By turning to parallel their approach track, we were now in a pinch: to turn either way would give at least one of these monsters a chance to hit something.

"Right two degrees rudder," the captain called.

"Right two degrees rudder, aye, sir," the helmsman responded, barely inching the wheel to the right. We were doing twenty-three knots now, and I was hoping against hope that our slight turn would take us out of the path of those incoming torpedoes without swinging our back end right into one of them. For thirty seconds we waited, our hearts in our throats.

"Bridge, Sonar Control: One degree left bearing drift, they're passing us to port."

I heaved a huge sigh of relief. Up on the bridge we, of course, couldn't hear them, but the sonar girls must have been shitting little green apples by then, listening to those things come right at us. The captain expanded the turn to the right and then checked with Gun Control to see if they'd seen any more of that Kawanishi.

"No, sir, but some of our guntub guys are reporting they still hear him."

Not what I wanted to hear, but, in a way, suspicions confirmed. According to our intel files on the Kawanishi, he could carry two thousand pounds of bombs, *or* two of those big fish. If he was still in the area, he might be contemplating a strafing attack with those 20mm cannons and all those machine guns. I suddenly felt a little better about our situation. He'd have to come right at us and eventually over us to use those weapons. Between our three-inch, quad forties, and 20mm guns, we should be able to shred a target as big as a Kawanishi flying boat.

Main Control called and asked how long we'd be at maximum speed. The chief engineer was tactfully reminding the bridge we did not have unlimited fuel on board. The captain slowed to fifteen knots and set us up in a big circle to see if that guy was coming back or not. Then he turned to me. "How's this little interlude affecting our approach to station six?" he asked.

"If we're willing to transit faster, we can make up the time," I said.

"Faster is noisier," he pointed out. "And if the Japanese high command hasn't alerted him, this flying boat might. How's about this: We turn north from here. Go a hundred miles or so *above* where we think station six is, then approach it from the north."

I hesitated before answering.

"Okay," he said. "Out with it."

"First: The whole point of this picket line," I said, "was for one or more of them to warn Tokyo that the American fleet was coming north and which way they were headed. The American fleet is already assaulting Saipan. Station six may or may not know that stations one through five have been eliminated, but either way, his mission is OBE. He may even have already been recalled.

"Second: That Kawanishi today almost got us. There'll be more of those guys out here as the invasion of the Marianas proceeds. The farther north we go, the closer we get to the path the Japanese fleet will have to take to attack Spruance. That Kawanishi may wait until tonight, when he logically could expect the picket-line submarines to be on the surface recharging batteries, and broadcast two things: one, the Marianas invasion has already begun, and two, there's an American destroyer headed toward the eastern end of the picket line."

"So now," I said, "we'd be dealing with a Japanese submarine whose mission has been overtaken by events, who failed the emperor by not giving warning that the American fleet was coming for the Marianas, and whose captain might now be looking for a way to redeem himself."

The captain nodded. "And with a new ally—the flying boats. Those guys can stay airborne for hours and hours. They can even land at night, shut down, and just float around, saving gas, and resume ops in the morning. Plus, there'll be a relief for the guy we shot at today. So, second-in-command: What do you recommend?"

"I recommend we tell Tulagi where we are, that we've encountered Japanese scout bombers, that we're getting low on fuel, and request new orders."

"And we'd make Admiral Spruance copy-to on that message?" the captain said. "Remember him? The four-star who told us in no uncertain terms to go get the remaining *two* subs?"

I had no answer to that question, which is, of course, why he'd posed it that way. "Everything you're saying makes logical sense," he told me. "But I doubt that anyone's keeping score on what *we're* up to, given that the entire fleet is engaged in tearing up the Marianas and fighting off the Japanese fleet, sooner or later."

I nodded. No arguing with that.

"And," he continued, "we're an anti-submarine destroyer escort. If we even think we have the opportunity to sink a Japanese sub, then that's what we do. Yes, this one might be a whole lot more dangerous than the past ones. It's even possible that Kawanishi reported our position to station six, and now we might indeed be the one being hunted."

I closed my eyes in defeat. I certainly understood. I'd chosen a course of action that was best for the ship. He was telling me we weren't out here to do what was best for *Holland*. We were out here to kill as many of these survivor-strafing, prisoner-beheading bastards as we could. There was a Japanese sub out here somewhere. We'd already killed more Japanese subs than any destroyer in the Pacific Fleet. Whoopee, except I suspected that very few PacFleet destroyers still had any idea of who *Holland* was. The captain didn't care about that as long as the opportunity to kill one more was presenting itself. Time to get back to our bloody business.

"Yes, sir. Got it."

"Okay, good," he said, his eyes blazing. "So, let's stop screwing around here. Compute a course to where we think station six might be. Figure out the best way to get there, given that he might be coming after us for a change. Radar, on or off? Sonar, on or off? Weave? Zigzag? High speed or slow speed? Depth-charge attack or hedgehog? Or both? It might all be for nothing if that Kawanishi got a warning out and our final target is already running for home; I'll give you that, but I don't care. You guys didn't see what I saw at Pearl. If you want to think this is personal, I won't dispute that. I want them dead. I want them *all* dead. I want them crushed into flattened skin sacks full of microscopic bone fragments at the bottom of God's Pacific Ocean. Okay? Let's go."

I went back down to Combat, the captain's furious words still ringing in my ears. I knew he wasn't mad at me; my argument for quitting this lethal game was correct. He had to know that. Spruance had come and gone. The entire world knew the Americans were ashore in the Marianas. The picket line's mission had evaporated. I couldn't imagine the skipper of station six hadn't also figured that out, and, if that Kawanishi had managed to warn them about us, he'd be an idiot not to head for wherever his home base was. None of this reasoning mattered. The captain wasn't in a reasoning frame of mind just now. Apparently, Captain Ahab was going to get his accursed white whale or die trying.

I understood his silent fury. I sympathized with it, but I was also afraid. What if this final submarine captain, realizing that he might be the last unit left out of his entire submarine squadron, decided to wrap a white scarf around his head, give his crew a fiery speech, toast them with sake and banzais, and order them to prepare for one glorious, final battle. The crew of an American submarine would have helped their XO escort the captain to his cabin and locked the door after hearing that kind of screwball proposal. Japanese submariners? Everything I'd read about the Japanese war ethic told me they'd take a deep breath, bow, gulp their sake, write something poetic and elegiac in their diaries, and then ready themselves for battle.

25

CO

Down in my in-port cabin I swore at myself mentally for losing control like that; no one would have blamed us if we got the hell out of Dodge now that Japanese scout bombers were up and apparently looking for us. Having sunk five of their subs I would expect nothing less once they figured it all out. The brainiac among us was using his noodle to think things through, while the big bad captain was just itching to kill more Japanese, if only because there were still more Japanese out there that needed killing—picket station six being the closest to us.

It was going on lunchtime; I called the CPO mess and invited myself to lunch.

Protocol demanded I wait for the president of the chiefs' mess, Chief Roscoe Santone, to bang on my door and escort me back to the goat locker. The pickings were slim so soon after GQ, but I wasn't there for food, and I think they sensed that. I also suspected they'd already heard about my loudly fanging the XO for even suggesting we just let that last pigboat slip away. Once we were all seated, I made it clear I wanted to speak and they were supposed to listen. This wasn't about cake.

"The Fifth Fleet," I began, "with Admiral Raymond Spruance of Midway fame commanding, is ashore on Saipan. According to our last commodore, the entire Japanese surface fleet, or what's left of it, has decided to come out of their refuge on Borneo in response: carriers, battlewagons, cruisers, and destroyers, as many airplanes as they have left, and probably some submarines. They will probably try to draw Spruance away from Saipan for that one last decisive and glorious battle they dream about.

"My guess is Spruance won't fall for that and will try to deal with whatever they bring with his carrier air, both offensive and defensive. But as the Japanese fleet spills out into the southeastern Philippine Sea, we're gonna see more of what we saw this morning. Nobody's gonna divert a fleet carrier to go hunt down and kill one lone DE. But we are in air range of the southern Philippine Islands: Leyte, Samar, Mindanao, where they surely have air bases for their multi-engine, land-based assets. And if that scout-bomber this morning was any indication, they have five very good reasons to come looking for us now that they're out and about in the Philippine Sea.

"Theoretically, there's one picket sub left. Now remember: Their mission was to tip off the Japanese fleet in Borneo as to which way the American fleet was headed—the Philippines or the Marianas. Now that American infantry is ashore on Saipan, that question's been settled, hasn't it? In all probability, the Japanese high command has realized that, pulled the sixth sub off station, and told him to go north and see what he can do about all those American ship's clustered about Saipan. And that's why the XO is pushing for us to get clear of whatever's coming, especially since the last sub no longer has a mission.

"On the other hand, that last Japanese sub may be in the same quandary we're in. By that I mean out of sight, out of mind, or as the XO likes to say, down in the noise level. When the Japanese fleet commander gets his morning briefing, he'll be focusing on an impending fleet-versus-fleet battle, not crafting orders for one lone submarine. Similarly, I suspect no one on Spruance's staff is giving much thought to *Holland,* either, not with lebenty-thousand infantry engaged ashore and the Japanese battle fleet on the move."

Chief Bobby Garrett, the chief gunner, raised a hand. "If I may, Captain, from what you're sayin', if the big boys are about to get to it, then that sixth station sub's last orders to remain on station and report are still in effect. I'm assuming we don't have new orders, either, what with all this big-deal shit shaping up. Seems to me like we're back to where we were when Tulagi shitcanned us, a free agent so to speak. Let's go get that fucker."

There was a quiet chorus of "damn rights" and "hell, yeses" around the table. Music to my ears.

I raised my hand. "I have to reiterate—we're gonna be punching way above our weight if the Japanese show up in force to get some revenge. It might get truly noisy. It might be us in the water this time wiping fuel oil off our faces. I truly can't argue against the XO's logic on this one, and we all know, me most certainly included, he's one smart sonovabitch."

"Screw that noise," Santone growled. "Last time I checked, our first name is 'Destroyer.' Sir."

26

XO

I summoned my brain trust after lunch. As I saw it, there were two problems. The first was the by now familiar planning for making an approach on a surfaced submarine at three in the morning. We knew how to do that. All that was left was to work out courses and speeds, sensor employment, and all the what-ifs that might arise. The second problem was tougher, and it, too, consisted of what-ifs. What if the final boat on the picket line decided to reverse and come hunting us? Assuming he'd made contact with that seaplane bomber scout, he'd have a general idea of where we were or at least where we'd been when that Kawanishi had tangled with us. If the other five members of the picket line task unit had gone silent, it wasn't much of a reach for that Kawanishi to tell the last station we were probably behind that silence.

The time and motion problem was a bit more complex. We could steam at whatever speed we chose to close that final picket station. The submarine, on the other hand, assuming he chose to come after us, would have to do it submerged, where he could at best make three or four knots in order to preserve his battery. We were going to have to lay out a succession of possible intercept points. If we went fifteen knots to get to where we thought station six was, and he was coming our way at four knots, where would we meet? And if that point happened after dark, when he could come up on the surface, recharge his batteries and then begin to advance in our direction at twenty knots, where would we collide? If we went twenty knots instead of fifteen, we might arrive over top of him just as the sun went down. Would he come up? How much battery would he have left? When did we energize the sonar, if nothing else but to make sure we hadn't *already* collided? Aaarrgh.

I told the guys we had to establish several cases, and then do some math. Case one: He stays on station, and we do our normal, 0300 approach to datum. Case two: He leaves station and heads toward station five submerged, thus making only four knots or so. Case three: We speed up and try to arrive at station six earlier than 0300, hoping to catch him on the surface, running on his diesels because his batteries are badly depleted. Case four: Well, shit.

My mind was spinning. There were just too many variables. What-if, what-if, what-if squared. I could see they were equally frustrated. And yet we had to be careful here; if we were coming at each other, he'd probably hear us before we detected him. Then all he had to do was stop, hover, open all outer doors, and wait for us to present a favorable target. We'd dodged that last torpedo attack by only one or two degrees, but if we happened to pass in front of him at two thousand yards without even knowing he was there, he could fire an entire spread, and we'd never know what hit us. I realized my lack of sleep was catching up with me. It was also possible my heart just wasn't in it. Now I felt disloyal.

"XO?" Hal said. "Let's get the captain into this. He's got a feel for this kind of thing."

Gee, why didn't I think of that? I wondered. I would have loved to be able to call him down and present him with a brilliantly staffed plan of action. On the other hand, I simply didn't know what to do. As an excuse, I could always fall back on my ninety-day wonder reservist antecedents. I looked at my watch. "Okay, we'll proceed northeast at current speed for two hours. That'll let the skipper get some shut-eye. Then we'll meet again but with him present. Right now, I'm going below. I'm beat."

I woke up to the sound of the phone squeaking. Once again, it took about ten seconds for me to gather my wits.

"XO," I croaked.

"Wake up, sleeping beauty," the captain said. "Supper in the wardroom in thirty minutes."

I looked at my watch: 1730. Oh shit, I thought. I may have even said it out loud because the captain chuckled.

"No, no," he said. "Not shit. Spaghetti and spicy Italian meatballs. Straight from the can. God knows how long they've been in that can, but the cooks said the meatballs were talking to themselves, so they decided it was time to boil them before they broke out and hurt somebody. If it's any comfort, I slept just about as long as you did. Hal told me the planning didn't go so well, so let's get some chow and try again."

The cooks had done their best. They'd opened cans of spaghetti sauce and canned meatballs and thrown them into a steam kettle. The pasta was actually freshly cooked, but there was no disguising the metallic taste of everything else. We manfully tucked in. The only saving grace was that the night baker had managed fresh bread. Every time I despaired of ever getting good food again, I reminded myself that the Marines and Army grunts on Saipan were prying their food out of those tiny little C-rations cans with their dirty fingers down in muddy foxholes to the accompaniment of Japanese mortar rounds.

The Fleet Broadcast had been publishing periodical "progress" reports from Saipan. Anyone reading between the lines would know they were locked in a grinding, blood-and-guts fight to the death whose outcome wasn't all that certain. *Six* hospital ships had been called in. And here we were, eating off wardroom china with real tableware and with a steward waiting to pour some coffee. I felt better after some sleep, but I still didn't know what we should do next. The captain seemed refreshed after his nap, so I was optimistic.

The usual suspects gathered in Combat after dinner. The captain, as was his custom, cut right to the heart of the matter. "The possibilities are endless," he said. "But if we wrap ourselves around all the possible moves the enemy could make, we'll never generate a satisfactory plan. So, recall the first rule of intelligence: never try to guess what your enemy *intends* do. Focus instead on the worst thing he's *capable* of doing to you with whatever forces he has available. Trying to determine what his intentions are is a fool's game because he probably doesn't know yet what he's gonna do.

"In our case, we're facing a single Japanese submarine, who may or may not have already fled back to Borneo. The Philippine Sea is swarming with both American and Japanese forces, which tells me that he's not going to operate on the surface during daylight. Based on the way our planes react to a submarine on the surface, ours or theirs, by the way, it's just too dangerous. Which means that only now, as the sun is going down, can he surface and move in any direction at twenty knots, not just three. If we hypothesize that he leaves his station in the next hour or so and goes twenty knots on the surface, we can compute where he'll be for every hour that he does that, right, XO?"

I nodded, visualizing an expanding ripple starting at station six.

"And we're headed toward him at twelve knots to arrive at station six at around 0300, correct?"

Again, I nodded. My eyes felt like they had sand in them.

"Then where our predicted track cuts the outer ring of his possible advance is where we go to GQ and begin substantial evasive maneuvers and sensor management. If he's there, the game is on. If he isn't, we can still get to station six at 0300 by simply changing speed. Get cranking."

There was a chorus of "aye, aye, sir's," and then the captain went to the bridge.

The signal bridge called down as I was laying out the plot. They reported they were hearing an aircraft, position unknown. The GQ alarm went the next moment. Was that Kawanishi, or was one of his brethren back? I went up to the bridge while everyone went to their GQ stations. It was dark but not quite full dark, and there was a bright moon now that the skies had cleared, just to make things interesting. Since there was an aircraft nearby, the captain had slowed the ship to five knots to reduce the phosphorescence created by our wake. Even so, the aircraft would probably see us before we saw him, especially if he kept his distance. The captain and I stepped out onto the bridgewing to listen, but neither of us heard airplane engines. I called the signalman who'd made the original report down to the bridge.

"Could you tell which direction the sound was coming from?" I asked.

"No, sir, XO. It was just a droning noise. We kept that speaking tube in case another one came, but it didn't help."

"Were you hearing it just before you came down here?"

"In and out, XO," he replied. "SM2 Wright thought he heard it too, but he wasn't positive."

"Okay, Sigs," the captain said. "You did the right thing. When in doubt, always report it. Keep using that cone. One guy listens for five minutes, then another guy takes over, and so on. Good work."

"Thank you, sir," the kid said, beaming. Then he scrambled up the ladder leading to the signal bridge.

"You think he's looking for us?" I asked.

"Possibly," the captain said. "This could be the same plane or a replacement scout."

"Should we expect another torpedo attack?"

"Maybe, or it's possible he's out here to locate us and then cue station six as to where we are. Or to sic surface ships on us, or bombers, or the goddamned black plague. Hell, I don't know, but if he's deliberately staying out of visual range, then he's reporting to someone."

I scanned the dark horizon from northwest to northeast. What might be lurking out there? "Maybe we should just hightail it," I said. "Hate to see a pair of Japanese heavy cruisers show up and us with only one torpedo left."

He snorted, but then grew serious. "Maybe we should," he mused. "The picket line is no longer pertinent to anything at all, as you pointed out earlier. We're getting no intel whatsoever on what Japanese fleet forces might be out here in the Philippine Sea, or, for that matter, how the Saipan invasion is really going. I'm starting to get a bad feeling about how exposed we are."

That sent goose bumps up my neck. The atmosphere was electric. We were barely moving. The night air was barely moving. Ahab had a bad feeling?

"You remember what Spruance did at Midway?" the captain asked me. "After that first day, when we'd wrecked all those Japanese carriers?"

"No, sir."

"He withdrew. He turned his entire formation to the east at twenty-five knots and ran that way for the entire night. And it was a good goddamned thing he did, because Yamamoto and Nagumo had dispatched their battleships and cruisers to head east at best speed to close and then destroy the American carriers and their escorts with heavy surface gunfire and torpedoes, something they were known to be good at. Afterward, someone asked Spruance what prompted him to do that."

"He had a bad feeling?"

"Yup. He had a bad feeling. *I'm* having a bad feeling." He stood up and stretched his arms. "Come south, toward Tulagi, twenty knots," he ordered. "I think we're too deep in Indian Country and that nobody cares. Remain at GQ until further notice."

"Aye, aye, sir," I said, with a feeling of great relief. A few hours of sleep had worked wonders on him. I just hoped he'd made that decision in time.

27

CO

Gawd, I hated doing that. In one sense we were running from the enemy, driven by the specter of Japanese heavy cruisers of Savo Island fame, the ones with those towering black pagoda superstructures and endless numbers of eight-inch guns, appearing out of the night for some gunnery practice. Did the Japanese know that dear, old—actually not that old—*Holland* was the ship that had sent five of their submarines and hundreds of their submariners to their doom among the drowned mountains of the Philippine Sea? At the same time, I tried to ignore what my chiefs were going to think.

I remained on the bridge as we hurried south, away from the much-diminished picket line and toward, hopefully, safer waters. I knew that at some point I'd have to craft a message to the commodore in Tulagi and explain our movements. I'd never felt so operationally alone. In the North Atlantic we'd been constantly surrounded by dozens of rust-bucket merchantmen, manfully trying to maintain their convoy stations, every one of them knowing he was a target, and yet never far from a brace or two of scruffy British corvettes, banging their way through the merciless seas of the far north. Dealing with whiteouts, icebergs, German bombers, U-boats, and finally hollow-eyed, starving Russians at Murmansk, always asking: Is that it? Is that all you could send? But ever since coming out here to join the fabled (just ask them) First Team, we'd been pretty much left to our own devices. If it hadn't been for our successes, I still believed we could have decamped for Pearl and beyond without anyone being the wiser until we asked for a tanker.

Even with my eyes closed I could feel we were conducting a broad weave as we ran away from bogeymen to the north of us. *Holland* had a gentle vibration in her port screw at higher speeds, and it was making my coffee mug jitter in its holder. I reached for the bitchbox.

"Main Control, Bridge: What's our fuel and water status?"

"Main Control: Aye, wait one please."

The chief engineer came on. "As of twelve o'clock reports this morning, fuel is forty-five percent; feed is sixty percent."

"Thank you," I said, and switched off. "Naviguesser: How many miles to Tulagi?"

Because we were still at GQ, the navigator himself, Lieutenant junior grade Russ West, went to answer my question. He pulled the wide-area chart, transferred our latest position to the big chart, and then walked his dividers across the chart. "Eighteen hundred, three hundred miles, Captain."

I gulped. I'd forgotten where we were: the Pacific Ocean. Which was still vast. Back to the bitchbox.

"Main Control, Bridge: We have eighteen hundred miles to go; if we're starting at forty-five percent fuel, what's the best speed we can make and not run flat out of fuel?

"Sir, our range is theoretically thirty-seven hundred miles at fifteen knots with a full gas tank and a clean bottom. So, at fifteen knots we'll run out of gas at around eighteen fifty. Except that assumes all the fuel we have is usable. Practically speaking, it isn't. When you begin to scrape the bottom of the fuel tanks you stir up accumulated gunk and residual seawater. So, I'd say twelve knots tops to be sure."

Six, six and a half days, I thought. And, right this minute, we were going twenty knots, burning much more fuel than twelve knots would. I needed time to think, preferably with my tactical team. It was now full dark but still pretty bright out. And I was still really tired. "Slow to five knots," I ordered. "Right three degrees rudder and hold that. Steady zero six zero. Officer of the deck: Secure from GQ, set condition two. Contact the XO and tell him to assemble the tactical team in Combat."

We kicked around the various options open to us as the ship made a giant circle to frustrate any lurking submarine's fire-control system. We hadn't gone that far from where, let's face it, I'd lost my nerve. We'd still been several hours away from where we thought station six might be. Since then, we'd all fixated on the eighteen-hundred-mile journey back to Tulagi. Then it hit me.

"Wait a minute, wait a minute, *wait* a minute," I said. "If it's eighteen hundred miles to Tulagi, how far is it to Saipan?"

Eeep grabbed the big area chart and measured. "Eight hundred miles," he said sheepishly.

I nodded. We'd spent our entire anti-submarine patrol heading east or northeast. It stood to reason that we'd be closer to the Marianas than the Solomons. That's what prolonged fatigue can do to you.

"Okay, that's better, much better, and we know there'll be tankers up there since the whole damned fleet is there. XO, get with Russ and set us up with a straight-line track to Saipan. Initial speed fifteen knots until we refine our actual fuel consumption numbers."

Hal raised his hand. "Sir, we broke off our search for station six because we thought that the scout plane might bring Japanese cruisers," he said. "To get to Saipan we'll have to pass through those same waters. Should we perhaps do a dogleg—go east, maybe, then northeast, then north to stay away from where that scout plane saw us this morning?"

"Good point, Hal," I said. "But that Kawanishi can cover a lot more ground at a hundred fifty knots than we can at fifteen. If he's lost us, and is serious about it, he can just do an expanding square search until he regains contact. I think the best course of action is to join Task Force Fifty-Eight as quickly as we can. The closer we get to Saipan, the sooner they can give us air cover if we run into hostiles."

I could tell from facial expressions that Hal's proposal was the more popular course of action, but there was something I wasn't telling them. Going back through or close to station six would give me an opportunity to kill another Japanese sub, assuming he was still there. I looked over at Eeep, from whose expression I could tell that he knew *exactly* what I was thinking.

"Tell the Chop to open the messdecks so anyone who wants to can get fed. Make sure everyone knows that we're not out of the woods yet and that we may need GQ again on really short notice. XO, we'll head for Saipan as soon as you have a track. Fifteen knots, narrow weave. Radar on; sonar passive."

I went up to my sea cabin and flopped down on the bed. Condition two meant that half the crew would be at their GQ stations, but under relaxed rules. The other half would be able to maybe catch a little sleep and get something to eat. After two hours they'd go relieve the guys on station so they could do the same. It wasn't great, but if we were going to head back into Indian Country, we'd have a fighting chance if we got jumped while guys were napping under their guns instead of in their berthing compartments. I started to drift off until I remembered I'd better tell somebody what we were up to. I started to call the XO, but then realized he, too, needed a break. I called Radio Central instead and asked for a message blank. Then I sat at the tiny fold-down desk.

The first question: Who would I send this to? My boss in Tulagi, of course. But I also needed to alert the task force besieging Saipan that an orphan DE, low on fuel, was trying to join up.

Okay, I thought, first things first. I called the bridge and asked for our current position, latitude and longitude, and our current course and speed. Then I called Main Control and asked for an updated fuel state, and explained that I wanted info about usable fuel, not how much black oil was in the tanks. Someone knocked on the door. It was Eeep.

"Thought you might be putting together a sitrep," he said. "Can I help?"

I grinned. "You betchum, Red Ryder," I said. "I haven't been thinking too clearly lately."

He sat down on the bed. He'd brought a clipboard.

"First question," I said. "Besides Tulagi, who do we send this to?"

"Operationally, the commodore in Tulagi is our immediate boss," Eeep said. "So, the 'to' addressee is ComDesRon Forty-Five. The info addressees should be whoever is commanding destroyers in the Saipan invasion, plus whoever is commanding the replenishment group. Those task group and task unit numbers should be in the Fifth Fleet op-order, and I've got Hal looking them up. I'm assuming we're gonna do a UNODIR?"

"Yep," I said.

"We need a reason, something besides fuel."

"The CO has lost his nerve? Emilys circling in the dark sending targeting information to, what—a horde of Japanese cruisers?"

Eeep gave me a look. "This isn't about nerve," he said. "This is about exercising good judgment in the face of serious fatigue and a low fuel state. I'm thinking something like this: *Holland* is being shadowed by Emilys. We have no info on what other Japanese forces are in this area. We intend to proceed to joint TF Fifty-Eight. We intend to search the area of station six of the Japanese picket line en route. Will advise results."

I thought about it. The big boys of Task Force 58 may or may not know the significance of Emilys, the dreaded Kawanishi scout bombers, but anyone who'd been at Guadalcanal back in 1942 would surely know. We were proposing to enter the battle zone, where the carriers and battleships of both sides were operating. For all we knew, Saipan might already have been secured and the fleet had moved up to take Tinian and Guam. Or it hadn't, and we could be driving into contested waters, where either side might bomb us just for not knowing who we were. *Holland* had obviously fallen through the cracks. This would be a dangerous undertaking, much like spider-mating. At the end of the day, however, sat those fuel numbers, and the Big Blue Fleet was our closest gas station.

"Send it," I said. "Op-immediate. See if anyone cares."

28

XO

I was worried about the captain's last comment: See if anyone cares. It was the sheer scale of this war that was causing us to be ignored, not anything deliberate. Upward of eight hundred warships were savaging the garrison of Saipan, who were savaging them right back, in all probability. If the Japanese fleet had come out to contest the matter, aircraft carriers were assaulting each other over great distances with literally hundreds of planes. Giant Japanese battleships threatened the relatively unarmed amphibious shipping encircling Saipan and the other Mariana Islands. I didn't think our precarious position was a matter of nobody caring, but we were so far down in the chaotic noise of fleet combat operations that we were, for all practical purposes, invisible.

I'd put that business of searching station six for one last sub in as a face-saving gesture. I knew the captain would repeat our usual creep-up-in-the-night tactic as soon as we got anywhere near station six's predicted position, our low fuel state not-withstanding. I still didn't think there'd be anybody there. The picket line had failed, mostly because lowly *Holland* had sunk most of the picket line. There could be no doubt at the Japanese high command as to where Spruance was. So why leave a Japanese sub out there? The best explanation was also a bit depressing: for the same reason *Holland* had been left out here.

I went back up to the bridge to find the captain, but when I stepped out into the pilothouse, the OOD put a finger to his lips. The captain was sound asleep in his chair. Got it, I indicated, and went back down to Combat. "I want to set up the approach to station six," I told them. "Just like we've done five times before. Deep creep, catch him on the surface, kill him with guns if we can."

The CIC watch officer, Lieutenant (Junior Grade) Mike Weiss, looked at me. "What's changed?" he asked.

"The captain doesn't want to pass through those waters without even taking a look."

"We're headed north with the radar transmitting," Mike pointed out. "We've always been radar silent on the way in—occasional sweeps only. Why change that?"

"Because we're headed for Saipan, so it's possible there might be Japanese surface ships out here. Personally, I have no problems with our radar driving any Japanese submarine that's under water; if we see nothing on the radar when we near the station, we bring the sonar up into active mode and execute a search. What's our ETA to datum?"

That question brought some navigational work on the big plotting table. It struck me that I maybe should have awakened the captain for this planning session, but I sensed a few hours of sleep might be better for him than yet another meeting. God knows I could have used some sleep, but I was younger and tougher. Braver, too. Right.

"ETA to the estimated position is 0400 at this course and speed," the CIC watch supervisor reported. "If we broaden the weave for the last ten miles, 0430."

"We'll set condition one AS at 0230," I said. "With all this maneuvering and dithering we've been doing, I'm not confident we know where the estimated position really is. Did we get evening stars?"

One of the guys called the navigator, who told him the haze had prevented star sights. That meant we were working off several hours of dead reckoning.

Wonderful.

I looked at my watch: 2230. I let out a long breath. We really didn't know exactly where *we* were, either. That wasn't a "running aground" ship's safety issue out here in the Philippine Sea, where water depths were measured in miles, not fathoms. *My* instincts still told me to turn east and go east for at least a hundred miles before then turning back north to get to Saipan and friendly forces. These waters were dangerous for a lone DE if you considered we might be running up on a lurking and alerted Japanese sub, supported by Kawanishi flying boats, and the other possibility that there was a brace of Japanese cruisers or even a destroyer squadron prowling out there looking to settle accounts. But I was the XO, not the CO. I kept telling myself: If the captain wanted to go take a look, we were going to take a look.

With the captain asleep on the bridge, I had to remain awake—somewhere. Combat was as good a place as any. I walked over to the radar display. Green circular screen, a dull white spoke rotating slowly clockwise. If we'd been in a formation, I could have verified that the thing was working. But out here in the middle of nowhere, I really couldn't know that it was. The display was here in Combat; the electronic cabinets were down three decks in what was called the ET shop. This was the space where our two electronic technicians worked on any broken electronic gear—radios, the radar, the pitometer, fathometer, and even the sonar if the sonar girls couldn't diagnose or fix a problem. The shop also held the ship's main gyro, which fed course, speed, pitch, and roll data to indicators on the bridge. The ETs had an oscilloscope down there, where they could see and measure the actual outgoing radar transmitter signal. I called them and asked them to verify the transmitter was putting out energy. They said it was.

Next, I called Radio Central and asked them to bring me the read-board. This was a steel medical record holder, in which they sandwiched the most recent teletype-printed pages from the Fleet Broadcast. I realized I was going through the motions, mostly to stay awake. It wasn't working.

"XO?" It was the CIC watch officer, Mike Weiss.

"Yes?"

"Why don't you climb into the CO's chair and get some shut-eye. We've got you covered in here. We're four hours from setting 1 AS; we need you rested before any shit starts."

I stared at him. Them. There was more than one of him in my blurred vision.

"Right, Mike," I mumbled. "Good call."

I climbed up into the captain's chair, which was placed in the center of Combat, in case he wanted to sit down here when we were working a tactical problem. I was out in ten seconds.

It was the captain who woke me up, and I felt a sudden wave of embarrassment: nobody sat in the captain's chair except Himself. As I got my eyes focused, I could see he was grinning. "Buncha ratty bastards around here," he announced impishly to grins among the CIC team. "We're setting one AS, silent, in fifteen minutes. Lay below and wash up. With any luck we're gonna jump another one of these bastards."

I mumbled something and then hurried down to my stateroom to wash my face and try to wake up. The captain's steward appeared with a cup of fresh coffee and two warm doughnuts. I don't know which tasted better, but I was happy to see both.

We set condition one AS (anti-submarine) as planned. I was back in Combat, my eyes actually working now. The captain had gone back to the bridge after a look at the tactical plot, which showed our planned approach track to datum. I could feel that we were doing a broad weave as we closed in on what might yet turn out to be an ambush. We'd been talking about that possibility for so long that I almost wished it would happen so we could settle the issue once and for all. Almost, but not quite.

There were two radarmen watching the display console. Manned and ready reports were coming in from the topside stations—Sonar Control, Gun Control, the three-inch guns, depth charges, hedgehogs, side projectors, 40mm, 20mm, and the all-important searchlight operators. Also reporting in was Damage Control Central, Main Engineering Control, and the so-called repair parties, one forward, one aft. These consisted of a dozen firefighters standing next to their repair lockers, dressed out to fight fires and flooding. The ship was buttoned up, meaning all ventilation except to the main spaces had been secured to prevent smoke from spreading, all interior hatches had been closed and dogged down, and everyone was wearing battle dress: steel helmets, life jackets, pants' cuffs tucked in, and long-sleeved shirts to reduce burn injuries.

Comfortable it was not. Here in Combat, we had air-conditioning, but for the guys topside and inside the ship it was miserable. I often thought that wartime crew fatigue was mostly due to the hours and hours spent at general quarters.

"Radar contact," one of the radarmen shouted. "Bearing—"

"Well?" I said.

"It's gone, sir," he said.

"Give me your best estimate," I ordered.

"Zero two, maybe zero three zero degrees true, range fifteen hundred yards. But, sir—"

"That's okay, that's good enough," I told him and then indicated to the plotters to lay down the contact. Then I called the captain on the bitchbox, punching in Sonar Control's button as well.

"We may have just had contact on a periscope," I said, giving him the range and bearing.

"Sonar go active," the captain ordered, and then I felt the ship turning and accelerating.

"Bridge, Combat, Sonar Control: torpedo noise spoke! Bearing zero four zero, Doppler high."

We were still turning when the torpedo actually hit us, slamming into our starboard side with a horrifying crash that shook the whole ship, but then the next thing I heard was the hedgehog battery firing a full pattern. I'd stopped breathing, like everyone else, when that big fish punched its way into our side. Hedgehogs?

But the torpedo hadn't exploded. Why not? When it did, *Holland* would be broken in half and we'd all be swimming for our lives. Then I heard the port side depth-charge projectors firing a full bag and simultaneously felt the ship slowing down. And then, to my amazement came multiple thumps almost directly beneath the ship, followed seconds later by the thunderous blasts of depth charges, set relatively shallow, much too shallow, going off right next to us. Everything not bolted down in CIC went flying, and men found themselves on the deck from the shock of the depth charges.

Good *God,* had we just depth-charged ourselves? All I knew was that I had to get my terrified ass up to the bridge.

29

CO

The approaching torpedo was coming at us from bearing 050 true, so I yelled for flank speed and a turn to that bearing, hoping to comb what I expected to be a spread, not just one fish. I actually lifted my body up by my arms in the chair in expectation of the end of the world. And then the damned thing hit us, starboard side, with a crunching thump that reverberated throughout the ship.

But no explosion.

How the hell could that be?

I jumped out of my chair and ran to the starboard bridgewing, fighting to stay upright due to the strong heel to port. We were still turning? Main Control came up on the bitchbox and reported they had a torpedo warhead sticking into the engine room, and it sounded like the thing was still running. They were experiencing serious flooding. At that moment, one of the torpedomen blasted through the pilothouse hatch and yelled for the captain.

"Here!" I yelled back. He stopped in the pilothouse door, his face as white as a sheet.

"That fish is still running," he shouted, even though he was only two feet away. "Those props are counters: when they hit their count, it'll go off! You gotta get them to stop!"

It took me a second, but then I understood what he was saying, *and* why the torpedo hadn't exploded: we'd been too close. Torpedoes wouldn't arm until they were safely away from the launching platform, and the torpedo determined that by counting the revolutions of its own propellers. Somehow, I had to turn hard enough to make the back half of that fish contact our hull and jam the props.

"Right *hard* rudder," I shouted. By then the motors were driving us at full power, so a thirty-five-degree rudder definitely heeled us. I heard things falling in the pilothouse and men shouting.

"Sigs," I yelled. "Light up the starboard side."

One of the signal searchlights came on and revealed the long, black back half of the torpedo down at about the waterline, looking like a big wet snake that had gone into a hole after its prey. Two counter-rotating propellers were spinning at the back, spinning so fast that they were just a blur.

Counting.

"Starboard engine back full," I ordered. "Port engine ahead flank." This should tighten the turn even more, putting enormous pressure on the part of the fish that was sticking out of our side. There wasn't anything else I could do

If the props reached their ignition count, we were done for. Thousand-pound warhead, already stuck into our guts. I couldn't imagine what the guys in the engine room were experiencing with that big, black thing, framed by a stream of seawater that was rapidly flooding the space. The same pressure I was using to bend that damned thing into the hull was driving tons of water into the ship.

Suddenly, a shower of sparks, as the tail end finally was pressed up against our steel hull and the props screeched to a stop. I shouted to Sigs to douse the searchlight.

I exhaled, finally. But now what? If I slowed down, would those props crank back up? We were essentially turning in place, both motors fighting each other at full power. I could hear damage reports coming into the bridge from DC Central, but I couldn't focus on that right now. I could only hope that the combined hedgehog and depth-charge attack had at the very least sent the submarine packing. We'd been so close that his fish hadn't armed, and when I'd realized that, I fired all the weapons that could possibly bear.

The XO appeared in the bridgewing hatchway, and for once, he was simply speechless. I looked again down the starboard side at the torpedo. The propellers had ground themselves down to nubs on the side of the ship to the point where they were glowing red. Suddenly, they both broke off. I felt a seismic lurch down in my guts.

"Rudder amidships!" I shouted. "All ahead standard."

For a moment I could only lean over the bullrail and try to control my breathing. I slowly became aware of men out on deck searching for damage. I'd ordered the port-side side projectors to fire, set on shallow, because that's where I thought the sub must be as a consequence of our hard turn to starboard. I now wondered if they'd done more damage to us than the torpedo.

Main Control reported that they had the flooding under control with pumps, but that a lot of water was still coming in. And then there was the problem that the entire torpedo, some twenty-four feet long, was still stuck into our innards. We had to get that thing extracted, except the moment we did, we'd have a brand-new wide open twenty-four-inch hole to deal with.

"I think we got the bastard," someone said. It was Eeep, finally able to speak.

"If not, we scared the hell out of him," I said. "But until daylight, we have to assume we didn't. Right now, we have to get rid of that damned thing. Get How up here. Helmsman, right five degrees rudder."

"Right five degrees, aye, sir." I'd steadied up, but that made us a better target, so, just in case, I went back into circling mode. Garcia appeared, his bulk filling the doorway.

"Bosun Mate, I need that torpedo gone," I said. I'd seen him down on the starboard side earlier, so I didn't need to explain the problem to him.

"Gotcha covered, Skipper," he rumbled. "We'll get a sea anchor tied to its ass-end and then let Mother Pacific pull 'er right out."

"How will you get a sea anchor tied onto that thing?"

"Piece'a cake, Cap'n. I've already got the boys bringing up one of the quarterdeck awnings. We'll make a balloon outta that with some twenty-one thread, and then they're gonna lower me in a bosun's chair so's I can sit on that bastard. Then they'll fairlead some line down to me so's I can tie it on. After that, they'll haul my ass back on board, and we'll deploy the awning. If you want a smooth pull, you'll have to slow way down. You want it to jerk out, gimme ten knots."

"Sounds like a plan, Boats," I said.

"We're on it, Cap'n," he said, and then he was gone. I turned to the exec. "XO, explain to Main Control what we're gonna do. They'll need to get ready for some serious flooding when that thing gets jerked out."

"Aye, aye, sir," he said. "Just a suggestion, though: that fish punched through right at the waterline. It must have been porpoising. If we could put a port list on us, say, five degrees, that hole will be just out of the water."

Great idea, I thought. "Make it so, XO. And then I need damage reports and an ETR for the sonar."

It turned out that most of the damage had indeed been caused by driving almost right over our own depth charges set for fifty feet. That had been my fault. Depth charges were stored on their tracks or in the projectors preset for fifty feet. I'd told them to fire a half bag to port only, but not what depth to set them for, so they'd gone out set for fifty feet. The sonar receiver was repairable, but so far, the sonar-girls hadn't been able to find enough spare vacuum tubes for the transmitter. The radar was also down, but they did have the necessary tubes. Radio Central said they could receive the Fleet Broadcast, but the high-frequency transmitter antennas were out of action due to broken ceramic insulators. There were lots of interior lighting fixtures broken, and one of our two shaft bearings was leaking excessively.

As to the submarine, we'd need to go back to where we'd eaten that big fish to see if we had any evidence. Both Eeep and I thought we'd heard hedgehog warheads going off, but everything had happened so fast that we could both have been imagining things. Full daylight would tell the tale, although I wasn't eager to go back to where we'd been torpedoed. We needed to get a report out, but that would have to wait for Goliath and his deck-apes to extract that extinction device from our hull. I called our supply officer and told him to get some breakfast going.

Eeep came back to the bridge as first light appeared. We were still going in a wide circle, only now we had a port list, courtesy of the snipes moving both fuel and feedwater around. That had stopped the water that had been spraying into the engine room long enough for the pumps to get the bilges dried out. He told me Chief Garcia was ready for the big event. I went out onto the starboard bridgewing to watch. They'd mounted a portable davit so that he would be suspended directly over the torpedo, which was still wedged against our hull. Those propellers had almost eaten their way through our hull, leaving two big shiny gashes in the hull.

I directed Main Control to evacuate both the engine room and the fireroom. If that thing went off, *Holland* would be done for, but there was no reason to have men standing ten feet away from it when it went. The sea anchor was one of our quarterdeck awnings, white canvas and shaped like a trapezoid. The bosuns had hand-stitched it into roughly the shape of a balloon, maybe twelve feet across, and then tied twenty-one-thread, a light line, to each grommet in the awning, bringing all the strands to a central point and attaching them to a steel ring, like rigging a parachute.

The chief was swaying gently in his bosun's chair, the same one we used for ship-to-ship highline personnel transfer. He had a hank of twenty-one thread in one hand and a mug of coffee in the other. He looked as happy as a clam at high tide. I nudged the photographer to get a picture of him. Because the ship was listing to port, he'd be bumping his way down the steel sides until he could actually straddle the torpedo. The bridge phone talker announced that First Division was ready to attach the sea anchor. I told them to wait one. Then I got on the 1MC.

"This is the captain speaking," I began. "Chief Garcia is about to be lowered down to the torpedo that's stuck in our side to attach a sea anchor. The torpedo appears to be disarmed, for the moment, anyway. Appears to be. If it goes off when the sea anchor pulls it out of our hull, there is going to be a tremendous explosion, so I want all hands to get into their life jackets and get topside on the *port* side, bow or stern. The warhead on this thing is big enough to blow the ship into two pieces. I want the depth-charge gunner's mates to set all charges on safe. If you end up standing next to one of the life raft floats, be ready to cut it loose if this thing goes off. In the meantime, if you're topside, watch for a periscope. The Japanese bastards who torpedoed us may still be alive. That is all."

I told the phone talker to tell Garcia to give us fifteen minutes to get everybody out of the interior of the ship, knowing as I did that if that thing went off, he'd be the very first to know. I then asked Eeep if we'd gotten a report out. He said, no, they were still trying to get a transmitter to hook up to one of the emergency HF antennas. Apparently, this involved convincing the transmitter that it was indeed attached to a serviceable antenna.

"Okay," I said. "We're not going to do this until I know we've sent out a report that has our position and that we're trying to extract a torpedo from our side. If nothing else, that will bring a PBY or two. Go down there and tell the chief what the delay is all about, and then go to radio and get a message out however you can."

Eeep hurried down to the main deck to explain what was holding us up. In the meantime, daylight was upon us, and with it, the opportunity for a submarine to see us: a damaged submarine that desperately needed to get up on the surface, going in quiet circles, waiting for vacuum tubes. Suddenly the smell of bacon came wafting up to the bridge. Given our situation, it was immensely comforting. I looked back down over the side. The chief was now puffing on an ugly cigar, while hanging in a canvas and tube steel chair ten feet away from a thousand pounds of Japanese high explosive. He looked up at me on the bridgewing. I grinned. He grinned right back. I mouthed the words: "You're brave." He laughed, knowing full well how the rest of that expression went.

30

XO

The Radio Central leading petty officer, RM1 Billy Parkes, and I stood in front of an electronic equipment rack filled with the transmitter consoles for our newly upgraded high-frequency radios. He'd sent the other radiomen topside after hearing the captain's instructions.

"Why won't it work?" I asked. "Is it broken?"

"No, sir," he said. "The transmitter itself is okay—they're all shock-mounted. But it can't get on the air without an antenna. And not just any antenna: there has to be a wavelength match for the transmitter's signal—that's a specific, physical length of antenna wire. The wires are there, but all that blast broke the ceramic insulators for the actual antenna wire. The antenna itself has to be insulated from the ship's hull or else the entire transmitter signal goes to ground. I've got guys topside trying to piece together one good insulator. We get that, we can get back on the air. You got a message drafted?"

I realized I didn't. I grabbed a message blank and checked the block for operational immediate. From: USS *Holland.* To: ComDesRon 45; Info to: Who? I scrambled to think of who to send this to who was out here, not eighteen hundred miles away back in Tulagi. Then it hit me. I wrote down: ComFifth Fleet. Spruance, himself. Or at least one of his staffers.

> Holland torpedoed. Fish did not detonate but is stuck in our starboard side. Attempting to remove. Believe sub was sunk.
> Intentions:

I stopped there—our intentions were not for me to say. I decided to take the draft to the captain.

"They got it," the radioman announced. "The transmitter is coupled. Where's the message?"

I told him to wait one, that I had to get the captain to sign off. When he nodded, I headed back up to the bridge. I learned that the lower spaces had been cleared, and we were waiting for the sea-anchor team to get Chief Garcia back up on deck. He'd attached the shroud line ring to a shackle, and then made the shackle to the torpedo's afterbody, just ahead of the fins. Our shipfitters had been alerted to bring flat stock and a welding rig to the starboard side for the patch, but in the meantime, most of the crew was over on the port side, helping with the port list. The captain was waiting impatiently; the sooner we got rid of this thing the better. We still had no way of knowing if the fish would simply sink or blow up with the sudden movement. Garcia stood up from the chair and gave me a thumbs-up. I motioned for him to get over to the other side, but he shook his head. Someone had to throw the actual bundle of canvas over the side and do so in such a way that the wake would catch and fill it. He wasn't going to leave that job to one of his "boys."

"The moment that sea anchor starts to fill I'm going to put right full rudder on," the captain said. "Swing the hull of the ship as far away as possible in case the warhead fusing system is still alive and mistakes the sudden shock for a contact hit on a target."

I hadn't thought of that, I realized. The captain gave Garcia the signal, and he picked up the heavy bundle of canvas. He made sure the shroud lines leading over the side weren't tangled, and then he threw the entire thing over the side like a shrimp fisherman throws his cast net. The canvas blob began to drift aft until the shrouds were extended, then it ballooned up into a close approximation of a parachute.

"Right full rudder," the captain shouted.

For a scary instant I thought the lines were going to break as they popped up out of the water, vibrating like violin strings. Then, with an earsplitting metal screech, the torpedo came out in a shower of sparks and immediately disappeared, taking the sea anchor with it into the depths. The lights in the engine room shone brightly through the two-foot-diameter hole in our side. The lower lip of the jagged hole was only a few inches above the wake, and the port list increased as the ship leaned into the starboard turn. I could just imagine what that sudden lurch to port felt like to the crew mustered on the port side.

"Rudder amidships," the captain ordered, then turned to me. "No point in driving back over it if it decides to—"

A deep, almost subliminal boom rose out of the sea off our starboard quarter, followed by a massive boil of shocked seawater fifteen seconds later.

"Good call," I muttered. The captain grinned and then ordered the boatswain mate of the watch to pipe all hands and tell them to reman their GQ stations.

"GQ?" I asked.

The captain nodded. "It's getting light. We're gonna go back and make sure we got that sonovabitch."

He must have seen the shocked look on my face. We had no sonar, no radar, a large hole in our side at the waterline, an unknown number of things broken in the interior of the ship

"C'mon, XO," he said quietly. "You didn't think we were just going to leave with our tail between our legs and go lick our wounds, did you? It's coming daylight. If he's still down there, he'll be in a world of hurt, too. Post enough lookouts so that we have every twenty-degree sector covered. Cooks, snipes, skivvy-wavers, sonar-girls, and radio-pukes—I want eyes on the water, all around, nonstop. If he pops a periscope, I intend to attack with both depth charges and hedgehogs. You go down to Combat and reconstruct our track, and then set up the search square. Quarter-gasket!"

"Coffee coming up, Captain," a voice answered from inside the pilothouse.

I handed over the message draft. He glanced at it, nodded, and said he'd take care of it. I went down to Combat, stepping over broken light bulbs littering the passageway. I began by canvassing the various GQ control stations as to where things stood. Sonar Control said they could receive signals from the sound head, but only on the filtered circuit. There were fourteen broken vacuum tubes in the transmitter cabinet; they had only six spares, so pinging was out of the question. The ET shop said they'd have the radar back up within the hour, probably at a reduced capability, as long as they didn't find any more problems. Main Control reported they'd weld a plate over the hole from the *inside*; it was just too hard to drape an arc welder over the side, with his gear. One slip or even one rogue wave could electrocute him. I concurred. As soon as the plate was in place, they'd get the port list off the ship.

Damage Control Central reported there was a fair amount of shock damage throughout the ship but most of it superficial: overhead lights, battle lantern bulbs, cracked door hinges, watertight hatches out of true. Gun Control said they were ready to work. The port-side depth charge projectors had been reloaded, as had the fantail racks. Hedgehog was undamaged, and the guns reported no visible problems. That's good, I thought, 'cause we were going to go looking for trouble. It took the oil king twenty minutes to calculate fuel remaining and the news wasn't good: we were just below 40 percent.

Computing a track back to the area where we'd been hit was proving to be difficult. We hadn't managed morning stars, so we were still pretending to know where we were by dead reckoning. I presumed the captain's plan was to go back to where we thought we'd been attacked, and then settle down to wait the submarine out, using radar to detect the inevitable periscope. Why am I presuming? I wondered. Go ask him.

I stopped by my stateroom to clean up a little before going to the bridge, but when I got there, they told me he'd gone down to Radio Central. When I got back down there, he was standing in the transmitter room. The duty radio operator was busy keying in a message. The other radiomen were elbows deep in equipment cabinets, trying to get more than one long-haul transmitter operational. When the captain saw me, he put up a wait-one finger, and then handed me the message draft once the operator had sent it out. He'd kept my opening statement about having been attacked. The message now read:

> In position 7.49N-145.7E Holland torpedoed. Counterattacked with D/C and H/H. Believe sub was sunk. Fish did not detonate but penetrated the engine room on starboard side. Eventually removed it. Sustained widespread shock damage due to shallow D/C. Radar operating in REDCAP. Sonar is listen only. Guns, H/H/, D/C operational. Port shaft may be broken. Intentions: return to position where attack occurred, then wait for 12 hours to see if he surfaces. UNODIR will then proceed to Saipan. Fuel is 38%. Request fuel RDVU instructions.

"That ought to do it," I said. "I'll have a course recommendation in a few minutes, based on DR track."

"DR," he said. "Dead reckoning. Whoever coined that term knew what he was talking about, didn't he? How long, roughly, if we creep back at eight knots, with a weave?"

"Lemme go see," I said. "And I'll make sure we get evening stars this time, or the naviguesser's going for a swim."

"Yes, please do," he said. "We'll maintain that visual watch until nightfall. After that, we'll listen and wait. Keep the radar on the air as soon as we get it back up."

The navigator, Russ West, joined me in Combat to reconstruct our movements since getting hit. Unbeknownst to me, he had actually managed to get evening stars the night before, so we started there with a fresher DR plot. The only hole in the track was from the time the fish hit us to now: all the plotters had been too busy picking themselves and their gear off the deck plates. I finally jabbed a finger down on the chart and told them to start from here, with "here" defined as the last plotted position before the attack. We drew a line from that point to where we'd estimated the sub had been lurking, and that became the course order: eight knots, with a broad weave. We'd get there in about four hours. I gave that information to the captain, and he concurred. I put Hal in charge of setting up all the extra lookouts. We relaxed GQ so the crew could get some chow, but both three-inch mounts remained fully manned, as did the depth-charge team. We gave the four-barreled 40mm mount crew head-of-the-line privileges on the messdecks, with instructions to reman their mount as soon as possible.

I decided to go below to the engine room to see what was going on. The ship still had about a six-degree list to port, which meant that travel down ladders was a two-handed endeavor. The engine room smelled of seawater, oil, and the distinctive smoke generated by melted steel. They'd pumped the bilges down to normal levels, and they now had a large steel plate tack-welded to the starboard side. The welder was now laying down the full perimeter beads, his arc screened from the rest of the space by a wet blanket from which emanated clouds of blue-white smoke accompanied by the continuous crackling of an electric arc. The chief engineer told me they'd start working on the ship's trim as soon as the repair was deemed watertight.

"How about that shaft bearing?" I asked.

"It's actually the stern tube, where the propeller shaft penetrates the hull, that's leaking. It's not really a bearing, but a steel tube lined with *lignum vitae* staves, and some of them probably have whiplash damage. We'll set up an eductor into that plenum chamber. Take a dry dock to repair that."

"Okay—is it squealing or making any kind of noise?"

"Not much," he said. "I figure as long as it's leaking, it's lubricated."

"I'll have sonar do a spectrum sweep, see if we're making unusual noises."

"The stern tubes are in the baffles, XO."

I mentally slapped my forehead. Of course it was. Okay, we'd just have to take our chances—the sonar was blocked from listening in an arc stretching twenty degrees from the centerline to either side, acoustic wedge known as the baffles.

"Any other significant damage?"

"Number one evap has a vacuum leak, so it's producing feedwater at a reduced rate. We should be able to find that pretty quick, but this plate took precedence."

"Will it be watertight?"

"No, sir, it will not, but the leakage will be minimal."

"Okay," I said. "Get us flat as soon as you can. Coffee mugs keep sliding all over the place."

He grinned and assured me he'd do his best to mitigate that serious crisis.

I went to the wardroom and dished up a plate of mystery-meat stew served with rice. I sprinkled it with hot sauce in order to disarm my taste buds. Whatever it was, I could assume it was safe to eat. Beyond that, one did well not to ask too many questions. The night baker had had loaves of bread on the rise when the Japanese fish hit. He'd had to discard the entire batch.

Depth charges, I thought. We'd given ourselves a punch in the guts setting them at fifty feet. The captain must have thought the sub was in the process of diving from periscope depth after firing that fish. There may even have been more than one torpedo, but everyone who'd heard that thing was coming at us had been dealing with control problems of a different sort just then. On the other hand, maybe we'd smacked him hard enough that he was, like us, picking up pieces.

The captain seemed convinced that the sub might still be there. If we could reenter his patrol station and just hang around, he'd ultimately have to come up, especially if he'd been damaged. As usual: too damned many ifs, I told myself. The sub skipper had to know he'd hit us with that fish, but also that it had failed to detonate. After that he would have been very busy. His tormentor had left the area, leaving the sea humming with the energy released nearby from a slew of depth charges. Had he decamped for home base? Obviously, the captain thought otherwise.

I went to my stateroom and flopped on my rack. Just for a moment, I told myself.

31

CO

The day was drawing to a close as we made our way back northeast, the sun setting behind us across a calm sea. I'd grabbed a bite in the wardroom before resuming my post on the bridge. I'd not had much appetite, so whatever it was had done the job. I think when you experience a surge of terror-induced adrenaline, food fades from your priorities list. If that torpedo had had time to arm and hit us where it hit us, *Holland* would have sunk in less than a minute. The front half would have capsized immediately and gone down with all hands; the back half might have stayed afloat for a few minutes, but the shock would have opened seams, dismounted main propulsion motors and generators, snapped the propeller shafts, and broken the legs of anyone standing on the steel deck. Everyone who'd survived that initial blast would have drowned, simply because they couldn't swim. As the captain I lived with the possibility of the ship being destroyed every time we tangled with a submarine. I supposed I should have been celebrating the five victories we'd achieved. No other DE had achieved such a record, I told myself for the umpteenth time. If the subs had been planes, *Holland* would be an "ace." Somehow, after that torpedo, it didn't seem so important anymore.

And yet, I was now sensing a certain coolness from Eeep. My decision to go back to the scene of the crime had obviously upset him, and, through him, probably the entire wardroom. We'd done our damn job, smashed the picket line, and survived a terrifying near miss. No one would have thought anything about it if we'd headed for the safety of the Big Blue Fleet, if only for fuel. I knew that the crew thought my pursuit of all those subs had been a personal vendetta in revenge for what the Japanese did to my crew at Pearl. He's a Sicilian, they'd mutter. Those guys can't help themselves when it comes to revenge. The word on our damage was certainly out: the sonar couldn't ping, the radar was working only at half power, to the extent that we had a dozen extra lookouts substituting for the radar with handheld binoculars, and there was something wrong with one of the propeller shafts. Sounds like a good time to declare victory and seek shelter with the rest of the fleet.

But, no: the captain says we're going back to see if we killed that guy or not. And if we didn't, he wants to fight it out when that sub pops up looking for air. And how will he come up if he does come up? With six torpedo tubes locked and loaded, that's how. Our sonar might, *might* hear him, but his sonar, living down in the sea where our pings, had we had any pings left, must penetrate layers, detect the sub, and then make their way back to our sonar in some recognizable form through all that ambient marine-life noise, will definitely hear us. He ambushed us once, which proves that he knows how.

I couldn't, of course, actually know what my crew was thinking. Many of them were focused on the next meal and some rack time. What we were doing, and why, was simply way above their pay grade. For a moment I was sorely tempted to just break it off, head east at fifteen knots, and then north to the Marianas. But then I recalled the nightmare sight of my minesweeper guys in the water, floundering around in their skivvies, their ears ringing and their limbs like rubber from the blast of a bomb that had catapulted them into the harbor, and then watching them suddenly spouting blood from their mouths, noses, and ears as those Japanese killers hit them with 20mm rounds. For fun.

I asked the quartermaster for an ETA to the new datum. "Ninety minutes, Captain."

"Very well," I said. "Pass the word: we'll set GQ in ten minutes."

It was late afternoon when we passed over datum, or at least what we thought was datum. I had extra lookouts posted to search for any signs of a kill, but my nose told me there were none. Wreckage might disperse, but a diesel fuel oil sick would still be out here with the sea as calm as it was. I called down to Combat and asked Eeep how certain he was of our position.

"Not very, Captain," he said. "Recommend an expanding square search, two thousand yards on a side."

"I concur," I said. "How's the radar picture?"

"A bit weak," he replied. "We can't really tell until it sees something, and right now, there's nothing out there."

"I think there will be once it gets dark," I said. "Run the square for an hour, then collapse it. The radar's our only hope unless we damaged him. Is there a layer?"

"Two," Eeep said. "A weak one—three degrees differential—at one eighty feet, a strong one—ten degrees—at two sixty feet."

"How far did we go from the torpedo strike?" I asked. "Could he have surfaced while we were dealing with that fish?"

"It's possible, sir," he said. "He could have come up, lit off the diesels, and gone in the away direction at twenty-two knots."

"And the sonar is in listen-only, correct?"

"Yes, sir, and that only on the modified panel. The ping transmitter is hard down, and the receiver can hear but can't display what it's hearing. We'd hear an approaching torpedo, but beyond that, we can't know how capable it is. Or isn't."

Wonderful, I thought. Two layers meant he could stay down and remain quiet for as long as he had air and battery. If we were going to see him, it would have to be on radar. The next question was how long should I keep the ship at GQ? The crew probably wasn't completely exhausted, but they soon would be with the ship buttoned up, no ventilation, no food, and all this after the siege of dealing with that torpedo.

"XO, I want you to set up a modified, three-hour condition watch: Combat, the two guns, the forty, and the hedgehogs ready on station. Otherwise, set condition three. I think this is going to turn into a waiting game, so I want the crew to be able to get some downtime. If he pops up on radar we can go back to GQ. I'll remain on the bridge; you get some downtime. When my eyes get too heavy, I'll give you a call. Okay?"

"Yes, sir, that makes sense. We have the luxury of relaxing a little. He does not."

"Exactly; now—say it."

"What could go wrong?" he replied promptly.

I grinned. That was more like it. I wasn't the only one who wanted to finish this bloody business.

We moved randomly through the datum area for the next two hours, changing speeds and courses as randomly as we could. The seas remained glassy calm, the moon in and out of high clouds, and a light overcast covered the area. Earlier in the evening we'd received an update on the Saipan landings and the preliminary casualty figures were eye-opening. They weren't declaring the island secured yet, which explained why my message hadn't elicited any response. In a way that suited me just fine, except for the low fuel state. I expected that, when someone did read our message, we'd be ordered to break off and head for the Saipan operating areas.

"Bridge, Combat: Radar contact, bearing zero three zero, range eleven thousand yards. Wait one: It's gone. We had it for two sweeps. Could just be a ghost."

I acknowledged, having been jolted out of a doze. A radar ghost was just that: a momentary video return on the scope, and then—nothing.

Sometimes more than one would appear, looking like a line of contacts that was headed in toward us. There'd be solid paints, bright little blips on the screen, that would then dissolve after a few minutes into a blank screen. The radar techs said it had something to do with ambient conditions—temperature, pressure, humidity, and sea state. In other words, they couldn't really explain it.

"Bridge, Combat: Regained contact, bearing zero three five, range still eleven thousand."

Eleven thousand yards—five and a half miles away. Was it a ghost or a periscope? I didn't think we'd be visible at that range in the strange, dim, gray moonlight, but our radar signal might be detectable.

"Contact lost," Combat reported, and this time it was Eeep on the bitchbox. This sure sounded like a sub putting the stick up just long enough to look around and then quickly pulling it down. Taking a look or teasing us so that we'd head over there and try our luck against a spread of torpedoes?

"We'll stay right here," I told Eeep. "Constant motion, constant changes in course and speed. Whatever he's up to, the one thing I know is he needs to surface to refresh his air and his battery."

"You think he knows we're here? That he'll come down here and start a fight?"

"No," I said. "I think he's desperate to come up on the surface. Think about it: If he could surface, light off his diesels, turn northwest, and run on the surface at twenty-plus knots, we'd be eleven thousand yards out of position to chase him with a speed advantage of only two knots."

"And if we did chase him, we'd be asking for a salvo from his stern tubes," Eeep said. "He'd let us get close and then fire a spread. Whichever way we turned, we'd catch one."

My heart sank a little. Eeep wasn't here to fight, after all. I mentally recited the "if" mantra. *If* what we were seeing on our reduced capability radar was a periscope and not a ghost, and *if* this final picket sub had evaded our desperate launch of depth charges and hedgehogs, and *if* he'd stayed around, and *if* we were even in the right place, what were my choices? Eleven thousand yards. Five and a half miles, just over there. He could just hear the sub's captain: C'mon, Yankee devil. Kick her in the ass and come to me. You've killed five of my brethren submarines. The picket line is no longer needed. Time now for a true fight to the death. I'll put the scope up one last time, in case you've lost the will to fight. Come and get me. Unless of course you're afraid. I am not afraid. This is now a matter of honor.

"Captain?" a voice said from behind my chair. It was Eeep. Suddenly I didn't want to hear any more logic. His face was gaunt in the dim red light in the pilothouse.

"XO, go back down to Combat," I said. "Plot the last radar contact as a point in the ocean and then take us there. Then draw a circle with a three-thousand-yard radius based on that point. Come to eighteen knots, get us on that circle, and we'll then run that circle until he surfaces."

Eeep started to protest, but I silenced him with a look. "Don't you get it, XO?" I snapped. "The only difference between him and us right now is that we can breathe. Sooner or later, he won't be able to do that anymore. Let's go."

32

XO

For the first time since we'd begun this pursuit of the picket line, I was worried that the captain had lost his sense of perspective. We were seriously low on fuel. Our sonar didn't work. Our radar was iffy. Our people were exhausted. I didn't want to even think about a change in the weather, especially if another tropical storm showed up. But, orders were orders, so I set up a track to the radar ghost points and off we went. At eighteen knots we'd be there in just under twenty minutes, not counting time and distance lost to weaving and turning.

And then what? I wondered. Get on our "fence" and drive around all night until the sub ran out of air and battery power or began taking shots at us, or both? If he came all the way up to the surface, our radar should see him, and then, what by now was the familiar drill: searchlight, gunfire, torpedo evasion. Surely the sub's CO knew that's what would happen. And the one question I did not want to pursue was: Is there a submarine even here? Were those just radar ghosts after all, causing us to burn off the last of our fuel? The captain apparently thought the possibility strong enough to warrant what I was beginning to think of as a stunt.

Nor was the sub without fangs, either. They could lie low for a couple hours and plot the sounds of our screws until they had the circle, relative to wherever they were lurking. Then pick a sector of the circle where they could predict where we would be if they fired a spread of torpedoes at time X. That would prove he was actually here, but we still had no way to determine exactly where he was without an active sonar. So maybe I should recommend random speed changes on the fence, to disrupt such calculations.

You're overthinking this, I told myself. The captain has twelve years of experience at sea; just sit back, watch carefully, and—

"Combat, Sonar Control."

"Combat, aye," I answered, surprised to be hearing from the sonargirls.

"XO, this is Tommy," the ASWO answered. "We've got something—weird, on the passive side."

"Define 'weird,'" I replied.

"Well, it sounds like, well, somebody's dropping depth charges. North of here, bearing between three four zero and zero two zero true. Not close. Maybe even two ships, listening to the patterns."

"Depth charges," I said.

"Yes, sir, it's like when we roll six from the back end. We have no idea of how far away they are, but Chief Roscoe agrees—those are depth charges, and maybe even more than one ship dropping them."

"Stand by," I said, and then called the captain on his sound-powered telephone. He sounded a little befuddled when he answered. He'd told me to get some downtime and he'd keep watch. Well.

I told him what sonar was reporting. He thought about that for a few seconds, and then said: "Go north at eighteen knots." I sent orders to the bridge watch team and we turned north. I kept the weave in place.

Depth charges. That had to mean American destroyers were north of us. How far? No way to tell. Were we that far off in our estimate of where station six was? I realized that was the wrong question—were we that far off in estimating our *own* position? That was much more likely. Then I notified Sigs to be ready for a visual challenge. It was another thirty minutes before our radar picked up two contacts to the north at a range of ten miles. I alerted the captain we had them on radar. He told me to start a track on them to see if they were conducting a standard fence attack on something. Sonar confirmed they were still dropping depth charges.

"When we get into eight thousand yards, set full GQ; in fact, pass the word now that we'll be going to GQ in fifteen minutes."

"Combat, aye," I said. We were already at modified GQ, but if those two destroyers had a real contact up there, then we'd better approach ready for action. I called the signal bridge to send down a messenger with a message blank. Then I wrote the following:

> USS Holland reporting for duty. We have no active sonar, and radar is redcap. Weapons systems are operational. We have D/C and hedgehog available. Request tactical frequency.

"Take this to the captain," I told the seaman. "Tell him I recommend we send this by flashing light as soon as recognition signals are exchanged."

The challenges arrived and our reply was duly accepted. The ships identified themselves as the USS *Blake* and the USS *Cogswell,* both *Fletcher*-class destroyers. The signal gang then sent the message I'd drafted. The *Cogswell* came back with a tactical frequency, which I told radio to patch to the bridge and CIC. Moments later, the radio speaker burst into life. *Cogswell* had a destroyer division commander on board, which made him the task unit commander. He called on the radio, using plain ship's names instead of call signs, seeing that we were the only ships out here. I waited and then the captain answered.

"Establish a fence at four thousand yards," the commodore ordered. "Our contact is deep and quiet. Our fence is fifteen hundred yards diameter. We will pass sonar cues to you shortly. Intend to keep periodic depth charges going. Two layers not helping. Acknowledge."

I heard the captain go back with a WILCO, and then he called and told me to set it up. Speed twelve. Constant turn on the fence. I looked at my watch: 0230. Sunrise was at 0545.

The first cues came in five minutes later from a different voice—probably the *Blake*. He gave us ranges and bearings from us to where they thought this guy was, and I began a plot. If we'd had an active sonar, we'd have been expected to take our turn on the active fence and start going in and making depth-charge passes. As it was, we weren't much help, but it was good to know where the enemy was. The *Blake* said their contact was intermittent and they were going to stop dropping the occasional depth charge to improve the sound conditions. It went on like that for two more hours, with the indirect plot indicating the sub was barely moving. The captain came down into Combat from the bridge.

"This guy must have been able to recharge everything before these two DDs showed up," he said. "He's probably down at two eighty, maybe even three hundred feet, counting on those layers to keep the tin cans guessing."

That was all possible, I thought. "Or," I said, "these two guys haven't spent much time hunting submarines. I *am* glad they stopped dropping depth charges."

"Well, I can understand doing that," he said. "Keep that bastard down there awake, and remind him we can stay here for damned near ever, but he can't. You were supposed to get some sleep."

I shrugged. Being in the vicinity of an active submarine prosecution didn't make for good sleep. The captain looked at the DRT plot. Our constant circling had just about worn a hole in the tracing paper. Our guys were plotting the position and tracks of the two DDs, and, of course, our track. The submarine was represented by red Xs, which hadn't moved much.

"It's coming daylight," he said, stifling a yawn. "Let's set a modified condition one. Keep the hedgehogs, the quad-forties, and the ashcan crews at their stations. Open up ventilation, and tell the cooks to get cracking. This could take all goddamned day."

The captain left to get some food and coffee while I set up the watch stations. It was unlikely we'd have to actually join the fray, blind as we were underwater. All these newfangled electronic whizbang devices were wonderful, but they had glass jaws. Those damned vacuum tubes were Achilles' heels that must be fleet-wide, because there weren't enough to completely stock every ship with a replacement set for each piece of gear. As I stared at that heavily scribed circle on the tracing table, I could suddenly see, however much we changed courses and speeds, we were essentially moving through the same water on each revolution. I called the bridge and told them to reverse course to a counterclockwise rotation. That reversal probably saved us. Sonar Control woke up the entire watch five minutes later by coming up on the bitchbox reporting torpedo noise spokes, one, possibly two, up-Doppler and then, almost immediately, null Doppler, meaning those fish were going to miss.

My guts ran cold. They'd been down there the whole time, listening to all three of their tormentors, before realizing that one of them, namely *Holland,* was running a predictable course. The other two tin cans were only fifteen hundred yards away from the deep-running sub; we were out at four thousand yards, but their torpedoes, if set on slow, could run for twenty *miles* if they had to.

"They're going to pass to starboard. Definitely two."

I ordered the bridge to turn out of our fence circle and head southeast at eighteen knots but with a constant three-degree rudder.

I got on the tactical circuit to report being fired on, but I might as well have not bothered. Both destroyers had heard that instantly recognizable scream as those oxygen-fueled, twin-screw turbines pushed the big fish through the water at almost fifty miles an hour. They both turned in for an immediate attack, one after another, secure now in the knowledge that the contact they'd been chasing for hours was, in fact, a submarine. They laid down a large pattern as we opened the range. The captain burst through the CIC door.

"What are we doing?" he asked.

"Getting out of the way," I replied. "We can't hear anything with that pattern they just laid down, so—"

"Bridge, Combat, Sonar: Cavitation noises astern of us, steady bearing. On the starboard quarter, up-Doppler."

"He's running for it," the captain announced. He glanced up at the rudder angle-indicator. "Get your rudder amidships, and slow to ten knots. Tell hedgehog to stand by."

There was no time to create a plot. The sub was going as fast as it could underwater, cavitation noise be damned. He was trying to drive right under us as a way to mask his departure, and then probably give us a salvo once we were directly behind him. The two DDs were already going back in for another barrage of depth charges.

"Tell me the instant Doppler changes," the captain told sonar. "The very instant!"

We waited, but not for long. "*Lost* cavitation noises; no Doppler," Sonar reported. The captain smiled a most unpleasant smile.

"Fire hedgehogs, full pattern," he ordered. Once the rattling thumps up on the main deck subsided, he ordered a wide turn.

To our vast relief, at least a dozen underwater explosions went off. "Got you, you Japanese sonovabitch," the captain growled. He turned to me. "XO, report that we got him." He then left for the bridge.

I made the call to the commodore in *Cogswell,* who immediately asked if we were sure. I told him the sub had tried to escape their fence by running up our stern and that we'd fired a full pattern of hedgehogs.

"Yes," he said. "And?"

Wow, I thought. "And, they don't go off unless they hit something. We had about a dozen underwater detonations."

"Combat, Bridge," the captain called. "We have stuff coming up. Tell the boss we have debris in the water."

I relayed that message to the unit commander and then went up to the bridge. The familiar stink of diesel oil assaulted my nose as I stepped out into the bright sunlight. "Stuff coming up" hardly described it. The water all around us was littered with various kinds of wreckage and not a few sodden bodies. A dozen hedgehog hits basically had taken this sub apart. Then the familiar boil of dirty water and geysers of oil-soaked air began to rise out of the depths, followed a few minutes later by that long, hollow booming noise indicating complete breakup at depth. Not much doubt there, I thought. We slowed to bare steerageway to let the photographer get the all-important "proof." I looked out the bridge windows to see the other two ships headed our way. The captain ordered a turn to get out of their way, assuming they wanted to steam through the debris filed and get some proof of their own.

"Bridge, Combat: Radar contact, three four zero, sixteen thousand yards. Wait one—it's gone."

"Evaluation?" the captain asked.

"Ghost, Captain. We've been seeing them all morning."

The two destroyers slowed and then came to a sliding stop. *Blake* turned right, *Cogswell* left to execute a circle through the actual debris field, which was, if anything even bigger now.

The commodore came up on the tactical circuit. "Not much doubt about this," he said. "Well done, *Holland*. How many does this make?"

The captain seemed surprised that the other skipper even knew about our previous kills. "This will be six," he replied. "We think, but don't know, that this was the last of the picket stations."

"Bridge, Combat: Ghost is back, but this time he's closing. The captain looked over at me to answer Combat while he kept talking to the commodore .

"Combat, Bridge: Are you sure this is a ghost?" I asked. Something wasn't right here. Closing?

"With this radar, who knows, XO," the ops boss said. "Shit, it's fading away."

"In which direction?" I asked.

"West, but we didn't have time to develop a track," Ops said. Then came the report that confirmed my suspicions.

"Bridge, Sonar Control: torpedo noise spoke! Bearing three five zero, high *up*-Doppler!" the chief yelled over the bitchbox.

The captain heard that and whirled around just in time to witness *Blake* blow up in a huge blast of fire and smoke as a torpedo hit her, followed almost instantly by a second blast that completely obscured the stricken ship. The captain ordered all ahead full, right standard rudder in case more were coming. *Cogswell* did the same but in the opposite direction. As we turned away, what was left of *Blake* finally emerged out of the enormous waterspouts. All we could see was the front fifty feet of her bow and the back fifty feet of her stern, both standing almost upright in the water as they slipped beneath the waves. The captain looked aghast. I'm sure we all did.

"There's *another* sub out here?" he asked the stunned air. None of us knew what to say. He did: he ordered full GQ.

The *Cogswell* had turned back around and was making a slow pass through the second debris file that had been *Blake*. I could see their deck crews frantically tossing life jackets and even a couple of life rafts over the side, which is the first time I realized there were survivors in the water. It seemed impossible, but there they were. But not very many of them. The captain slowed us down and turned south. *Cogswell* was already looking for the perpetrator, a hunt we couldn't join. Suddenly her guns swung out, pointed north, and began firing, just as the signal bridge called. "Bridge, Sigs: Three bogeys, bearing three five five true, inbound, low level, multi-engine. Identify as Bettys."

It wasn't hard to find them once *Cogswell* started to get the range. Three black dots, right down on the water, increasingly being surrounded by exploding five-inch AA shells. One of the planes banked to its right and headed west, possibly trailing smoke. The other two kept coming as the captain turned again so all our guns could bear once they got closer. *Cogswell*'s five-inchers were starting to depress their muzzles as the planes came in. I could see our gunners were itching to get into it, but the bombers were still too far out. Then the Betty on the right side of their formation suddenly sported a hot red flare followed by the loss of its right wing. The plane went into an uncontrolled bank to the right and crashed into the sea. The final plane kept coming. The captain ordered our three-inchers to open fire, but our rounds still fell short. *Cogswell* was starting to turn to keep her guns on target and then her forties started up; she almost disappeared in all the gun smoke. The bomber jinked to its own right and headed directly toward us, and now our three-inchers could add some steel to the game. The captain had kept the turn going and now did something that stunned me. He turned the ship to present our entire broadside to the attacking bomber, whose nose was alight with cannon fire aimed right at us. At the same time, he ordered all back full emergency. By presenting our broadside he'd given our guys their best shot at knocking him down. It also presented the bomber with the thinnest target, assuming he was about to drop bombs. And by backing down, hard, he defeated the bomber's efforts to lead us because he would be assuming we'd be going as fast as we could in the *ahead* direction.

By the time he released a stick of bombs he was obviously going to pass just in front of us. He got the drop range right, but by the moment the bombs hit the water—four or five of them—we were no longer there. All the bombs went off in a series of earsplitting blasts right on top of the water, stunning everyone on the bridge and the topside spaces. The captain reversed the engines just as all the guns flipped to the other side and followed that bomber out with streams of tracer fire. A true steamship couldn't have done what he'd just pulled off, because the big steam turbines took time to spool down, then close the admission valves, open the astern valves, and then spool back up. Our electric-drive motors, on the other hand, could do that in seconds and be applying full reverse power with the movement of a single rheostat. The ship would have to dispel all its forward momentum before actually beginning to go astern, but it would have the entire power plant thrashing the water, dragging her backward almost instantaneously. A steam turbine ship wouldn't start responding for at least ninety seconds.

One image had supplanted the frightful view of *Blake*'s fiery demise: Chief Bobby Garrett had shed his 20mm gun harness and dropped to the deck as that approaching bomber filled the sky. Bettys carried cannon on both ends, and the area around the highest 20mm mounts was getting pretty hot as that thing closed in. Garrett, lying on his back among all the shell casings, had calmly stitched the underbelly of the Betty as it flew past just fifty feet in front of the bow, a steady stream of his tracers unzipping the plane's entire length. As it disappeared into the flak from the rest of our guns, I thought I saw a flicker of gasoline flames erupt up under the wing roots.

"Where's that third one?" the captain yelled as our guns went silent. I hadn't seen what had happened to the other Betty, other than it had kept going in the away direction. Where indeed was that third one? I called Combat, but the radar was clear except for *Cogswell*. I put my binocs on *Cogswell* and spotted *two* antennas on her mast: a surface-search radar antenna like ours and above that what looked like a bare inner-spring mattress. That had to an air-search radar, so if anyone was going to spot that third bomber, it would be *Cogswell*. I realized my throat was sandpaper dry, and I was struggling to catch my breath.

"Breathe," the captain said, with that wolfish grin. I nodded, realizing to my amazement that he was loving this shit. I had to sit down to catch a breath.

33

CO

To be honest, I was still trying to catch my breath, too. My ears were still ringing from the combined effects of all our guns firing at once and that stick of bombs, which had to have been five-hundred-pounders. I smiled as I thought about what the snipes had probably experienced. They were used to five-hundred-pound depth charges, but those usually went off at depth. The Japanese bombs, probably with contact fuses, had gone off just about on the surface. *Cogswell* probably thought we'd been hit, they were that close.

"Combat, Bridge: Concentrate all eyes, electric or otherwise, to the north and west. There's still one more bomber out there."

Then I called Gun Control and told Bat Watkins to police brass, refill hoppers, and stand easy on station until we found that missing bomber. The commodore came up on the tactical frequency. "Well, that was fun," he said, but without much humor in his voice. "Did I see you actually back down?"

"We're electric drive," I replied. "We can go from full ahead to full back in thirty seconds. I think it saved our asses."

"I think you're right about that. We're short one Betty. If he was the one that fired those two long-lance torpedoes, he may have gone home or he might be lurking, waiting for us to let our guard down. Request you resume recovery ops for *Blake* survivors. We're gonna keep an eyeball out for number three. I'm just about convinced he was the one who fired those two torpedoes that got *Blake*."

"As opposed to there being yet another sub out here," I said.

"Bite your tongue, Captain."

"Bite my tongue, aye," I responded, although I thought the commodore was right: Three destroyers picking through the remains of a Japanese sub would have made a great target. The fact that the bomber had been ten to fifteen miles away, and the three destroyers concentrated in a slowly-moving cluster, it would have been child's play to launch torpedoes that ran at fifty miles an hour.

"Do what you can for anyone still alive in the water," he said.

Both of them, I thought, but acknowledged the order. While *Cogswell* assumed a circular patrol around our field of catastrophes, one theirs, one ours, her two radar antennas turning earnestly, I ordered the deck gang to man the rails and look for possible survivors. I still couldn't get that picture of an entire destroyer being blown to flinders in two seconds out of my mind. I'd seen gasoline tankers do that in the North Atlantic but never a warship. I was also conscious of how badly shaken my crew was as we crept back into the area where *Blake* had been sunk. It was one thing to search for possible survivors of a sunken ship. It was quite another to watch it happen.

Our medical team appeared on the fo'c'sle: hospital corpsman first class Snedecker and his assistant, hospital corpsman third class Farron, called Doc and Baby Doc, respectively. Then Chief Louie shouted from the fo'c'sle and pointed up ahead, where there were black specs in the water. They were a few hundred yards ahead of us, so I bumped up our speed and then slowed back down again. I wasn't thrilled to be almost stationary when there were Japanese bombers in the area, although having *Cogswell*'s air-search radar provided some comfort. The chief had his crew mount the "mushroom" davit on the port bow. The davit was padded, canvas-covered, and shaped like an upside-down mushroom. A man in the water could climb onto it, hug it, and be quickly hoisted up to the main deck. If necessary, one of the crew could ride the mushroom down to assist in helping the survivor cling to the hoist.

Now that we were closer, I could see that some of the "survivors" were clearly dead. *Blake* had been at general quarters, which meant that all hands would have been wearing steel helmets and kapok life jackets. But having a ton of high explosives go off right under your feet, creating a big enough blast to blow a 2,100-ton destroyer right in half, meant any men who'd been topside would have been killed by just the shock of it. They were floating only because of their life jackets.

I counted perhaps two dozen bodies bobbing in the oil slick. It reminded me of Pearl and what my crew looked like as those Japanese fighters flew away. There were some survivors, however, and soon Chief Louie's crew had them out of the water and laid out on the main deck while Doc Snedecker and the Baby Doc performed triage to see who he could help and who were hopeless. It was a pitiful sight: a row of sailors lying on their backs, leaking various fluids across the sloping deck. Young, white-faced bosun mates were helping as best they could. The signal bridge reported another cluster of men in the water a few hundred yards to the east, so we carefully made our way in that direction. There was some debris in the water but not much. She'd gone down so fast she'd taken most of her bones with her, as well as anyone who'd been inside the ship. One minute you were standing in front of your boiler, watching the steam-drum water level. The next: Well hello, Jesus.

The second patch of floaters was clearly all dead. I toyed with the idea of picking up the bodies, but there was the unsettling knowledge there was potentially a third bomber still out there. I ordered the OOD to begin a spiraling circle with standard rudder, to see if we'd missed anyone still alive. I looked back down to the fo'c'sle to see that there were only six survivors who hadn't been covered in blankets. The docs and some of Chief Louie's men were deploying stretchers to get them to sick bay.

Shit.

Eeep was sitting in one corner of the pilothouse on an overturned trash can, his back supported by the corner of the chart table, sound asleep. The OOD saw me looking, but I just shook my head. I didn't need him just now, so I let him sleep. It was afternoon, which surprised me. Everything that had happened seemed to have occurred in ten minutes. I told the quartermaster to mark the position where *Blake* had gone down. I asked what the water depth was out here. Nineteen thousand feet. Almost four *miles* down. I wondered how close her remains were to the submarine we'd killed. For one surreal moment I could almost visualize the two ghost crews rising up out of the lightless ooze, climbing through the blackened bones of their ships, and gathering warily on the seabed for a ghost beer, followed by some sea stories and fond reminiscences about wives and sweethearts.

"Officer of the Deck!" a young voice called from the port bridgewing. It was one of the lookouts, and he sounded excited. The OOD, Lieutenant (Junior Grade) Eddy Cooley, the comms officer, headed out there. I followed.

The lookout had his binocs up to his face, but he was staring almost straight up. "Sir," he said. "What is that?"

Eddy and I both looked up into the late-afternoon sky. The haze was bright, but I couldn't see anything in the sky. Neither could Eddy. We lowered our binocs and tried to see where the lookout was pointing.

"It's right there," the young lookout said. "It's—it's flashing."

Flashing? As in something metallic? Then Eddy saw it. "Jesus H. Christ," he whispered. "It's a plane." He put his binocs back up, searched, and then found it. "Betty!" he shouted. "Diving!"

I finally saw it. It was still way up there, so high we couldn't hear it, but as I studied the shimmering image in my binocs I could see it was almost vertical and trailing a thin line of smoke. And coming down right at us.

"*Right* full rudder," I yelled. "All ahead flank, emergency!"

The lee helmsman frantically banged the handles back and forth as the bridge watch stared upward in horror. The snipes had not been asleep: I could feel the sudden acceleration as those big electric motors converted the sudden surge of power to torque. I ran inside and grabbed the radio handset to alert *Cogswell* what was coming. That produced a "Say again?"

I had no time to explain matters. *Holland* was in a sharp turn to starboard, sharp enough to force me to hang on to a stanchion stay upright. There was no way the guns could deal with a bomber coming straight down at probably five hundred miles per hour. And now we could hear it: a howling scream of piston engines turning at well over redline. He was coming down so fast I wondered if he could correct for our hard turn. What if I reversed the turn?

"*Shift* your rudder!" I shouted.

"Shift my rudder, aye, sir," the terrified helmsman squeaked. I heard someone out on the port bridgewing shout: "Hit the deck! Hit the deck!" The ship had just begun to straighten up before leaning into the reversed turn when there was a truly loud crash above us, followed by a large, dark green blur passing no more than twenty feet from the starboard side and then raising a thundering vertical mountain of seawater. Then something came down on top of the pilothouse, and I suddenly saw rigging cables, pieces of what had to have been our radar antenna, a section of the mast and a flurry of smaller bits before that huge waterspout fell back on the ship and turned the light coming through the portholes green. We were still turning when I heard the shouts of "man overboard" coming from down on the main deck.

"All ahead one-third," I ordered. "Turns for three knots. Rudder amidships. No—belay that, *left* standard rudder. Someone give me a bearing to any people in the water."

We were already turning; the quickest way back to the point where men had gone over the side was to keep turning, get close to them, and then stop. I was startled by yet another metallic crash on the pilothouse overhead. There were still small waterfalls pouring down ladderways and through drain holes in the deck of the starboard bridgewing. There were no signs of the bomber. I went out to the starboard bridgewing, sloshing through water all the way, and looked down on the main deck. Chief Louie had his rescue team setting up the mushroom again. Eeep was down there with them. I called Sigs.

"Do you have men in sight?"

"Yes, sir, bearing . . ." There was a pause. ". . . Bearing one one zero true, maybe three hundred yards."

I ordered the helmsman to come to that course and told Combat to direct us to a point bearing one one zero, three hundred yards. The OOD could now see heads in the water, so I told him to take over, conn us alongside, and let Chief Louie work his magic. I had a sudden, adrenaline-inspired need to pump bilges. I climbed up to the signal bridge to find the piss-tube. While I was standing there, my legs beginning to tremble, I saw *Cogswell* approaching from astern. I looked up: Our mast had been sheared clean off fifteen feet above the flag bags. I realized I was really shaking now; that had been so damned close. If I hadn't reversed the turn, he'd have probably hit us amidships and cut the ship right in half. I banished that thought and went back down to the bridge. We'd lost our UHF communication antennas along with the radar. Even the signal bridge could not put up a flag hoist signal until we got some new halyards run. We'd lost one of the searchlights and the starboard-side signaling light; we could still send flashing light from the port side.

Eeep met me on the bridge.

"We're getting our guys back on board," he announced.

"Very good," I replied. "How many of *Blake*'s crew are still alive?"

"Six, I think," Eeep said with a sad face. "Two are gonna make it. The other four are suffering from blast damage, broken bones, bad burns. Doc says he's doing what he can for them, but two's probably gonna be the final count."

Two out of about 350. It reminded me of a sobering statistic from the HMS *Hood-SMS Bismarck* battleship engagement way back in May, 1941. *Bismarck* had punched a fifteen-inch, armor-piercing round into one of *Hood*'s magazines. Three out of *Hood*'s crew of 1,500 survived. And my poor little *Holland*—these damned Japanese were chipping pieces off us at an increasingly dangerous rate. On the other hand, who could blame them, after what we'd done to them.

Cogswell was sending us a flashing light. They wanted us to come alongside and transfer *Blake*'s wounded. They had an actual doctor on board. Our doc, a hospital corpsman first class, nodded eagerly when he got that word. Since it was getting late in the day, I proposed a boat transfer—I didn't think the wounded could manage a highline ride. The problem was that we'd both have to slow way down to do that. If there were still hostiles in the area, we'd be asking for it. The commodore, however, agreed. Boat transfer it is.

We both slowed to bare steerage way a few hundred yards apart. *Cogswell*'s motor whaleboat was launched and then made four runs, one patient at a time, until we had them all on board *Cogswell*. Their sick bay was bigger and better equipped than ours. I went down to the port-side boat davit by which we were lowering the wounded in Stokes litters into the whaleboat bobbing alongside. I made sure I said something to each one of them, told them I was the captain and it was gonna be okay. A real doctor was going to take over their care, so everything was gonna be better. I tried not to make eye contact with the men standing around, every one of whom understood these were just words. It was the least I could do. It was the *only* thing I could do, and it was hard to keep tears from my eyes when I actually got a good look at them. They were just kids.

Eeep walked me back to the bridge when we were through with the transfer. I pointed up at the damage to mast and superstructure. "How did he manage that?" I asked him.

"He was coming straight down, and then you maneuvered," Eeep replied. "He tried to recover but just couldn't do it in time. His starboard wing did all that damage. Fortunately, he'd been carrying torpedoes, not iron bombs."

I stopped at the base of the ladder going up to the bridge. "You think they'll be back?

"Not that sonovabitch," Eeep said with a cold grin I hadn't seen before.

"Damned right, XO," I said admiringly.

We secured from GQ, and the crew set about making repairs. The radio-pukes got one UHF radio on the air, which meant I could still talk to the commodore. Our long-haul HF comms were back to hard down, not because of the antennas but because the shock of the plane's hit had shattered the one big ceramic insulator we'd been able to find. The radio gang was once again hard at work trying to get a second emergency HF antenna up, but without insulators we'd only be able to listen, not transmit.

At sunset we held a burial at sea ceremony for *Blake*'s dead. It was a hurried affair this time, but I still performed the entire ceremony. Right after dark the commodore requested I come aboard *Cogswell* for a conference. This time we used our boat, and soon I was sitting in the commodore's cabin. He excused his staff officers and then opened a bureau drawer from which he extracted a bottle of Kentucky bourbon.

The commodore was a hawk-nosed, bushy-eyebrowed full captain. He was, like most of us out there, noticeably thin. His uniform looked too big for him, but he had bright blue eyes and a ruddy, warrior's face.

"Your good health, Captain," he began.

"And yours, sir. Thank you. It's been—interesting."

He laughed, a short, sharp bark of appreciative humor. "You guys," he said. "You guys are famous in DesPac. Five, no, *six* submarines? That's just goddamned amazing. Which might explain why we're about to get some protection. Spruance is sending a CLAA, the *San Juan,* and three, count 'em *three* tin cans to escort us back to the loving arms of the

Fifth Fleet. They'll be here at dawn. We're moving in their direction right now."

"Wow," I said. "For one DE?"

"One very special DE," he said. "More importantly, the Japanese have apparently figured out who it was that sank six of their boats and killed seven, eight hundred of their submariners. They want revenge."

"I get that," I said. He laughed.

"Yeah, that's what they're saying about you. The Sicilian guy. Call sign: Sweetie, back at the trade school. Got a vendetta going on the entire Japanese navy."

"That's overblown," I said.

"Truly?" he asked.

"Well."

"Well. Right. Listen: Saipan was a bloodbath ashore. Thousands and thousands of casualties. Every Japanese on the island ready to die for his goddamned emperor and thousands of Marines trying to oblige them. But it was bad, really bad. Six big hospital ships within fifty miles of Saipan. The Japanese had a former fleet commander in charge ashore, if you can believe that."

"Is there any good news?"

"Oh, yes, indeedy," he said. "They sent the entire First Mobile Fleet—battleships, carriers, cruisers, destroyers, and every carrier aircraft they could round up to break up the Saipan invasion."

"And?"

"And Spruance creamed them. Sank three of their carriers. Chased their battleships back to Borneo. Shot down over five *hundred* of their carrier aircraft, and the ones who survived that had no decks to go back to. For all intents and purposes, the Imperial Japanese Navy is finished. Next stop will be taking back the Philippines. After that, it's probably gonna be the big prize itself."

"Was Saipan the only objective in the Marianas?"

"Negative—apparently we've got to take Guam and Tinian, too."

"Well, shit, why?" I wouldn't normally have said that to a senior officer, but then I realized the whiskey was having its effect. I hadn't had a drink since leaving Pearl. He didn't seem to notice.

"The whole point of the Marianas invasions," he said, "was to set up air bases for the new B-29s."

My expression must have revealed that I had no idea of what a B-29 was. He smiled.

"You had anything to eat recently, Captain?"

I tried to think back as to when I'd last eaten. I couldn't really answer his question. Meatballs came to mind.

"Right," he said. "Sit back, relax, finish that, and we'll fix something up. In the meantime, tell me *Holland*'s status."

I closed my eyes and described the torpedo hole, the shock damage to our electronics, losing some people to a submarine's guns, of all things, our only radar and all our long-haul comms antennas being sheared off. "I can't tell you the actual state of the sonar—we can't even turn it on for lack of vacuum tubes, except in the listen mode. But otherwise, main propulsion, guns, depth charges, hedgehogs, all ready to work. Wait—we might have a problem with the port shaft, too."

"I didn't see your gun director," he said.

"We never had one," I replied. "Our gun battery is secondary armament; everything's manual."

I could see that that news surprised him. "What's your fuel status?"

I opened my mouth to reply but then couldn't answer him. He must have been more than a little shocked—a destroyer skipper who didn't know down to the gallon how much fuel he had left?

"Don't worry about it," he said. "It's possible you folks have been a bit preoccupied lately, right?"

He'd said that with sympathy. I was sure Eeep could have answered him. He told me again to sit back, finish my whiskey, and they'd have some chow up directly. Then he left the cabin. I sat back, as directed, and instantly fell asleep.

He gave me an hour, and then there was a steward setting up some real food at the captain's table. The whiskey glass had mysteriously disappeared. I couldn't actually remember finishing it. In the meantime, he'd gotten Eeep to send him a visual signal containing a full fuel, ammo, feedwater, provisions, and existing damage report. I felt a little guilty after eating, thinking I should have saved a doggie bag for Eeep.

"Okay," he said, as if I hadn't been out for an hour or more. "*San Juan* should arrive at dawn. Then the whole gaggle will head for Saipan, where there's still a bunch of our ships. The fleet is doing the softening-up work on the next two islands, Guam and Tinian, but they'll get you fixed up sufficiently to get you back to Pearl and a real shipyard."

"I guess we could stay," I said. "A new radar antenna, some vacuum tubes, those glass insulators—we'd be back in the game pretty quick."

"I'm sure you would, Captain," he said. "And Admiral Spruance may decide to do just that. Let's wait and see."

I nodded, but then a question occurred to me. "Why were those Bettys out *here,* of all places? You told me we've just about destroyed Japan's ability to conduct carrier warfare. And yet while that stupendous battle was going, we were visited by Kawanishi seaplane bombers and now torpedo-carrying Betty bombers. Land-based bombers, at that. Where are they coming from? And why?"

He thought about that for a moment. "I'm guessing here," he said finally. "But I suspect that they are basing out of the Philippines, themselves. I'm also guessing, even amid a fleet engagement, someone finally told their big boss that one, lone American destroyer escort had just managed to find and kill an entire squadron of their submarines. Can't you just see it? The Japanese admiral getting this unlovely news from a junior staff officer as he's hurrying down a passageway. The admiral stopping short, turning around: 'What did you just say?' The staff officer, now officially guilty of bringing bad news, begins bowing and scraping, wondering if he is about to lose his head, tells him again.

"'Where?' the admiral asks.

"'In the southeastern Philippine Sea,' the staff officer says. 'Tokyo set up a picket line to warn you of Spruance's approach, and—'

"'Find that ship,' the admiral hisses. 'Kill it, kill it at once and any ships with it. Use those cowards hiding in the islands, especially the Army's aircraft—they've been no goddamned use to us so far; see if they can manage one destroyer.'"

I was stunned. "So this *is* about revenge?" I asked.

"They've just had their asses handed to them," the commodore said. "The First Mobile Fleet has just been humiliated by Raymond Spruance. But one DE? *San Juan* is coming with three destroyers. I make four. You make five. Well, four and a half."

I had to smile at that. But then he was serious again.

"Listen, Captain, getting back to the fleet might not end up being the cakewalk you'd expect. Let's get you back aboard, and then we'll head northeast. Speed ten."

"I've got twenty-three available," I said. "As long as there's a gas station at the other end."

"Anything above ten makes a nice, wide phosphorescent wake," he pointed out. "By the way we've already got a snooper, hanging around at about thirty miles out. Let's not make it easy for them, at least not until we have that cruiser with us."

34

XO

The captain looked gaunt when he came back aboard. *Cogswell*'s smart gig made a quick approach to our sea ladder. The bow hook grabbed our sea painter, made it to a cleat, and then one crewman stood on the lowest rung until he was sure our CO had made it safely up the side and through the lifelines. His appearance must have alarmed them, too. On the other hand, he seemed in good if tired spirits as we walked up the port side, so there hadn't been any ass-chewing over on the *Cogswell*.

"Wardroom," he said. "I need the department heads and three chiefs: Louie Garcia, Bobby Garrett, and Hammer Santone. Wake 'em up if you have to. It's not over."

He didn't have to explain what that meant. I'd been expecting a twenty-three-knot transit toward Saipan and the protection of the entire Fifth Fleet. But then I noticed we were still creeping through the darkness at ten knots, not twenty-three. I felt a chilly tingle in the back of my neck. I'd also been feeling a rumbling vibration from the port shaft for the past hour, too.

It took twenty minutes to get everybody assembled in the wardroom. Some had been asleep; others had been on watch who needed first to be relieved on station. The captain was slumped in his chair, smoking a cigarette and nursing some freshly made coffee.

"I apologize for interrupting anyone's sack time, richly deserved as it certainly is," he said, taking a lung-deep drag on his Lucky Strike. "We're about seven-hundred miles from Saipan. Right now, *Cogswell* is acting as our escort, which is an interesting turn of events since supposedly we're the destroyer escort. At dawn there'll be a light cruiser and three more DDs out there. Apparently, we need protection."

That statement made everyone sit up a little. Protection? From what?

The captain then related the events of what later came to be called the Battle of the Philippine Sea. He described the bloodbath that had been the conquest of Saipan, one that was apparently still ongoing. He told us how the Japanese First Mobile Fleet had come out from its hidey-holes in the Philippine Islands, the Palau, Hong Kong, Singapore, and Borneo.

"Our carriers, along with a couple of our submarines, beat them to death. They lost three carriers and hundreds upon hundreds of carrier airplanes—and their pilots. They should have known better: Spruance was the same guy who gave them their first bloody nose at Midway."

"Why this Saipan place?" Hal asked. "I would have thought that the Philippines would have been the next big deal."

"The commodore said that they needed the Mariana Islands, all three of them, to prepare airstrips for something called the B-29. Apparently, from there, this new bomber can reach Tokyo."

That took a moment to sink in. Reach Tokyo?

"That's right," the skipper said. "The commodore said that capture of the Marianas meant that we were at 'the beginning of the end.' And, that the Japanese high command knows it."

There was a moment of silence around the table. The captain watched and waited. The chief engineer, Casey Stormes, finally voiced the question uppermost in everyone's mind, including mine. "So why—" he began.

The captain raised a hand. "The commodore thinks that someone at the Imperial Japanese headquarters has figured out that one lone, DE, namely us, killed six of their submarines while no one was looking."

"Hah!" Chief Garrett proclaimed. "They want revenge. They want revenge, just like, um, us." Obviously, he'd realized what he'd just blurted out, and to whom. An embarrassed look crept over his face. But the captain simply smiled and said, "*Vendetta, esattamente.*"

"The Betty bomber," he continued, "can be either a Japanese Navy bomber or an Army bomber. It's based ashore. We got a real close look at one today. *Blake* was sunk by one shooting torpedoes from miles out—and hitting. They've also got those Kawanishi seaplanes, which are bombers disguised as floatplanes. They've got those planes all over the southwest Pacific. It's not like they're gonna order a carrier strike on one DE. First of all, apparently, they're fresh out of carriers. Second of all, they don't have to. As I was leaving the *Cogswell* the commodore told me they were watching a snooper on their air-search radar."

Chief Louie asked what a snooper was.

"It's an enemy reconnaissance aircraft," the captain said. "It can be anything—fighter, bomber, seaplane, even—that sits just out of range and reports back to its base where our ships are. If they decide to attack, the snooper continuously updates the locating information and can even guide a strike in. That's why I got everybody up."

"Do you want to set GQ for the night?" I asked.

He shook his head. "We've got a pretty capable escort now, and by dawn we should have even more protection. With all those radars, we'll get plenty of notice. No—our people need rest. Set GQ an hour before dawn."

The captain went to his cabin. I excused the chiefs and sat with the department heads for a few more minutes. We decided to set a normal wartime steaming watch, but with an iffy radar and a listen-only sonar, there wasn't much point in manning all the guns, depth charges, hedgehogs, and torpedoes—or torpedo—we only had one left. If we were jumped in the middle of the night, probably the most useful weapon would be the quad-forty. I told Bat Watkins to man up the forty, but to let his guys sleep on station with one sentinel always awake.

I still thought there was something not quite right about how we were going about this transit to Saipan. If the entire Japanese fleet had just been chased back to their bases, why was a light cruiser and three destroyers coming to escort us home? We had an almost fully up engineering plant—why not just make a run for it, especially while the Japanese were licking their wounds? There'd be a tanker or six around Saipan, and at twenty knots, we could be offshore of the landing zones in forty hours. And what was this snooper crap? They hadn't needed a snooper to make either the Kawanishi or the Betty's attacks. Hal Welles tried to stifle a large yawn, which set everybody off. I gave up. Fatigue trumped logic. Time to verify the status of the watch and then get some sleep.

Ten minutes later, or so it seemed, the bridge watch called me to remind me that GQ was going down in fifteen minutes. I got up, washed up, and hauled my weary body up to the bridge, where some angel had cranked up a fresh pot of coffee. The captain came up right behind me. I could hear activity throughout the ship as men went to their GQ stations. The captain had introduced the process of a planned GQ along with the concept of the silent GQ. There was a lot less drama; it took longer, but as long as the GQ was precautionary, that didn't matter. The bridge watch team was in the process of turning over the watch to the GQ bridge team while I tried to figure out which end of the spoon did the best job of stirring in some sugar. Our favorite little red light came on next to the captain's chair.

"Bridge, Sigs: Flashing light from *Cogswell*. Five contacts inbound, bearing three four zero, range twelve miles."

"Bridge, aye," the captain responded.

"Five?" I asked. The captain blinked and then frowned.

"When's first light?" he asked.

"Thirty minutes, Captain," the quartermaster of the watch told him. "Sunrise thirty-five minutes after that."

The captain grunted and lit up a cigarette. If there were something wrong, *Cogswell* would have been issuing warnings. It was definitely frustrating not having a radar; we were beginning to recognize how really dependent we'd become on our electronic eyes and ears.

Half an hour later we saw recognition signals being exchanged between *Cogswell* and another ship that was still not visible. The captain asked the signal bridge to identify the oncoming ships with the Big Eyes as soon as they could. Then we waited some more. The day's heat was already starting to crank up, as if to honor the fact that we were all sweating happily away in full battle dress.

"Bridge, Sigs: We identify two *Atlanta*-class light cruisers, *San Juan,* and the *Oakland,* plus three destroyers of the *Fletcher* class. Looks like the three tin cans are out in front, with the two cruisers in line ahead behind them."

Just then one of the cruisers' escorts sent us a challenge, most likely to make sure we were the *Holland*. If this approaching formation was talking on the radio, we did not have the frequency. By now we had the one UHF circuit up with *Cogswell*. I assumed that one of the two cruisers would take charge of the whole group, and that's what happened. They used a flag hoist signal in order to maintain radio silence. *San Juan* ran up a complex formation signal. *Holland* would be the "guide," on course 340, speed twelve knots. *Cogswell* plus the three new guys would surround us at four thousand yards distance. The two cruisers would operate independently. The captain keyed the bitchbox to alert the signalmen to hoist the "G" flag when the flag hoist was executed.

"A DE as the guide," he said, shaking his head. "That has to be a first. Ask Sigs to find out who the flag is in *San Juan* when they get a minute."

The OOD had been keeping his binocs glued to the *San Juan,* waiting for the "execute" signal, which was when *San Juan* would haul down all her signal flags. Our job then would be to turn to course 340 and set our speed at twelve knots. The only job of the guide was to maintain a steady course and speed. The rest of the ships in the formation would assume and then maintain their stations using *Holland* as the formation's point of reference. In a fleet formation, the guide would usually be a carrier or a battleship.

"Execute!" the OOD sounded off and then ordered course 340, speed twelve. For *Holland* it meant we'd raise the guide flag, take up and maintain course 340, and speed twelve. The other destroyers would scurry to their respective stations. *San Juan* didn't maneuver at all; *Oakland,* the other light cruiser, turned west and then northwest.

Once everything settled down, we looked like any self-respecting task unit. The cruisers were beauties, although at 7,400 tons, they were smaller than true, six-inch gun light cruisers. They looked a lot more like really big destroyers, lightly armored, seriously fast, with a beautifully sheer hull line. But it was their armament for which they were famous. They carried six five-inch, double-barreled gun mounts, three forward, three aft, plus two more waist mounts, one on each side, for a total of sixteen barrels. These guns were radar controlled with a director at each end. They had eight torpedo tubes, four to a side, the usual complement of 40mm and 20mm secondary AA guns, and both air- and surface-search radars. From the side view, they fairly bristled. During the early Guadalcanal battles, the Japanese referred to them as "machine-gun" cruisers due to the enormous rate of fire they presented. Their main vulnerability was their thin skins: in a surface fight against Japanese cruisers, they depended on speed and maneuverability to survive. But as antiaircraft escorts, they were unmatched, and as aircraft carriers were now dominating naval warfare, they'd become immensely valuable.

"Why two cruisers?" the captain mused. "And heading north*west*? That's toward the Philippines. Twelve knots? There's something else going on here, I swear to God. What do you think?"

"Everything is on such a grand scale out here," I said. "Name any two places, and it's a thousand or more miles between them, if not more.

Everything—the number of soldiers going ashore, the number of casualties, the number of carrier aircraft, the number of tons of supplies floating around out here—the unit of issue always seems to be 'thousands.' I've never felt more insignificant in my life."

"Yeah, exactly."

"And the other thing I've realized is that our opinions on the matter at hand are neither required nor desired. Sigs reported that there was a one-star rear admiral riding *Oakland.* A flag-officer to escort one not-all-that-badly-damaged DE to Saipan? And there's this: I asked Sigs to ask *San Juan* for the primary tactical UHF frequency now that we have one UHF radio working. You know what we got back? 'Will advise.' In other words, when we want you to squeak, we'll tell you when and how loud."

The captain gave me a strange look. "You play chess?" he asked.

I shook my head. "Never had the time to learn," I said.

He nodded. "Okay," he said. "It's full daylight. The dreaded dawn attack has not materialized. So, set condition two. Both three-inch plus the quad-forty. Otherwise, half the crew at their GQ stations, the other half turning to or getting some rest. Relaxed battle dress. Ventilation on. Get everyone fed. If there's something coming, we are clearly not expected to do anything but remain afloat. It might just be that none of this stuff is about *Holland.* For now, gen up a material status sitrep. You know that flag is gonna want one."

The day was clear, bright, hot, and humid, with a flat-calm sea. *Oakland* had gone out to the horizon while *San Juan* remained close by, milling about on random courses. I smelled bacon and was immediately hungry.

35

CO

I went below to my cabin and took a totally unauthorized hot shower, meaning I stood under the hot water for five full minutes. Then I shaved, standing in front of my stainless-steel sink, a razor in one hand and a cigarette in the other. Once I was dressed, I buzzed the wardroom and asked my steward to bring some breakfast. With GQ secured, what were called the "hotel services" had been turned back on: ventilation, fresh and flushing water in the heads, major doors and hatches opened, steam in the galley, and normal lighting in the passageways and berthing compartments. After breakfast I took a turn about the decks. The designated gun stations were manned, with one petty officer designated to be awake while the rest of the gun crew slept like logs. Maybe not the very best defensive posture in a war zone, but my people were dead on their asses. Some downtime was more valuable than all hands being at ready-air, if only because if something popped, they'd be awake soon enough to deal with it.

Somebody had informed Eeep that I was going walkabout. I knew the drill. He'd queried the phone network, where the various talkers were sending discreet heads-up notices that the captain was on the loose and where. Eeep joined up, and we proceeded to walk the main deck, the 01 level, the fantail where the depth charges kept watch on their oiled rails, the side projectors where even more depth charges sat in their cradles, waiting to be punched high in the air over the sides. We then dropped down into the main holes, as they were called: the boiler room and then the engine room, where those big, gray electric motors hummed quietly. Down to Sonar Control, where Chief Roscoe was tinkering with some electronics while happily cursing the device to the four winds and beyond. Two of the sonar-girls snored from the darkened corners of the compartment.

We went up and forward to the main deck to visit the three-inch mount and the hedgehog "sandbox." We found Chief Louie Garcia sitting on the anchor windlass, nursing a cup of the dreaded boatswain locker coffee, which reputedly could support a spoon vertically, the spoon being necessary to break through the crust in the cup in the first place. Some of his bosun mates, known fondly as "deck-apes," were curled up on the warm, steel deck like a pack of sleeping sled dogs as the ship pointed northwest, her bow rising and falling gently to the rhythm of deeply hidden swells. It was a pleasant enough scene until, way out on the horizon, *Oakland* blew up, followed a moment later and much closer, by *San Juan* doing the same thing.

Only they hadn't blown up—they'd both *opened* up with their main batteries of eight twin-barreled, five-inch guns, creating so much smoke they disappeared into a heavy cloud of their own gun smoke punctuated by rapidly repeating pulses of bright yellow fire. Our own GQ alarm went off, almost inaudible in the thundering din coming from nearby *San Juan*. I ran for the bridge; Eeep headed for Combat; even *Holland* accelerated. The weather decks looked like an overturned ant hill as the crew sprinted to their stations. Out of the corner of my eye I saw all the destroyers kicking into high gear and turning to present their own guns to the west and also opening fire. At what? I wondered as I snatched up my binocs and began scanning the horizon. Some of the cruisers' shells started to pop down low on the horizon, soundless blooms of bright red fire that turned into puffs of intensely black smoke. And then I saw what all the fuss was about. Low, almost at sea level, came the silhouettes of several twin-engine bombers out at around eight or nine miles, head-on.

Since our little transit formation had disintegrated once the tin cans scrambled to meet the threat, I felt I was free to maneuver too, if only to stay out of everybody's way. But then I remembered what Bettys down on the deck meant: torpedoes, not bombs. I had two choices: run across the inbound tracks or turn toward them and try to comb the lethal swarm that was probably already coming on at some ungodly speed. I chose to comb. *Cogswell* suddenly appeared on our starboard quarter, a huge bone in her teeth, and then made a hard turn to port right in front of us to parallel our course, passing close enough I almost ordered an emergency astern bell. She never stopped shooting, which meant several outbound shells passed right over us. It was probably a good thing we didn't have a mast anymore.

The bitchbox light came on: "Bridge, Sonar Control: Multiple torpedo noise spokes dead ahead, high up-Doppler."

I acknowledged, but there was nothing more I could do but watch—and pray. Out ahead I saw several gasoline fires on the sea as the two cruisers found the range and began to splash the oncoming raid. The destroyers had managed to create a shooting gallery, two ships on a side, forcing the Bettys to fly between their massed batteries of five-inch guns plus an untold number of 40mm and 20mm cannon fire. Not a one of them survived the passage down this canyon of AA fire.

"*Down*-Doppler!" Chief Santone shouted over the bitchbox down in Sonar Control.

I realized neither of my own three-inch mounts had fired, but that was understandable. The destroyers were using radar-directed gunfire control systems to feed a central main battery computer down in gun plot. That computer meant their barrels were pointed far enough ahead of the Bettys that the five-inch shells arrived at the same point in space as the bomber, inviting the tiny radio transmitters in the shells' noses to say: Now. Suddenly we were enveloped in burning gasoline smoke as the bombers, one after another, burst into flying thunderballs of avgas just before they crashed down into the sea.

And then it was over: everybody stopped shooting. I had to force myself to release the death grip I had on my binocs. There were fires on the sea everywhere.

"Bridge, Sigs: Light from the *San Juan*. PriTac 243.6 is megacycles. Air defense common is 213.5 megacycles."

It took me a moment to understand, but then I got it. I called radio and told them to patch that primary tactical frequency into both Combat and the bridge and to guard the other one up in CIC. We could only listen to the second one—we still had only one working UHF transmitter.

San Juan was calling a radio check. She was using the call sign "White Lightning." I had the OOD respond with our call sign, "Hook."

Finally! I thought. We had radio comms with the rest of the ships. But what came next sent a chill down my spine.

"This is White Lightning: warning red, warning red. Air raid, high, inbound, bearing two niner three, range: thirty-six miles. Composition: many. Break. Signals follow, immediate execute to follow: Formation able-able two-tack-four zero. Stand by—execute! Hook, over?"

The OOD picked up the radio handset and replied: "Hook, roger out."

Truth be told, I wasn't sure of what to do next. Were we still the guide? In which case, we'd be expected to hold course and speed. All these other ships would maneuver to set up the AA defense formation around us. I asked Combat to break the signal and tell me what "formation AA2" meant. Eeep was already on it. "Basically, it means all ships maneuver independently to maximize AA fire."

That made sense, and the destroyers going helter-skelter in all directions confirmed it. *San Juan* was turning to present all but one of her twin turrets toward the northwest and coming up in speed. It became clear as I watched that the best move for us was, once again, to stay out of everybody's way and conform to the cruiser's movements. I told Sigs to keep the Big Eyes on *Oakland,* still way out on the horizon, and to let me know when she started firing. There was enough of a haze I couldn't see her. Eeep sent word there were two groups of enemy aircraft approaching at altitude. Sigs suddenly reported that *Oakland* had opened fire, along with her escorting destroyers. The speaker erupted into life: "Hook, this is White Lightning. Aircraft are Judys. Commence evasive maneuvers."

"This is Hook: roger out," the OOD acknowledged.

Judys? I thought. A Judy was a single-engine *carrier* dive-bomber. How was this possible?

"Bridge, Sigs: Large bomb splashes close aboard *Oakland*; two planes going down close aboard. *Oakland*'s throwing everything they got at these bastards."

Then *San Juan* opened up with the by now familiar fountain of gunfire, and finally I could see the attacking aircraft, small dark cruciform dots coming down almost vertically, pursued by those nasty red flashes. Bat Watkins had seen them, too, and now our two three-inch guns had their barrels elevated at fifty degrees and were blasting away, spitting out empty brass powder cases onto the forecastle. Out of nowhere a blazing Judy sliced down into the water between us and *San Juan* and then exploded underwater, raising a shell-splash eighty feet into the air. I glanced out the front portholes in time to see *San Juan* heeled over in a tight turn as she evaded two bombs, one on each side, that fully obscured her until I realized she was headed straight for *us* at twenty-five knots. I shouted a turn-away course order to avoid a collision, and we passed each other at a distance of no more than two hundred feet. The noise from her guns was incredible.

As we steadied up, and I remembered to breathe, two bombs bracketed us, their underwater explosions strong enough to push us left, then right, rattling everything in the ship and drenching the weather decks. The Judy who'd dropped them flew smack into the water right ahead of us like a knife, as if the pilot had blacked out. Then I felt a nasty vibration coming up from astern, and we began to slow down. I looked around to make sure we were clear of the cruiser and then turned the ship away toward the east.

"Bridge, Gun Control: Come north—our guns can't bear!"

I grinned then. Oblivious to what those two bombs had done, my gunners wanted back into the fight. I adjusted course a little and could then hear the quad-forty joining in, and then both three-inch mounts went back at it. We were rewarded by a direct hit right between the anchor hawsepipes as a five-hundred-pounder dulled the pointy end of our bow and thankfully disintegrated before it could go off as it reached the water. *Cogswell* appeared out of nowhere again and chased the responsible Judy until one well-placed, five-inch round blasted its tail off, leading to a very satisfactory pinwheel crash ahead of us. I was surprised to hear the cheers and shouts of the gunners over all that gun noise. I hurried out onto the port bridgewing. *San Juan* was close by but no longer firing. But way out there, among the many smaller fires on the water from downed planes, there was an ominous cloud of black smoke rising from something much bigger.

Oakland had been hit.

Oh, no, I thought. God, no, *please*.

God didn't listen. As I stared through my binocs at that pillar of black smoke there came a yellow-white flash. A magazine? With all those guns, the *Atlanta*-class cruisers were one big floating ammo storage locker. Moments later a dark gray cloud of fire, smoke, and falling debris began to drift eastward. I couldn't see *Oakland* anymore, but I could see two destroyers hurrying in to assist her, probably to look for survivors. *Dammit!*

"Bridge, Main Control." It was Casey Stormes.

"Bridge, aye," I replied, climbing back into my chair.

"We have a serious vibration on the port shaft. Starboard shaft has one, too, but not as bad. The port shaft alley is flooding, but I think the eductor can keep up with it. Who were those masked men?"

"Japanese carrier bombers," I said. "And, no, I can't explain that. We need to secure the port shaft?"

"Yes, sir, we do. After steering is reporting that the tiller's main hydraulic pump is 'singing.'"

Two five-hundred-pounders, I thought. One on each side, close aboard. Sometimes a near miss did more damage than a direct hit, like the damage caused by depth charges going off right underneath us. Ship hulls were not rigid. They flexed to survive, but that could mean real problems for rotating machinery-like propeller shafts.

"Do what you've got to do, Casey. It looks like the *Oakland* caught it, but we still have *San Juan* and the destroyers."

"Main, aye."

The hot, metallic smell of the gun barrels was nearly overwhelming. I didn't know if our guys had hit anything, but the Japanese had surely known we'd been trying.

Eeep called, "Bridge, Combat: Recommend slowing to ten knots; we're on one-shaft ops." I acknowledged and gave the order.

Looking around, I realized it was now late afternoon. The downed Japanese planes were no longer visible as small oil fires on the sea. *San Juan* came by, probably to look us over. There were men out on her weather decks, wrangling brass powder cases into the deck-edge netting. Her gun barrels were burned black, the paint still smoking in the late afternoon light. I glanced up front where we had our own paint-blackened nose. I told Sigs to tell them we had one damaged shaft and some minor flooding.

The admiral was on *Oakland* but not communicating. The CO of *San Juan,* the senior skipper in our group, took over. He dispatched another destroyer to go to the aid of *Oakland*. He then put his cruiser practically alongside us at a distance of three hundred feet. To the west one of those astonishing Pacific sunsets was gathering in the tropical sky. The CO asked if we could make fifteen knots. I told him fourteen was tops. The cruiser then pulled away and ordered everyone to head 350, speed fourteen.

I called Eeep in Combat: Had we made any progress at all over the last twenty-four hours toward Saipan? We had, as it turned out. We were now 690 miles away from the safe haven of the fleet, which was a good thing, because we were down to 38 percent fuel. I wasn't too worried about that because *San Juan* could refuel us if absolutely necessary.

As night fell, I ordered the ship to set condition two and told Eeep to get everybody fed and then to refill all the ready-service ammunition lockers. I was still trying to get my head around the air attacks of the day—Judys? Was there a goddamned carrier out here somewhere after all? If so, where the hell were our carriers?

Eeep came topside, his face a study in fatigue. We both noticed the smell of cooking down below. Eeep and I lit up cigarettes. It was actually the first time I'd seen him smoking. Everyone knew it was bad for you, but nothing, and I mean *nothing,* calms your nerves like a belly-button deep draft of good American tobacco.

"I can't figure all this out," Eeep said. "I would have expected to be offshore Saipan by now." That dreaded red light came on the bitchbox.

"Bridge, Sigs: Light from *San Juan*. 'Enemy air contacts west, composition few. Probably snoopers.'"

"Great," I said. "They're not done."

"Where the hell are they coming from?" Eeep wondered. I couldn't answer him.

"Okay," I said. "I wouldn't expect night attacks. Dawn might be a different deal. We're headed toward friendly forces at fourteen knots. Eight hours, we'll be a hundred miles closer. Yippee."

"The Philippines," Eeep said. "The Japanese have probably scraped airstrips all over those islands. If we sank all those carriers, then these guys are coming from bases in the Philippines. Nothing else makes sense."

I called Main Control to get a sitrep on the port shaft. Casey reported that he thought the shaft was either cracked or possibly even broken. The starboard shaft wasn't altogether healthy, either. The rudder assembly was tenuous, as well. Those two big blasts, right alongside, had rendered the entire back end unreliable. "If we can settle on a course and hold it," Casey said, "We can probably make it to Saipan. Is it close?"

"Not very," I replied. "But getting closer. Is there any serious flooding going on?"

"Little weeps and seeps," Casey said. "Those two bombs opened up a lot of seams, sea chests, every weak point in the hull. Our patch on that torpedo hole is now spraying water everywhere again. We're gonna try a mattress patch with shoring. I now have six men on sounding and security instead of one. Eductors are doing their duty, but as everyone knows, eductors bear watching."

"Amen to that," I said. More than one ship had been seriously flooded by one of her own eductors left unattended. "Stay on it, Casey," I said. "There's an unlimited supply of flooding water right outside."

"I'm looking at some of it, Skipper. But we got this: Everybody down here has been to hack-it school."

Then we got a message from the *San Juan*: *Oakland* was under tow toward Ulithi Atoll. I gave a silent, mental cheer. She'd survived, but it was going to cost our little gaggle two destroyers to get her there to safety: one to tow her and one to defend her. And if there were night snoopers in the area, they'd know there were easy pickings out there. I needed sleep, but couldn't imagine getting much with Japanese prowling out there in the dark.

36
XO

The bridge sent down word that the captain had turned in to his sea cabin. I called Combat to see where we were in relation to Saipan and what kind of formation had been established. The watch officer told me everybody was headed east to put a little more distance between us and those Philippine air bases. The admiral was back in charge and wanted another hundred miles between us and the Japanese, and then we'd turn north toward Ulithi, which fortunately was sort of on the way to Saipan. Gawd, I thought, this is a big ocean.

The formation was creeping at eight knots because of *Oakland*. One destroyer had her under tow, and that was about the best they could do. A second destroyer patrolled in a big arc to the west of the stricken ship, staying between the cripple and the snoopers in expectation of a dawn air attack. *Cogswell* stayed with us, while *San Juan* and the third tin can patrolled west of us in a loose AA formation. The night was pretty dark, with almost no wind and no moon. It was marginally cooler than the night before, but everyone was still sweating and itching.

I made a hurried tour through the ship, including after steering, where I could hear that singing steering motor before I even got down there. They'd set up a manual tiller rig just in case. I was a little surprised to see how much water was in the bilges of the steering engine compartment. The two watch standers told me they had a portable eductor set up and were pumping pretty much full time. I asked where all that water was coming from. One of the watch standers, a very young fireman, said innocently, "Outside?" The other watch stander rolled his eyes, and I fled before I embarrassed the kid by laughing. I had asked.

Topside there were men sleeping in the quad-forty mount, and both three-inch guns had ready service rounds in the trays while their crews slept out on deck, using their kapok life jackets as pillows. Seeing the stub of the mast was disturbing, almost as disturbing at seeing all those overboard discharges spewing water over the sides down by the waterline. It looked like every eductor on board was working overtime. It's called the water-hammer effect: water is incompressible, so the shock wave from a near miss is actually more effective than a direct hit. That was how Billy Mitchell sank those old battleships during his air-power demonstration back in the early twenties. He told his pilots to drop their bombs close alongside, not actually on the ships. The underwater shock waves had opened every rivet in their hulls, creating an insurmountable amount of flooding. My main concern, of course, was that if we took another substantial hit or near miss in the morning, our ability to keep water out of her was already pretty much maxed out.

I sat down up on the forecastle on one of the mooring bitts, my back to the starboard lifelines. Around me were sleeping shapes, some around the forward three-inch gun mount, some near the hedgehog "sandbox." I was coffee'd out, as the expression went, and I really wanted a cigarette, but all the ships were at darken ship. I could hear some muffled conversation from some of those dark forms lying on the still warm deck. I noticed the bow was rising and falling in tune to some deep swell from ahead. Then someone said: "Goddamn, look at that."

I looked, and there, on the distant western horizon, three magnesium flares burst into painful white light, illuminating the underside of an overcast we didn't even know was there. Like silent ghosts, they drifted down toward the sea, leaving a trail of bright white smoke that writhed under their parachutes in agonizingly slow motion before going out. There was no way for me to tell how far away they were.

"What is that, XO?" a voice asked out of the darkness. I'd had no idea they even knew I was there.

"Air-dropped flares," I said. "The Japanese snoopers letting us know they're there and that they know where we are."

"Fuck me," someone muttered.

Amen, I thought.

An hour and a half later there were more fireworks. Apparently, the admiral had dispatched one of the destroyers to go back west, slow enough to not make a phosphorescent wake, until she was at the maximum extent of her gun range from the snooper. She then fired five white-phosphorous rounds at maximum range and altitude, which exploded in a huge display of searing white light and smoke between the tin can and the snooper, probably one of those Kawanishi flying boats.

"Bet they shittin' and gittin' now," a voice proclaimed in the darkness.

I felt a sudden surge of respectful affection for this admiral. I went back to my cabin, rousted out my GQ gear, and lay down on my rack. Ten seconds later, or so it seemed, the bosun's call pealed its all-hands whistle, and then announced that GQ would go down in twenty minutes, *and* there was chow and coffee on the messdecks. I got a courtesy call from the bridge and rolled out of my rack and almost fell down. A quick head call, and then I went through the messdecks, where the cooks were offering appropriately dressed French toast and piping hot fresh coffee from the sixty-gallon urn. I continued up to Combat trying not to drip syrup on my shirt. God bless the Chop, I thought, he and his guys had to have been up since 0300 making all that.

The captain was already on the bridge when I manned up my station in CIC. The watch officer told me that the formation had been collapsed into an antiair warfare circle, with *Oakland* and her destroyer tug in the center now, and *San Juan* and her destroyers close in at ranges of two thousand yards. We'd been designated part of the "screen." *Oakland* had reported she had regained electrical power and most of her guns were ready to work. Both her propeller shafts had been broken by the bomb hit, so she remained under tow, but she had five of her eight mounts available, plus radar.

"When's daylight?" I asked. One hour was the answer.

San Juan reported the radar indicated our snooper had withdrawn. One of the CIC watch standers asked if this meant they weren't going to attack. RD1 Mickey Hennessey, the CIC supervisor, shook his head. "Nope," he said helpfully. "He's just getting out of the way."

With that happy thought, we waited for another half hour. This being blind business was putting everyone on edge. I went topside to the bridge. The captain was in his chair. The dark circles under his eyes seemed more pronounced. I could sympathize—*Holland* pursuing a submarine was his show, and he'd proved damned good at it. This business of being in a lame-duck formation with no way to help and a hundred leaking seams did not forecast yet another great Navy day.

"Think they'll come?" I asked.

"Why would they not?" he replied. "If they bring enough planes, *Oakland*'s toast."

Then the radio erupted: "This is White Lightning. Warning red. Warning red. Air raid, bearing: two niner zero. Range: sixty miles, closing. Composition: many. Altitude: medium high. Break. Guns tight, I say again, guns *tight*. Break—*Holland, Oakland,* over?"

Our OOD rogered for the message, as did *Oakland* a few seconds later. "Guns tight" meant no shooting. "Okay," I said. "I'll bite—guns *tight*?"

"Look," the captain said, pointing up to the northeast. I looked, and then saw literally dozens of yellowish contrails headed our way. Way up there—they had to be twenty-five thousand feet. High enough to catch the first rays of sunrise.

"That's probably American carrier air," the captain said. "With any luck, the Japanese are about to get ambushed."

We both went out to the port bridgewing. If the Japanese were west-northwest of us, they might not see what was coming, because they'd be looking into the rising sun. How appropriate, I thought.

Within a minute we saw all those contrails appear to falter and then begin to drop straight down on the Japanese formations. We couldn't see individual aircraft, but the contrails began to disappear as our fighters rolled in on them. Soon there were individual black lines falling out of the sky. The captain called Gun Control. "Bat, watch for low fliers. They may have sent some of the bombers in on the deck while everybody's watching the air show."

"Gun Control, aye, Captain," Bat replied. "We're on it."

The admiral must have had the same thought, because he came over the tactical circuit to order all ships to watch for low-flying intruders. "Guns free for low E," he said.

The action upstairs was getting hotter. There were more of those descending black plumes; in some cases, we could see the fireballs they produced as they fell silently into the sea some twenty miles away, which was about the limit of our visual horizon. It was almost surreal as we watched full-scale aerial combat happening silently four, maybe now only three, miles above us. Everyone jumped when some of *Oakland*'s twin five-inchers erupted into an earsplitting barrage. Then the destroyer that had her in tow joined in. They were shooting at something very low, with what looked like half the projectiles going off just above the water all the way out to a suddenly clearly visible pair of Betty bombers, at about fifteen thousand yards.

Torpedoes, I thought. They're going after *Oakland,* who couldn't maneuver. Finally, one of the two ships got lucky. A Betty took one on the chin and then went cartwheeling into the sea.

"This is White Lightning," the radio suddenly blared. "Check firing, check firing, *check* firing."

My talker relayed that order to Gun Control. As I tried to wrap my brain around that order, two Navy Corsairs came whipping down out of nowhere and got behind the remaining Betty and poured so much fire into it that it exploded in midair. The two fighters had to pull up sharply to avoid the fireball. Both of them then executed hasty victory rolls, made incredible banking turns to their left, and then went hunting for any other down-on-the-deck interlopers. We could hear the cheers from our topside gun stations.

"This must be that famous First Team they were talking about back at Tulagi," the captain muttered. "No more snide remarks from him."

Behind us there were still small red gasoline fires burning on the sea several miles away. The admiral again ordered guns tight. Is it over? I wondered. The captain shouted to the lookouts and the signalmen to keep a sharp eye to the west. One of the signalmen shouted back that many aircraft were closing in on us, followed by a report from the Big Eyes that there were Corsairs out there. Their distinctive gull-wing profile made it easy to identify them. Within a minute a couple dozen fighters, maybe more—Corsairs, Hellcats, and some strange-looking, twin-hulled planes I didn't recognize—came overhead in a big wave. Everyone topside was jumping around, cheering and waving their hats as planes roared overhead. None of us had actually seen carrier aircraft in action. Or, for that matter, fleet destroyers and cruisers in action.

For the rest of the day there were two pairs of fighters above us—way above us—as we churned purposefully toward the Ulithi anchorage. The captain ordered me to secure from GQ and then to get the ship cleaned up and the crew fed, and to tell the department heads to prepare a detailed summary of battle damage sustained. He didn't want to show up, be offered help, and not be able to immediately tell them exactly what we needed. I, for one, was just glad to get some clean clothes on and a sit-down hot meal without having to keep one eye on the western horizon.

37

CO

The Ulithi lagoon, located in the Caroline Islands, is essentially a submerged volcanic caldera, some nineteen miles wide. Small bits of the crater's blackened rim poked up above the water here and there, creating several tiny, ridgelike islands, some even dotted with palm trees. As advertised, there was room for an entire fleet within the lagoon, perhaps two. There was one larger island, Sorlen Island, where it looked like there was an airstrip, with several yellow bulldozers hard at work making the runway longer and wider. Some low, white buildings and a high tower were on one side of the airstrip

Four ships were anchored in the lagoon: a full-sized, *Prairie* class destroyer tender, an oiler, and a fleet tug that was nursing a single large, U-shaped segment of a floating dry dock. Marry ten of those segments together, and she could lift a battleship. Once assembled, the dry dock could then sink itself until the flat bottom of the U section was forty-two feet underwater. A damaged ship could then be pushed into the ten submerged U sections, carefully aligned with submerged blocks, and then the dock would be pumped dry, slowly lifting the damaged ship right up out of the water.

The fourth ship was a heavy cruiser that was down by the bow and listing to port about five degrees. I speculated she'd be the dry dock's first customer once the other nine sections arrived. She had a huge, black burn mark on her portside hull just behind turret two, probably courtesy of a long lance torpedo. We slowed to bare steerageway as *Oakland* was pushed alongside the tender's port side to begin repairs. Our small screen of destroyers went in different directions to their own designated anchorages, while *San Juan* went alongside the oiler to begin refueling. I thought maybe we had been forgotten until a signal light up on that tower began blinking at us. We were ordered to go alongside the tender. I set the special sea and anchor detail and conned us over to a spot five hundred yards astern of the tender. She put up a flag hoist signal indicating we should come alongside her starboard side and then executed it.

I took the conn myself, as I wasn't sure if my exhausted junior officers were up to the task of mooring to an anchored ship. It sounded simple until a breeze came up and your target began to swing to her own anchor. The ship was the USS *Hercules* (AD-16). Unlike earlier in the war, when some tenders had been converted passenger liners, *Hercules* had been built from the keel up as a destroyer tender. At nearly twenty thousand tons she was packed from stem to stern with machine shops, foundries, electronic repair shops, optical shops, electric motor bake, dip and rewind facilities, re-gunning shops, boiler repair, piping and shaft repair, and a host of other machinery repair and fabrication facilities. There simply wasn't much that a tender could *not* repair on a destroyer. Plus, she had vast storerooms, filled with spare parts normally only available at a shipyard. Like vacuum tubes, I sincerely hoped.

We slid alongside without hitting or scraping anything. Lines and fenders went over, and for the first time since Tulagi, seemingly ten years ago, we were no longer technically underway. Interestingly, the first order of business was to take on fuel. We had an operable engineering plant, so if trouble popped up, we were expected to get underway and steam in the away direction from this big, gray sitting duck even though she sported four five-inch guns of her own. I sagged in my bridge chair once we were officially moored alongside. There were line-handling parties wrestling a brow over to a hatchway opened in the side of the tender down on the main deck. As soon as the brow was over, the tender's shop personnel began swarming aboard to be greeted by the chiefs and then taken inside and belowdecks to see the problems for themselves. A lieutenant from the tender who'd been designated as the ship's superintendent for *Holland* came up to the bridge and presented me with an invitation to have lunch with the service squadron commodore, one Captain Marshall King. I hadn't noticed a burgee flag as we were making our approach, but sure enough, there was one with the number six. I respectfully accepted and then handed over our repairs wish list. Then I went below to get a shower and find some clean clothes. My guys had been alongside tenders before and didn't need me telling them what to do. Between the chief engineer, the supply officer, and Eeep, everything that should be in motion was probably already in motion.

A service force squadron was composed of ships whose designator began with the letter "A," for "auxiliary": repair ships (AR), destroyer tenders (AD), oilers (AO), ammunition ships (AE), and fresh/frozen provisions ships (AF). An ensign from ServRon 6 staff took me up several decks to the commodore's cabin. I was puffing a little when we entered Captain's Country, where a Marine sentry stood watch in the passageway. Couldn't possibly be all those cigarettes, I thought. Nah.

Captain King looked every inch the Texan that he was: large frame; big, sunburned face, complete with a Wyatt Earp mustache, of all things; and exuberantly friendly. It was clear he was wearing cowboy boots, albeit highly polished cowboy boots. There was a small collection of cowboy hats on one of the bulkheads. His cabin was air-conditioned, well lit with several portholes, and pleasantly large, with a bedroom, a sitting/conference room, and even a dining room. He welcomed me effusively, told me he was by Godfrey honored to have a famous ship like the *Holland* alongside. He spoke with what I guessed was a Texas accent—southern but with an edge to it.

We spent a few minutes on the usual "where you from" pleasantries, and then lunch was served. Afterward he filled me in on what was going on in the western Pacific and the prospects of this Ulithi anchorage becoming a major fleet base within the next month or two.

"Tomorrow or the next day the rest of the floating dry dock sections will arrive," he said, "along with a submarine tender, a second destroyer tender, an AR, which is a fully equipped structural repair ship, an aviation detachment of fighters, airfield controllers, transports, and four hospital ships. Sometime thereafter the bulk of the battle fleet will arrive, followed by the first troop transport units for the invasion of the Philippines."

"Well," I said, "this anchorage certainly looks big enough."

He laughed. "You have no idea of how many ships will soon be here. Something like seven, eight hundred, I'm told."

"So we've heard. We've been on our own-some for so long I can't imagine eight *hundred* ships in one place."

"The Japanese were here for a while," he said. "But the Marines took the entire archipelago basically unopposed. The Marianas are perfectly positioned in terms of providing a staging area for the final push—the Philippines, the Japanese perimeter islands, and then the Japanese mainland islands. But the big deal is that the Army has a new bomber—four-engine, long, *long* range, with a big payload. That's what taking Saipan, Tinian and Guam was all about—airfields for just that one bomber. From Tinian they can reach Tokyo—and back."

"The Japanese must be getting worried."

"Saipan was a bloodbath, Captain. Far worse than Guadalcanal. If Saipan was any indication, the Philippines, Okinawa, and any of the strategically important home islands are looking at astronomical casualties. We're hearing the Japanese lost thirty thousand dead on Saipan, and we lost almost four thousand. It's probably kinda like when Lincoln was told of the casualties at Shiloh: the entire country, north and south, got a real shock."

"Where is the fleet now?" I asked.

"Spruance is offshore the Marianas right now. Halsey will soon take charge of the fleet—you know how that works, right? Spruance in command—it's the Fifth Fleet; Halsey in command, it's the Third Fleet. They spell each other."

"So, we've been told," I said. "But I've always wondered why. Surely the Japanese know by now that the Fifth Fleet and the Third Fleet are the same thing?"

"One would think so," the commodore observed. "No, I think the real reason is that these guys aren't young men anymore. Halsey was born in 1882, for Chrissakes. Spruance, 1886."

"Yes, that makes more sense."

"Word is, they're gonna stand up a Pacific Fleet headquarters complex on Guam, once they're sure all the Japanese are men. There's a rumor that Nimitz, himself, will set up his headquarters on Guam. Pearl's just too far away—almost four thousand miles. So, what's your damage?"

I described the various problems. He thought the mast was repairable out here. The propeller shaft could be fixed in the floating dry dock—if they had the makings for a shaft. "That one will probably require a shipyard," he said. "Which means they won't try to fix anything major out here. Vacuum tubes for the sonar, a stronger patch for your torpedo hole—can-do-easy. But frankly, I think *Holland*'s stateside bound. Not like you haven't earned a breather—*six* submarines sunk? Goddamned amazing."

My disappointment must have shown. I knew that if *Holland* left the theater of operations, it was unlikely she'd ever be back.

"Listen, Skipper," he said. "I personally think this horror will be over in a year or so. After what just happened over the Philippine Sea? The Imperial Japanese Navy is a force in name only. The only truly distressing fact is that, the closer we get to Japan, itself, the bloodier this thing is gonna get. We got a taste of that on Saipan. They're all fucking nuts. I think Spruance is gonna tell your guys what a great job they did, and then tell you to take 'em home. You, a destroyer escort, do not want to be out here for what's coming."

"I'd think they'd need every ship they can muster," I said.

"Lemme explain something," he said. "We send out a carrier strike, every pilot who launches fully intends to blast the target *and* get back to Mother. The Japanese are pretty much out of carriers after the Marianas. So, every strike *they* launch? It's understood to be a one-way trip. Fly out there, find the Americans, climb to altitude and then dive straight down with a big bomb bolted to your undercarriage and fly your plane straight into that ship. Tell, me, Captain: Is there anything *Holland* could do to defend against that?"

I shook my head. That Betty had tried just exactly that, and all we'd been able to do was to jump sideways, hold our collective breath, and pray.

"The ships that matter now are ones like those *Atlanta*-class light cruisers. And the carriers, of course. Even the battleships and the heavy cruisers have been relegated to being AA platforms. There is simply no role for a DE, especially one with no radar, manually directed guns, and only two, single-barreled, three-inch guns. Here's my prediction: You'll go back to the States to become a celebrity, the *only* US Navy destroyer that's managed to sink six submarines. You will be featured in harborside war-bond drives. Then she'll be decommissioned because the need for experienced people for all the new construction trumps any possible contribution you could make to what's coming. You've done your part and then some, times six. Ask your crew: You guys see anything wrong with that picture?"

I nodded. I knew what the answer to that question would be.

"This tender will do everything they can for you. They might even be able to cobble up a new mast. They'll restore your radar if they can find an antenna. They'll rustle up the tubes you need for your sonar, and they'll get your comms back up, too."

"But not if were just gonna slink back to Pearl," I said.

The commodore smiled. "Those decisions are well above your pay grade and mine, Skipper. The Army guys have an expression for this situation: Take your pack off, soldier. You've done far better than most ships of your size and weight. And you, personally, compadre, look like you got rode hard and put away wet—no offense."

"None taken," I said, suddenly experiencing a wave of weariness I'd not fully felt before. "Thanks for all the good gouge, Commodore. We've been in the dark so long it's good to know what's going on."

"Well, glad to help. I have the CO of *Oakland* coming up in an hour, so thanks for coming.

I summoned Eeep once I got back aboard and went to my hot and stuffy cabin. He began to report the status of repairs, where there were problems, mainly due to a lack of spare parts; and what they were all doing to work around the problems. I buzzed for my steward, and he brought us both a coffee. Then I related to Eeep all the amazing information I'd had from the commodore.

"Going *back*?" he said. "We've got some stuff broke, I'll admit, but it's not that bad. Now, that heavy cruiser over there? I can believe she's going back. Looks like her whole front end is burned out and still flooded."

I then shared the commodore's analysis of the utility of a small destroyer escort to what was probably coming once the fleet got closer to Japan. He sat there in silence, looking like someone had hurt his feelings. I could sympathize. "What'll happen then?" he asked.

"Well, I guess we could always go back to the North Atlantic," I offered. "There's probably a U-boat or two still out there." He gave me a look; we both knew the invasion of Europe had happened a couple of months ago. Suddenly I decided it was all too hard.

"I'm gonna take a really long nap, XO," I said. "Call me in the morning if anything significant happens."

"Aye, aye, sir. Will do."

At 0530, he did call. "You're gonna want to come up and see this, Captain."

"Are we setting GQ?"

He chuckled. "No, sir, not this time. But the entire Fifth Fleet is entering the anchorage. We haven't sounded reveille, but I think the whole crew is out on deck. It is quite a sight."

Master of understatement that he was, Eeep, along with damned near the entire crew, was out on deck in the dawn's early light as a procession of huge gray shapes began to pass silently by our little nest and disperse into this vast anchorage. First to come in were the big-deck carriers: chunky behemoths nearly nine hundred feet long and displacing close to forty thousand tons. We could just barely hear 1MC announcements coming from their open hangar decks against a background of ventilation fans and aircraft engines doing maintenance turns. We marveled at how many planes were crowded up on their flight decks. Even the tender began to rock slowly as they passed by—*twelve* of them, each carrying almost a hundred warplanes and crews of nearly forty-five hundred men.

Then came the battleships, a mixture of the new construction *Iowa* class, some *North Carolina* class, and some of the prewar dragons with their cumbersome-looking tripod foremasts. Their huge main armament guns were elevated at ten degrees, while their sides bristled like porcupines with five-inch and smaller guns. Next came the heavy cruisers, also bristling with eight-inch and five-inch guns. The light carriers came in next, twenty of them, followed by four entire squadrons of destroyers in four separate columns, and then a dozen or so light cruisers spreading out to stations along the perimeter of the anchorage to set up an antiair defense ring. The service force ships came in last, too numerous to count, with their parade into the huge anchorage taking almost two hours. I suddenly appreciated the importance of logistics to a fleet.

It was noon before the entire fleet had come in. I'd gone down for breakfast at around 0900. When I got back to the bridge, they were still coming. Somebody must have promulgated a master plan because each ship went to a specific spot in the lagoon to drop her anchor. We had the harbor common radio circuit patched up to the bridge, but there was no talking. We either had the wrong freq up or there was simply no need for talking.

The last ship in was an *Iowa*-class battleship, the *New Jersey,* escorted by two *Atlanta*-class light cruisers like the *San Juan,* plus three destroyers, tucked in tight. She was sporting a four-star's flag from her forward mast. Up above us, the tender's crew was called to attention to starboard over the topside 1MC speakers, and then told to hand salute. The sixty-thousand-ton armored beast passed about five hundred yards away, and everyone topside on her weather decks came to attention and returned the hand salute. Fortunately, most of my guys followed suit when the order came over the tender's topside speakers. I don't think we'd ever rendered passing honors before.

Then Eeep called and asked if he could bring me up to speed on repairs. I told him to meet me in CIC.

38

XO

The captain looked genuinely rested for a change. I think seeing the entire fleet steaming by had rejuvenated everybody. After months of hearing about it, there it was, and it seemed to stretch for miles. The First Team indeed.

"So, XO, we getting anywhere?" he said.

"Actually, we are. The sonar is back up. They're installing the new insulators for the long-haul antennas, and the metal shop is working up a design for a temporary mast. It won't be as tall as the original but tall enough to mount a surface search radar antenna so we can see in the dark again."

"Good news," he said approvingly. "The main shafts? They gonna dock us?"

"No, sir," I told him. "Their divers are going to replace the *lignum vitae* staves in the stern tubes and strengthen the external shaft support structures. They don't have the capability to work on the shafts themselves, just the main bearings. Both rudder stocks are slightly deformed.

The most serious problem with the shafts, themselves, is that they, too, are deformed, longitudinally."

The captain nodded. I could see he knew what that meant. Propeller shafts on larger ships are hollow, which means that in a twenty-four-inch-diameter shaft, there is a half-inch hole bored down the entire length of the shaft to allow the shaft to accommodate the sudden torque of a full or flank bell without breaking. If those two bombs had caught the shaft during a deflection, then that deflection became permanent. Basically, the shafts were no longer straight. "So, a shipyard it is," he said. "Damn."

"That's what the ship's supe is saying. They'll get us seaworthy, but we're not fit for combat operations."

"And the patch?"

"They're installing two new bilge pumps, bigger than what we've got, in case the patch fails or partially fails. They're also going to weld some strongbacks on the patch itself."

"Okay," he sighed. "I guess the commodore was right, after all. What's the time line?"

"We should be ready for sea in three, four days," I replied. "We've already refueled from the tender. All we're missing are orders."

"The tender will make its report to the commodore," the captain said. "Who will in turn ask ComDesPac back in Pearl for instructions. It's kinda pro forma—we need a shipyard, the tender has other 'customers' waiting, so there it is."

"Does Admiral Spruance get a vote?" I asked, remembering that message when they passed us in the dark.

"Admiral Spruance has much bigger fish to fry right now, XO, especially if they're getting ready for an invasion of the Philippines. Plus, I understand Admiral Halsey is inbound. That's probably a seismic event all on its own. The issue of one broke-dick DE is gonna be handled way down the chain of command. If it were one of his big-deck carriers, now, that would be a different story. By the way, shouldn't there be some paperwork I need to sign?"

I groaned. "Yes, sir, I completely forgot. Just seeing the fleet come in completely distracted me."

"Another sight of a lifetime," he said. "The Japanese are doomed, and it's about goddamned time."

Somebody needs to tell the Japanese that, though, I thought, remembering the sight of the Betty screaming down at us, obviously bent on murder *and* suicide.

The next three days were frantically busy as the tender hurried to complete what repairs they could make in order to clear her sides for other damaged ships that were still on their way. The captain kept himself above the fray as the department heads, and I chased pop-up problems, work-change orders, equipment tests and provisions. But, interestingly, there was no ammo aboard. In fact, we were told to download most of our hedgehogs and our single torpedo—more indications we were headed home. Having seen the Fifth Fleet, soon to become the Third Fleet under Halsey, I was beginning to agree with the captain's prediction that they'd scrap her when we got back and redistribute her experienced crew to the flood of new-construction heading west.

On the fourth day, we got a real surprise: an invitation from the fleet commander to come aboard the flagship for a formal call on Admiral Spruance. I say we—it was for both CO and XO. This was beyond exciting news. Raymond Spruance was one of those almost mythical admirals that we'd only read about. King, Nimitz, Spruance, Halsey were names spoken in tones of reverence ever since that first slugfest victory in the Solomon Islands. Both the captain and I scrambled to find suitably clean and pressed uniforms. Neither one of us was satisfied with the result of that hasty search and we both felt a little ratty when the flagship's barge came alongside.

Captains of ships had gigs; admirals rated a barge. The name "barge" was misleading in the extreme. A US Navy barge had a long, shiny black hull with a highly polished white-topped cabin aft, crewed by a coxswain, boat engineer, and two, sometimes three seamen, all dressed in class-A uniforms. If the admiral was a four-star, there would be four silver stars mounted on the barge's bows. At the stern, there would be an American flag mounted on a staff topped with a brightly shined medieval halberd.

The captain and I waited at the accommodation ladder on the starboard quarter as the barge rumbled quietly alongside. I think half the tender's crew was watching from the decks above, as most had never seen an admiral's barge before. The coxswain, a boatswain mate first class, gave his engine maneuvering orders to the engineer via a bell, which he sounded using an elaborately woven lanyard, while he manned the wheel. It was fun to watch as the coxswain steered the big boat alongside the accommodation ladder, slowing and then backing the single-screw engine via a series of bells to get her stopped precisely at the ladder, where one of the seamen leaped down onto the platform and made her fast so we could board. I went first. By protocol, junior officers boarded first so that their weight would stabilize the boat as she bounced around. That way, the senior officer only had to step aboard to maintain his all-important dignity.

The anchorage around us was swarming with boats as dozens of ships ran their errands between the service force ships: personnel boats, Mike boats, gigs, floating ambulances, great big utility boats for larger cargoes, and even a couple of tugboats. The anchorage was a beehive of activity, made possible by that circle of hidden reefs which protected the entire enterprise from the deep Pacific's swells. We went down into the plush after cabin and watched out the portholes as the barge began its trip back to the flagship, causing every boat in the vicinity to back down and come to a stop. Soon we were coming alongside the *New Jersey*'s armored sides, a far cry from *Holland*'s lightly constructed steel hull. The battleship's armor belt alone protruded from the ship's sides far enough for a man to stand on. This time the captain went first, and we could hear the cruiser's quarterdeck sounding two bells and announcing: *Holland,* arriving. We ascended the accommodation ladder to the quarterdeck, which was substantially higher above the water than *Holland*'s, saluted the ensign on its flagstaff astern, and stepped aboard.

A lieutenant commander greeted us. "Welcome aboard, Captain," he said, saluting and then extending a hand. "The admiral's in a briefing that's gone a little over. Like to take a main-deck tour?"

"Absolutely," the captain said. "How many miles is it?"

The staff officer grinned, and then we started forward. It was an unusual experience. All I could feel was this mass of steel all around and above us. We threaded our way through five-inch twin mounts, themselves surrounded by or supporting 40mm and even 20mm mounts. It seemed that every square inch of space along her sides was covered in guns and local gun directors. I was fascinated to see that the deck itself was covered in teak. Anything wooden would have been stripped off any warship for wartime use, except that the teak, three inches thick, had been deemed too hard to physically rip out. Above us was the 01 level, itself a forest of smaller AA guns. And above that towered the two stacks, with sixty-inch-diameter carbon-arc searchlights, boats, and antennas hanging off them. Forward and above that was the armored conning tower, with a huge, optical range-finder mounted on top along with various kinds of radar antennas. That range finder had to be almost a hundred feet above us.

We walked out onto the forecastle, where the two forward sixteen-inch gun turrets were, one superimposed right above the one in front of it. Turret two's three barrels were elevated, but turret one's were flat along the deck allowing us to walk up to the business end and see for ourselves how big those muzzles really were. I was surprised to see that the forward deck was sloping up as we walked toward the two 40mm gun mounts on the bow next to the anchor-handling gear. When we turned around to face aft, we both had to crane our necks to see the ship's top-hampers. She was magnificent. Lethal, but still just plain magnificent.

We saw a white hat up on the bridge level waving. The staff officer then led us aft—and up, way up, to the flag level in the forward superstructure. We entered a passageway that had wooden batwing doors displaying a sign saying FLAG COUNTRY, where we encountered armed

Marines in the passageway. I detected an atmosphere of quiet importance as we walked forward on what looked like spit-shined tile decks. The air-conditioning was impressive. We passed several offices on either side of the passageway, filled with staff members vigorously pursuing paperwork. As we approached the admiral's cabin, a tall, distinguished-looking captain with pronounced dark circles under his eyes stepped out of a side office and introduced himself as Captain Holloway, the assistant chief of staff for operations. He welcomed the captain by name, nodded politely at me, and then took us into the inner sanctum, where Admiral Spruance was standing behind a surprisingly plain steel desk. I became aware other officers were following us into the cabin.

They say some men have a natural aura of power and authority about them. Spruance was certainly one of them. He exhibited none of the bombast of Halsey or the "I shall return" theatrics of MacArthur that we'd all seen in the wartime propaganda movie clips. He had a friendly if reserved smile and graciously welcomed the captain, and then me, and then told the staff who we were and what *Holland* had accomplished.

"That's never been done before," he concluded, "by anyone. They rolled up this Japanese picket line pretty much by themselves, with little operational help from either in-theater, shore, or afloat commands."

He paused for a moment. "In defense of that, sometimes, when you realize you have a true warrior in place for a mission, the best alternative is to point out his quarry to him and then turn him loose. That's what I did, and six submarines are what they bagged. That's nothing short of amazing.

"Therefore, I am today promoting Lieutenant Commander Mariano deTomasi to full commander, USN, and his executive officer, Lieutenant Ephraim Enright, to lieutenant commander, USNR. Gentlemen, step forward."

An aide, who'd obviously done this before, quickly removed our collar insignia and replaced them with our new ranks: golden oak leaves for me, silver oak leaves for the captain. The admiral congratulated us on our achievement, and then presented the captain with a Legion of Merit medal and me with a Bronze Star.

"I understand that *Holland* did not escape undamaged," he continued, "and that she will soon return to the States for repairs and, possibly, modernization. Commander deTomasi will be relieved by his executive officer, Lieutenant Commander Enright, after an appropriate and brief turnover period. Commander deTomasi will then take command of the new-construction *Sumner*-class destroyer, USS *Copeland,* who will arrive here in five days following the death at sea of her commissioning CO due to a tragic accident. And finally, I'm recommending that *Holland* be nominated for a Presidential Unit Citation and a Navy Unit Commendation. Gentlemen, will you join me for lunch?"

We followed the admiral into his flag dining room for what turned out to be a light lunch. My head was still spinning at what had just transpired; I could tell the captain had been equally astonished. But the real surprise of the day came afterward, when Captain Holloway invited us in for a "chat" in his office as we were leaving. I felt a tingle of alarm—Navy tradition held that big bosses handed out promotions and medals; senior staff officers were known to inquire about professional loose ends, should there be any.

Captain Holloway invited us to join him at a conference table, ominously, to my eyes anyway, covered in green felt. The captain brushed the green felt surface with his right hand, and then glanced at us. "Relax," he said. "I thought you might be wondering why we kept you out there after you got the sixth and final Japanese sub."

The captain looked up with sudden interest. "Yes, sir," he said. "We've both been wondering that."

"As in, there were supposed to be six subs in the picket line; *Holland* had disposed of six subs. So why weren't you hightailing it to the Marianas and the cover of friendly forces?"

"Yes, sir," the captain said again. "Exactly that."

Captain Holloway smiled. "You might be amused to know that some—*ahem*—unnamed senior staff officers were making book as to whether or not you'd come in with a whiskey tare fox message when you ended up lingering out there."

"Lieutenant commanders don't send WTF messages to four-stars," the captain said.

"You might be surprised there, Captain. Anyway, let me explain. When Fifth Fleet hit Saipan, the Japanese reacted by sending their entire battle fleet east to dispute that invasion. Long story short, over the next week we wrecked that fleet, and most importantly, shot down hundreds of their planes, carrier- and land-based. More planes were lost when the survivors flew back to their carriers and discovered they'd been sunk. Tactically, all of that was very satisfying, but more importantly, this fight had a truly consequential strategic result. Planes can be replaced relatively quickly. Pilots, on the other hand, especially experienced pilots, cannot. We think they now have two, possibly three fleet carriers left. And at the moment, enough pilots to man maybe one or one and a half.

"Now, here's some secret stuff. The Fifth Fleet is about to become the Third Fleet. Admiral Halsey in for Admiral Spruance. And the next big deal is the invasion of the Philippine Islands. The 'when and where' does not concern you. What concerns *us* is that whatever planes survived what our aviators are calling the Great Marianas Turkey Shoot, are now going to have to operate off land airstrips in the Philippines. Problem is, we don't know where those are, especially in the southern Philippines, and we'd really like to pay them a visit, preferably *before* we bring in an invasion force. That's where *Holland* came in," said Captain Holloway.

The captain shot me a "Hunh?" look. Captain Holloway got up to get some coffee from a sideboard; we joined him. I was surprised at how quiet the battleship was. In *Holland,* there was always noise: work in progress, people talking, sometimes shouting, machinery noises. Then I remembered that a lot of the bulkheads on a battleship were inches thick, not one-eighth inch like on a DE.

"I actually proposed to bring you back to rejoin the fleet once you got that last sub and we began receiving reports of Kawanishi flying boats.

The admiral asked the question: Why are there Kawanishi looking for *Holland*? Nobody could answer that question, so we went back to the drawing boards to figure that out. The answer turned out to be one of those 'right hand not talking to the left hand' situations," said Captain Holloway.

"Admiral Spruance knew about what *we'd* been doing?" the captain asked. "Amid all that was happening at Saipan?"

"Admiral Spruance has one of those steel-trap minds that remembers everything," Captain Holloway said. "Never forget that. Anyway, I detailed an officer to check with naval intelligence and ask if they'd by any chance used *Holland*'s achievements in their Pacific theater-wide propaganda efforts. I expected the answer to be no. The events were too recent, and *Holland* was still way out there. Turns out, I was wrong, but Navy Intel weren't the guilty parties. You've both heard of Tokyo Rose, I assume?"

We nodded. We'd even listened to some of her ridiculous broadcasts.

"Turns out, General MacArthur, he of the 'I shall return' drama, still has many contacts in Manila and elsewhere. He has much personal history with the Philippines, as did his father, for that matter. MacArthur's been preparing for his return to *his* islands ever since the fall of Corregidor. To that end, he immediately established wide networks in the islands, from big cities like Manila all the way down to small villages along places like the San Bernardino straits, between Luzon and Samar. He has Army Rangers in-country, working with an increasingly emboldened underground. They report progress in the war against Japan via a network of island-wide couriers, pamphlets, underground radio broadcasts, and, hell, jungle drums, probably.

"The 'news' emanates from Manila and is fed by MacArthur's staff from Port Moresby and Australia. The purpose is to keep morale up among the Filipinos, whom the Japanese are treating with their usual savagery. When MacArthur proclaimed that he would return, the Filipinos assumed months, not years, so this effort has been a high-priority deal at MacArthur's HQ."

"And General MacArthur figures in this how?" the captain asked.

"The word about Holland's one-ship killing spree apparently got loose in the Pearl Harbor intelligence world. You have to understand that Pearl Harbor today is a hotbed of various commands and staff officers, probably ten times the size of Husband Kimmel's Pacific Fleet staff on December 6, 1941. I think that's one of the reasons that Nimitz is moving his fleet operational headquarters to Guam as soon as it's truly secure."

"It's not yet secure?" I asked.

"There are apparently still some live Japanese on the island; that number has to go to zero before they'll let Chester Nimitz set up shop there. Anyway, MacArthur keeps a sizable 'liaison' staff in Pearl, or actually, up at Fort Shafter. That way he can keep tabs on what the ever-devious Navy is up to, especially if it impinges on his famous 'vow' to return to the Philippines. He operates on the theory that the Navy is working tirelessly to sideline all his grand plans."

"That sounds like a bunch of bureaucratic bullshit to me, Captain Holloway," the captain said. "If you'll pardon me saying so."

"I will pardon your extreme but understandable ignorance, Captain," Holloway replied, patiently. "Now let me finish."

I thought that was a great time to pay close attention to stirring my coffee.

"Long story short, the Army liaison crew in Hawaii passed the news of *Holland*'s accomplishments to MacArthur's headquarters out here, along with the oh-by-the-way information that she was still out there. MacArthur's people turned that into some kind of inspiring tale for Filipino consumption: one lone, heroic US Navy ship out there somewhere in the Philippine Sea, overwhelming an entire squadron of Japanese submarines, sinking six and killing close to a thousand Japanese submariners. Naturally the Japanese security services in Manila are intercepting all of this underground traffic moving around the islands."

"So," the captain said, "some genius on MacArthur's staff said: 'If the Japanese are reading the Underground's mail, let's give 'em something to read.'"

Captain Holloway gave the captain an approving look. "Precisely," he said. "And one of the things they gave them was what the *Holland* had done to an entire squadron of Japanese submarines. More importantly, *where Holland* had managed this, along with lots of crowing and insulting language."

"And they swallowed it?"

"Yes, indeedy, and having just had their imperial asses handed to them, it's my opinion that they were hungry for some retribution, *any* kind of retribution they could send up the line to make Tokyo feel better. But this breach of operational security suddenly presented us with an opportunity to solve one of our most pressing problems. The downside of this opportunity was that we needed to keep *Holland* out there for just a little longer. Can you guess why?"

The captain frowned for a moment, but then those black eyes lit up. "Bait," he snapped. "You needed to use us as bait for something."

Captain Holloway nodded. I watched in growing alarm as the captain's fists began to clench and unclench. "It gets better, Captain," Holloway said. "We actually set up our own version of a picket line."

When the captain heard the words "picket line" I thought he was going to erupt out of his chair. Captain Holloway put up a restraining hand. "Please rest assured," he said, "that I'm not taking a dig at you or your fine ship. The picket line you destroyed was made up of submarines. Ours was composed of aircraft, deployed on a three-hundred-mile arc of fighters under the radar supervision of three specially equipped Army B-25s acting as airborne command centers. When the Japanese sent Kawanishis and Bettys out to find you, every one of them came from one of those unlocated strips and even dirt fields in the southern Philippines. Our picket line let them through and then—and this is the crucial part—followed them discreetly back to those landing strips in the jungles of the Philippines. No shooting—just precision and stealthy reconnaissance. The Japanese actually sent lots of search planes out to find *Holland*, and they sent them from lots of places. I'm not talking about big air *bases*. Their planes are now operating out of small strips, mostly, which are widely dispersed against the expected invasion. The important bit is that these strips, however little, are now crammed with all the carrier orphans that survived the Turkey Shoot. Emilys and Bettys, which are land-based, were transferred south. So were Kates, Jills, Judys, and Vals—that's why you saw carrier aircraft."

The captain's face was still a bit red, so I intervened to ask a question: "How many bases did you uncover?"

"Thirty-six, which admittedly was something of a surprise. Like I said, these aren't like the fields we're building on Guam and Tinian right now. But if the Japanese could get just one Judy with a five-hundred-pound bomb in on a fully-loaded troop transport, you're talking a genuine catastrophe. We'd previously found four and those only because the local resistance steered us in the right direction. Now we have thirty-two more."

"I still can't believe you'd use a damaged US Navy ship as bait," the captain grumbled.

"Let the record show, Captain—we did send you some support, yes?" Holloway said. "Granted, *Holland*'s just a destroyer escort, but you were never completely alone after the Kawanishi showed up. And once the Japanese got serious, you had two light cruisers and four destroyers escorting *you*."

The captain nodded his acquiescence. "We had no idea," he said. "The sheer scope of what's going on out here. Our first time at war was in the goddamned Arctic. It was us and a bunch of crazy Brits driving odd-lot frigates, corvettes, sub-chasers, and the occasional ancient destroyer that probably fought at Jutland trying to cope with Hitler's U-boats, who were not to be trifled with. But this—this—"

"I know," Holloway said. "The entire industrial might of the United States of America has been marshaled to utterly destroy Hitler's Germany, Tojo's Japan, and all their works. One of our biggest problems every day is what they're calling 'command and control.' Global war. Hundreds of combatant units. Now you understand why Nimitz swaps Halsey and Spruance out periodically—it's just overwhelming."

"Thank you for explaining why we stayed out there," the captain said. "I'm tired—we're all tired. But you guys—*Jesus!*"

Holloway smiled and nodded.

"How did you bet on the book about whether we'd squawk or not, sir?" I asked.

"I bet you wouldn't, that you'd figure out something was going on that was well above your pay grade and keep quiet. Close?"

The captain grinned. "More like all our long-haul comms were down. We didn't squawk because we couldn't."

At that Holloway started laughing, and I suddenly had the feeling things were gonna work out, despite all our best efforts.

39

CO

Bouncing around in the barge within the still-busy anchorage was almost unsettling after being aboard that mountain of floating steel. Eeep was staring into the middle distance as he considered the fact he'd soon be in command of dear old *Holland*. Old *Holland*. Hell, I thought, she was only two-plus years old. And I was being given command of a brand-new *Sumner*-class destroyer. Strangely enough I was a little worried about how *Sumner*'s commissioning crew would receive me. The prospective commanding officer of a brand-new ship was called the PCO in the shipyard. He was the prime mover in that critical period when a large piece of inert metal began the transition from steel hull to a fully functioning ship and crew. He was usually a larger-than-life figure in any ship's life. To have a stranger now walk in and take command after all that work done by the PCO might incite some resentment, especially if the PCO had been really popular.

Popularity had never been my strong suit, as evidenced by my academy nickname. Nicknames for midshipmen inevitably indicated the exact opposite of what the nickname implied. I'd tried to be pleasant when taking my first command, an oceangoing minesweeper, but my efforts to present a smiling, friendly face had had some of them thinking I really wanted to bite somebody. It didn't matter, not after the first time when I drove my sweep into a known minefield to begin a job of work. We didn't blow up; the captain was a hero. But after watching most of my crew die in the flaming waters of Pearl Harbor so that Japanese fighter pilots might have some "fun," my focus had changed to one of unalloyed vengeance against Japan and its savage minions.

Everybody in *Holland* knew that. They even joked about it. I'd also heard the "Captain Ahab" references, although only the officers had probably understood that. My chiefs, on the other hand, knew what it was all about, especially Bobby Garrett, even though he wasn't Sicilian. When somebody with my background finally concludes that vengeance, *vinitta,* is necessary, you don't talk about it. You keep your own counsel, if only because silence is always scarier than someone indulging in bombastic threats and dramatic posturing. When a Sicilian undertakes vengeance, he withdraws from the routine cares of everyday life. He appears to be calm and not terribly concerned with what's going on around him, but anyone who knows him well will recognize the signs and remain at a safe distance

Gunner Bobby Garrett was probably the first chief in the goat locker to see it, and he, by God, wholeheartedly approved. He had cause, like I did: two brothers, also slaughtered by the marauding, treacherous Japanese at Pearl. But now I wondered if my new crew would be aware of or understand any of this. In my heart of hearts, I was beyond grateful for what Admiral Spruance had done. There were still too many Japanese out there, infesting these vast seas with their dreams of conquest, blood, and imperial glory. Thank you, sir, a thousand times over, I thought, because there's much that remains to be done and I *ached* to continue doing it.

Once we got back on board, I went up to my cabin to take stock and absorb it all. It became clear that the decks were already ablaze with rumors as I made my way forward and up one deck. The captain had gone to visit the flagship a lieutenant commander and come back a three-striper with a medal on his shirt. Four bells now, not just two. And *what*?! The XO was going to become the new CO? A reservist lieutenant? Yeah, yeah, but, c'mon, who better? Besides, Eeep and the crew had something important in common: very few of them were careerists. When this horrible mess was over, most of them, reserve officers and enlisted draftees, if they lived through it, would go back to being civilians. They liked him, and more importantly, they respected his technical knowledge. They highly appreciated his willingness to dive into a black box and help techs who were absolutely buffaloed by technology they didn't understand—and then usually ended up fixing the goddamned thing or even improving it. They also secretly admired the way that he, as XO, managed to get between them and the CO when I became angry about something. I could just hear him: "Hey, Chief, don't sweat it, I'll talk to the captain. It's gonna be okay. I'll manage him." I suspect that none of them knew that the two of us, acting in quiet concert, "managed" those perceptions from start to finish. The captain's on the rampage? The XO would intervene, pouring oil on the waters. Or the opposite: The XO wanted someone flogged; the captain, bless his benevolent soul, would step in and rein that wild man in. In both cases we'd have consulted quietly with the chiefs to determine the appropriate form of justice for such high crimes as talking back to a petty officer, having a dirty berthing compartment, or being late to relieve the watch. Being a CO, or for that matter, an XO, always involved a certain amount of acting talent.

God knows I would miss Eeep and could only hope that whoever was exec in *Copeland* could step up to that same degree of professional collusion. If not, I might be facing a tough few weeks. On the other hand, I told myself, you've been the captain for a while now, haven't you. First time, you were getting the hang of it on the sweep, then banging around in the North Atlantic with a bunch of salty Brits right out of the

Horatio Nelson school of command. Then out here to a high command who appeared to wish you'd just go away. Now, you and your ship are famous out here. How often do you really think this brand-new, shiny-faced commissioning crew would be able to surprise you? There will at best be about 5 percent of the ship's company who could claim with a straight face to be "experienced." And if nothing else, you can always go Sicilian on them, which is to say, become the consummate quiet man. Just look at them when they bring you a problem and wait for them to make a recommendation on how to fix it. When some big operation is unfolding, sit down with the wardroom officers and get them to explain how they're going to handle it, not how you want them to handle it. They're young, green, probably afraid, and they will rise to the occasion or they won't, and then you promote the ones who do.

Most importantly, get close to the chiefs as soon as you can. If you have the goat locker in your pocket, all else will follow. I sighed. There was lots to do, very soon. But right now, I realized my main job was to prepare Eeep for success here in *Holland*.

Piece'a cake, I thought, with a grin.

The admiral had mentioned a suitable turnover time for the change of command, which Eeep and I both kind of smiled at. Respectfully, of course. There wasn't anything he didn't already know about our trusty little DE, and there wasn't a helluva lot I didn't know about him. We spent two days signing over the accountable equipment, such as binoculars, small arms, and other pilferable equipment. We mutually inspected the main spaces, magazines, and the state of the crypto hut. We jointly compiled a precise list of damages not yet repaired and other matériel deficiencies. We reviewed admin records and the pay accounts. I had to write detachment fitness reports on all the officers, which meant that Eeep had to prepare drafts for each of them.

USS *Copeland* showed up at the end of the second day and anchored not far away. I surreptitiously spent an hour between reviewing fitreps in the bridge chair inside the pilothouse, studying her, helped by tidal currents that swung her around her anchor so I could see every shiny new feature. My heart warmed at the sight of her. The *Sumner* class looked every inch the fleet destroyer, with clean, sleek lines that made her look like she was hastening forward, even while anchored. I cringed a little bit when I thought what we looked like in return.

Except for those six red, rising sun submarine silhouettes painted on either side of our forward superstructure. There wasn't another superstructure so decorated in the entire fleet.

So there, new guys; top that!

Only if you make it happen there, Captain, my inner voice whispered . . .

40

XO

On the day before the appointed day for the change of command, moved up by a sudden requirement for *Copeland* to get underway that very afternoon, the chiefs and I made hurried preps for the sendoff we'd cooked up. A change of command ceremony back in home port was a big deal, with lots of ceremony, speeches, sometimes personal awards, and a reception at the club afterward. In a war zone, it was sometimes as simple as the new CO and the departing CO meeting in the captain's cabin, along with the exec and the department heads, and saying the magic words: I relieve you, sir, and, I stand relieved, sir. That was all it took, along with a single-line entry in the ship's log.

As if to emphasize that we *were* in a war zone, the damned Japanese managed to infiltrate a submarine into the Ulithi Atoll anchorage, despite its supposed security, and torpedo a fully loaded oil tanker. The tanker proceeded to explode all over the place, spewing burning oil everywhere and causing several sudden and very much unplanned changes in the fleet anchorage plan. Unfortunately for the sub, he then broached in full view of the entire Fifth Fleet. Two destroyers at anchor promptly opened fire and sank him forthwith.

My job was to convince the captain to meet Chief Louie in the bosun locker, of all places, which was located all the way up at the bow of the ship. It was accessed down a steep ladder from the fo'c'sle near the anchor windlass and the two hawsepipes. I went to get him in his cabin and found him in clean and pressed khakis, his seabag at the ready and a brand-new brass hat on his head, courtesy of the ship's store on the tender. I told him we needed to make a detour up to the bosun's locker before going back to the accommodation ladder and the waiting gig from *Copeland*. He gave me one of his looks confirming he knew full well that there was some kind of *despedida* afoot. His job now was to pretend to be surprised.

We walked together up the main deck to the anchor windlass, right in front of the forward three-inch gun mount. He went first down the hatch; I followed. Down below Chief Louie had his deck-apes assembled. Some of them had to perch up in the mooring line reels because it was a pretty cramped space, with its triangular front bulkhead, otherwise known as the bow, and the piles of ropes, lines, ladders, anchor tackle, shackles, and cans of paint wedged along the frames of the ship. Chief Louie presented the captain with a most elaborate bosun's call, the lanyard woven into a bright white embroidered bib mantle sewn out of individual threads of bleached canvas, extracted one at a time from some awning material. Someone in the machine shop had engraved something on the actual call. He probably thought it said "Captain." Turned out, what it said was simply: "Call Me Ahab."

I thought he was going to tear up when he read that. It was *the* perfect departure gift for an officer who'd sunk his vengeful fangs into an entire Japanese submarine squadron and harvested them all. But that wasn't the best part. We climbed up that steep ladder leading to main deck, me in the lead this time. When he stepped out into the tropical sunlight, the entire crew was lined up in class-A uniforms. To get to the accommodation ladder back on the quarterdeck, he had to shake the hand of every man jack of them. Chief Santone made introductions just to make sure the captain knew to whom he was saying goodbye. In more cases than I would have expected, he didn't need prompting and had something appropriate to say to each of them.

We finally made it to the ladder and then four bells went off: Commander, United States Navy, departing. The boat shoved off and headed the four hundred yards over to *Copeland,* where it seemed that a large number of her crew was up on deck. I could see what had to be her XO up on the bridge.

Roscoe turned to me and saluted. "Orders, Captain?"

"Holiday routine, Chief," I replied, which was Navy parlance for take the rest of the day off, as tradition demanded. "That was a fine farewell you arranged."

"Thank you, sir," he said. "And don't you think all those boots over on *Copeland* didn't notice, either."

AUTHOR'S NOTE

Naval history buffs will recognize that this story is based on the actual exploits of the destroyer escort USS *England* (DE-635) in the summer of 1944. She was of the *Buckley* class and did indeed manage to sink six Japanese submarines over a two-week period, although not all by herself. She was part of a three-ship task unit that had been cued to the Japanese picket line by Naval Intelligence in Pearl Harbor, where the Navy was reading the Japanese fleet's codes. As things turned out, however, each time the task unit cornered and attacked a sub, it was always *England* who made the actual kill. In fact, when they made contact on the last sub, the task unit commander ordered *England* to stay out of it in order to give the other ships a chance to score for once. They worked the sub over all night and into the following morning, but the sub managed to keep evading. Frustrated, and fearing this one might escape, the task unit commander radioed over to *England*: "Oh, hell, go ahead, *England*." She made one hedgehog pass, all misses, then a second, which was followed by a massive explosion underwater, thus ending the siege.

The first submarine sunk in this operation was not part of the picket line, but rather the I-16, a large submarine with a distinguished war record of nine war patrols. She was big enough to carry a two-man, two-torpedo midget submarine on her deck. At the time of the picket line, I-16 was engaged in resupply missions to starving elements of the Japanese army, wherein they would dump rubber bags full of rice offshore and then try to launch a midget sub to attack any nearby Allied shipping. One of her midget subs was recovered after the war off Guadalcanal and is currently on display outside of the Submarine Force Library and Museum in Groton, Connecticut.

The hedgehog weapon system was introduced in the Pacific theater in late 1943 and worked as described in this book. The British had been using hedgehog since 1942, and it had turned out to be a decisive upgrade to anti-submarine warfare. The Royal Navy's statistics after World War II showed that one enemy submarine would be sunk for every sixty standard depth-charge attacks. The stats for hedgehogs were one submarine sunk for every *six* attacks. The British reported the only drawback to using hedgehogs instead of depth charges was they lacked the morale-destroying impact on the sub's crew of having to endure the terrifying ordeal of multiple large explosions, sometimes for hours. This was more than compensated for by the fact that, unless one of the hedgehogs actually hit the sub, the water at depth remained acoustically undisturbed. This meant the destroyer could remain "in contact" with its quarry and that another attack could be made immediately.

There were actually seven subs assigned to the picket line, but as Eeep suspected, one of them was recalled when it finally became clear to the Japanese high command that the Americans knew about the picket line and were happily rolling it up. There is a detailed but relatively short history-gram on *England*'s accomplishments provided by the Navy's historical branch. It also tells you a little about each of the Japanese submarines and their wartime history until they encountered USS *England* and company. It can be found on the web at:

history.navy.mil/about-us/leadership/director/directors-corner/h-grams/h-gram-030/h-030-1.html

PTD